Undine of Deadrise Bay

Todd Woofenden

Signal Light Books
Bowdoinham, Maine

Undine of Deadrise Bay

Print Edition
ISBN: 978-0-9789192-8-3

Cover Design by Braden Todd Curtis

CONTENTS

Show us your form and carve in the mark.
Show us your strength and ink 'round the core.
Show your endurance through day into dark
And unfurl the spiral another turn more.

Then hang up your blades. Retreat from the fire.
Save us the burden of death's dirge to sing.
Too hot are the flames and too high the pyre,
For to gain the fourth level, the river's the ring.

       —Tallach fighter's lament, traditional

Prologue

Una felt her foot slip on wet moss, and reflexively reached out and put a hand on the trunk of the tree. It was barely anything, just the tiniest, quietest thump of her palm against the rough bark. But she knew it was over. She couldn't see her pursuer. Even if she had been standing on the terrace, she might not have been able to see Caterione, jet black and silent in the night. But the instant her hand touched, she could feel the eyes looking up at her.

"Don't make me climb up there and get you, Una. I'll thrash you."

Caterione's latest torment hadn't caused any real harm. No one but the other girls had been there to watch her push Una out of the bath house and lock the door. No one else even knew about it. But Una wouldn't let the insult go unanswered. This time, she thought, her response had been especially clever—right up until now.

The idea for her revenge came from a chance overhearing of a conversation as she was making her way to the bunkhouse to get clothes. She was hiding behind her master's hut waiting for an opportunity to slink past, when she heard a voice she didn't recognize.

"You understand, we have long-standing trade agreements," a woman said. "We rarely accept new buyers."

Una sidestepped to the edge of the hut and peeked around the corner. Was this the runner from up north? The place had been abuzz with rumors that a runner from the Lesser Mire compound would be coming.

"I'm aware of that," said the woman's host, a dark-haired woman in a brown gi, "and of course I know your textiles are the finest."

This was Una's master, the fighter Aideen, a refugee from the ninth sector and a teacher of the Gatto fighting style. Master Aideen had accepted Una as a student two years ago, with the caveat that to remain with The Hidden, Una would need to prove herself both in her fighting skills and in her willingness to assimilate with the traditions of the Gatto.

"I demand this of anyone I train," she had told little ten-year-old Una on the day she had arrived. "Caterione comes from a fine fighting tradition, child, but the others were strays just as you were. All must show respect to the tradition and resolve to the task. Show that and you'll be Gatto."

But while the master took care to guide her along that path, the girls were less interested in helping the newcomer to assimilate. They were there because of their quality and skills, but this grubby stray had gotten in on a cheat. Una had been sent by the gunners. And yes, the message was that she was to be held to the same standard, but they knew how that would go. No one said *no* to a gunner.

Una glanced around warily, and leaned forward to get a better look. Master Aideen had spent months negotiating. To train a group of orphaned girls was one thing. But to be recognized as a legitimate Gatto house and accept paying students required certain trappings, most importantly the textiles to build the fighting pavilion and display the colors. The Lesser Mire produced woven materials of unmatched quality.

"As you can see, we keep a low profile," Aideen added. "The meeting will be discreet. Come, I'll show you the meeting place up on the terrace."

The terrace! Una hesitated only for a moment. Maybe another Gatto girl would utter a sigh of relief and hurry to the bunkhouse, but Una followed. *Your future is up to you*, the gunner had told her. You didn't get ahead by taking the safe route.

Padding along on bare feet, she followed as her master led the runner above the forest canopy. She and the other novices spent much of each day here, training on straw mats in the art of fighting. The ground had been cut to a smooth, even plane, and was paved with tightly set brick with not so much as a single weed growing in the joints. But when it rained they sparred in the rain, and when it snowed they sparred in the snow. The girls were as eager as their master to see a roof over their heads.

"Will this do?" Aideen said. "With your textiles, we'll raise the Gatto pavilion of The Hidden on this very spot." She left it to the runner to take in the magnificent view of the forest below.

"It will do," the runner said. "My master will meet you tomorrow at sunset."

Una grinned and slipped away. Tomorrow at sunset! Her revenge would be doubly sweet: She would get back at her foes, and get them in trouble at the same time.

The other girls would come to realize that they were also to blame, for taking the bait. Una's taunting in the bath house earned her another eviction. But this time as they shoved her outside, yanked her towel away, and slammed the door shut behind her, there was something wrong. It was only at the last moment that they realized Una had her gi pants on under the towel. And it was not until Lilly had snapped the bolt shut that they considered the weight of the towel they had stripped from her and tossed to the floor. For inside it was another towel, rolled into which was a big, ragged rat.

Una snatched her gi jacket from a bench outside and had a good head start when the screaming started. The door burst open, and the four pursuers whipped towels around themselves and tore off after her.

Up on the terrace, Master Aideen was halfway through the Gatto tea ritual. Her dour, tight-lipped guest was watching the setting sun and taking a long moment to decide if the tea suited her, when she was distracted by something. A figure darted onto the edge of the terrace and abruptly cut off to the side, vanishing into the woods. Then four girls ran onto the terrace, dripping wet and howling—and stopped dead at the rising figure of their master, her face screwed into a death scowl.

"All right. You caught me. I give." Una exhaled loudly, perched up in the tree. "But you deserved it." She squatted and took hold of a lower branch. "I'm coming down."

In a light-footed hop she landed on the ground and rose to face her accuser—and was bowled over from behind. Three figures swarmed her, two taking her legs and one her arms.

"I give. Let me go! I said I give!" she protested.

"Turn her over," Caterione ordered.

Una thrashed and fought, but couldn't throw them off. They wrenched her onto her back and shoved her down.

"Get her belt off."

One of the girls shifted forward, and Una almost got a leg free. But Caterione's foot slammed down on her shin. Una's eyes watered, but she stifled the scream into a growl.

"Hurry up. Get her belt off."

The gray belt was roughly pulled loose and tossed aside, and her gi jacket yanked open. Then she clamped her teeth shut as a balled-up cloth was pressed over her mouth to silence her.

The beating went on and on, the arm whipping down, everything around her quiet except for the thump of the weighted sock hitting her stomach and ribs. Her eyes teared, and Una held her breath and tried to prepare for each blow—until pain took over, reason went away, and she heard herself start to cry. Still the blows kept coming, until finally even her muffled keening had stopped.

Then a voice spoke right next to her ear. "We're not going down for you," Caterione hissed. They released her and vanished into the woods, leaving her to roll over and curl into a ball, sobbing.

1. The Western Shores

Saor Tieg strode along a high walkway overlooking a steep drop to the ocean, in no hurry. On that day long ago when the eighteen-year-old slave boy Tieg delivered the last coin to his master and became Saor Tieg, Tallach freedman, he had vowed never to run again.

"And what if a wolf is chasing you?" His old master had said with a little smile, dropping the coin into a drawer.

"I'll break my vow," Tieg told him, and with a tip of his hat, departed.

Now in his early fifties, his hair turned to silver and the slave clothes of the Tallach cartel replaced with a fine silk suit, he had no need to run. People came to him. Even, it seemed, emissaries from the north.

"I'm told you spent time overseas," a young man in a northern officer's uniform said, strolling along beside him. "On mainland Ben Attallach."

Ten paces back, a unit of northern soldiers broke step, as if merely out for a stroll themselves. They kept their hands clear of their weapons and prayed there would be no cause to draw them.

"I grew up on a merchant ship," Tieg explained. "The master ported all along the Western Shores, including here in Deadrise Bay. Boys were taken from the southlands and put on Tallach ships in this very port. In fact, it wasn't far from this bay that I was taken."

The northern officer turned and looked at the man. "By the slave cartel."

"One moment I was little Tieg, a mischievous eight-year-old venturing out onto the wharf, and the next moment I was marching onto a Tallach slave ship tied to a line of boys. It took ten years running for the regional governor to earn enough to buy my freedom."

"You were a messenger, then. So you were able to earn money on the side."

"A runner can carry two or three messages as easily as one. And the master didn't begrudge me taking extra work as long as his own epistles were delivered first."

"And how did you land a position as a runner? I understand that not many Tallach slaves are given the opportunity to earn."

"Being raised by a merchant seaman had its advantages for a boy traveling in a ship. While the other boys were retching on empty stomachs, I was sleeping like a baby, and taking advantage of the uneaten portions at the daily meal. Of course they recovered eventually, but when we disembarked I had considerably more energy than most others."

"You must have been terrified."

"Perhaps I should have been. But walking down the gangplank onto the shores of Ben Attallach wasn't much different than walking down the plank of my master's barque. One port seemed the same as another to a ship boy."

"You must know a lot about the Tallachs. Ten years! That's a long time."

The older man laughed softly. "Is it? It must seem so, for a young officer. And your master just as young."

The officer looked around warily. "Maybe we could speak of that indoors."

"Of course." Tieg waved an arm and led him up a stone staircase to an inn overlooking the bay.

A pair of servants rushed to open the doors, and the soldiers stopped outside. Tieg led the officer through a large dining room filled with wooden tables and chairs. They stepped into a smaller room, much more richly laid out. A varnished table aged to a golden brown graced the middle of the room, decorated with vases of cut flowers. Around it were upholstered chairs.

Tieg motioned for the officer to sit, and they looked down at breakers on the rocks, and rows of merchant vessels tied off to the wharves and moored out in the bay. A man in the vest of an innkeeper rushed in with a bottle of wine and poured. "How may we serve you today, sirs?" he asked with a bow.

"No need to trouble yourselves for a freed slave," Tieg said. "Whatever's on hand will be fine."

"Yes, sir." The innkeeper bowed and rushed out of the room.

The officer took this to be a little game, joking with the servants about what a commoner he was, the most powerful merchant on the whole of the Western Shores.

And Tieg hadn't failed to notice the silver bar with three small ruby cabochons set into it, pinned to the soldier's lapel. That was the mark of a northern commander, one of the triumvirate's inner elite.

"So tell me, Commander Riley," he said, "what brings you to Deadrise Bay? Even being right on the border with the northlands as we are, I don't recall ever seeing a man of arms of the young Tynan lord in these parts."

"Pardon, but the Tynan lord is not my master. Not directly. I'm a man of his gunners."

Tieg nodded. "Of course. The girl gunners of the northern triumvirate, who stand at the lord's heel. Although I suppose they're young women now. Immensely powerful young women."

The officer looked around again, and leaned in. "Gunner Ailmili has asked me to convey to you her greetings, and to request an audience."

"In Deadrise Bay?" Tieg's eyebrows went up.

"Yes, sir."

"With a legion of soldiers, I suppose." The eyebrows went down again. "That might be a regular matter across the border, but this isn't an ideal place for such a thing."

"No soldiers, sir. Just the gunners. They prefer to travel on their own."
Commander Riley gave a strained smile.

"Ah!" Tieg laughed, "I'd heard about that. Very secretive, those two.
And they're going to cross into the southlands and visit the Western Shores
without an escort?"

The commander's smile widened. "They visit wherever they please
without an escort, sir. It's been all I can do to convince them to allow me
to announce their plans in advance in cases like this. They'd just as soon
simply appear at your table one night."

"Would they? Here at my table, the gunners of Tynan? That would be
interesting."

"Of course I'd prefer to accompany them, but we slow them down, you
see." The young officer grimaced. "So it will be just the gunners."

"I see," the silver-haired man smiled and nodded. "And yet I assume
there will be a contingent of soldiers just out of eyesight."

Commander Riley shrugged. "Not so close as to raise the ire of the two,
and yet close enough to be on hand quickly, should the need arise. But my
men won't be looking to get into any entanglements. Please be assured
that we mean to arrive and to leave without incident."

"And the purpose of this meeting?"

"The gunner has told me to request an audience. That's all I know."

Tieg nodded slowly. "All right, then. And when should I expect these
elusive northern gunners magically to appear at my table?"

"Tomorrow night. In this room at seven o'clock."

"Tomorrow night," Tieg echoed.

The landscape from the wharves up to the town at Deadrise Bay had
been a steep, grassy slope. But through the generations, stone retaining
walls and fill had been added, forming a series of wide, flat terraces with
stone walkways and stairs winding from one to the next. Down near the
water, rough sheds, tents, and awnings over fire pits dotted the terraces.
When ships were in port, the food terraces were abuzz with sailors.

As one ascended, the type and quality of the structures improved, as
did the social rank of those present. On a grassy plateau up near the inn,
under an ivy-covered pergola, Saor Tieg stepped up to a polished mahogany captain's chair. There were chairs on either side, already occupied.
The men jumped up and bowed, and after Tieg had settled in, they seated
themselves again.

A servant approached with a bottle of wine and a platter of fruits and
cheeses. He served, then at the slight raising of Tieg's hand, stepped off to
stand in the shadows.

"Wait until you sample this wine, my friend. There's nothing like it," said one of the men flanking him. He wore the brown vest and white shirt of a Tallach merchant, and tailored pants tucked into brown leather boots. "The vineyards are the finest in the southern plains."

"We think you'll find the quality of this label to be much to your satisfaction, Saor Tieg," the other added, stiffly. This man was also dressed in Tallach garb, but simpler, with a plainer cut to the vest.

"No need to be so formal, Leon. I've known your captain for, what, eighteen years now, Armand? Since that girl of yours was a toddler. Just call me Tieg."

The captain nodded, and Leon relaxed. "Tieg, then. Yes, sir. And pleased to be your servant."

"Tell me about the shipment."

"We've arranged for a, uh …" Leon looked around warily and dropped his voice. "We've arranged for an unexpected change in course," he winked.

Their conversation was interrupted as a servant stepped forward. "Miss Undine," he announced.

The men rose and turned. Down the stairs strode a dark-eyed girl of twenty, her dark hair tightly braided and wound into a circle on her head, and pinned with a steel rod. Like Tieg, she wore clothing of the Tallach upper class. Her white shirt was neatly pressed, with mother-of-pearl buttons down the front. Over it she wore a tailored vest of black and blue satin, and black pants of the same material, the cuffs snug to her shins, leaving her legs bare from mid-shin down.

Normally she would have worn leather sandals, but a glance at her feet told the men why she'd chosen to go barefoot. A blue and black dragon's head on her right foot with the tail sweeping up the side of her leg stood out with the reddish-pink inflammation of a new tattoo. Her left cheek bore a similar hue, a black spiral of tight diamonds having been newly extended for a total of four turns.

"Well, well," Armand said, as the girl stepped under the pergola, "so you've passed the fourth trial of Tallach fighting. And what's that on your foot? Undine, spectacular!"

"Father," she said, flashing a smile and stepping up to Tieg.

"I knew you'd do it," Tieg said, opening his arms for the girl. "And a dragon-serpent, no less!" He gave her a hug, and turned to his guests. "Didn't I tell you that my Undine could face whatever trial one might cast in her path? And do it with style. A fourth-tier Tallach fighter, and a dragon-serpent! Come, child, sit—or perhaps you don't want to sit just now, with a fresh dragon's tail running up your leg."

The Tallach men laughed.

"Why don't you show us? I'll bet the artistry is sublime," Armand said with a sly smile.

The girl put a hand to her ear. "Did I hear an old sea captain proposing to me? Because the only way you're going to see where that serpent ends is to win my hand, sailor."

They all laughed again, and the servants rushed to place a chair across from the men. The girl perched on the edge and stretched her leg out.

Tieg nodded at the second man. "Undine, this is Armand's new road man, Leon."

Leon bowed, and Undine nodded. "You arranged for that excellent silk," she said. "The midnight blue with the gold weave. Am I right? I hope there's more of that."

"From the high villages. Yes, miss. But don't say that I told you." He winked, and took his seat.

"Bring me some of it, and I'll be silent as a stone."

"So, tell me," Armand said, sitting down and leaning forward. "Reaching the fourth tier of Tallach fighting is nothing to sneeze at. But what earned you the dragon-serpent? Surely you're waiting for us to ask. A fourth-level Talla is rare. But I may have seen one girl in all my life who's earned the dragon-serpent. What did you do?"

Undine gave a melodic laugh, and then winced and put a hand to her cheek. "Might you fetch some of that rose balm?" she said, looking at a servant. "I'm afraid I'm a bit raw."

The servant bowed and hurried up the steps.

"So? Tell us then, my girl," Saor Tieg urged. "Tell us, so I can brag about you for the rest of the day."

"What did I do?" She grinned. "You know about the fourth trial? The last part, where the aspirants race between the torches and pass through a wall of fire into the river."

"*The river's the ring*, as the old poem goes," Armand said. "*Show us your form and carve in the mark*, and so on. We used to chant that as children, when we were pretending to be Tallach warriors. I don't remember all of it. Something about putting away your blades and giving up when you reach the third tier, as I recall."

"Good advice," Leon interjected. "The third tier is quite respectable enough."

"But I remember it ends with, *to gain the fourth level, the river's the ring*," Armand said. "Isn't that right?"

Undine nodded. "I'd been thinking about it as I was training. We practice it, except of course in practice there's not actually a burning trench of oil between you and the river. You don't see that until you're in the trial."

"It's a test of courage and resolve," Armand said, "not to mention

11

physical skill. The fire pit's no small thing to leap across. I've heard that many don't earn the fourth ring in a single try, or climb out of the river with their hair burned off. And some bear markings of failed attempts."

Undine nodded knowingly. "One of my instructors. The side of his face, and his arm. He told us that he was lucky to have been able to carry through and roll into the water, or he'd not have made it at all. I think they picked him to be an instructor for the fourth trial candidates because of that. Show what happens if you fail, and put a little fear into us."

"But it seems you made it through," Tieg said, sitting back, satisfied. "And you still have your lovely black hair."

The girl grinned slyly. "The rules say that the runner must pass down the corridor and into the river. I read it over and over, during practice. I kept thinking, there's nothing that says the runner has to leap through the fire."

"What, are you going to break through the torch wall and scurry around it?" Armand pursed his lips. "That would earn you the loss of your third ring, and a fancy scar on your face from the removal of it."

"She could dig under," Leon proposed. "Burrow down like a rodent, and come out under the water." He made burrowing motions with his hands and grinned at the girl.

Undine folded her arms and scowled. "I suppose if either of you should ever choose to walk the path of a Tallach fighter, you had better learn to jump through flames."

Tieg laughed. "Come now, Undine. Tell us the story. How did you trick your way past the fire pit of the fourth trial? I've got to hear this."

"As I was saying," she glared at the visitors, admonishing them to be quiet and let her finish, "the rules say you have to run down the corridor and land in the river. There's nothing that says you have to go through the flames. So I snatched one of the torch poles, flipped it around and planted the burning end into the ground, and vaulted over the fire pit."

The men stared at her for a long count of five, and then burst into laughter, slapping their knees.

"One of the judges said I should be disqualified, but the others disagreed." She pursed her lips at the laughter. "And they conferred, and realized I hadn't broken any rules. No one had thought of going over the fire, but there was no rule stating that the runner must pass through the flames. So they passed me, and awarded me the dragon-serpent for novel thinking."

"That's my Undine. If there's a way to get around the rules, she'll find it." Tieg rose and offered a hand to the girl. "Undine, you're a gem. Here, why don't you go get that rose balm and a good meal, and I'll finish my conversation. It's good to have you back. Things are more entertaining already. Shall I see you this evening?"

"Maybe. But I'd like to see Tyra. I haven't seen her in forever."

"She'll be down on the wharf, no doubt," Armand said. "And won't she be excited to see that new ring on your face. Again, congratulations, Talla."

Undine hunted the wharves and found her friend on the deck of a four-masted schooner, leaning against the wheelhouse, lost in a book.

"There you are. What are you doing on the *Ocelot*? Getting into Captain Neel's library again?"

The girl looked up, startled, and then leaped to her feet with a shriek and wrapped her arms around Undine. "You're back!" A steel pin clattered to the deck, and red braids tumbled down her back. "When did you get back? It's been so boring here without you. No one to make trouble." She pulled back, noticing the inflamed patch on Undine's face, and the new ink. "You did it," she hissed. "You passed!" She reached out and ran a finger over Undine's cheek.

Undine swatted her hand away. "Ow, damn it! Do I go poking you when you have fresh ink?" She poked the girl in the forehead, where a little blue flower had been tattooed.

Tyra flinched, and then laughed. "But you did it. And—raptors, a dragon-serpent?" She set her book down and grabbed Undine's hand. "Come on. We have to show Erling. He'll choke and die. Fourth level and a dragon-serpent, and you're only twenty!"

She hauled Undine across the deck to an open hatch, and called down. "Erling! Uh, I mean, Captain Neel. Are you down there?"

"Cap'n ain't aboard, missie," came a deep voice. "Gone up to the village. Likely ain't gonna see his face back here until the noon bells tomorrow."

"Oh," Tyra said, disappointed. "In the village?"

A gray-haired head popped up through the hatch. "Maybe he's gone to fetch somethin' for a pretty girl."

"What are you talking about?" Tyra folded her arms. "What pretty girl?"

"What pretty girl indeed. I seen you two lookin' at each other. You'd better watch yourself, missie, or you'll find yourself attached to a new ship. Won't be no more playin' the field with the sailors then, mind you."

"Who says I'm playing the field?" She stomped her foot dangerously close the man's hand, and he dropped back down and laughed. "And tell me where he is. *A sea captain commands even in his sleep.* That's from *The Book of Tallach Seamanship*. The captain doesn't run off to the village and not tell his first mate where he's going."

"He'll be up to that saloon by the distillery, I 'spect." came the man's voice up from below. "Don't tell him I told you."

Tyra stormed off, and Undine followed her onto the dock. "Playing the field," she huffed. "Like I'd be interested in a bunch of sailors."

"I've seen you looking at Captain Neel too, Tyra."

"Books." She whirled. "He has books. I'm interested in his *library.*" Tyra glared at her friend. "He's practically forty, Undine. You think I want to marry an old man?"

"Come on," Undine grinned. "Never mind Captain Neel. I want to talk to you about something." She pulled Tyra along, and as they made their way up the terraces, she leaned in. "I heard something. I have a plan."

"Not the card games." Tyra pulled back on her friend's arm. "I was just joking about making trouble. They'll put you in jail, Undine. The first mate of the *Oncilla* was watching you last time. I know him. I'm under his thumb for a month straight, each time we make the passage. He knows you're cheating."

"Not the card games. I swear. This is something better." Undine grinned. "Much better."

"*Better* as in, we get a dressing-down by our fathers for an hour, or *better* as in living behind bars? Or do we get strung up on a yardarm?"

"Oh, shut up. Just come on. My father set the celebration for tomorrow, so we have the whole night to do whatever we want. We'll go to the village and have a meal, all right? My treat. There's a fire pit pavilion tonight. You'll love it. And we'll stop in and say hello to your ship captain if you want."

"He's not *my* ship captain. My father is my ship captain, thank you very much. I wouldn't be caught dead sailing on the *Ocelot.*"

Undine grinned. "It's identical to your ship, Tyra. And I don't think you want to be saying things like that out loud. What would your capt… what would your *librarian* think, if he heard you slandering his schooner? Probably put you over his knee."

"He'd have to fight me first," Tyra grumbled. "I might not be a fourth-level Talla, but nobody puts the daughter of a Tallach sea captain over his knee."

"You'll have to learn to fight, then."

They ascended to the top of the terraces and headed down the main road.

The town proper of Deadrise Bay, just south of the border with the northlands, was a long, dense stretch of houses, storage facilities, stores, and mills, reaching out on either side of a river. The buildings cascaded down a series of drops to a wide outlet to the ocean. Goods from the mill were transported by cart along a road that wound along the river and ended at the mouth.

But not all goods that passed through Deadrise Bay were moved along the traditional trade routes. The outer village was the other side of the coin. Meandering to the east were miles of woods dotted with clusters of houses and hidden business operations. Things that couldn't be traded publicly were traded there.

"It's close to ten miles to the fire pit pavilion," Undine said. "Let's take the carriage."

Tyra scowled. "I thought your father said you were forbidden. You know, after that thing in the village last time, with the … you know."

"*I* can't take the carriage. But *we* could, if you're up to it."

Tyra sighed. "You're going to get us in trouble on your first night back."

"And that's why you love me." Undine guided them down a side street toward the livery stables.

"Fine. But I'm not going down for you."

Undine's eyebrows lowered and she slowed, her hands tightening into fists and her teeth clenching. Then she breathed in, got control of herself, and adopted a strained smile. "It's my first night back. He won't banish me for going to dinner. We'll take the little one, so we won't need a driver."

They strode into the office of the livery stable, a room with a few benches and a table, and a small desk for the ledger. A man in a black waistcoat was leaning against the wall, smoking.

"Aren't you supposed to do that outside?" Undine said, folding her arms. "The hay, and all. Isn't that how the stables in the old city burned down?"

The man pushed off with his foot and ambled forward a step, and his eye twitched as he saw Tyra step up beside Undine. He looked at them guardedly. "What can I do for you? Saddle your mares? Headin' out for a ride?"

"Hitch up my father's day carriage," Undine said. "I'm just back from the trials. We're going out to celebrate."

"But, miss, the master has said that you're not …" Then he caught Tyra's look, and he clenched his eyes shut.

"That I'm not to miss out on a well-deserved dinner?" Undine prompted.

The man sighed. "To be sure. Just that."

As they headed down the road seated on the plush cushion of an elegant open carriage, Tyra sat back, giggling. "We're going to get in so much trouble."

"Tyra, you saw him with General Lonnard's wife. And as I recall you telling it, the mounting didn't involve helping her get her foot in the stirrup."

"Ha! Yes. There's a passage in *Tales of the Tallach Wanderer* I could quote, but I'm not supposed to have read that," Tyra grinned.

"He'll hope we bring the carriage back in one piece, and then he'll scratch the line out of the ledger," Undine said.

"But if your father finds out …"

"He won't. Now don't be an old woman. And never mind those books you hide in your berth. I'll show you some real excitement. You've got to see the fire pit pavilion. It's amazing." Undine snapped the reins, and the horses broke into a trot.

The pavilion tent was lit with paper lanterns hanging from the ridge-pole, and the tables underneath were crowded with people. Fires down the hill by the water sprayed sparks upward, and boys in peasant shirts and snug caps hurried back and forth, carrying the grilled fare up to the diners. Servers moved about, filling bowls and taking away plates stacked with bones.

Undine and Tyra were pressed side-by-side, occupying a scant end of a bench that held another ten closely packed people. They looked across a table piled with food at another dozen people. Three more tables were filled, and a crowd waited in the gloom outside the tent, ready to fill spaces as they became available. It seemed that the whole village was eating out tonight.

"I've always wanted to go to one of these things," Tyra said, grinning, leaning in to her friend. "It's so visceral."

"*Visceral*? Tyra, you and your reading."

"But, it is. The platters of food, and bowls of honey spirits and beer— and everyone crushed together. And eating off the bone with our hands. Even on the *Oncilla* the men use utensils. At least if the captain's watching, anyway. I'd wager there wasn't anything like this before Lord Torin's victory over the dictator Shular."

"Quiet," Undine warned. "Not so loud. Someone might be listening."

Tyra rolled her eyes. "We just stole your father's carriage, and then stole these peasant dresses, and covered our face markings in whatever this stuff is."

"Face paint. Girls of your … of our kind aren't allowed here unat-tended. They'd never have let us in. But shush."

"You're worried about someone hearing us talk about the northern lord's overthrow of the black-gi? Everyone knows the story, Undine. It's not a secret."

"Tyra, you spend too much time with your nose in a book. Pay atten-tion. Everyone knows, but nobody *talks* about it. There are still plenty of blades, and some of them don't take kindly to that subject. And for your information, the only new thing about the fire pit pavilions is that they set them up in the open now, instead of hidden in the forest. When I was little, I saw things just like this, before Shular's defeat. Not that I ever got into one. You had to have money, and you had to be invited. And they had hired guns all around." Undine turned to her friend. "And the entertainment was decidedly more *visceral*."

"What, did they have mad orgies? Or boil prisoners in oil?" Tyra smirked. "You're making up stories." She bumped her shoulder into her friend. "You never saw a fire pit pavilion. Number one, your father runs the trade from Deadrise Bay to halfway down the Western Shores. He could get an invitation easily. And when did you ever not have money? But even if he wanted to, I'm supposed to believe he'd let his daughter—" She leaned in, and whispered, "… his *Tallach* daughter, native-born in mainland Ben Attallach—get anywhere near a fire pit pavilion in in the days of the dictator?"

"Shush. You talk too much. Pass me the bread."

Later, amply sated by the feast, Undine nudged her friend, and they rose and departed. Undine passed a coin to the boy watching their carriage. They climbed in, Undine snapped the reins, and they rode away from the smoke-filled clearing.

"All right, fine. Tell me about this big plan," Tyra said, feeling good. Her friend was back, and they were full and a bit tipsy from honey spirits, racing down the road at a reckless speed under a bright moon.

Undine slowed the carriage to a walk and leaned in. "During my trials I heard the soldiers talking. There's always a unit of soldiers keeping watch. And I heard two of them talking one night."

"You were sneaking around at night?" Tyra grinned. "Why am I not surprised?"

"Listen to me. The soldiers who work the trials do it for extra money. It's not their regular duty. This unit works the road from Deadrise Bay up through the borderlands."

"To the north?" Tyra's tone became guarded. "Undine, you're not proposing getting involved with the northlands."

"Let me finish. You have to know that the trade routes don't stop at the border, right? Your father is captain of a merchant ship. All that stuff doesn't get sent southward. Lots of things are sent to the north."

"I've heard the rumors. Crates smuggled through the borderlands and boxes of silver pieces hidden along the way as payment. But that's just stories, Undine."

Undine giggled. "But it's not. It's real, Tyra. The soldiers on lookout, it's their regular assignment. They go into the borderlands in the middle of the night, and at a hidden place they collect the payment for shipments sent to the northlands."

"Sure they do. Undine, soldiers talk. They probably also consort with beautiful wood fairies with skin that glows."

"I'm telling you, it's real. These weren't soldiers boasting at the saloon. They were complaining about it. *That forsaken, pestilent forest. Curse the northlands.* That kind of thing. And they said something else. There's going to be a drop. Gold! Not silver pieces, but actual, real gold."

"We can't take the gold," Tyra said, dully. "We'll be shot, Undine. And besides, that would be stealing from our own people. Like from my father, and from Captain Neel. And your father, too. You can't steal Tallach gold."

"Honestly, Tyra. Obviously I'm not suggesting we steal gold from Tallach soldiers."

"Fine." Tyra folded her arms. "So tell me your amazing plan."

"All right, listen. You know there's no direct trade between the northlands and the cartel. It's forbidden. And so you can't just have a big meeting in the borderlands and hand off the payment. It's all done clandestinely. The northerners pack the payment into a parcel of some sort, like a leather bag, or a roll. And they have a prearranged location. You know, put it under the big rock by the oak tree, a hundred paces from where the stream joins the river. That kind of thing."

"And you know the location?"

"Listen to me. The northerners place the payment at the arranged location, and then they have to leave, since they can't be seen with Tallach soldiers. The soldiers come and pick it up later. Once they receive it, it's Tallach money. But while it's sitting there, before they arrive, they haven't technically been paid yet, right? And who's to say what could happen? Somebody could stumble on it. It's still northern gold until the Tallach soldiers have possession."

"And you know the location," Tyra repeated, scowling.

Undine laughed. "The thing is, yes! Yes, Tyra, I know exactly where it is. I heard them describe it, and I know the place. All we need to do is stake it out and grab the payment before the soldiers arrive. Maybe we plant a cover story, like somebody saw some border rats nosing around the place. Something like that. In any case, it's not the Tallach soldier's problem if the gold isn't there when they get there. The northern traders can't say, *well, we left it there, so you've been paid.* That would end the trade line for good."

They rumbled along the road for a long time, Undine waiting expectantly, and Tyra thinking, nodding her head. "And there's some reason you need the gold?"

"Because it's *there*, Tyra. Because I can. Don't you want to have a little fun?"

Finally Tyra blew out a breath. "All right. When is this drop?"

"Tomorrow night."

2. The County

The cabin had no public utilities and no satellite dish. It had been built half a century ago as a hunting camp, on a plot of land at the end of an old fire road. It was a forty-acre chunk cut out of a bigger chunk of an even bigger tract of land that had all been farmland and woods. Through the generations pieces were carved off for sons and daughters, and then the pieces sold as families dwindled or moved away.

By city standards, it was extremely rural. The nearest neighbor was five miles away. But by northern Maine standards, it wasn't all that remote. There was a local store with some of the basics, and larger stores for stocking up within a few hours' drive. It was just a matter of planning.

Horace knew the winters in northern Maine would be harsh, and at sixty-nine he felt the cold more acutely than he had at fifty-nine or forty-nine. But he was in good health, and he liked the Maine wilderness. He had hiked and camped in Maine as a boy. Somehow it felt right to retreat to the north.

When the broker flipped to the page showing the cabin in the woods, she saw his interest, and turned up the charm. "Look at this one. Wouldn't this be a lovely, secluded retirement spot?" the woman gushed.

She was taken aback when Horace broke into laugher. Retirement? Horace Rand was not going into retirement. He was going into hiding.

His trainer, were the man still alive, would have slapped him on the back for a job well done. In Horace's younger years, the man had admonished him relentlessly to take more care. Horace had a rare talent for observation. He just needed to learn to use it.

"Listen, Ace," the man once told young Horace after a failed simulation, "you got past ten hostiles. Fan-fucking-tastic. Good job. And clearly you're a fine shot. But you rushed the last part. And the best approach in the world doesn't count for shit if you blow the mission by being reckless in the end."

"The trap door was a cheat," Horace snapped. "And don't call me *Ace*."

"What, you want me to call you *Horace*? Sounds like an old duffer studying history. If you want to be taken seriously as an agent, take my advice and stick with *Ace*."

The young man flashed him a glare. "What's wrong with studying history?"

"And nothing is a cheat, Ace. You understand me? The enemy doesn't follow a set of rules. You can't make assumptions. Get in. Get set. Check. Check again. Execute the plan."

"I did that."

"Execute a plan other than jumping out and shooting everything in sight, okay? The agency wants a chameleon, not a killer."

What his trainer didn't say—didn't have to say—was that Horace was already adapting. His young trainee wasn't angry at being scolded; he was angry with himself for missing something.

The next time through, his trainer stood slack-jawed at the finest execution of this particular drill he had ever seen: flawless, and the best execution time on record.

"You were right," Horace grudgingly admitted. "I was rushing things last time."

"Well, shit," the man said, offering a congratulatory slap on the back.

Young Horace started with what he called *the blue-collar side of the trade,* mostly sitting through endless hours of surveillance. Sometimes jobs went bad, and he was thankful for his hand-to-hand training, his skill in fast driving, and his hours on the shooting range. But his superiors saw the same thing his handler had: Horace Rand had a scary ability to pick up on the fine details of a scene.

"It's like he can read minds," Horace once overheard them saying. He smiled and said nothing. His father had told him that one day he might discover unexpected connections to other people. "I don't mean social connections," his old man had said. "I mean reaching out, but not with your arm, see? My daddy had it, and I have it. One day you might see something you don't expect. Watch for it, son. It's a gift."

In his young career, Horace thanked his father for passing it on to him. His father was right. He could sense what people were about to do. It gave him an edge.

But it wasn't until his son was a teenager that he truly understood the vivid nature of his father's *gift.* It wasn't just a question of anticipation. He started to see things. At first he dismissed it. Maybe he was dehydrated, or had gotten up too quickly. But then it happened again and again. At random moments, Horace saw the world through his young son's eyes. Some little thing would set it off: He would clear a stack of dirty dishes from his son's room, or retrieve his jacket from the front stairs to hang it up, and his focus would shift and zoom in on something of the boy's life. Some of the scenes were harmless: sitting in school, or walking along the road. Others were startling: brutal fist fights with other boys, or shooting animals in the woods for fun.

As his son reached his middle teens and the scenes grew darker and darker, Horace came to think that his insight wasn't a gift, but a burden. He silently cursed his father for passing it on to him. What was he supposed to do? He was a single parent with an important professional career. Vergil was a disturbing young boy, but Horace didn't have the time or the energy for mollycoddling.

Then his son grew up and left home, and it wasn't his job to tell his grown son what to do, was it? So he closed the door to Vergil's room, gave the house a thorough cleaning, and the glimpses into his son's life faded and stopped. There were no more warning signs to ignore. Everything was calm and peaceful again.

Soon *The Ace* was living the life. He advanced to more complicated and less dangerous missions, engineering complex cons to trick his way into private board meetings to gather intel, and setting elaborate traps for high-value targets. When he reached age 60, the agency celebrated the early retirement of one of their best ever white-collar agents.

Then came the knock on his door. "Mister Horace Rand?"

Horace held the doorknob as a pair of police officers stood on the stoop. "Yes."

"Your son is Vergil Rand?"

"Yes." Horace scanned the street out of habit. One cruiser, lights off. Nobody on the sidewalk, or anything else out of place. Was he being summonsed? He thought all his cases had been wrapped up.

"May we come in?"

"No, I'm sorry." This was a reflex. Never give up ground if you don't have to.

"Do you know where your son is, sir? Is he here, by any chance?"

"My son? You're looking for Vergil?" He could have told them that Vergil was overseas working for an investment firm, but they hadn't said what they wanted. Horace was too well trained to offer unsolicited information.

"Your son is at large, sir," the officer said. "If he's contacted you, we need to know. There's been another killing."

"A killing? What, a fellow stock broker?"

The officer winced. "Do you know what your son was in prison for?"

Horace's face changed. "Prison?"

The officer dropped his voice. "Your son isn't a stock broker, sir. He was convicted of murder in the shooting death of a government agent. And now another assassination has taken place, just a few weeks after his escape. You and your family could be in danger. If you've seen him, sir, it's important that you tell us."

Horace stared mutely at the man.

"I can't talk about the details, sir, but your son is wanted for a very high level killing."

An abruptly silenced scream from the hall behind him caused Horace to snap out of his daze and spin around. His daughter-in-law stood in the doorway to the kitchen with a hand clamped over her mouth and her eyes wide. That afternoon she left, with a bag over her shoulder and her little daughter Camilla in her arms.

Horace didn't zoom in on the scene shortly after, of his son getting shot, but he felt it. On the second visit, when an officer stepped up cap-in-hand, Horace just nodded, closed his eyes, and quietly shut the door.

No one proposed that he was responsible for his son's killings, but Horace understood what he had done. Instead of using his odd connection to his son to help steer the boy in the right direction, he'd done everything he could to switch it off, and Vergil had turned into a killer.

Now all he could do was to try to atone for his son's deeds in the one way he knew how: take down the men who had ordered the kills. These were extremely rich, extremely powerful, and extremely dangerous men. Not even Horace Rand could hope to confront them face-to-face. There would be no dramatic hailstorm of bullets. But Horace didn't need to get into a room with them. The long game had become his trademark, and this time he had nothing to lose and no reason to rush. It took him years to track down the men who had hired Vergil and to gain their confidence. And he knew that when he finished the job he would have to run, but that was okay. He was an old man, and he had no one left to come home to, anyway.

In the end he chose a classic scam. He started with small, successful real estate investments that paid off handsomely for his marks, and eventually lured them into a large-scale project with shiny marketing materials and a staggering price tag. He talked up the deal, gathered the investments, and then when his adversaries were all in, the accounts were emptied. Ten years from the day the officer had stepped up to tell him of his Vergil's death, the families of his son's victims received large, anonymous payments, an inner coterie of the rich and dangerous were ruined financially, and Horace vanished.

"Yes, this is satisfactory," he said to himself as he stepped into the cabin, his new home in the woods. It smelled of old pine and cooking grease with a hint of cigarette smoke. Sunlight slanted in through grubby windows onto a tattered rug and an old recliner. "Lots of work," he muttered. "Lots of work to be done. But it will do. I think I can live here."

He backed his pickup truck up to the front door and got busy lugging his things in and clearing out most of what the former owner had left.

Everything from his old house had been left behind: the photos, the artwork, the furniture—even the portrait from his wedding day. It was not that he didn't want these things, but he knew the men who would be hunting for him. To stay safe, he couldn't merely move to another place. He had to be a completely different person. No one could ever step into his cabin and see a portrait of young Horace Rand and his bride on the mantel. All of that had to go.

Just one thing made it from Massachusetts to Maine, a plastic container with a snap-lid, which held the meager physical possessions handed over to him upon his son's death. He had shoved it in a compartment under the truck seat when the police had given it to him, and had forgotten about it. Then as he was packing things from the cabin into the truck to haul off to a secondhand store, a box of old flatware spilled, and as he fished around to collect forks and knives, he pulled the seat up and came upon the container.

For an instant he thought of unloading it along with the tattered recliner and the rug and other things. But no, he couldn't do that. Instead he shoved the seat back down, and when he returned to the cabin, he pushed the container under the coats in the mudroom and went back to cleaning. He would get rid of it later.

By evening the cabin was mostly cleaned out, and he was heating up a can of soup on the propane stove and looking forward to sitting outside and watching the sunset.

"The men who hired my son to kill people have been dealt with," he asserted out loud, as he poured soup into a bowl. "All of that is done. I've moved on." Maybe saying it out loud would help make it seem more real.

He sat on the stoop and ate, and listened to the sounds of the woods. It was quiet and calming, and he thought this might actually work. Maybe he could be at peace here. He felt good, even.

But the moment he stepped back inside, his mind turned to his son, and the calm feeling soured. Somehow the cabin itself reminded him of Vergil.

"What's the connection?" he mused, frowning. "We never went on camping trips, Vergil. I've no fond memories of staying in a cabin with you."

As he shoved the door shut, he glanced at his rifle resting against the wall. Maybe that was it. This one was a brand-new Ruger .22, not his old rifle. But maybe it had sparked a memory: He had taught his son to shoot. They had practiced at the shooting range, and Horace had lectured his son relentlessly about being prepared. *A strong offense is a fine defense*, he'd told the boy, over and over. *Get set. Check. Check again. Make a plan. ...*

"And wasn't that a fine lesson," he grumbled, turning to pour himself a bourbon. It hadn't occurred to him that Vergil might interpret his advice as a directive to kill people with a sniper rifle before they had a chance to put up a fight.

He sat down and sighed. "It will fade," he assured himself. "It just needs time."

The move-in complete, Horace drove into town. He had his eye on a dusty antique shop, and sure enough, he found what he was looking for. On a corner shelf were a stack of old maps, and among them a nice topo map that included his own piece of land. Back at the cabin he drew a grid-work on it in pencil, marking two-mile by two-mile squares, and prepared for a methodical exploration of the area around his cabin.

Some squares he skipped, because people lived there. He didn't want to draw attention by prowling through people's back yards. Some were flat patches of land covered in woods or growing back from a clear-cut. But in other areas there were streams and ravines, tumbles of glacial boulders, and sunny meadows. Horace worked his map, and for many days he enjoyed the solitude and serenity of the Maine woods.

But one morning as he stepped outside, the calm feeling of the outdoors in the morning wasn't there. He was struck by something his old trainer used to say: *You don't need to go looking for trouble, Ace. Just stand still and wait for it to find you.* He could sense it, something about the old fire road he had found. He'd stumbled onto it yesterday, and today he planned to see where it led. And now something on that road was calling out to him. He put his backpack and an empty box on the seat of the truck and drove to town to pick up supplies.

"Yes, *supplies,* for the woods. That's the ticket," he laughed to himself as he set a bottle of bourbon on the counter. "Old Paul Bunyan would approve of a little nip, wouldn't he?" Then as he turned to find snacks, something caught his eye. There was a girl at the front of the store, ducking behind a display. "Camilla?" he said reflexively. "Is that you, dear?" He took a step in the girl's direction. But it couldn't be his granddaughter.

When he had fled to the cabin in Maine, there had been one lost contact that he regretted. He wondered if his little granddaughter even remembered living in his basement with her mother. His daughter-in-law had been content to rely on Horace's charity in spite of her estrangement with Vergil, until the day the officers showed up. When she discovered that Vergil had not merely abandoned her and Camilla, but killed people for a living, the woman packed a bag, and scooping up the two-year-old girl, shoved through the front door and left. "Don't ever try to contact us," she hissed. "Not you or your evil son."

The accusing, dark eyes of his little granddaughter staring back at him as her mother stormed down the walk haunted him. And ten years later, those eyes still haunted him. He had cut off little Camilla along with everyone else. But it wasn't a maudlin feeling of familial longing that bothered him. No, it was a nagging concern that his line hadn't ended with his son. Camilla could be a problem.

Horace shook his head and blinked. Clearly this couldn't be his granddaughter.

The girl turned and flashed a look of surprise, and drawing her shoulders in, she ducked down an aisle. Odd, he thought. Why had Camilla come to mind? For years he had been plagued by memories of his son, and now the ghost of his granddaughter was showing up in the aisles of the local store? What did she even look like? This girl looked to be in her mid-teens, older than his granddaughter would be. She had dark hair, and it looked as if she had on a white bikini, although it seemed early in the morning for a swim.

Then it struck him. It was the stance. That was the same nervous look Camilla's mother always had, arms clutched across her front and shoulders in, trying to look small.

"That girl is frightened," Horace muttered, impulsively moving to the front of the store. "Child, do you need help?" He turned the corner of the aisle, but she was gone. Unsettled, he returned to the counter and paid, and carried his box of things back to the truck. He set the box on the seat and transferred the items to his backpack, fired up the truck, and pulled onto the road. "I wonder, Camilla," he mused out loud, "does the world frighten you? Is that what's got me bothered? Are you out there somewhere, as frightened as your mother always was?"

He started back toward his fire road, but remembered another road that ran close to today's square. It would save hours of walking, and give him more time to explore. And sure enough, he found an overgrown drive that would make a good starting point. There was a chain across it, but it was old and rusted, and wasn't locked. He drove in and put the chain back up, and rode through tall grass to a clearing. A pile of moss-covered, rotting wood marked the spot where a hunting cabin had once stood. It was a fine base for his hike. He took a morning swig of bourbon and set off into the woods, mulling over the matter of his one remaining blood relative on the planet.

"You'd have no cause to be frightened if you were up here, Camilla," he said out loud. "I'd see to that. Maybe I could show you some of these places. Would you like that? I wouldn't mind having a companion on my daily excursions."

He checked his compass and stepped into the woods, talking to absent Camilla about hiking as a kid. Soon he found the old road. But it was different today. Broken sumac and alders in the wheel ruts showed that someone had driven in.

"This morning," Horace said. "There was no disturbance here yesterday." He adjusted the straps of his pack and trundled along, following the contour of the wheel ruts. "Good, then. An adventure. Let's see if we can find out who you are and what you're up to."

The road wound around a steep, rocky hill. As he approached the top of a long rise, he heard water tumbling down rocks, a stream up ahead. That might be a nice place to stop. Then something raised a warning signal in his mind. He pulled the rifle off his shoulder and racked a round into the chamber. Someone was up there, and something about it wasn't friendly. He crested the hill and stopped at the edge of the woods where the trail ended at a clearing next to a mostly dry streambed.

To his left was a big pickup truck with a cap on the back, much like he had expected to find, except that it was a late model. He'd expected something a hunter would drive, an old work truck. But this wasn't a hunting party. Horace relaxed his grip on the rifle. The stream flowed over a stony rise and dropped into a little pool, forming a natural shower, under which a naked woman in her late twenties was standing. Two men in their forties were watching her, one sitting in a canvas chair and grinning while the other hopped around with a camera, tipping it one way or another and chattering away.

"Oh, nice, nice! Tip your head. Oh, baby, that's nice! Turn, turn. Show me that fantastic pair. You got it, baby. Come on, get in the water and show me."

A nude photo shoot? But wait. The sun was on the wrong side. This was a good looking woman, but no fine photos would result from this effort. If the man were to move around to the other side, the sun would catch her body nicely. Wasn't it obvious?

But the woman wasn't making a serious effort, either. She rolled her eyes and stood contrapposto, hands on her hips like a scolding mother, and glared at the man with the camera as if she found the whole thing terribly annoying.

Horace scowled, too. What lonely hiker wouldn't appreciate a secretive look at a young woman enjoying the day au naturel? But this seemed more like something out of a low budget porn film. He stood and watched anyway, but couldn't help feeling disappointed. Then the wind changed, and he heard the woman talking.

"Why the hell did you let her out of the truck, Arlan?" the nude woman said, scowling at the man in the camp chair. "We're supposed to be shooting today, not taking goddamned photos."

Horace lowered his eyebrows. His earlier sense had been right. Something was off.

"I didn't think she'd run off without her clothes, Kaley, okay?" said the seated man. "Why don't you babysit her yourself next time?"

"We're supposed to be *shooting a film*," the woman repeated. "Sweet little French girl gets banged in the woods. We're supposed to make all kinds of money with Juliette in it. And then you let her go?"

"Fuck you. I didn't *let her go*. She ran off when I was filling the tank," the man snapped back. "But just shut up, all right? Where's she gonna go? She's got no money, no food, she don't hardly speak English, and she's in her underwear, for chrissakes. She's probably hiding in the bushes back at that gas station. I'll go get her later."

"Kaley, I need you more *in the waterfall*," the man shooting pictures complained, holding his hands to demonstrate how he wanted to frame the shot.

"Screw the waterfall, Mack." The woman stomped out of the stream and snatched a towel from a rock. "You told me I was gonna do this fantastic sex scene with that kid, not freeze my ass off while you two get a hard-on. You think you're some kind of goddamned art photographer now?"

"I'm taking test shots. I'll shoot video when we have Juliette back." Mack lowered the camera. "And Arlan's right. She's got nowhere to go. She'll do her part when she's hungry enough."

Horace scanned wider, studying the campsite. The scene in the store suddenly made sense. He absentmindedly moved his finger to the trigger guard. If the frightened girl he'd seen was as young as he suspected, maybe he ought to just blow these three away right now, and leave them to rot in the woods. Three shots should do it, even with just the .22.

But no, he wasn't a murderer, and he didn't have the whole story. "Don't rush things," he muttered. He turned and fast-walked back to his truck, and sat behind the wheel to think.

"Now what? Call the police?" he said out loud. He shook his head. "I don't have a phone. And I can't call from the store. That would draw too much attention." He huffed out a breath. "Go find the girl myself?" He gave a snort of derision and turned the key. "Oh, yes, that would work nicely. *Come here, little girl in your underwear. Get in the truck with the sketchy old geezer.*"

He put the truck in drive and rumbled back down to the chain across the road, and soon was heading back to town.

"I have to call the police," he said out loud. "What is she, thirteen? Fourteen? My god."

"Pas de police," said a weak, high voice from behind the seat.

"God damn!" Horace pushed hard on the brakes, and the truck stuttered and shimmied to the side of the road. "Who's back there?" he demanded, and silently kicked himself. What were the options? He turned to look at the girl from the store, but a hand shot up.

"Je ne suis pas habillée!" said the same young-girl voice.

Horace snapped his head back to the wheel. "Not dressed," he said. "Right. I'm sorry." He fluidly switched to French. "Je conduis. Vous restez là. D'accord ?"

"Mais pas de police."

"Pas de police. C'est promis." He said. "And I understand you might need food. Uh, voilà. Il y a des vêtements dans le sac et de la nourriture." He picked up the pack and pushed it over the seat, and hands took it. "Put something on. And there are snacks. Help yourself."

"Merci," the girl said, almost in a whisper. "Vous allez m'aider?"

"Votre nom …"

"Juliette."

"Je m'appelle Horace. Heureux de vous rencontrer, Juliette. Yes, I'll help you, honey. Of course."

Horace smiled, and almost laughed. He considered that he ought to feel a surge of adrenaline at this unexpected drama. Instead the girl's voice prompted a powerful feeling of nostalgia. Yes, she was in trouble and needed help. It seemed clear that she didn't want to do a cheap porn film with those three in the woods. But speaking in French to a young girl brought him right back to Paris when he was little.

He pictured his mother in the living room tutoring a high school girl in English. Horace had been infatuated with his mother's students, those magical older creatures in their school uniforms. He would trundle in with a picture book, and the girl would laugh and pat the cute little boy on the head as he climbed into her lap and asked her to read. And without missing a beat, his mother would shoo him away and work the scene into the lesson.

"Allez lire votre livre toute seule, Horace. Je suis occupée," she would prompt.

And the girl would slide him off her lap. "Go read your book by yourself, Horace. I am busy."

"Bien, bien," his mother would say, and Horace would offer a weak protest and retreat to the kitchen.

Horace pulled back onto the road, and they drove in silence. This time he drove to his own fire road and pulled up next to his cabin.

"Come inside," he said, as he pulled to a stop. "Venez. Allons à l'intérieur. Come tell me what's happened."

He felt his curiosity rise to anger as the girl told her story. He had to stop himself from jumping out of his chair or pounding his fist. It was such an old, awful con. It started with shoplifting in this case, although it might just as easily have been drugs, or a story about her brother being in trouble, or any of countless variations. The target was a young exchange student stuck working for the summer near her school in Québec, unable to afford to go home for the break. Juliette had slipped out of the dressing room wearing a shirt from the store under her own—and the men casing the mall looking for a mark had spotted her.

A man in a uniform stopped her. It probably wasn't a real store security uniform, but how would Juliette know? He cuffed her, and ordered her to come with him; and she was led to a back room. Horace pictured a storage room, not a security office. And then came the predictable set of steps.

As the girl stood there terrified, the man shouted and threatened her. She faced five years in prison, he told her, and she would lose her place at the school. She would be expelled, and her parents would be notified, and she'd be marked for life as a thief. No school would accept her.

The man brought her to tears, and then the first man stepped in with the good-cop routine. Maybe we can make this go away, he told her. His friend works for the store, and said his brother was looking for a girl about her age to do some work. It wasn't anything difficult. Just a small part in a film, but they needed to do a shoot out of town, a camping scene. She'd be gone for two or three days, maybe. He could make it work. He would call the boarding house himself and explain, so she wouldn't get in trouble. Nobody would need to know that she'd been caught stealing.

"Oh, *honey*," Horace sighed, face-in-hands, as she brought him up to the present.

The girl sat shaking in his big chair, dressed in one of his plaid shirts and a pair of his khakis with the legs rolled up. He had given her a bowl of soup and toast and butter, and she had eaten every scrap. The empty dishes sat on a snack tray next to the chair, and he caught her glancing longingly at them. He rose to heat a glass of milk for her. When it was ready, he filled a bowl with cookies and stepped back in and gave them to her. She smiled and said thank you. She was starting to look a bit less terrified.

Horace sat and watched her eat. He smiled as she caught him staring. "You're not my little Camilla, dear," he said, "but here you are. What shall we do with you?"

To fill in the story, he spoke to her in French, asking about her family and her home. She was in an exchange program, she told him, over from France for a year. Most of the girls in the school went home for the summer break, but she couldn't afford to fly home and back, so they put her up at a boarding house where she did housekeeping to pay her way, and she was supposed to spend the summer studying and not getting into trouble. And then came the incident at the store.

She broke into tears again, and it took a while to get the rest of the story from her. At first things seemed to be going as promised. The movie called for a scene in the woods, a couple and their daughter going camping. She was excited. She would play the daughter. They'd set up a tent. It sounded like fun.

It wasn't until they had snuck her past the border that she realized it was all a lie. As they drove, they worked on her, leading up to telling her that she had to do a nude scene or they'd leave her in the woods on the wrong side of the border. Then the woman spilled ketchup on her dress and told her to take it off quickly while the men were in the store, and she'd try to get the stain out with soda water. But she didn't give it back. Instead she made her stay in her underwear. She said it might help with her attitude.

When they stopped again to get gas, Juliette ran into the store and saw Horace, and heard him ask if she needed help. Afraid the men would catch her, she ran back out, but couldn't think what to do. She figured the truck must belong to the old man in the store, so she hid behind the seat.

"Good plan," Horace said.

Juliette finally fell asleep in his chair, and Horace sat thinking. Midafternoon he made sandwiches and more soup, and they sat and had a long, quiet lunch. The girl was starting to settle down. That was good. She insisted on cleaning up after the meal, and Horace poured himself a glass of bourbon and sat in his chair while the girl washed the dishes. He felt drowsy, and started to nod off. When he realized more than an hour had passed, he stepped into the kitchen and found Juliette scrubbing the floor.

"What are you doing? You don't have to do that, Juliette," he said. He motioned for her to come sit down again.

"Je dois te payer pour m'aider," she said.

"No, no. You don't need to pay me a damned thing. Just come sit down. Viens t'asseoir."

Juliette seemed unsure, but Horace nodded his head, and she followed him back to the living room.

"All right, then," he said, absentmindedly shifting from French to English as the girl resumed her perch on his big chair. "I've got the picture, Juliette, and we'll take care of this, all right? You need clothes, a way to get home, and we need to take care of those predators. And I think you might need to find a different school for the next term, eh? You need a change." She looked at him blankly, and he repeated it all in French.

"Tu peux faire tout ça?" She stared.

Horace smiled. "Oh, yes, I can do all that, sweetheart. I can do it blindfolded and standing on one foot. You watch me." He didn't translate for her, but Juliette got the idea. She smiled back, and started crying again.

The girl was terrified when he rose to leave, but he had things to do, and needed her to sit this part out. He explained that he needed to execute a solution—or rather, the first of several parts of the overall solution. "It's not one gigantic problem, Juliette," he told her in French. "It's several separate problems, each of which needs a solution. I'm going to take care of one of them right now, and then we'll tackle the others. You wait here, all right?"

Juliette seemed doubtful, but she gave him a weak smile and agreed to wait in the cabin.

First he drove back into town to do some things; and then he returned to the campsite in the woods. They had set up a large tent, and inside the woman was arguing with one of the men. Outside there was a hamburger in a cast iron pan burning to a crisp on a camp stove, while the second man sat slumped in a camp chair, asleep, still holding a spatula in one hand. His cell phone was on the ground where it had slipped from his other hand. It wasn't even quite seven o'clock. There was still plenty of daylight left. But beer bottles scattered all over explained his slumber.

This made things rather easy, Horace thought. He slipped over to the pickup, quietly opened the door, and with a gloved hand slid a package under the front seat. Then he checked the two figures shouting in the tent, and confident that they were fully occupied, he stepped over to the sleeping man and pocketed his cell phone. He found the woman's shirt and bluejeans draped over the back of a chair and took them, and before disappearing back into the woods he returned to the truck and neatly slashed two of the tires.

Juliette was up next. Horace couldn't risk making the call himself, even on the phone he'd taken from the pornographer. So he fetched her from the cabin and drove back to his temporary parking space at the fallen down hunting camp. He assured her that she wouldn't even have to get out of the truck.

She breathed in and out, and pressed 9-1-1. Horace had written her lines down, spelling them phonetically for her. "Please you must help me," she said in a little-girl voice. "They take dirty pictures of me. I get away, but they come get me, I think."

He heard a voice on the line asking her questions, and then the voice switched to French, and Juliette played her part. She told them the story Horace had outlined for her, ending with getting away from them and getting a ride. A nice man was taking her to a bus station. But she knew where the people who had kidnapped her were. They had stolen guns and liquor from a store in town, and had dirty pictures. She told them the name of the store, and told them where the campsite was.

The voice on the other end tried to get her name, insisting that the police would need to speak with her. But Juliette ended the call and handed the phone to Horace. He wiped it off, lowered the window, and tossed it out.

"Well done," he said, and gave her an encouraging pat on the shoulder. "Maintenant, nous attendons," he said. "Now we wait." She nervously took hold of his hand, and Horace smiled. "La partie la plus difficile est terminée," he added. "The next part is easy. I just want to see this, all right? That's why we drove back here. Then we can have dinner. How does that sound?"

It didn't take long. Horace had deliberately tripped the burglar alarm after lifting several pistols and two bottles of Jim Beam from the store in town. He didn't know if the men already had guns. If they did, it wouldn't matter. The police would face armed suspects. But he wasn't going to help arm them, should they happen to find the package before the police got there. And so he picked out three .38 specials and two .45 magnums—and ten boxes of 9mm rounds. So the men weren't geniuses, were they? he told himself, chuckling as he packed it all into a fabric grocery bag, which now sat under the front seat of their truck.

Juliette held tight to Horace's hand. Soon they saw the blue lights. They watched the police rush past, and then Horace pulled back onto the road and drove back to the cabin.

"That should take care of those three. Come. I've got clothes for you."

Dinner was a fine French quiche, another taste of home, and Horace smiled and praised the girl for preparing an excellent meal. He gave her a glass of wine, which she accepted without the usual *really?* look that he would expect from an American girl her age. By the end of the meal, he had gotten a genuine smile out of her. And then when he told her the second part of the plan, she burst into tears again, and hugged him.

The second part was much simpler, from Horace's point of view. Throwing money at a problem didn't require any tactical skill. But he could see how it might seem dramatic to the girl. The hardest part was getting back on the grid to arrange the transaction. In the end he opted to take the simple route. He drove back one more time to the fallen-down hunting camp, found the discarded cell phone, and made a call.

He might be living off the grid, but his money was not. And those who managed it for him didn't ask questions about where he was, or why he was calling from a strange cell phone. He told them to wire two hundred thousand dollars to a family in France. "Include a note that it's for Juliette's education," Horace said, and no questions were asked. Nor did they question why he wanted them to arrange for a female agent to meet a young girl at a bus station in Portland, Maine, and escort her to her home outside of Paris. He simply explained what he wanted, told them to make it happen, and told them to place a special ad in the New York Times when the girl was safely home. He'd expect to see it in Sunday's edition, if not Saturday's.

. . .

It hadn't rained all week, but everything in Virginia was damp.

Summer humidity blanketed the little town southwest of Richmond in a haze of vapor. Mack stumbled around the trailer in his boxers, sweat dripping from his hairy chest, turning all the lights off as if it might help cool things down. When he stepped into the cramped living room and clicked off the table lamp by the TV, a sullen, high voice broke the hot silence.

"You know what would make it feel cooler? An air conditioner."

The big hulk of a man turned his gray eyes to a skinny twelve-year-old girl slouching listlessly in an overstuffed chair in the corner. She pulled up the hem of her undershirt and mopped it across her face, pushing back the black hair plastered to her forehead. "They do make air conditioners, you know."

"We can't afford air conditioning, Camilla," the man growled. "And Jesus, could you put some clothes on? Jimmy's coming over to watch the game. You can't be sitting around in your underwear."

"It's a hundred and ten," she said. "And if I die from the heat, the agency won't pay you anymore. And look who's talking. You think I want to look at that?"

"I bet they have an air conditioner at the agency. Wanna go see, little wise-ass? Maybe I could leave you there."

"What, you're gonna walk? Or do you mean maybe you're finally gonna fix the car?"

"Jesus, Camilla. Didn't Marie just buy you a bathing suit? Why don't you go jump in the lake."

"Asshole," the girl muttered under her breath as she hauled herself up and stomped out of the room. But the lake wasn't a bad idea. She pushed into the tiny laundry room that they had made into her bedroom, and tried to slam the door, but it stuck with a thump, too swollen to close.

Mack had turned off the fan in the window, and she aggressively turned it back on and put it on high. Then she turned on her lamp, and reached up and pulled the chain to turn on the bare bulb overhead, too. She looked around, but she had played out the little protest as far as it would go. There was nothing else to turn on.

The fan slowly got going, and she felt a stream of warm air as she rifled through the plastic stacking drawers that served as her bureau. Clothes tumbled to the floor, and she pulled out a cheap yellow bathing suit with a ruffle around the waist, and exhaled loudly. "It's like for a six-year-old," she muttered. She had begged Marie to get her a bathing suit, but instead of buying her a new one, the woman had dug this old thing out of a box at a yard sale.

"Probably cost her a whole dollar," Camilla grumbled.

She turned and shoved harder on the door. All she needed was to have Mack walk in on her and catch her pulling the bag out from under her mat.

She upended the shopping bag onto her sleeping bag, and smiled. "Now *this* is a bathing suit," she said, picking up a sleek, jet black two-piece.

Her friend Sasha had been shocked when Camilla had showed it to her in the parking lot. "Where'd you get that? I didn't see you buy a suit. Wow, it's nice. Oh, god, Millie, you didn't steal it, did you?"

"Steal it? Of course not. You think I'm stupid? I'd get nabbed, and some assholes would try to con me into doing a porno."

"You … what?" Sasha flashed a look of confusion and horror. "A porno?"

"Never mind. Just something that popped into my head."

"Millie, you're so strange sometimes." Sasha folded her arms and scowled.

"My brain is fried with this heat, Sash. I didn't steal it, okay? Some doofus in the store bought it for me."

"A guy in the store bought you a bathing suit? A perv?"

"No, just a guy. He's piling stuff on the counter and going back for more, and the girl scanning the stuff is too busy blabbing on her phone to be paying attention. So I waited until the guy was at the back of the store, and I said, hey, can you scan this and put it in a separate bag for me?"

"No way." Sasha's eyes went wide, and she flicked her red braid over her shoulder.

"It's not like I lied. I didn't say I was his daughter, or that he said he'd buy it for me or anything. I just asked her to scan it. And she put it in a bag, and I left. All paid for. Totally legit."

The trick now, Camilla realized as she pulled it on, was not to be seen wearing it by Mack or Marie. So she tugged the old yellow one-piece on over it, and checked herself out with a hand mirror.

"Oh, shit," she said. The yellow suit was cheap and thin, and she could see the black suit through it. But it would have to do. She yanked on the doorknob and forced the door open, stepped into her flip-flops, and listened. Mack was flipping channels, looking for the game. Good. He probably wouldn't even notice her leaving. And with the lights off, he wouldn't notice that she had a new suit on under the old suit, anyway. But she had a lie ready, just in case: "You can see through it," she'd whine. "I'm not gonna swim in it without underwear on."

He'd buy it. He'd probably complain that she looked like a slut wearing black underwear under a yellow suit. But he wouldn't go so far as to question whether it really was underwear. Mack was not that smart.

She slipped out, closed the door behind her, and draped a towel around her shoulders. Now she just hoped to god that nobody would see her. The yellow suit was awful. It was bad enough that she was shorter than everyone else her age. The suit made her look even more like a little kid.

But in spite of her fast pace, halfway down the first block she was discovered. "Hey, stick girl!" came the unwelcome voice of her neighborhood adversary. "Gonna take a shower? Probably got no running water inside at home, right? Does your foster father wash you down in the yard with a bucket?"

"Go away, Kevin," Camilla said, not looking around. She picked up her pace.

"You can come to my place. We got a hose out back for the dog. I'll scrub you with flea soap."

She halted and spun, and folded her arms. "Get away from me," she snapped. The boy caught up with her and loomed over her, grinning. He was only a year older, but thirteen-year-old Kevin was big for his age, and twelve-year-old Camilla was tiny. She stood in his shadow looking up at him, her face contorted into a scowl. "I wouldn't be caught dead going to your house. And I can see why you need flea soap. I bet the whole place is infested with them, just like you are."

"Nice bra," he said. "Except what do you need a bra for?"

"It's not a bra, dickweed. It's a bathing suit."

"You got a bathing suit on under your bathing suit? Wow, that's great," he joked. "Is that what all the stick girls are wearing this year? And what's under the black one? Oh, wait. I know. Nothing! Just a stick girl. Here, let's take a look." He reached for her, but only caught the hem of her towel as she jumped back.

Camilla spun away and let go of the towel. She considered dropping into a karate stance and taking a shot at his balls, but instead she turned and broke into a run. Kevin was three times her size, but he wasn't fast. She could beat him easily in a flat-out sprint, even in flip-flops.

The boy slowed at the end of the block and broke into an over-loud, taunting laugh. "Catch you later, stick-girl! Don't go and sink and drown in all those bathing suits!"

"Asshole," she huffed, slowing as she turned the corner.

The neighborhood bully was one reason she spent so much time in the trailer. Mack and Marie were annoying and cheap, but all they did was shout a lot and threaten to send her back to the agency. Kevin, on the other hand, never turned down an opportunity to torment her.

Sasha's house was the last on the block, a little cottage that had been converted to a year-round home. But compared to the trailer Camilla lived in, it seemed palatial. They had a separate kitchen and dining room. She pushed through the front gate and flashed a smile at her friend's father, who was practicing his putt. He'd converted the small patch of grass in the tiny yard to a makeshift putting green by burying a red plastic cup in the middle.

"Hey there, sweetie," he said with a wink. "How's your day going?"

"Great," Camilla lied. Mr. Harris made her feel jealous of her friend. He was *nice*. He didn't say, *Hey, Camilla, don't you look especially ridiculous in that cheap, horrible suit.* He just smiled and said hello, and pretended he didn't notice. Sasha had an actual blood-related father, and he wasn't an asshole.

"Sasha's inside," he said. "She was hoping you'd want to go swimming. Why don't you stop on your way home, and I'll grill us some hot dogs? There's plenty."

"Yeah? Thanks, Mr. Harris." She gave him a smile. Swimming, and then food! The day was shaping up.

Sasha pulled open the door just as Camilla was reaching for the knob. "What in the name of everything creepy and old is *that*?" her friend said, pointing at the yellow suit.

Camilla rolled her eyes and pushed inside. "This is what Marie thinks is a bathing suit." She shoved the door shut, and slithered out of the yellow one-piece. "Hide it somewhere. I have to put it back on before I go home."

"You walked here in this? Outside?" she held up the suit. "God. Your foster dad actually lets you wear this?" Sasha stuffed the old suit under a stack of sweatshirts and jackets packed onto a shelf in the tiny entryway closet.

"What? No, obviously Mack hasn't seen it. He'd throw a fit if he saw me in a see-through bathing suit."

"God, yeah," Sasha agreed. She pulled back handfuls of red hair and made a pony tail with a rubber band.

"And then my grandfather would show up in a pickup truck and take me away, and Mack and Marie would get arrested."

"Whoa, what?" Sasha stopped in the middle of twisting the rubber band for one more loop. "Millie, your grandfather? You told me you haven't seen your grandfather since you were two."

Camilla expelled a loud breath and closed her eyes. "Never mind. It's stupid. Just something I was thinking about."

"You are so, so strange."

"He's not gonna come save me from Mack and Marie," Camilla growled. "Just forget it."

"But listen," her friend said, picking up on Camilla's distress and pitching her voice up in a strained effort to sound cheerful, "your new suit is super nice, isn't it? I wish I could get random strangers to buy suits for me. Come on. There's supposed to be a lifeguard until four. We've got three whole hours."

The lifeguard was a bored high school boy lounging on his perch on the guard tower, reading a magazine. The town beach was busy, but it was all families with little kids. The boy looked up hopefully as a pair of girls approached, one in a black bikini and the other in a blue one-piece. But then he sighed. More little kids. He turned back to his magazine, and missed the big boy stepping up behind the two girls.

"Only one bathing suit this time, stick girl? You lost one already?"

Camilla clenched her fists and stepped onto the sand. "Go *away*, Kevin," she barked. "What, did you follow me here? Jesus."

"What do you even need a suit for?" said a higher voice. "You could go bare like a little kid. Who'd notice?"

Sasha and Camilla stopped and turned. "Miles," Sasha scolded the smaller boy tagging along behind Kevin, "Just 'cause your protector is here doesn't mean you can be a prick. I'm gonna tell my brother you were bothering us again, and he'll beat the shit out of both of you."

"Him and whose army?" Kevin said.

"God, really?" Camilla rolled her eyes. "Why don't you both go away. You can't go on the beach anyway, Kevin. You got banned for smoking. Take your little buddy and get lost."

"Kev told me you had two suits on," the smaller boy said, grinning. "How come, when you don't even need one?"

"Shut up, Miles," Camilla said. "You're like a parrot. Can't you think of anything original? I'll beat the shit out of you myself."

"Got anything on under that one?" the younger boy persisted.

"Maybe we should see." Kevin went for her again, and she was too slow this time. He caught hold of her top and yanked, wrenching her forward and pulling her over, and broke into mean laughter as she fell to her hands and knees.

Kevin laughed, and Camilla rose and went rigid. She stood there frozen—and then lunged forward and rammed her forehead into the laughing boy's face.

There was a hushed instant of incredulity, as attention turned from Camilla with her top askew to Kevin clutching a hand over his face, blood gushing from his nose. He howled and fell to his knees, and Miles took a step backward, lost his balance and landed on his backside in the sand. His smug grin was replaced by a look of horror as Camilla took a half step toward him, her body language asserting that he was next.

Sasha grabbed Camilla's wrist and pulled her away. "My god, Millie," she hissed. "I think you broke his nose!"

"You heard the sensei," Camilla scowled. "You have a right to defend yourself."

"Yeah, I missed the class where he taught us to head-butt people. Come on!" Sasha pulled her away from the boys.

"So sometimes you gotta improvise. Sue me."

The lifeguard turned at the sound of the shrieking boy and saw the figure on his knees spewing blood onto the sand. He dropped his magazine and hopped down as parents on the beach turned and started to run over. Camilla saw people converging on her, and her eyes bugged out. She pulled her arm free and ran.

...

Horace decided to skip his usual walk in the woods. Juliette had given him a hug when he dropped her at the bus stop, and that was that. The cabin seemed especially empty.

"Isn't it strange, Camilla," he said out loud, pushing the door shut, "how a random, brief encounter can tug at you. I've known Juliette for just one day, and still I miss her."

Maybe he would pour himself a bourbon. Just sit and do nothing. He stepped into the mudroom and hung up his light jacket—and his thoughts shifted to his son.

"What, now?" he complained. "What is it, Vergil?"

He felt the same sense of grief that had plagued him since the police officer had stood cap in hand on his stoop. But this time another feeling was in close competition: annoyance. Couldn't he enjoy a moment of bittersweet reflection on his brief encounter with the girl? Juliette was unconnected. He had stumbled into someone else's drama, and had intervened and helped to set things right, and that was the end of it. He would never see her again. But couldn't he at least mull it over for a little while? Was it too much to ask for one single day in which his dead son was not the center of his attention?

Instead the crushing feeling of guilt and horror was even more intense this time. He stopped dead in the mudroom and broke into a sweat as he was drawn into a scene from his son's life for the first time in decades. He saw his son, plain as day, perched on a mountainside staring through a rifle sight. Someone was about to die. He was about to watch his son kill someone.

"No, no, no!" He said, rushing outside and shaking his head to get rid of the scene. "I broke this off years ago, when my boy left home. Why is this coming to me now?"

He wandered back into the mudroom, and his knees buckled as he felt it again, like a wave. What was this? It couldn't be related to Juliette. And it couldn't be the guns, or the time he had spent with his son on the shooting range—none of that. He was seeing remnants of old things. Why?

Then he looked down. "Oh, no," he gasped, as he saw it. It was indeed something else. It was something obvious. Shoved beneath the coats in the mudroom was the dusty plastic container of his son's things. Ten years ago, with a solemn nod of sympathy for the old man whose son had turned into a killer, the police had handed over that container the prosecutors had determined weren't relevant to the murder case: an old fountain pen, a piece of driftwood, a chunk of granite, and other trinkets.

"Maybe you'd like these to remember your son by," the officer had said.

Horace had forgotten about the container he had tucked under the truck seat. And now somehow he had forgotten about it again. How stupid! He should never have taken it to Maine in the first place, and when he'd found it, he should have gotten rid of it immediately.

"They aren't random trinkets, Vergil, are they?" He backed up, staring at the container. "You didn't collect those things on happy vacations around the world. They're from your kill sites."

That container under the coats held tokens gathered by his son the assassin, and the connections hadn't died with Vergil. His son's keepsakes were calling out to him. Horace felt his heart race, as angst transformed into something more like fear. It was all he could do to stop himself from grabbing the container, heaving it out into the yard, and slamming the door.

Bourbon turned out to be the plan for the day, after all. He sat outside on the steps and downed half a glass. Soon he felt more calm, if less clear-headed.

"It's a step," he muttered, returning indoors, "a step in the right direction. At least now I have a framework. I know it's not random."

As the panic subsided, Horace felt an urge see if he could find Vergil in these things. His son was dead, but maybe these old connections could help him understand—or he might be drawn into something he didn't want to see.

When he couldn't resist any longer, he resolved to start with just one item. He would dip a toe in the water and check the temperature. He opened the container and drew out a chunk of rock in a plastic zip-lock evidence bag. He set it down, snapped the lid shut, as if the other items might try to escape.

For a while he just looked at the stone. He held up the bag, not daring to open it. The tag on the bag indicated that it had been recovered from a commuter train car after an incident in which the subject had escaped. An agent had apparently collected the rock from Vergil's apartment, and had then thrown it at him during a chase. Horace studied the mica-flecked chunk of granite. It looked like an ordinary rock. He touched it through the plastic, and it still seemed like nothing special. Finally he opened the bag and tipped it into his palm. Nothing happened. He felt nothing different, and didn't see anything but the woods outside his window, and his chair, and the other things in front of him.

"Maybe it's gone," he said, with a sigh of disappointment and relief. "My son is gone, and all that's left is the random flash of recollection and the anguish. Maybe these objects are meaningless now." He set the stone on the windowsill. Later he picked it up again, still felt nothing, and set it back down.

One night there was a terrific thunderstorm, with dramatic bolts of lightning crashing into the woods, and long, lingering booms. He went to the window and clutched the stone in his palm, and then sighed out loud when nothing happened. It left him feeling a bit stupid. Why would the weather around his little cabin somehow bring this relic of his son's experiences to life?

The stone became his own keepsake, an object to turn in his hand absentmindedly as he stood looking out the window.

And then one day as he tossed it from one hand to the other, the woods in front of him seemed to change. It was not young, new growth, but old growth—very old growth—like the King's pines in the New England of the seventeenth century. All of a sudden he wasn't standing in his cabin. He was standing on a trail partway up a mountain, looking at an ancient forest.

Then as quickly as the image came to him, it blinked out again.

"Oh!" he cried out, startled.

He tried again, and got another flicker. This time it was a glimpse of a road marked with wheel ruts. It seemed to be early morning. The road was empty except for a single wagon covered in canvas, rumbling along well ahead. And then it vanished, as if he were a gnat zipping across someone's field of vision and a wave of the hand had brushed him away. This kept happening: A flicker, then gone. The connection was too weak, it seemed. He was unable to keep contact for more than a series of fleeting moments. He put the stone down and moved on to other things.

It seemed purely by accident that he connected to the little girl. It had been one of those rare days when he had been hiking in the woods and had seen people on the logging road. A young couple in hiking boots stood on a small bridge experiencing the great north woods, admiring the creek that ran beneath, while a sullen teenager leaned out of the window of their Subaru and informed them that she was hungry and needed to go to the bathroom.

Horace had watched them for a minute and then retreated. Tourists driving the backwoods roads of northern Maine would find it frightening to see an old man emerge from the trees, and he didn't want to talk to them, anyway. But seeing the kid in the car made him think about his grand-daughter again. Maybe that had something to do with it. He had stumbled across the young French girl Juliette and she had somehow reminded him of Camilla; and now here was a girl in a car. Camilla would be around that age, almost thirteen. Things seemed to point toward his granddaughter lately.

But when he finally made a strong connection, it was not to Camilla. He stepped inside after his morning hike and looked out the window. And just as he was leaning over to pick up the chunk of granite, a muscle in his leg cramped. He bent over in pain and clutched the stone—and looked into a dark night with a figure looming overhead, repeatedly whipping a weighted sock down. The girl on the ground was not Camilla, and not Juliette, either. Who was she? The pain in his leg seemed to mirror the beating the little girl was getting, and it was only when the beating finally stopped and she curled into a ball that he was able to relax enough to center himself in the scene.

"Can you see? Open your eyes," he said.

3. Dinner and a Show

Saor Tieg paced back and forth beneath the pergola, looking down at the torches and the food tents. Normally there would be a crowd of people, the noise rising up the terraces in a pleasing, steady roar. It was the sound of sailors spending their pay. It meant goods from the mainland making their way overseas, and money flowing to the Western Shores. This is what had made him rich.

Tonight the sailors would be delayed in their meals, although none would complain. All down the terraces and along the wharf, decorations were going up. The drab tents of the lower tiers had been taken down and replaced with canopies in brilliant colors, and thousands of small paper dragons in oranges, yellows, and reds, intricately folded and strung together, festooned the walkways and canopies.

Tonight would be the Tallach version of the fire pit pavilion, a gigantic feast of spit-roasted meat, barrels of fine beer, endless bottles of wine, and baked goods of all sorts.

All of this should be enough to occupy Tieg's attention. But he had something else on his mind. The Tynan gunners would be arriving soon for a secret meeting. What did they want? Tieg had never met the northern lord or the fighters who ran at his heel. But he understood how the northern triumvirate worked. These two young women, not even thirty, commanded the full power of the northern king himself. Ailmili, the smaller one, was practically worshipped by the northern army. A casual comment about the gunner could cause a barroom brawl if northern soldiers were about. And Rachanna was known for being quiet and reserved in conversation—and ruthlessly efficient in a fight.

And it had been these three, the northern king and the two young women, who had overthrown the southern tyrant. The southlands were now free, and new governors had been appointed. But the gunners of Tynan held powerful sway in the south. A meeting with them could spell the start to something big—or an end to it.

"The meal is prepared?" Tieg halted and turned.

"Yes, sir. Everything is ready." A servant bowed.

"And the table is set. And the wine is breathing."

"All to your orders, sir."

"And what o'clock do we have?" He started pacing again.

"Nearly seven, sir."

"Where are they, then?" he said under his breath. "All right. I'll wait in my dining room. You'll see them in immediately."

"Yes, sir."

He scanned the waterfront one last time, and headed up the steps. The small dining room was decked out richly, fancy blue and black damask draped over the windows between the room and the larger dining hall. The curtains had been drawn over the exterior windows as well, to give the diners some privacy. The best china of the inn was laid out, three places at one end of the large table. Heavy candles in brass stands cast a warm light.

Pulling back the curtain, he looked down at the commotion along the waterfront. The noise of the preparations and the breakers on the rocks blurred into a dull murmur through the thick glass. He turned as the hand on the clock ticked to seven o'clock.

"Where are they, then?" he repeated, and almost drew his blade as he detected a pair of figures standing in the shadows in the far corner of the room.

"Saor Tieg," the smaller one said, as two women in their late twenties stepped into the candlelight. "Thank you for consenting to meet with us. I'm Ailmili, and this is Rachanna. Gunners of Tynan." They bowed.

The gunners wore black robes with wide collars. Long sashes embroidered with silver vines hung around their necks and draped down the front. The gunner Rachanna was imposing, tall and solid. Her dark hair was pulled into a tight braid down her back. Ailmili, a head shorter and thin, had her blonde hair tied tightly on top of her head. Her face was half obscured by a silver-edged white band covering her eyes. Tieg knew why. The blonde gunner's deep blue eyes were marked with silver lines like crosshairs. The fabric band hid her devil's stare. In their reflection in a mirror behind them, Tieg could see the ebony handles of northern hunter blades at their shoulders, three red stones set into each.

He bowed. "Gunners," he said. "I hope I've not kept you waiting." He snapped his fingers, and a servant entered immediately. "The wine," he said, and turned back to his guests. "Shall we sit? And let me say, I'm deeply honored to entertain the northern lord's gunners."

The gunners stepped to the table, and the servant hurried to pour the wine.

"I'm told you prefer to travel on your own. But I'd be delighted to offer hospitality to your soldiers—if by chance there might be some on hand. There's no need for them to be outside."

Ailmili offered a smile. "If they want to follow us around, they can find their own hospitality. But thank you."

He nodded. "And may I invite you to stay after the meal? There's to be a celebration tonight. My Undine."

"The Tallach fighting trials," Ailmili said. "Your daughter, isn't that right? Give her our congratulations. The fourth level, I hear. And a dragon-serpent."

Her companion gave a grunt of approval.

"You've heard? It would be a great honor, were you to greet her."

The gunners looked at each other, a silent communication, and the smaller one nodded. "Time allowing, we'll stay and offer greetings to your girl. Thank you."

Tieg beamed. "Undine will be very excited. She doesn't know you're here, of course. It will be a wonderful surprise. Gunners of Tynan attending her celebration! Now then. Shall we eat? And then talk."

The meal was elegant, a fish stew with a pastry crust, thick-sliced bread made with onion seeds, and an excellent wine. When the servants entered to offer seconds, all three diners declined. Tieg called for coffee, and they sat sipping the hot beverage.

At length, Rachanna nodded to her companion, and Ailmili set her cup down and pushed her chair back. "Fourteen years ago, slave traders raided a southern town and stole from it. This was during the later part of the reign of the dictator Shular." Ailmili stopped and looked around, noting the servant by the door.

Tieg bowed. "The end of whose reign, gunners, I thank you for." He made a hand motion to the servant, and the man bowed and left, closing the door. "I have no fond memories of the dictator and his black-gi henchmen. And as for slave traders, I'm sure you know that I was taken myself—much earlier, of course. But I've interrupted. You say, slaves taken from the southlands …"

"Fourteen years ago," Ailmili repeated. "The one we seek would be twenty-two now."

"There are many stories. Children lost overseas."

"A report has come to us unexpectedly after so many years, of a sighting of this slave."

"In Deadrise Bay? That would seem unlikely. No one would allow a slave to be seen in this port."

"Not here. Overseas in Ben Attallach. Seen in the highlands, well inland." Ailmili sipped her coffee and looked at the man. "Identified, and later confirmed. We know the location, more or less."

"I see. I've not been overseas in many years. At one time I knew the roads there all too well. But I can't claim recent knowledge of Ben Attallach."

"We want to retrieve this person, and we ask your help in arranging it."

Tieg pushed his own chair back, both relieved and concerned. It didn't seem that they were proposing an end to his empire on the Western Shores. But to get involved with matters overseas might lead to the same end. "My help. You might imagine that my relationship with the powers that be on the mainland is complicated."

"You run the trade for over a hundred miles. Goods that flow into southlands and northlands alike come through ports that you oversee. The ship captains deal directly with you. All of this we know."

"Yes, yes. But …"

"You control well over half of the entire flow of commerce from Ben Attallach. You know the ships and their officers. I'm sure you have spies and agents on board."

"Well, now, let's not head too far down that road." He folded his arms.

"Of course you do. As do we, sometimes. It was an agent of ours who made the report. Credible information. The man who owns the slave is a governor there, Lord Crinan of the Green Hills Manor."

Saor Tieg's face clouded. "Crinan. I've not met him, but I understand him to be a troublesome governor."

"I wish to recover this child of the southlands from this Lord Crinan."

"Retrieve the slave. And how do you mean to do that? Lord Crinan is the governor of a tract that stretches from the Green Hills all the way up to the northern peaks."

"We're here to ask your assistance."

"In retrieving a slave from Lord Crinan? I'm afraid I've no means to approach such a person, even if you were to offer a considerable ransom."

"A bounty, but no ransom. The Tallachs have no claim to souls stolen from the southlands."

Tieg blew out another breath. "Being a freed Tallach slave myself, I'm sympathetic to the injustice of a stolen life. But gunners," he looked at them, imploring, "There are layers upon layers of masters and guards. Slaves in that region are not easily recovered."

"That's why we've come to see you. You have the assets, the connections."

There was a moment of silence as Tieg stared at the gunner. He looked at each of them, then dropped his eyes. "As noble as it would be to return a stolen soul of the southlands to his father, I've no means to do so. My men—even those you might think of as agents—work in the transport of goods, not people."

"Goods are sometimes moved clandestinely," Ailmili said.

"Another road I'd not venture too far down." Tieg smiled thinly. "Of course I take your meaning. The mercantile trade is messy around the edges."

"And surely to work in a field with messy edges," Ailmili smiled back, "requires skills of the variety we seek."

"Again I take your meaning, gunner, but the similarity isn't so great. My men don't work the quiet trail. They are not trained to be subtle. I can't call on them to penetrate a governor's defenses and move a man silently and secretly."

"The quiet trail." Beneath her veil, Ailmili's eyebrows rose.

"I've heard of it, yes. It's been mentioned to me. Your clandestine network for moving people. Why not use them?"

"Because they aren't Tallach," Ailmili said. "They don't know the land or the people. But isn't it much the same to move goods as people?"

Tieg shook his head. "My men work in a coarser manner, gunner. I don't send them to pluck a select treasure from a guarded compound and direct its transport to me. To be blunt, the roughness around the edges in the merchant trade doesn't involve quiet, secret events. Were you planning to invade the Green Hills," Tieg smiled, "they might be a fine fit. They're skilled in loud voices and long blades. Not in clever planning and subterfuge."

"But surely there are transactions, arrangements ..."

"Not of the variety that would be required in this case. No, I'd have no confidence in my men trying to carry out that kind of plan."

Ailmili started to say something, but the dark haired gunner reached over and made a sign on the her arm, and she stopped. She nodded, and simultaneously they stood, stony-faced. "We thank you for your hospitality, Saor Tieg. We'll greet the fourth-level girl and take our leave."

Tallach soldiers accompanied them to the pergola. People had begun to crowd the terraces. Music filled the air, sailor tunes and old mainland favorites rising up from the wharves. The beer barrels had been tapped, and the torches had been lit to form corridors of fire that marked the way for the revelers and symbolized the passage of the girl through the fourth level of Tallach fighting.

Suspended above the pergola, a giant paper dragon in red and yellow was illuminated from inside by a brilliant oil lamp. Underneath was a row of upholstered chairs, several occupied. Those seated immediately rose. The gunners scanned the faces and attire, and picked out two ship captains, a woman who might have been the wife of one of them, and two men in the garb of local industry magnates.

Tieg motioned to the gunners and gave a sweeping bow. "The gunners of the northlands join us," he announced in a low voice.

Eyes widened, and as a group the guests bowed. Ailmili and Rachanna nodded and sat.

The others leaned in, murmuring to one another, and Tieg stepped forward and raised a hand. Instantly, servants swept in carrying torches. Tieg stepped up onto a carpeted pedestal and raised both arms. The music stopped, and everyone turned. A cheer rose.

"Men and women of Deadrise Bay," he called out, and another cheer rose. "Friends of Ben Attallach, our most welcome visitors ..." another cheer, "villagers and wharf rats ..." a laugh broke out among the onlookers, "and distinguished guests," he turned and bowed to the gunners, "tonight we celebrate the fire trial of my beloved daughter, a girl of Ben Attallach. Tonight we celebrate my Undine!"

A cheer rose, and rose again.

He raised a hand for quiet. "My Undine, once the young rascal of a girl whom many of you chased out of your stalls ..." more laughter, "... has come into her own. No longer is she little Undine, filching bread from the vendor's baskets and playing tricks on unwary sailors. We must all forgive and forget her youthful mischief. For tonight we celebrate Undine, Talla of the Fourth Order!"

The cheers and the shouting continued until a brilliant light shot up from one of the docks. Everyone moved to the side as a dozen young girls in bright yellow dresses rushed forward carrying torches. A space cleared, and the girls launched into a fire dance, spinning the torches, a tightly choreographed display that ended with all of them coming together, torches blazing in a single, rising fire. Then they scattered up the steps, as behind them a girl in a jet black fighting outfit studded with glimmering blue stones stepped forward. The crowd hushed.

Undine smiled widely as she stepped up the walkways, making her way to the pergola. She stopped on the tier just beneath her father and faced the crowds.

In the torchlight above her, Saor Tieg looked like a god of fire, hovering over the dark figure of his daughter. He pulled a short sword from its sheath and held it up, and everyone fell silent. The torchlight glinted on a sapphire cabochon set in the hilt, the mark of a Tallach blade.

"Undine, Talla of the Fourth Order, accept the blessings of your father. As testament to your achievement, I give you the blade of the family." He knelt down and presented it to her, and bowing, Undine took it and turned back to the crowds. Servants dropped down lightly next to her, and all of a sudden she was lifted. The torches illuminated a girl in blue-studded black, rising slowly to stand on the carpeted pedestal.

"To Ben Attallach, and the tradition of the Talla!" she said, raising the sword to a round of applause. "And to my father, Saor Tieg, who taught me to respect the traditions of my homeland, and whose strong hand kept me on the path and allowed me to be here now. My true challenge is not to cross the flames of the fourth trial, but to prove myself worthy, as the daughter of Saor Tieg." Another cheer went up. "And tonight I'll look to gain favor by following my father's strategy in speeches. That is, to keep it short and let you get to the feast. To Ben Attallach, and to Deadrise Bay!" She raised the sword again, and the crowds cheered and waved, and moved for the tents.

Undine hopped down and gave a laugh. She handed the blade to a servant. "I've no sheath at my hip, I'm afraid, so let's hope a hoard of brigands doesn't come upon us tonight."

Tieg smiled and took her arm. "And now, Undine, I'd like to introduce you to our honored guests."

He led her into the dim, cozy light beneath the pergola, where two figures rose. Ailmili swept up her veil, and Undine stepped forward and froze. The look of satisfied glee turned to something that looked like terror. She stared, her mouth fell open, and she dropped to her knees and pressed her forehead to the ground. "Gunners!" she gasped.

The others all stood up, startled.

"Rise," Ailmili said brusquely.

Undine rocketed up and stood at attention, her chest heaving.

"Undine, child," her father said, his eyebrows lowered, "indeed, the gunners are here to greet you. I'm not sure how it is that you know them."

The Gunner Ailmili's eyes pinned her in silver crosshairs. She raised a hand and abruptly spread her fingers open, as if tossing seeds to the ground, and pulled the cover back over her face.

Undine knew this sign. During training, a Gatto master would bark, *stance!* But in a demonstration, the master would flash the open hand. It meant, *compose yourself.* "I'm just … surprised, father. And honored." She forced a nervous laugh. "The gunners," she stuttered. "Here? What an honor. Let me serve you." She motioned to a servant, who hurried forward with a pitcher, and another stepped up with crystal goblets. Undine's hand shook as she took a goblet, filled it, and handed it to Ailmili. She quickly filled the other and handed it to Rachanna. "Gunners!" she gushed.

Her father looked at her with a critical eye. "Undine, we have servants for that. Come, tonight is your night. Shall we sit?"

The gunners took their seats, then the others, and Undine discovered that she was to be seated next to the blonde-haired gunner. She dropped down and sat rigidly, staring straight ahead.

On Tieg's other side, the guests spoke softly, glancing over and remarking at the strange response of the Talla to her guests. "It seems the fighters of Ben Attallach have a greater respect for the northlands triumvirate than I'd known," one man muttered to Tieg.

"Well," he said, adopting a more lighthearted expression, "she might be a fourth-tier, but she's still a twenty-year-old girl. It's not every young woman who has the gunners of Tynan attend her party."

"True enough. I'd never thought I'd lay eyes on them, myself."

At the other end of the row, the conversation was almost inaudible.

"Una," Ailmili said, accusingly. "I'd not expected to find you here."

"Gunner, please. Let me explain. I'll …"

"Hush," Ailmili demanded. "It seems you've become a native born Talla named Undine. That's a neat trick for a southern stray."

"Don't expose me. Please. And gunner, you know my first allegiance is to you."

"Is it? I don't recall ordering you to be delivered to Deadrise Bay so that you could become a fighter of the Tallachs. As I recall, we met you at the Rose and Star Inn. You were a little slave girl who emptied chamber pots. I arranged for you to be freed, and sent you to learn under Master Aideen of the Gatto. Did you take issue with my choice? I'd thought you would rise to the challenge of learning from a Gatto master."

"Yes. My eternal thanks, gunner. You saved me. My sword is yours."

"It seems your sword is a Tallach sword, presented to you by a freed slave. I'm not quite following the familial lines."

"Don't expose me. I beg of you. It would ruin my master. Saor Tieg is a father to me."

"Evidently there are many who think so."

Undine looked around, and then rose. "Father," she said, "I'll walk with the gunners, by your leave."

"Of course. The night is yours, Undine."

Everyone rose and bowed, and Undine gave the gunners a simpering smile and led them up the stairs. Servants made to follow, but she waved them away. "We'll walk along the drop," she said.

Undine led them around the side of the inn, and they descended stairs to a stone walkway that skirted the edge. They walked on for a minute, and then Undine stopped.

"I didn't want to leave. But the Gatto trainees … and I wasn't …"

Ailmili held up a hand. "Stop, Una. Just tell me. Master Caterione told me years ago that you had left. She said it was your choice. Was it?"

Undine swallowed a sneer. "In the sense that I ran off on my own, yes. It was my choice." She grimaced. "*Master* Caterione? She's a Gatto master now?"

"But you didn't want to leave?" Ailmili pressed.

"It seemed unwise to continue to take the beatings. One day I might want to bear children, or to be able to walk upright."

"They beat you?" inquired the dark-haired gunner.

Undine turned at the gunner Rachanna's first words of the evening. She let out a breath. "Yes."

Her final beating at the hands of the Gatto girls had been the night Caterione caught her hiding up in the tree. That was the night she ran, and the night the voice first came to her. It was eight years ago.

It wasn't exactly a voice; not like someone speaking directly to her. As a child, when she had been a stray in the seventh district, she and the girl who stood watch with her could read each other without speaking. They would turn and meet eyes, and over and over they would say the same thing at the same time. After a while they stopped talking, and just looked at each other and understood.

What had come to her the night Caterione had ruthlessly beaten her was something like that, a very strong suggestion, almost as clear as if actual words had been spoken. As she lay half senseless on the ground, clutching her abdomen and drooling on the dirt, all of a sudden she felt as if a man were there making suggestions. Her mind formed words from the impression.

"Can you see? Open your eyes," this new presence demanded.

"My eyes are open," little Una muttered. She rolled onto her back and pulled her knees up, and groaned. "I can't see anything."

"Your eyes are closed. Open them. Ah! There we go. Do you see? Branches and the night sky."

The words seemed to come from someone old. "A dream," the girl muttered, rolling back to her side and curling up again. "Or a nightmare."

"And what of it? Who's to say a dream perception is false, and those that come when we fancy ourselves awake are real?"

Una groaned again and tried to get up. Her psyche had chosen this moment to debate the question of reality versus perception? Was this a class, then? Had the beating brought about an anxiety dream with her tutor grilling her?

"Oh, please shut up," she growled. She pulled her legs under herself and rose to a crouch, and then sat back on the ground with a huff of air, spent. "I don't see anyone. There's no one here, is there? It's in my head. Nobody is talking to me."

"You're sitting. Good. Get up. See if you can stand."

She tried to rise, and blacked out from the pain. The voice stopped.

"Yes, gunner Rachanna," Undine continued, shaking away the memory, "they beat me. It was mostly my fault. As much as I've fantasized about taking my revenge on the Gatto girls of those woods, the truth is, I was always getting them in trouble." She turned to Ailmili. "I'm sorry, gunner. I'm just not cut out to abide by the rigid discipline of the Gatto. I couldn't resist responding to an affront. I'm afraid I'm a bit too … *visceral*."

Ailmili pursed her lips, stifling a smile. "All right, Una. I told you when I sent you on the quiet trail that it would be on your own merits, should the Gatto master choose to take you in. I didn't tell you that you were obligated to stay there. It's for you to choose your own path. And so you've chosen. A fourth-level Talla wasn't quite what I had in mind, but live on, Talla Undine, and join in the hunt tomorrow."

Ailmili bowed her head, and once again Undine dropped and pressed her forehead to the ground. When she lifted her eyes a moment later, confused as to why the gunner hadn't told her to rise, she was alone.

She sank down and sat on the stone ledge.

The presence in her head on that night eight years ago had proposed that she kill the Gatto girls, although she couldn't tell if he was serious. It almost seemed as if he were joking. "Poison. I could show you how. I see poison hemlock in that moonlit patch over there. Conium maculatum. Do you know about it? That would do nicely."

Maybe it was her own little fantasy. Wouldn't she have liked to settle the score. "I have to get away. They'll kill me next time," the little girl said out loud, making her way from the terrace to the river, clutching her abdomen.

"Not if you take the initiative and kill them first. Although if you'd like to consider some options, there are other ways to address the insult that would be more interesting, and probably more satisfying."

She stopped and whacked a palm against the side of her head. "Stop it. Stop it! Get this voice out of my head!" Distracted, she lost her footing and tumbled down the bank, crashing through the undergrowth and splashing into the river.

At first she panicked, disoriented under the water. But her hand brushed against a rope, and she took hold and pulled herself up. It was the anchor line for the boat the envoy from the compound had arrived in. Master Aideen must have convinced her and her men to stay after all. Una hauled herself into the boat, crying out at the bludgeoning pain as she rolled in. But after a minute to catch her breath, she drew in the anchor, dropped the heavy brass weight into the boat, and sat. She was in too much pain to work the oars, so she let the boat drift out into the river on its own. Soon the current caught it, and it slowly turned as it moved downstream.

When she woke, the sun was up, the boat was caught in the branches of a tree leaning into the water, and she was wet and cold. She lifted her head and put it down again. Her stomach hurt. Her chest hurt. Everything hurt. But she managed to climb out, and after hiding the boat as best she could, she trudged up the bank. She was hungry, and needed to find clothes. She couldn't escape from The Hidden half starved and dressed in a wet gi.

And that voice in her head. What was that?

"Not what. Who." The thoughts popped into her head just as before, and her mind translated them into words. "And the answer is Horace."

"Horace?" Una muttered. It was strange, but earlier she had had the impression of an old man. *Horace* seemed to fit.

"Yes, I'm a man, and yes, I'm rather old. And a bit reclusive. Maybe a tad crabby. I don't always take to people. Not unless I'm on the job, but that's different."

"I have a crabby old man in my head?" Una grumbled, picking her way through the scrub. "Oh, that's lovely."

"A crabby old man who knows how to make a tincture of poison hemlock. *Sola dosis facit venenum*, as they say. My son would have said it would be classic, although I suppose you couldn't exactly emulate Socrates with a group of little girls. I don't see them *draining the cup in one breath*. But I can show you better ways to get revenge, anyway."

"I don't know Socrates. And soladosis? What's that?" It was strange, as if she were carrying on a conversation. She climbed to a wagon road and trudged down it, tugging at her damp gi.

"Sola dosis facit venenum. The dose makes the poison. It's Latin."

"What's Latin? And what does *the dose makes the poison* mean? I have an imaginary old man in my head speaking nonsense. What about something useful? Maybe you could help me get to a village before I die on the road."

"All right. For starters, girl, turn your little butt around and look up. Don't just wander aimlessly."

She did, and immediately stopped. Above the trees in the other direction she could see thin plumes of smoke rising in the distance. "Oh. Well, damn. I'm going the wrong way."

In those early days of her flight, Horace peppered her with questions: Who was she? Where was she? What part of the world was she in? What was the calendar date? Una was alone in the woods, and so she humored this new thing and wandered along telling her life story out loud to the trees, as if dictating a memoir of her first twelve years.

There were a lot of repeated questions. "The forest of the hidden? Where is that? And the year 99 of the Dreugan empire? What is that supposed to mean? Is that from a fantasy book? I don't know what kids read these days. I have a granddaughter about your age. Maybe she reads the same stories."

Una prattled on, keeping herself and this imaginary person company. She asked questions too, learning what she could about her new companion. Horace was sixty-nine years old, and lived in a place called The County. It was an enormous, unpopulated country, at least as remote as the forest she was walking through. There were endless miles of woods broken up by areas that had been cleared of trees, and dirt roads with sturdy little wooden bridges built over the streams. Horace had chosen to live there precisely because of its remoteness. No one would find him there.

He had a son named Vergil, who had been killed years ago. Una couldn't quite follow this part of his story—or her story, or the story of the delusion in her head—whatever it was. It seemed this Horace was looking into his son's death, and somehow he stumbled upon Una. Something from his son seemed to be connected to something from Una.

"I can't pinpoint it," Horace told her. "The connection is old. Maybe it's something you've touched upon. I used to catch snippets of things from my son when he was alive. Quite vivid impressions, sometimes. Very strange. Things much like you're showing me now."

"You caught things from him? Impressions?"

"We have similar ways of perceiving things. Ho! Watch it, there, girl! Someone's approaching."

Una ducked into the woods to hide as a wagon rumbled past.

In spite of her complaints about the things she didn't understand, and her general sense that this presence in her head was a function of having been beaten half to death, she realized quickly that when Horace gave her an urgent command to do something, it was wise to do it. Of course it was really just her own instincts, wasn't it? Her subconscious mind had cooked up this Horace character, and was using him to warn her of things that her conscious mind wasn't picking up on. But Horace repeatedly pointed out dangers, so whatever he might be, she paid attention when he barked.

"Observation is a skill you might wish to develop," he said, subtly chastising her when she walked right past a patch of edible berries. "Look around you, girl. Get the blinders off. You need sustenance."

Una ate handfuls of berries, and started to feel a little better. As her head cleared, she considered that maybe she wasn't supposed to understand everything her Horace mind told her. She started to fancy Horace as something like a muse, an inner voice offering inspiration. And weren't inner voices supposed to be elusive? They didn't tell you things like, "you've counted your coins incorrectly," or "you need to brush your hair." Inner voices were supposed to get you to consider your place in the world, to help you navigate.

Horace proved her point later in the day. She was hungry. Berries were fine, and she had found some edible greens. But she needed something more substantive. When she came upon a young man sitting at a campfire, a merchant porter who traded in the region, she crept up, trying to work out a plan. She could wait for him to leave. Maybe he would leave the bones of the rabbit he was slowly turning over the flames. Her mouth watered.

"There won't be anything left," Horace told her. "He'll toss the bones in the fire, and then cover it with dirt. Why don't you ask for food?"

"I'm a stray," she muttered. "No one will give meat to a stray."

"A stray? Listen to yourself, child. I see a young fighter in a karate uniform. Play your part. See if you can convince him."

Una grinned. It was a good idea. She and the girls had conned many a traveler on the road out of little trinkets. Una herself had shown them how to do it. It had gotten them all into big trouble when the master found out about it.

She straightened her gi and strode out into the clearing, holding a long stick. The man looked up and rose. With the stick, she drew a line in the dirt in front of herself, and then stepped one pace back.

"I speak for The Hidden, who are all around you. You are not to cross the line." She held her eyes wide, staring at him without blinking.

"Who are you?" The young man reached for a knife, but didn't come at her. A little girl was challenging him?

"I am Maya of The Hidden, daughter of Mala, second to the master." Una gave a bow, keeping her eyes trained on him. "Mala and her warriors are all around." She waved her arms out and swept her eyes slowly from left to right, suggesting that others lay in hiding on all sides. "Mala demands payment for lighting a fire on the grounds of our ancestors."

This was entirely made up. The Hidden had very few ancestors buried anywhere in the region, as they had fled from the southlands not many years back; and they didn't make sacrifices to the dead, anyway. But nobody knew much about them. Who was to say that they didn't demand sacrifices for violating sacred ground?

"Your ancestors?" the man protested, glancing around nervously. "I'm a porter. I'm guaranteed safety along this road. It's a durable agreement."

Una could see the concern in his eyes. He was skeptical, but it was working. "You are not on the road," she said, and continued to stare at him, waiting, watching as he thought it over. The trick at this point was not to blink. Whoever blinked first lost.

The young man looked around at the quiet forest, and sighed. "I'd no intention of trespass. No one told me. What does this Mala require of me?" He scanned the trees, trying to see the hidden warriors.

"A meat sacrifice. The small beast there will do. Mala is gracious. You may keep a few pieces for your meal."

Soon the young man was grumbling and putting out his campfire, and Una was tucked behind a sheltering berm stuffing rabbit meat into her mouth.

"Very nicely done," her Horace mind told her. "Oh, yes, there's material to work with here."

And then just as she started to grow accustomed to him, Horace went away. She had gotten away from The Hidden, had crossed the border into the southlands, and was making her way to the west, and one day the old man in her head was gone. She talked out loud to him, but he didn't answer. She tried to draw up the feeling, but it didn't come. What had happened? Was she finally fully healed from the beating? Was her head back to normal again? She supposed she ought to feel thankful for the recovery, but instead she felt lonely. She was by herself, wandering toward the Western Shores with no prospects and no plan, and nobody to talk to.

Now eight years after the beating, as she sat alone on the ledge where the gunners of the north had vanished from sight, she felt something oddly similar, a disjunction in her head. Had she dreamt the gunners, too? For the gunners of the north to show up on the very day of her celebration seemed absurd. Had it been her imagination?

But no, they were real. The gunners who had rescued her from slavery when she was a little girl had returned and discovered her in her new life. What did it mean? She rose and headed back to the stairs.

4. Another Old Keepsake

Sensei Taniemon took Camilla aside after class. She bowed and sat on the mat, and the sensei sat across from her. "You have fire in you today, and focus."

"Sensei." She bowed her head.

"You and your friend are doing well. Are you ready to earn your belts tomorrow?"

Camilla nodded.

"The belt is a sign of achievement. But it's also a sign of respect."

"They told you." Camilla dropped her eyes.

"Your mother spoke to me."

"She's not my mother. And I didn't start it," Camilla snapped. "He came at me."

"And you broke the boy's nose with your forehead. This is a karate move? Which kata is it from?"

Camilla looked up and caught her sensei pursing his lips. "It's not from a kata. I saw it on TV."

"TV." Sensei Taniemon folded his arms.

"You told us karate's not for fighting, and if we use it to hurt people, we couldn't stay in class."

"So you head-butted the boy? Camilla, it's permitted to defend yourself. Did you do that?"

"I … Yeah. I had to, didn't I?"

"I'm told he threw you to the sand. Then you rose."

"And then I broke his nose. Was I supposed to let him beat me up?"

"When the boy threw you to the sand, was the right time to defend after or before?"

"Was it … oh," Camilla dropped her eyes again. "Shit. Okay, I get it. You're telling me I should have blocked or something, so he couldn't grab me in the first place."

"And why didn't you?"

"Because I was angry," she admitted with a loud sigh, "so I wasn't concentrating. I wasn't watching his eyes like you always tell us. So I let him get inside my defenses. Damn it."

"And when you broke his nose, was that needed?"

"He tried to pull my top off. He completely deserved it."

The sensei looked at her for a long moment. "Is karate about retribution?"

"Fine. So I could have walked away, or told the lifeguard, or something. But what would you do if someone twice your size kept coming at you?"

"Leave or defend. Attack only if it's necessary."

"So you're not gonna give me my belt."

"Prove you've earned it, and you'll wear it with honor. But Camilla, karate is in your mind. Tune your mind to it. Use it to defend yourself when you must. Next time the woman who is not your mother tells me of an incident, let her tell me you fractured the boy's arm with a fine inside block, or cracked his rib with a kick. A karate move."

"Yeah?" Camilla grinned. "You sat me down to tell me I should have broken his arm?"

"I sat to tell you karate is in your mind," the sensei said, rising. "Not to fight is best. But if you have to fight, use what you know, and use it well. Now go practice your kata. Tomorrow is your belt ceremony."

"Okay." Camilla nodded. "But wait. Can I show you something? It's a kata."

"Class is over."

"It's not a kata from class. It's one I saw. I want to know what it is. Can I show you? It's not very long."

The man nodded and stepped back. Camilla got into a karate stance, bowed, and then executed a set of moves, starting with a few simple blocks and punches, and then advancing to combinations with shifts between the moves. She stopped and bowed again, and looked up at him.

"Show me again," he said; and she did. "Where did you learn that?" Sensei Taniemon's eyebrows were up.

"I saw a girl practicing it, and I memorized it. But I was just watching. She didn't say what it is. Is it good?"

"It's quite interesting and graceful."

Camilla detected a note of surprise—or was it concern?—in her sensei's expression. "I didn't make it up. I swear. I saw a girl do it. Is it bad, or something?"

"No, no." Sensei Taniemon adopted a pleasant smile. "It's very nice. Tell me if you learn others. I'd like to see them."

Even Mack thought the police officer in the room was overkill. The school principal, the vice-principal, the boy's parents, and a woman from the agency weren't enough? Yes, Camilla had issues. But the boy with his nose taped up was three times her size.

"Wouldn't you think he'd be embarrassed?" he whispered to the foul-tempered woman sitting next to him. "Shit, I'd have hidden at home for a week if I got my face bashed in by a little tiny girl when I was his age."

"I think," Marie hissed, through clenched teeth, "that I'd like to bash the little tiny girl myself when we get home."

"Maybe keep that to yourself, Marie, huh?" He elbowed her and nodded at the officer standing just inside the door. "Ease up already."

Camilla was sitting two chairs down from Mack, arms crossed, lips thin, staring at the wall. The principal and vice-principal were talking in low, calming tones to the boy's parents, who were pointing at Camilla and expressing their displeasure in sharp terms. The woman from the agency seemed to be reading a report.

Finally, when the boy's mother had pointed at her one too many times, Camilla shoved her chair back and shot her arm out, pointing back. "You! Yeah, I'm pointing at you. How do you like it, you old witch?" she shouted. "You know what I think? I think your son is a creepy pervert who tries to pull girls' tops off. So I broke his nose. Next time I'll burn your house down, okay?"

The police officer moved a half step forward, but Camilla dropped down and darted past him and out of the room.

The agency woman looked up and nodded agreement when the vice-principal raised both palms and proposed that some anger counseling might help. And then all the chattering suddenly stopped when Mack finally finished processing, and rose to his feet, looming over everyone at the table.

He fixed his eyes on the boy. "Wait a minute. You tried to pull her top off? Jesus Christ, kid. You *are* a creepy pervert."

And then chairs slid back all around, and the police officer found that he had something to do after all.

When she stepped into the trailer hours later, Camilla found the woman from the agency sitting in the kitchen. Marie sat across from her, rotating a mug of coffee on the table, and Mack was pacing.

Marie started to say something, but Mack put a hand on her shoulder. "Let me do this."

"Fine," Marie growled.

"Camilla, here's the thing," he said. "That boy shouldn't be picking on you. That's got to stop. But it doesn't make it okay to assault him. You broke his nose, for chrissakes. And then you threaten his parents? That wasn't cool."

Camilla halted in the doorway, refusing to enter. "I warned him to get away from me. But look, just tell me I'm going back to the agency, and we can skip the big lecture, okay?"

"Not just now," the agency woman said, looking up from her reports. "But we're going to need to make some adjustments, Miss Rand."

"Maybe you can start with Kevin's nose. It needs some adjustment," Camilla smirked, and Mack gave a half-laugh and cut it off abruptly at his wife's glare.

The agency woman didn't seem to think it was funny. "Your foster parents have arranged a schedule for you, Miss Rand. You'll be seeing someone who can help you."

"Screw this." Camilla spun around and stormed into her room, and started stuffing clothes into a backpack. She wrenched the window sash up and let the fan fall to the floor, and in moments she was out the window, across the yard, and heading for the end of the block, her backpack slung over her shoulder.

Mack answered the phone call a quarter hour later. "She's there? Okay, thanks. I thought she might be," he said, and paused. "Okay, yeah, I know. She's upset. You don't mind? Maybe that's not a bad idea. For tonight. Okay. Thanks, man." He clicked off. "She's at Sasha's," he announced. "Her dad says she can stay over. Just let her, okay?" He countered Marie's deep scowl with a look of surrender. "We don't need to all be here together, all pissed off. Let her stay with Sasha and cool down. And she'll go see the therapist." He turned to the agency woman. "Starting tomorrow, if you want."

"I gotta get away," Camilla told her friend, as they lay in sleeping bags on the living room floor.

Sasha's father had suggested they might like to pretend they were camping instead of sharing Sasha's small bed. He poked his head in. "Turn down the air conditioner if it gets too cold, girls," he said, and drew a grin from the little girl from down the street, who couldn't imagine what *too cold* felt like. "And turn off the lights when you're ready to go to sleep, honey," he said, and blew Sasha a kiss and closed the door.

"Get away, like where?" her friend asked. "I mean, not to be mean or anything, but ..."

"It's not being mean, Sash. It's being honest. My dad's dead, my mom is gone, and there's no way I'm gonna be able to stay with Mack and Marie. If it was just Mack, maybe. He's kind of an asshole sometimes, but Marie hates me."

"So you'll find another family. Only, Millie, if you go back, am I gonna even see you again after that?"

Camilla rolled onto her back and folded her hands under her head. "You know how I told you I see things sometimes? Like, I get these flashes?"

"Yeah." Sasha's voice grew strained. "You said your grandfather started talking to you."

"I know you think I'm nuts. Like a schizo. But it's real. Things like, *I hope you're not scared like your mother.* What the hell did my mom have to be scared about? She took off 'cause she didn't want to have to deal with me."

"Millie, that can't be true."

"Yes it can. Why couldn't she have just left me with my grandfather? He doesn't seem like an asshole. But no, she has to run off when I'm little, and then leaves me with people like goddamned Mack and Marie."

"Millie, I ..."

"But it's not just my grandfather anymore, Sash. When I broke Kevin's nose and I had to run, I went to the playground. So I'm up on the monkey bars, and nobody's there, right? Like, the whole playground is empty except for me. And all of a sudden I see these girls. Two of them, maybe nineteen or twenty, or something. Not at the playground. They're in this jail. There's bars on the window, and a big, heavy door like you see in a dungeon in the movies. One of 'em's sleeping, or unconscious or something, but the other one is sitting up. She called the one sleeping *Tyra*."

"Yeah?"

"I wasn't imagining it, Sasha. I was looking right at her. At an actual, real person. She's got this tattoo on her face, like a spiral."

"Yeah?"

"Diamonds. A spiral of diamond shapes. It's really cool. I gotta look that up and see what it means. Some gang, or something, I guess. And I could hear her, too. Not crying. It wasn't like, *Boo hoo. I'm in jail. What am I supposed to do?* She was pissed. Like how I get when I screw things up. You know, upset, but I know it's mostly my fault, so I'm even more pissed."

"It wasn't your fault. Kevin started it."

"So I'm watching this," Camilla continued, ignoring her friend's attempt at solidarity, "and the one who's awake calls the other girl Tyra. Who the hell is Tyra, Sasha? I've never met anybody named Tyra. You know, though, she kinda looks like you. She's got the red hair thing, and the braid."

"What's wrong with a braid?" Sasha's eyebrows went down.

But Camilla didn't answer. Instead she froze, and her eyes blanked.

Sasha leaned closer. "Camilla?" She poked her, but Camilla just stared vacantly at the wall, unresponsive. "Camilla! Oh my god!" Sasha shook her.

"Gaa! Hey, stop it!" Camilla came around, and pulled away. "Cut it out with the poking!" Then she grinned. "Now I know her name. It's Undine."

"Camilla, you blacked out! What was that?" Camilla earned a punch in the arm.

"I didn't black out. I just kinda left for a minute. I went to have a look. You know the one I saw in the jail? Her name is Una. Everyone calls her Undine, but her real name is Una. I got that from my grandfather. And her friend who looks like you is Tyra. Aren't those cool names? We ought to make those our karate names. I'll be Una and you can be Tyra."

"Are you making fun of me?" Sasha fingered her red braid. "'Cause it's not very good, if you are. I have no idea what you're talking about."

"I can *see* them, Sasha. Like, almost anytime I want."

"So where are they, then?" Sasha sat up and looked around. "I don't see anybody."

"Not here. Don't be stupid. They're in some other place. But ever since that first time, I can see. I think my grandfather triggered it. He was talking to Una in her head the first time. You know, when I was on the monkey bars and saw her. I think he connected me to her somehow."

"Camilla," Sasha growled, "You have to stop this. I know you've been thinking about your grandfather, but these stories are creepy."

Camilla sighed at her friend's deep scowl. "I'll prove it to you, okay? Here, watch. I saw her practicing her fighting. I'll show you a kata that you've never seen before." Camilla hopped up out of her sleeping bag. "Watch this." She dropped into a stance, and then slowly executed a long set of punches and kicks. "See? Una does it a lot faster—and better—but I watched her and learned the moves."

"So you made up a kata." Sasha folded her arms.

"Nuh-uh. I watched Una do it. It's not Shotokan. I showed it to Sensei Taniemon, and he didn't even recognize it. It's something different."

...

The area he would explore today featured a quiet, sunny stone outcrop, the thin stretches of soil in the low spots covered in native Maine blueberries. Horace wondered how many people from away knew what a blueberry plant looked like: not the hybrid highbush varieties, but the low ground cover of plants at the tops of rocky hills all across the state. He sat on a flat boulder and pulled out his lunch, a thermos of hot stew, a chunk of sourdough bread wrapped in a cloth napkin, and a stainless steel flask filled with a particularly nice Irish single malt in place of his usual bourbon.

"Are you seeing things like this, Una?" he said out loud, scanning the sunny hilltop.

It had been weeks since his connections to the little girl had ceased. For many days he had spoken with her, as she wandered on her own heading south and westward in whatever land it was that she lived in. He did his best to help her navigate the dangers, picturing Camilla as he spoke with the girl. While clearly Una lived in another place and time, he couldn't help think of his granddaughter as he watched the girl out on her own, making her way.

He wasn't certain, but his sense of things was that he was looking at someone much later on the timeline. The settings looked like the distant past. The forest was old, and the structures and machines were simple and mechanical. There was no electricity. There were no internal combustion engines. There was no digital technology. Based on the surroundings, he might place the scene in the late 1600s in the western hemisphere. But there were too many anomalies to support that timeline. A young girl in the western hemisphere separated from Plimoth Plantation, say, would not be wandering the woods in a karate gi. And the places Una described—the fighting terrace of The Hidden, and her former home in a place she called "the southlands"—these didn't mesh with any history Horace was aware of. He had read a lot of history, and he was confident that he hadn't missed a continent.

The girl was naturally startled at first by their encounters, but in a re-markably short time she seemed to adapt. She stopped insisting that it was all in her head, stopped smacking her head to try and rid herself of him, and seemed to reconcile herself to it. She wandered along, talking out loud to him, offering a running narrative as she made her way. And Horace listened. He chimed in now and then as needed, especially when the little girl seemed about to get herself into trouble. But for the most part, he was just along for the ride.

When one day the old chunk of granite no longer connected him to Una, he felt an overwhelming sadness. The days suddenly seemed empty and uninteresting. He tried over and over to connect. Maybe it was temporary. Then as days turned to weeks, he was forced to accept that the connection was gone. He had dropped in on little Una's life, had had some fine times talking to her, and then they had parted ways.

It was a stretch of relentless, drenching rain that prompted him once again to pull out the container of things from his son. Wind howled, and the trees sprayed leaves and branches all over the yard. Water pounded against the windows and came in under the front door. It was summer, but the cold and wet made it feel like fall. Horace made a pot of chili and toasted some bread, and sat by the window to watch the storm.

As he finished and turned to decide what to do next, he felt his son's keepsakes tugging at him. Why not see what else he might connect with? It had been a risk to pull out the chunk of granite, but it had connected him to a mischievous little girl, and not a gruesome scene of killing and death. Would he fare as well a second time? Maybe he would discover something or someone else to distract him from his loneliness.

The piece of driftwood was unremarkable. When he was little, he had an aunt who lived on a spit of rocky land that jutted into the ocean. Horace would spend weekend afternoons exploring at low tide, watching the tiny fish trapped in temporarily disconnected pools of saltwater, and collecting things. His keepsakes never made it to the car. Somehow each time as they packed to leave, the plastic bucket filled with detritus smelling of rotting fish would be moved out of the way, and in his excitement for the ride home, Horace would forget about it. But the next time they visited he would be back at it, collecting his treasures.

As with the granite chunk, the piece of driftwood had been sealed in a plastic bag. Horace pulled the bag open and caught the faint odor of the ocean still clinging to the old piece of wood. He sat back and tipped the bag up, and dropped the wood into his hand.

The room swirled and vanished, and the glare of the ocean blinded him. He blinked and centered himself. Two boys, ten or eleven years old, were on the sand, laughing and playing at swords. Each had a long stick, and they were smacking them together in a pretend battle—careful, it seemed, not actually to hit each other.

"I rule the south!" cried the dark-haired boy, moving forward on his little friend. "No one can conquer me!"

"You're king of nothing!" shouted his light-haired opponent. "The world will never bend to your evil!"

"I'll sit on a mountain of gold and everyone will obey me," insisted the dark-haired boy.

Horace smiled, and brought his focus closer. Odd, these two. The dark-haired boy had the hair shaved all around his ears and in back, with the hair on top twisted into a top-knot. The other's was down past his shoulders and untied, so that the wind blew it in his face when the breeze kicked up. Odder still was their dress. The boys wore silk loincloths that reminded Horace of the Japanese mawashi of a sumo wrestler, every bit as outlandish as the more flashy examples he had seen. The dark-haired boy's was brilliant blue with a glimmer of black in the cross-threads, and his companion's was silver satin with tiny red stones along the hem.

Had they been trying to force each other out of a ring, he might have taken them to be imitating the art of sumo. But a pretend sword fight didn't fit. More likely this was their usual dress, and the boys were just playing on the beach. As the light-haired boy fought to regain his ground, the dark-haired boy suddenly turned, flung the stick away, and raced across the sand, laughing.

"Catch me, you slow northerner!" he shouted over his shoulder. "Just try, Neassan! You'll never get close!"

"Oh, I'll get you, Shulie!" His companion raced after him.

"Don't call me that! You want me to call you Neassie?"

Then they both stopped short at the sound of two rapid hand-claps. They turned and froze, and looked up at a man on the rocky shore, arms folded, staring down at them. The man wore a silk gi that matched the weave of the dark-haired boy's loincloth. He looked like an older version of the boy. Surely his father.

"He found us, Shular," Neassan whispered, standing rigidly, arms down at his side like a soldier. "What do we do?"

"Don't say anything," his friend hissed through clenched teeth. "Nobody saw. They can't prove we did it."

"Did what?" Horace asked out loud. He expected one or the other or both of them to do a double take, and look around to see who had spoken. But neither boy moved. "What did you do? Perhaps I can help you out. I'm clever that way," he said. "Trust me. I'm an expert at trickery." Nothing. No response at all. "Boys, do you hear me?" It seemed they didn't.

Horace watched as the man stormed down onto the sand and approached, angry. Without a word, the man stepped up behind them, wrapped a hand into the hem of each boy's loincloth and hauled them up. He headed back to the stony rise with the boys dangling on either side of him as if he were carrying buckets of water.

The scene changed. The boys stood stiffly with their backs to a wall, eyes wide, anticipating the wrath about to befall them, in a room that looked to Horace like the kitchen of a plantation home in the old south. A long table filled the center. Around it women were at work rolling dough while others chopped vegetables and meat. Beyond them, more women were hovering over hot stoves, and still more were scurrying around fetching herbs and gathering dishes. Overhead were racks attached to the ceiling, holding dishes and utensils. A canopy of woven onions and garlic hung along one wall, partly obscuring floor-to-ceiling shelving packed with even more supplies.

But the focus of attention was a washtub in which a little girl was sitting and screaming at the top of her lungs, as women hovered over her, dousing her with water and dabbing with a cloth at her swollen, reddened eyes.

"You stand there," the man who had retrieved them from the beach barked at the boys. "See what you've done. Move from that spot and you'll discover a new variety of regret." He turned and stormed out of the room.

Then the scene changed again. A woman quietly closed a door and stepped into an opulent hall. Bronze candle stands lit dark wood walls decorated with portraits and ancient weapons. The boys sat on the floor looking small, arms around their knees.

"What did you do? What did you put in her bath? Was it hot pepper? You tell me, you little beasts. I don't care whose sons you are. Do you hear me? That was a mean piece of business."

Then the scene shifted again. Horace shook his head, bewildered. This was a different kind of connection than he was used to. Typically he played the role of passive observer, as when so many years ago he had looked in on his son's life. Sometimes he was an invisible companion, as had been the case when he'd traveled with the little girl Una. This time it seemed more like a series of snippets played one after the next, as if he were seeing a reel of film with sections cut out and the pieces spliced together.

The next scene was predictable. The boys were bent over howling, as a different man administered a paddling. The fuss the boys were raising seemed a bit over the top. The man was pulling his strikes, putting on a show of mercilessly punishing them, while not actually doing much more than tap them on the backsides. Evidently the servant didn't want to get on the wrong side of these two, Horace mused. In any case, the guilty parties would walk away with little more than the scar of humiliation, which for boys that age wouldn't last long.

Then it shifted yet again. The boys were older. They sat at the table in the same kitchen. The colorful loincloths were gone, replaced by the type of outfit he'd seen the man wearing. Shular's was blue and black, and Neassan's was black and silver.

Shular filled a cup with wine and passed the bottle to his friend—who had his arm around an older version of the girl Horace had just seen screaming in the wash tub. She wore the plain outfit of a house servant. They looked to be fifteen or sixteen, and the girl considerably happier. She flashed a smile at the older Neassan, who squeezed her shoulder. Neassan filled her cup, and she offered a quiet *thank you* as he poured for himself.

Shular scowled and shifted in his chair, scraping the feet loudly. "Is there anything to eat back here?" he huffed.

One of the women working at the other end of the table immediately stopped what she was doing and hurried over. "What would the young lord like?" she asked.

"I'd like these two to stop slobbering over each other, for starters," he snapped, shoving his friend's shoulder hard, causing Neassan to knock heads with the girl. "It's revolting."

"Ow!" the girl complained.

Neassan spun and glared at the boy, and Shular shoved his chair back and rose. "Never mind. I've lost my appetite." He stormed out of the room.

Neassan pulled the girl close and kissed her where his head had hit hers. "He doesn't own you, Clarice," he said, in a low tone.

"Oh yes he does, young lord," the woman interjected, "Clarice and the rest of us too. Just as sure as we're standing here. Now, Clarice, you get to your work."

"You're slaves, then? Is that how things stand in the southlands?" The boy scowled.

"Lord Neassan, honey," the woman said, softening her voice, "you and your daddy come from another place. *Slaves* is not a pretty word, though, is it? Not a fine thing to say."

"If you're forced to live here and to work for him and his father, then you're slaves," Neassan countered, crossing his arms stubbornly. "What if I take her with me?" he said, catching the girl's arm as she rose. "What if she comes back to the Crossroads with my father and me?"

"What if I'd been born a queen, and my little Clarice a princess? What if we owned a grand old house like this, and had a kitchen filled with cooks of our own. But what-ifs don't count for much when supper needs cooking. So you go on upstairs, young lord, and see if you can snap that boy's mood into something more pleasant, will you? He is your friend, after all, and his temper lands on all of us."

Then Horace lost the scene, and found himself back in his cabin. He tried to return, holding the piece of wood and concentrating. But the odd, disjointed flow of snippets was over. He was standing in his cabin holding a piece of driftwood. The rain had abruptly stopped, and the sun was out. Steam rose past the window, and he felt the heat of the sun.

"Not a southern manor," Horace mused out loud. "We're not looking at Georgia in the 1850s. No, this is something else. Where did you get this, Vergil?" he asked to no one, setting the piece of driftwood next to the chunk of granite on the windowsill. "What's the connection? Is this from Una's time? Quite peculiar, those boys—except that the love triangle is the oldest plot in the book."

He pulled on his boots, slung the rifle over his shoulder, and stepped outside. Dropping in on the boys had left him in a good mood. His fears of seeing something horrible hadn't panned out. Instead he'd had a strange but entertaining show.

"Well, Vergil, we'll have to try again later. For now, it's time to get outside."

...

Camilla stared at her friend. Sasha was happily asleep, mouth open, drooling on her pillow. "Why can't I sleep like that?" Camilla grumbled, and rolled onto her back to stare at the ceiling.

She knew why. She could feel it. Things were ramping up in a familiar crescendo. The people from the agency would be coming for her soon. Then there would be a period of instability as they tried to place her, and eventually they would find another pair of suckers who either needed the money or wanted to "help," and she would be deposited in another temporary home. That was the best-case scenario.

But it felt different this time. The chaos was greater. She had gotten into scraps with other kids before, and had gotten in trouble in school enough times that she found it more boring than frightening. Even the plague of the neighborhood bully was familiar. But the visions in her head—scenes from somewhere else playing out in front of her—this was new. The agency shrinks had come up with long words to describe her condition, but *schizophrenia* wasn't on the list.

"Screw it," she said out loud, folding her hands behind her head. "I'm not schizo."

Still, she couldn't deny that this was a new level of escalation. She had the bully down the block gunning for her, the foster parents ready to throw her out, the school siding with the bully—and voices in her head showing her the girl Una in a dungeon. Was it a warning? Was her grandfather, or whoever or whatever spoke in these strange, lucid visions, showing her what was in store for her? She had told Sasha that it would be cool to take the names Una and Tyra as their karate names. But instead of idolizing these older girls, was she supposed to be learning something from them? Were her visions a warning that this time when it all went south, she might find herself in a version of Una's dungeon, and not on her way to another foster home?

"I have to get away," she muttered. She clenched her fists, clamped her eyes shut, and her head spun.

Smoke! There were voices around her, trying to cry out warnings, but the warnings were cut off in hacking coughs. "Out!" someone said. "Get out! Fire!"

Camilla opened her eyes and felt the burn of thick smoke. She couldn't see anything. Someone stepped on her leg, cried out and fell with loud crash and a scream. Sasha? The house was on fire! She tried to call out. *Sasha!* But she couldn't speak. She got to her hands and knees and crawled toward the spot where her friend would have landed. *I have to help her get out!* But nothing felt familiar. There should be mats on the floor, and sleeping bags. The sofa should be right next to her. Instead she felt rough ground, as if she were camping. She tried to rise, and felt the burn of the smoke in her lungs. Then she lost her balance and fell, and lost track.

"Shut up. Don't say nothing," a voice whispered in her ear. Camilla felt a hand over her mouth "They'll kill you, Una. You have to keep quiet."

She opened sore eyes, and closed them again. Everything was rumbling and spinning, as if she were tumbling down a hill.

"Just keep quiet. Pretend you're a boy. They don't know."

The voice was a boy's. A young boy's. The hand over her mouth let go, and she breathed in, coughed, and breathed in again. She wasn't falling down a hill. She was in a cart or a wagon, bumping down an unpaved road. With another slow breath she opened her eyes. It was dark, but not the pitch black of the smoke-filled room. Lines of dim light revealed the gaps between boards of a wooden wagon. She sat on the floor with six or seven others, all very young.

"They got all of us. Us boys, anyhow. And they thought you was a boy, too, I guess. Sorry, Una. I'd have told 'em, but I wasn't sure if he'd beat you and make you lie down on the ground like they done to Udelle and the others, or if he might have gutted you. You know, 'cause he'd be angry that he fetched a girl out of the smoke. The other scouts would make fun."

I'm not Una, Camilla tried to say. But she couldn't talk. They bumped along as the wagon moved down the dark road. As her aching head started to settle and her sore eyes adjusted, she studied her surroundings. It was definitely a wagon. Overhead was a tarp, and the sides and floor were wood planks. She counted seven others with her. They seemed small, none of them much bigger than she was—and Camilla was the shortest person in her class. Maybe they were younger. Then it struck her that maybe she was younger, too. This wasn't the aftermath of a fire at Sasha's house. The boy had called her *Una*, and said something about *Udelle*. Camilla didn't know anyone named Udelle.

One of the boys leaned forward and started coughing, and Camilla soon found herself doing the same, gagging and coughing. Then there was a long, confusing interval of dark, blurry shapes, and more coughing.

Later the wagon stopped, and someone unfastened a hasp and dropped a wooden tailgate. "Out," commanded a rough voice. "Y'all stink like shit and piss. Get in the creek and scrub it off. And those of you that's got 'em, strip off those nasty rags." He turned to another man. "Get that bag of grain sacks from under the seat. Let 'em fish through that for something to put on. And you boys, some of you grab buckets and flush out the wagon."

"Una, they're gonna see!" hissed the boy next to her. "You have to run."

The man stepped up close and waved an arm to hurry them.

"How can I run?" Camilla heard herself say—and flew back as the arm struck her across the face.

"Shut up, you! I said get in the creek and wash. Did I say talk?"

It was then that Camilla realized she was merely a passenger. She hadn't said *How can I run?*—and wouldn't have. The look in the man's eyes was plain enough. When someone gives you that look, you don't talk.

The boy grabbed her wrist and pulled her along as he jumped down himself. He hurried them both into the water. The boys ducked under and scrubbed at their hair. Camilla looked up at the men watching. She didn't understand. What was going on? A few things were clear. She was here by mistake. These men thought she was a boy. And if the boy was right, she was in more danger than the others on that count. And Una—if that's whose world she was in—was much younger, and lacked the skills of the older Una. This Una hadn't learned to fight, or even to think like a fighter. She wasn't doing anything strategic.

Camilla could see options. Why couldn't Una? Run into the deep water, duck under, and swim away. Maybe the men wouldn't chase her. Or move out beyond the other boys, at least. Be last. Maybe as the boys returned to the wagon, she could slip back in without the men noticing. Instead this Una was doing everything wrong. She didn't take off the grimy whites, and that would anger the men. She hovered in the middle of the pack of boys. That meant she was boxed in. And she was looking away most of the time, as if afraid. That meant not gathering information. Camilla screamed in her own head as Una turned and a man's eyes locked on her.

"Hey, you there," he demanded. Everyone in the creek froze. "I said take off the nasty rags and wash up. What are you hiding?"

The rest was predictable. Camilla found herself hauled out of the water and belted across the face again. Stunned and lying on the ground, she looked up at the arguing men.

"You took a goddamned girl? What's wrong with you?"

"Shit, I thought it was a boy. So just shut up, okay?"

"You can't tell a boy from a girl? Raptors, now we're one short. And you're gonna get your damned head beat in if Shular finds out. You know this is his slave run, right? The boss man himself, the lord of the south-lands. He finds out you tried to bring him a girl for a slave, and you're gonna regret bein' alive."

"So who has to know? We'll get rid of her."

"We? No, you will. Take her in the water and hold her under."

"But … what?"

"Your fuck-up. You fix it. Hold her under. And get some of the boys—the ones that actually got penises—to scrub out the wagon so we don't got to smell that all the way to the tenth."

"I've got to drown her? Aw, come on."

Then a third voice joined the conversation, as the driver stepped up. "Whoa, now. There ain't no call for no drowning. What are we, savages? Just take her out in the woods and gut her quick, all right? Go on. And take her out to where we don't got to look at it. Do it."

Camilla felt herself hauled up and dragged along by the man. Her head was fuzzy. He'd hit her hard.

"Fuckin' stray girl," the man grumbled, as he pulled her around the back of the wagon and headed into the woods. "You could have said you was a girl. But you wanted to get me in trouble, didn't you? That it? Big joke on me."

Do something! Camilla silently urged, as little Una stumbled along, half walking and half dragged. But Una didn't do anything. She let the man lead her into the woods. He spotted a boulder and pulled her to the back side. He grabbed her by the neck with one enormous hand and lifted her and shoved her against the boulder so her feet dangled off the ground. With his other hand he unclipped his knife sheath.

Now, damn it! Camilla urged, and then with all her resolve, whipped her knee up. And it worked! The girl's knee snapped up and caught the man hard, squarely between the legs. He growled and let go, and stumbled backward. Camilla didn't think about the next move. She grabbed the biggest rock she could find and flung herself at the man. A clean hit to the head brought him down.

Twice more she hit him, feeling Una's panic. Then she got to work. In minutes she had stripped the body. The clothes were much too big, but they would have to do. She pulled on the man's shirt and pants, and looked at the boots. They were enormous, but she had to have shoes. She used the knife to cut strips of cloth from his undershirt and wrapped her feet, and pulled the big boots on. Then she turned, listened, and ran.

Camilla snapped her eyes open as the air conditioner kicked on with a bang. She was soaked in sweat, flat on her back with her fists clenched and her heart pounding. Sasha was fast asleep next to her.

"Una," Camilla hissed. "It's a message! First the dungeon, and now this? You're telling me I have to go!"

5. The Twelfth Station

"Wasn't that a nice surprise for your celebration," Saor Tieg said, giving Undine a hug as she stepped under the pergola. "You certainly seemed taken with the gunners. You must know about them."

"Of course," Undine said, trying to sound casual. "Who doesn't? I mean, father, they became Tynan gunners at an age when I was barely through my second trial." She forced a smile and kissed him on the cheek. "Thank you for that. I'm sure it must have been a task to arrange it."

He hugged her again, and released her. "It's a great accomplishment to earn the fourth level, and greater still to be awarded the dragon-serpent," he said.

But Undine wasn't listening. She was sweeping her gaze across the throngs below, searching.

"Undine!" came Tyra's excited voice. The girl ran up the steps and wrapped her arms around her friend.

Hours later, two figures in black moved along a path into the forest. They stopped and slipped their horses into an empty paddock, reluctant to leave them at the trailhead where someone might spot them, and headed into the forest on foot.

"Undine," Tyra complained in a whisper, "I suppose with all the drinking, no one will notice you're gone. But this isn't quite the after-party I'd expect for a woman passing the fourth trial."

"Tell me that when we have a fat sack of gold pieces. Now, come on."

There was just enough moonlight penetrating the canopy to allow Undine to guide them to the place she remembered from eight years ago, when she had been a starving little girl making her way south. Little Una had stopped at the very spot. She had crept into a shallow cave to sleep, only to have a group of soldiers stop and build a fire not twenty yards from her hiding place. After hours of terrified wakefulness, listening to their low, harsh conversation, she peered out and saw them crawl into their bed rolls and go to sleep, and she was finally able to slip away. But she would never forget the place.

"We're close," Undine whispered, guiding Tyra through a dense stand of trees. "It opens up just ahead. Follow me."

As they approached a clearing, they ducked down at the sight of torches in the distance, flickering yellow lights moving through the trees. They heard low voices, and waited, watching. The torches came closer, and then a group of northern soldiers stepped into the clearing. They gathered around a stone cairn and hovered for no more than half a minute, and moved off into the woods again. Undine and Tyra kept silent, looking and listening until the sounds and the torchlight had faded to dark and quiet. Then they crept forward.

"We need to be quick," Undine urged. "The Tallach soldiers won't be far behind. Under that rock," she said, rushing forward to the cairn. "The flat one on the ground. This must be it." She pushed it aside and pulled out a leather satchel. "Got it! Let's go." She rose to leave.

They took two steps into the woods, and then something slammed into the back of their heads, and they went down.

It was summer, but the floor was cold. Undine awoke and put a hand to her head. There was a lump, and crusted blood in her hair. She held still, working to clear her thinking. The room was dimly lit by an oil lamp on the floor. Then she realized that all she had on was her whites. She curled up and sat, and discovered a prone body also stripped to her whites, red braids carelessly lying on the stones.

"Tyra," she muttered, and shuffled over.

Tyra was alive, but sleeping—or maybe unconscious. She groaned and rolled over, and Undine leaned in to check on her.

When the jailer pulled back the iron port in the door and looked in, he didn't see the shapely backsides he had been admiring on his earlier pass. He found the two young women sitting in the corner pressed side by side, clutching their arms around their knees.

"Awake, then. Hungry? Come over. I've something for you."

His prisoners declined, and the jailor kicked a port open at the floor and slid a tray in. Then he reached in and set a wide, squat pitcher next to it. He kicked the port shut again.

"Don't damage the tray. It's not a shovel, and you're not going to carve your way through the stone with it. And don't break the dishes. Ruin the tray or break the dishes, and the food stops coming. Understand?" He received only the stares of his prisoners by way of reply. "The small cups are medicine. A bit of laudanum for the bumps on your heads. One each. You'll feel better." He slammed the port shut.

"Laudanum," the voice in Undine's head said. "How interesting. You have laudanum?"

Undine sighed. "What are you talking about, Tyra? He just told us it's laudanum."

Her friend reluctantly turned to her. "I didn't say anything, Undine."

"Undine. Is that your new name? Surely this is little Una. Not so little anymore."

"Horace?" Undine buried her face in her hands. "It's happening again."

"Undine," Tyra said, leaning in. "Are you all right? You're babbling."

"I'm ... I don't know."

"I'll fetch the medicine." Tyra carried the tray and the water pitcher and sniffed the medicine. Satisfied, she gave Undine her dose. "Take it with some water."

"Go on. Laudanum should help considerably," the Horace-voice added, murky in her head.

Undine knocked back the liquid and took a long drink from the pitcher to chase it down. The jailor was right. Pretty soon she started to feel a lot better, and Horace faded away. Tyra took her medicine as well, and they sat silently and ate the food, and then fell asleep.

Hours later, awake after the drug-induced slumber, they sat shivering in the corner and once more heard someone outside the door. This time they heard the bolt slide and the door creak open. A northern soldier stepped in, and another pushed the door closed behind him and slid the bolt into place.

"Clothes," the man said, and tossed a pair of rough peasant dresses to them. "Sorry for the wait. Not used to having prisoners of your gender. Don't have uniforms for young women, and the captain wouldn't allow the night clothes. Go on. Put them on. I'll turn. Don't try to strike me, or the boys in the hall will beat you senseless. Understand? I've no weapons. Just put the clothes on." He looked at each of them, then turned his back.

They hesitated, then rushed forward, grabbed the clothes, and pulled them on.

"All right?" He turned back. "We'll bring blankets. It can be cold down here."

"Where are we? Why are you holding us prisoner? We're Tallach!" Undine scowled, her arms wrapped around her front. Her head throbbed from the effort.

The soldier held up a hand. "You won't gain anything by petitioning me, miss. I've no power to do anything one way or the other."

"But tell us what this place is," Undine demanded.

"What it is? What do you think it is, girl? You robbed a pay run. You're in the twelfth station. Don't act all surprised."

"But we're *Tallach*," she insisted. "And you've no jurisdiction!"

The jailor smirked, and rapped on the door. "Tell that to the quartermaster. See how far it gets you." He stepped out, and the door closed with the definitive bang of metal on metal. The little port scraped open, and the jailor's face appeared. "Did you think you could rob the pay run and get away with it? I thought you Tallach women were supposed to be smart." He slammed the port shut. They heard footsteps and another door slam, and they were alone again.

As Undine stood staring at the closed port, Tyra stepped up next to her and weakly punched her in the arm. Then she hit her again, harder. "Damn it, Undine!" She huffed off to sit in the corner by herself.

Slowly shaking her head, Undine turned. "This isn't possible. They'd left the payment already. It wasn't their jurisdiction."

The redheaded girl snorted and turned her back.

It was a long, cold day later that they were shackled, brought to a bath house, and ordered to wash. They didn't protest. They needed a wash badly. Clean clothes were laid out for them. Then cloth sacks were pulled over their heads, and they were led to a back room in the quartermaster's station.

The quartermaster, a sour man of thirty-five, looked at them with resentment. "Leave us," he said to the soldiers.

The soldiers closed the door behind them, leaving the prisoners standing in the middle of the room.

"Take the hoods off," he ordered, and they pulled them off and looked at the man. "What did you think you were doing?" he scolded. "I've been told who you are. I might expect that kind of thing from the border rats that run amok through those woods. But the daughter of Saor Tieg, and a ship captain's daughter? Do you want to start a war?"

"You've no right to hold us. We weren't on northern lands," Undine asserted. Tyra just stared glumly.

"Oh, so you're an expert in cross-border relations, are you?" he said. "If you were, then you'd know that by the treaty signed after the defeat of the dictator Shular, the borderlands are considered to be neutral by nature, in terms of jurisdiction. When a crime is committed in the borderlands, jurisdiction is assumed by whomever is on hand. And you, you ignorant young women, you were captured by soldiers of the gunners. The god-damned gunners of the Tynan lord!" he roared. "Damn it all, a simple trade transaction. What were you doing there?"

The man got up and started pacing. "Here we are, trying to come to terms with the growing reality of an increasingly legitimate Tallach trade cartel, and the settling of your people along the Western Shores in the new era of peace. We've ended the slave runs. We've made agreements not to sell arms to renegades. We've signed treaties to honor the borders. And to honor the borderlands!" He spun and pointed at Undine. "And then what? You two cook up a plan to steal the gunners' gold?"

"We didn't know it was …"

"Quiet! Did I ask you to speak? I'll tell you when you can speak. Damn it, girl. You and your friend have put us into quite a predicament." He stormed back and forth, seeming to grow even more furious. "Saor Tieg's daughter. Fire and daggers," he seethed. "You know you'll die for this, don't you?" He turned and slumped into a chair.

Tyra made a keening noise, and Undine stood in shocked silence.

"You'll die, it will start a war, and I'll spend the rest of my godforsaken life with the guilt of it." He turned his eyes to them again. "Do you think I want to put you to death? Do you? But I've no choice. The rear guard of the pay run saw you lurking in the woods watching the drop, and then running in and snatching up the purse. What am I do to, tell them, oh, no, those Tallach women dressed all in black were just out for a stroll. It was an accident." He made a growling noise and ground his teeth.

"You have to send word to my father. He'll pay whatever the ransom is."

The quartermaster seemed to wilt. "I can't send word to your father, Undine of the Tallachs. There's no ransom. It doesn't work like that. The penalty for highway robbery is death. If I send word to your father it will start a war right now, rather than in a month's time, or whenever the reality of it becomes known to them. We need that time to prepare."

Tyra leaned down and began sobbing.

"Please," Undine begged. "Please send word. I promise he'll make it right. He'll pay twice the amount of the purse. Four times! Whatever you say."

"The tribunal has already passed judgment. You'll be bled out tomorrow."

Tyra's sobbing grew to a wail of distress, and Undine dropped listlessly into a chair.

"I'll see that your accommodations are more comfortable tonight. And you may choose your meal."

Undine sat staring at the floor—and then her head whipped up. "I want to see Ailmili, the gunner."

The quartermaster's eyebrows rose. "You might have thought to seek an audience with the gunner before robbing her."

"I want to talk to her."

The man rose, shaking his head. "Don't be ridiculous. The gunner doesn't come around to the stations to visit border thieves."

Undine jumped up insistently and started shouting, demanding an interview. The doors flew open, the soldiers swarmed in, and she and Tyra were dragged out.

Their new accommodations were only slightly better. It was another stone dungeon, but with thatched mats on the floor, blankets, and a chamber pot and a bucket of water. They spent a long night, sometimes arguing and shouting, and sometimes sitting with Tyra sobbing on Undine's shoulder while Undine stared at the wall.

Just before dawn the jailor stepped in. Undine made a motion as if to rush him, and he whipped a rifle up from his hip. "Don't make me the one who has to live with this," he said. "Please, miss. I've done nothing to deserve having your blood on my conscience."

Undine halted and sighed out loud, and he stepped forward and shackled her, and then Tyra. He pulled the cloth bags over their heads.

"I'm sorry, misses," he said. "I truly am. I apologize for covering your heads. But we can't have the men seeing the spiral on your face, or the flax flower on yours. Those of us who saw already, we're sworn to secrecy. But you can't have the whole camp knowing. So the quartermaster has made up a story. He's told the station that it's untoward for soldiers of the twelfth to leer at peasant girls in their final hours—that to do so would be to dishonor you and themselves. And in truth, I believe you'll be the first females to be executed here in many, many years."

They were led to the same back room and seated with a soldier standing behind each of them, ready to force them to sit again if they should try to rise.

The quartermaster sighed, rose, and cleared his throat. "Two unnamed peasants of the borderlands, identified as Peasant Girl One and Peasant Girl Two, having been caught in the act of robbery, the witnesses thereto having filed their statements, are hereby sentenced to death by the letting of blood. The sentence will be carried out at midnight. Do the condemned wish to speak?"

Tyra's head hung, almost as if she were asleep. But Undine pushed up. Strong hands pushed her back down.

"I insist on speaking to the gunner. The Gunner Ailmili won't let this happen. I demand that you send for her."

"Silence, condemned," growled the quartermaster. "That won't do. Take them to their cell."

Undine thrashed and fought. Hands hauled her up to drag her out of the room. "No, you can't! You've no right. Unhand me!" The chains were pulled tight, and she cried out in rage.

Then the door swung open, and soldiers rushed in and spread out across the room.

"Gunner!" said the quartermaster, hastily rising.

"I apologize for the interruption," said a voice familiar to Undine. "Remove the covers."

Undine stopped thrashing as the sack was pulled off her head. She turned and fixed her eyes on the gunner standing in the doorway.

The quartermaster straightened. "Gunner," he repeated. "How may we serve you?"

"Gunner," Undine hissed. "Please, I don't deserve to …" She stopped short at Ailmili's hand motion, this time sharper than it had been under the pergola. This time it said, *shut up.*

"I've come for my agent. It seems she's made a misstep."

"Your agent?" The quartermaster followed her gaze to the Tallach girl.

"You know that my cousin and I visited Deadrise Bay recently."

"Yes, gunner. I'd been informed."

"This Talla has been recruited for a task. We don't need to trot out the details, except to note that it seems the matter of the terms of payment were unclear. Please convey my apology to the soldiers and to the Tallach merchants for this little misunderstanding. My agent made an error. Offer the Tallachs a tenth share extra for the trouble, and give the soldiers and the jailors a week's leave."

The quartermaster nodded at one of his soldiers, and the man nodded back and left the room.

"Undine will be handed over to me. And the other girl is to be held. And quartermaster," she looked right at him, "there's to be no word of this. Undine has been unable to explain her situation because I've forbidden it. No one is to speak of this."

The gunners' quarters at the twelfth station were a soldiers' bunkhouse, roughly converted to serve a temporary purpose. The bunks were pushed against the walls to make room in the middle for two beds. Nearby, a basin of water for washing sat on a small table. Across from it was a larger round table with chairs for the gunners, several covered dishes on a tray, a carafe of wine, and goblets. An extra bottle was uncorked and ready, should the gunners have a long night.

The windows, normally uncovered, were draped with bed sheets tacked along the top. From the outside, aside from the windows being draped, the sole indication that they were within was the guard. Two soldiers stood at attention on each side of the bunkhouse. It was more a symbol than a defense. No one in the station would dare accost the gunners.

At a fast march, a dozen soldiers accompanied Undine to the door of the bunkhouse. The captain stepped forward and rapped on the door. "Undine, Talla of Deadrise Bay," he said quietly to the closed door.

"Send her in," came Ailmili's voice from inside.

The soldiers stepped to the side, and the captain pulled the door open and motioned for Undine to enter. The door was closed behind her, and she stood in the entryway, unsure. A sheet tacked to the ceiling formed a barrier between herself and whatever lay within.

"We don't bite," Ailmili said, "and it's late in the game to be bashful. Come in and sit."

Undine pushed the curtain aside and approached cautiously. The gunners sat at the table. The black robes were gone. They wore white silk shifts, and leaned back on upholstered seats. Ailmili's eyes were uncovered. Undine felt her heart rate rise as silver crosshairs pinned her again.

"Well? Sit."

She stepped forward and dropped to her knees, and pressed her forehead to the floor. "Gunners."

"Oh, enough of that. Don't pander to us, Una. You're going to earn your pay."

She rose and stood rigidly.

"And enough with the standing at attention. We're sitting here in our underthings. It's not an inquisition." Ailmili smiled thinly. "Sit down, already."

"Gunner, you've saved me—again!" Undine said, unable to keep quiet. She took a seat. "Thank you. My blade is yours."

"Yes it is indeed. But we'll get to that in a minute. Would you like a glass of wine?" Ailmili picked up the decanter and poured. "I imagine the fare in the dungeons isn't the finest."

Undine gave a simpering smile. "Thank you." She sat and sipped at the wine, resisting the urge to slug down the whole glass and ask for another.

"When years ago we met you at Stockton Line, Una, the man running the crew at the inn told us the story of how you had arrived there. It was quite a story. A girl stray mistaken for a boy and carted halfway to the Western Shores on a slave wagon before they realized the mistake. And you, a small child, getting out of the predicament and then somehow finding your way to the inn. Very clever. And very unusual."

"And then you saved me from that place, just as it was turning on me."

"Yes, yes," Ailmili waved a hand. "But that seems to have been a mere detour. I delivered you to a Gatto master so that you might be trained in that style of fighting. And yet somehow you've managed to become a Tallach fighter of the fourth level, awarded the dragon-serpent. That, Una, is peculiar. One day I want to hear the whole story."

Undine nodded.

"But right now I'll settle for having you tell me why you left the Gatto master. You said they beat you. Tell me what happened."

Undine breathed in and out slowly. "I was accepted at first. And grateful to be there. Do you know, I was up in the trees the night you and the northern lord confronted the dictator on the Gatto terrace? I saw a great fight that night. I very much wanted to be like you." She dropped her eyes. "And so I stayed and learned more and more about fighting. I earned my jacket and then my novice belt. But I was always getting into trouble with the master."

"I can imagine Aideen was demanding, as she should be."

"I accepted my punishment. I didn't claim I wasn't responsible, or try to talk my way out of it. But you see, I wasn't the only one punished. The other novices were also punished each time I broke the rules. And they didn't like it. They beat me."

"And what exactly did you do to keep drawing your master's ire?"

"Oh, various things." Undine gave a simpering smile. "Sometimes by accident. But I admit that sometimes it was on purpose. I wasn't able to accept an affront. Not nicely."

"I see. Go on." Ailmili waved her wine glass.

"The other novices, they told me, *we won't go down for you.* They beat me and beat me, until finally I ran. I was twelve when I left. I wandered for a time, until a man at the Western Shores found me starving down by the sea. He told me his name was Saor Tieg, as he had earned his freedom from slavery on the mainland of Ben Attallach."

"So that's how you came to the house of Saor Tieg."

Undine nodded. "I told him I was a slave once, too. He took me in and made me his daughter. He told me it would help us both. I needed a home, and it would position him more closely with the Tallach tradesman to have a natural-born Tallach child."

"Natural born."

"I look enough like him. Did you see it? My nose, and my eyes. He told everyone that he'd been with a Tallach servant girl, and she bore a child. He said I discovered that I had a father overseas on the Western Shores, and I stowed away on a merchant ship to find him. I looked the part, bone-thin. It wasn't from a long voyage as a stowaway, but the effect was the same. So at twelve I became his daughter, and he raised me. And I learned to fight the Tallach way."

"Your friend. Her name is Tyra, I believe. Does she know all this?"

Undine shook her head, alarmed. "Please don't tell her! Nobody knows. And it would ruin my father if it got out. I worked my way through the trials to protect him. To get this." She pointed to the tattoo on her face. "Because with four turns of the spiral, no one will question my origin. No one would suspect that a girl with the fourth ring would be anything other than Ben Attallach-born. But Tyra wouldn't understand. Please don't tell her."

"Una, stop telling me not to betray you. If I wanted to put an end to you, that would be easy enough. You were managing that trajectory very efficiently on your own."

"You'll keep it secret?" She clutched the goblet tightly.

"For my own reasons. You see, a southlands stray who ran from the Gatto is of no use to me. But I can use a native-born Tallach woman. Here, eat. The soldiers seem to feel that Rachanna and I are too skinny, or else why would they ply us with such heaping quantities of food?" She slid the tray over and removed the lids, revealing a half-loaf of neatly sliced bread, cold meat, and a bowl of melting ice beneath a plate of crisp lettuce. "There's butter in the tin. Or if you'd prefer horseradish or olive oil, we'll call for it."

Undine bowed her head and began assembling a sandwich. "Thank you," she said. "You're right. The food in the dungeons isn't very good."

The gunners joined her, and for a few quiet minutes they sat and ate.

Finally she felt she couldn't wait any longer. "Gunner," Undine said, "I don't understand. You say you need a woman of Ben Attallach? And I said my blade is yours, and ... you want something of me?"

"When a payment is made, that's the expected outcome. You've received the payment, and so it remains for you to perform the task."

"But I don't have the gold, gunner. They took it."

"Your payment is secure. You may visit the quartermaster and take possession of the initial payment right now, if you wish. The balance, of course, is contingent upon successful completion."

Undine looked bewildered. "I don't understand."

"Didn't you hear me telling the quartermaster? We made an arrangement, you and I. You agreed to perform a task that I set for you, but made an error as to the planning for the receipt of funds. It's no matter," Ailmili waved a hand. "The soldiers are enjoying a week of leave, and the Tallach traders will have their payment. And I'm sure they're delighted with the unexpected bonus. A tenth share of that trade is no small sum. Of course you're on the line for that. It comes out of your end."

"My end? But, my end of what?"

"It was my cousin's idea," Ailmili said, nodding at Rachanna. "Rachanna sits here quietly, but she's always thinking. And now and then, genius ideas come from the head of Torin's left-hand blade."

Rachanna laughed quietly and raised a hand, and Ailmili slapped palms with her.

"We were at Deadrise Bay to enlist your father's help with something that we can't do on our own. But your father declined. And so it seemed we were to return to the northlands empty-handed. Of course the evening wasn't entirely a loss. What a surprise, when Saor Tieg of Deadrise Bay invites us to greet his Ben Attallach-born daughter at the celebration of her successful completion of the Fourth Trial, and who should rise to take his sword? Una, former slave girl at Stockton Line."

Undine smirked, but said nothing.

"It's quite a rise, from southern stray to Tallach fighter. Well executed. We left feeling that the mission had been a failure, but the entertainment had been quite good. And then a runner delivers a message that two young Tallach women are being held at the station for robbing the pay delivery. And who might these border thieves be? Imagine my surprise. Undine, the daughter of Saor Tieg, and a companion."

"It was my fault. Tyra shouldn't be blamed."

Ailmili held up a hand. "First we stumble upon a transformed Una, and then all of a sudden you're locked in a stone dungeon in the twelfth station, and the quartermaster is in a panic. But Rachanna, you see, is good with strategy. I was thinking, we've got to get her out of there. Grant you a pardon, or steal you away in the night."

"That wouldn't do," Rachanna said with a grin.

"Rachanna's idea was so much better. There you are in the dungeon, and here we are in need of a Tallach agent. And while it's a stretch to propose that someone could misunderstand the pay routes and stumble into the transaction of a merchant trade, well, we're allowed some latitude."

Undine nodded her head dumbly.

"The quartermaster is not stupid. He certainly didn't buy it. But he's more than willing to go along with it. He's probably off getting drunk, celebrating his escape from the fate of being the station quartermaster who put to death the daughter of the most powerful trade magnate of the Western Shores." Ailmili put her palm down on the table. "So there it is. You've accepted your pay. What's left is for you to do the job. I'm going to explain to you the job you agreed to perform, and you're going to perform it."

"But gunner, I didn't ..."

"Of course I can't force you. Your life as the daughter of Saor Tieg and fourth-level Talla seems quite fine. But maybe you'd prefer to be a borderlands bandit, and suffer the letting of blood for your crime?"

"No, please, it's just that I don't understand. You want me to do a job? Me? But I was a slave, and then I failed at Gatto, and then ..."

"Una, don't overcomplicate things. You robbed a northern commerce payment. Either you're my agent and you do what I tell you to do, or you and your friend don't get out of this. Is that clear enough? And your friend—Tyra, the daughter of Captain Armand of the *Oncilla*—will be held in lieu of your obligation until you complete your task."

"You're holding Tyra hostage? But it wasn't her fault."

"Many things that happen to a person are someone else's fault. Didn't you learn that in your time with the Gatto master, when your peers were being punished for your mischief? Other times, the notion of fault can seem almost irrelevant. One thing happens, and then another, and one tries to make something of it. But there's no way around it, Una. Tyra will get to know dark rooms while you're outside in the fresh air. The sooner you complete the task, the sooner she's returned to her father at Deadrise Bay."

"Dark rooms!" Undine stared, open-mouthed. "But, her father. He'll expect her. They're probably hunting for her even now. For me also."

Ailmili held up a hand. "We know the customs associated with the Fourth Trials. Those who pass through the fire have been known to take an entire year of excursions. And to travel with a second requires no complex explanation. I've already instructed the men on the pay route to seed the idea. Your first task will be to pen notes to the captain of the *Oncilla* and to your father to confirm it. You're taking your walkabout, and you've named the captain's daughter to be your companion."

"My walkabout?"

"Whatever you call it. Your wandering. Your travel. No one will question it. Note even Captain Armand. If anything, her father will brag of it. I hear that the ship captain's daughter spends more time reading than venturing out and experiencing the world. I'd wager her father will fly the fighter's pennant, and tell the story with pride to every man he meets. *My daughter, the second to a fourth-level Talla with a dragon-serpent. No bookworm, my girl.*" Ailmili smiled.

"I'll do what you ask. Of course I will. But not the dungeons. Please, gunner. Tyra won't survive down there. I'll do anything you want. But don't make her stay down there."

Ailmili sighed. "All right. Agreed. I'm sure the quartermaster would rather not have a young woman in his jail, anyway. That sort of thing tends to cause trouble in this kind of place. We'll remove her from the station jail and place her in confinement at another place that's more suitable. Will that do? But Una," her voice dropped, "if you want to see your friend again, you *will* complete the task. We'll lighten the burden on your friend as a courtesy. But you and your friend are joined in this. Succeed, and you go home together. Fail, and there are worse dungeons than those you've seen these past days."

"Yes, gunner," Undine whispered. "Tell me the mission. I'll do it."

"There will be parts of it that I think you might enjoy. You're going to visit your homeland, Undine. You and your second, a bookish girl with a little flax blossom on her forehead, will travel together."

"But, then Tyra is coming?" Undine looked even more confused.

"Yes, and I know just the girl to play her. I've sent for her already."

6. Ride

"Who is this Shular, then?" Horace wondered out loud, "and this Neassan?" His walk in the woods had been fine. Now he stood at the window staring at the piece of driftwood. "Two young aristocrats getting into mischief? Then the same two older, and the girl with a new kind of appeal. But Vergil, what are they to you?"

His son had been on both sides of that scene, Horace recalled, sometimes the boy with his arm around the girl, but more often the boy scowling at his friend for stealing his prize. And Vergil's struggle might have been similar to young Shular's. He had been attractive enough, but Vergil tended to scare girls away. After a date or two, the girl would seek someone more stable and less frightening. Of course Vergil eventually convinced a young woman to marry him, and Camilla came into the world. But it had taken considerable effort.

"And you couldn't maintain it, could you, Vergil?" Horace said out loud. He picked up the driftwood and turned it in his hand. "You couldn't hold onto either of them, any more than that boy in blue and black will be able to hold onto the servant girl, even though she's a slave in his own household. So, what is this, then? Is this a token of the time when you were a boy like those two, Vergil, playing on the beach? Is this a snippet of that promising young time when anything was possible?"

The late sun glared through the window, and Horace reached to pull the shade. He glanced at the chunk of granite, but had given up on it. Instead he picked up the driftwood again.

Two young men in black silk faced off on a high plateau overlooking a forest. The grass was knee-high, suggesting late spring. The blond man moved in and leveled a vicious attack, aiming blows at the dark-haired man's head and torso. But his opponent blocked and rallied.

This was years later. Neassan was a tall, muscular young man with his hair in a long braid. Shular was his equal in aspect, powerful and poised, his own hair also braided, but wound into a top-knot and pinned with a steel rod.

"I should send *you* overseas," hissed Neassan, backing off and circling. "You tell me where she is, damn it, or I'll have you thrown overboard with stones around your ankles."

"Save your breath. Your threats don't scare me," Shular countered with a tight grin. "And those little tricks you play to try to make me lose focus? Maybe that works on the rank and file. You can stop trying it on me."

"Tell me where she is!"

Shular stopped and circled the other way, keeping his distance. "I traded her," he said. "I traded her for things I wanted more. The slave traders have things from overseas, including a fine grade of fabric. I mean to dress my horse with it."

Neassan drew twin short blades with ruby cabochons set into ebony handles, and Shular drew two of his own, each hilt decorated with a single sapphire. Neassan flew at his opponent. Then figures emerged from the woods below and raced toward the fighting men. They wore black and silver like Neassan. More emerged from the other side dressed in blue and black, and closed in. Blades were drawn all around, and the dispute over a girl escalated into a battle on the plateau.

Horace looked on in mute astonishment at the ferocity of the fighting. As Neassan and Shular struck steel to steel, the soldiers hacked and stabbed, taking off limbs and running opponents through. Blood flowed, and men went down. But after only a minute or two, more soldiers in black and silver swarmed in. The remaining fighters in black and green closed on the young lords. They pulled Shular from the fight and turned and ran.

With a howl of rage, Neassan flung a blade at the retreating men. He missed Shular by mere inches, and the blade instead sank into the upper thigh of an older man at his side. Shular turned and cried out aghast as his man went down, but the rest of his men hustled him off the plateau.

The fighter he'd struck with the blade lay on the ground, growling in pain. Neassan's soldiers reached him, and surrounded the man.

"Leave the blade in if you want to live, Shiskin," one of them said. "Pull it out and your blood will flow."

"Get medics, damn it! Will you leave me to die here?"

Neassan pushed his way into the ring. "Master Shiskin," he said in cold acknowledgment. "It seems I may have inadvertently found the right mark. Your lord chose to trade his property. Was that your idea? If I know Shular, he'd have spent the rest of his days trying to coerce her. And she would never bend to him. Never. So I'm thinking the plan to get rid of her must have come from you. It has your feel about it."

"Fetch medics or escort me to my men," the man said, teeth clenched. "Assign soldiers to carry me there. I promise them a safe return. We'll leave the north, and young Lord Shular and you will have no need for further words."

"You have no men, Master Shiskin. You're my slave now." Neassan turned to his soldiers. "Send a message to *Lord Shular*." He spat the name with disdain. "Tell him he'll need to find a new trainer. Tell him I mean to trade my new slave for something I want more. It's a hot summer. Some of that fancy fabric from overseas might be handy to provide shade for Brannan's pigs."

The scene shifted. Neassan sat at the head of a long table in a stone room. Light from brass candelabras at either end cast a warm glow on him and twenty other men at the table. To the side sat another man, flanked by armed soldiers. This was Shiskin. His leg was bandaged, his foot up on a stool. His hands were tied, but still the soldiers stood guarding him.

"You mean to sell me into slavery. Is that it, Neassan?"

"*Lord* Neassan!" bellowed one of the soldiers, and pushed the point of a blade to the man's neck. "You'll show respect or I'll run you through."

"Is that what you mean to do," Shiskin said slowly, through clenched teeth, "*Lord* Neassan?"

The soldier withdrew the blade.

Neassan sighed. "Master Shiskin, how many times have I been under your canopy? How many times the three of us? I and my old, dear friend Shular on the mats," he spat the name with disdain, "and you guiding us. How many times?"

"Many times, young lord." Shiskin said. "Enough times that you might have learned respect." He turned and glared at the soldier, whose hand tightened again on the handle of his blade.

"Indeed. Is that what you thought I'd learn from you? Respect?" Neassan offered a low laugh, and the others at the table echoed in solidarity. "That's not the word that comes to mind."

"Oh, so you have words for me then, do you? You think that because you're …"

"Strategy," Neassan interrupted. "Master Shiskin, you're the finest strategist I've met. And although I realize I'm young, I've come across quite a number of men who suppose themselves to be excellent strategists. They pale in your shadow."

Shiskin fell silent, having expected an insult.

"And so let's consider. What benefit would I gain by selling you into slavery? Oh, it would be a sweet insult. And the poetic justice would be undeniable. That would be pleasing."

"I'm sure you would take pleasure in that," the man growled.

"But you toy with me, speaking of respect when you yourself have hurled such an insult. Shular will fume and spit, and who knows? Maybe he'll feel a pang of regret at having listened to your vindictive plan. After all, to take Clarice from me is to take her from him as well."

"Shular has no need for the distraction of uncooperative house slaves." Shiskin scowled deeply.

"And I have no need for false friends," Neassan countered. "But let's think strategically. Here it is. The moment Shular steps from the southlands into the north, you die. What do you say to that, Master Shiskin? As a strategy, I mean."

"You mean to hold me prisoner?"

"I mean to hold you hostage. As long as you live behind bars in the lower chambers, I believe my old friend Shular will stay on his side of the border. Many lives will be spared, and much misery."

"You mean not to sell me, but to hold me hostage," Shiskin repeated, involuntarily revealing his admiration for the plan.

Neassan waved at his soldiers. "Take him to his new quarters. And be on your guard. This man is the most dangerous prisoner you've ever had. And as for you, Master Shiskin, live on, you old snake, and we'll push the fight off until a distant tomorrow."

...

Miles sat grinning in the glory of his new possession. The dirt bike he had gotten for his birthday was shiny red and trimmed in chrome, a fresh symbol of power and status. It was secondhand, but his father had cleaned and polished it, and it looked close enough to new. The little engine puttered and barked in a noisy idle. He revved it, and turned to flash a self-satisfied grin at his admirers.

"You can't ride it," he gleefully told Camilla as she stepped up close. "You don't even know how." Over her shoulder he eyed her friend Sasha and an older redheaded boy.

"Let me try sitting on it," Camilla whined.

"Nuh-uh."

"Don't be a dick. Why can't I sit on it?" Camilla shifted the backpack on her shoulder.

Sasha's older brother glared at him, and Miles relented. "Fine. But just for a minute." He got off and held the handle bars.

"Fine," Camilla echoed sourly. She pulled the free strap of her backpack over her other shoulder, and threw her leg over the bike. Waving Miles away, she took hold of the handle bars and leaned down, imitating a rider in a race. She turned the handle bars as if banking a sharp turn. "Nice," she said. "And this is the gears, right? You hold the clutch like this, and toe this lever."

"Hey!" Miles objected. But before he could stop her, Camilla wound out the throttle and released the clutch, and screamed across the yard, spitting up dirt. "You can't ride it!" Miles shouted after her.

Camilla raced down the old tarmac of the dead-end road and kept going onto a dirt path into the woods. She kept up her speed until she had to slow for a turn. When she was entirely out of sight, she slowed and stopped, and looked back in Miles's direction. She couldn't see the boy's expression, but she imagined him hopping from one foot to the other and whining. Sasha would give her the details later.

Her English teacher would call this a nice piece of poetic justice. No, she considered, that wasn't right. Her English teacher would be horrified at the raw, child-killing potential of a dirt bike and a girl on it without a helmet on, and would warn her of the mistake all young people make, thinking they're invincible. The woman would say something about the younger generation, and Camilla would tune her out. But *poetic justice* wasn't quite right, anyway. It was a nice piece of *vengeance*.

She spun the back tire and shot up a hill. Miles wasn't her main target. But he'd been right there encouraging Kevin and laughing at her. She would bring his bike back, but not until he'd paid in full for taking Kevin's side—not until she'd had some fun, and not until enough time had passed that Miles would be good and worried that she might never come back with it at all. She would give him a chance to envision losing his prize on the day he'd gotten it.

At the top of the hill she stopped and killed the engine. This was a favorite spot. There was a clearing that looked over the town dump, a vast expanse of spoiled land piled with bulldozed trash, new heaps always waiting to be pushed around by the public works men. Sometimes the wind was in the wrong direction, and the odor would drive her away from her solitary perch. But today the wind was at her back, and she unzipped her backpack and pulled out a sandwich Sasha's father had made for her. She felt good. She and Sasha had gotten their belts, and now she was getting her revenge.

Teeing up this moment had been simple.

"Look, I'm really sorry," Miles had told her earlier, hanging his head. "I won't laugh at you again, okay?"

Camilla assumed his father had put him up to this. Miles's father was always belittling him. He had probably ordered Miles to apologize or he wouldn't get his birthday present—not out of a sense that Camilla deserved an apology, but simply because he knew the boy would find it humiliating to apologize to a girl.

She had stood there stoically, saying nothing for many long seconds before emitting a huff and turning away. "That's fine, but it doesn't make up for being a dick."

She already had her mind focused on the dirt bike. Miles had been bragging about it for weeks, annoying her to no end. He was always talking about his dad's motorcycle, insisting that his dad had let him ride the big bike already, so he knew how to ride. This was partly true. Camilla had watched him one day on the bike with his dad behind him, letting him steer and work the throttle. They had slowly gone up and down the street a couple of times. But the man would never let the boy ride the big bike solo. Miles wasn't any bigger than Camilla. He'd probably fall over before he could get going, Camilla mused.

She could have responded to his boasting that she had ridden a dirt bike before, plenty of times. But she kept this little secret to herself. Two foster families earlier, she'd had a foster brother whose passions were girls and pot, and getting together with both in remote places where his parents wouldn't bother him. To shut little Camilla up, he'd taught her to ride, in return for her promise never to tell his parents about the girls and drugs.

Now she sat triumphant, eating the sandwich and looking at the front-end loader abandoned for the night at the base of a pile of garbage. These moments almost made life worth living.

...

Vergil picked up a section of two-by-four and swung. His opponent reeled back and avoided the blow, and looked around for a better weapon. Vergil was bleeding from his left ear. But the blond terror's piece of lumber was longer and heavier than his opponent's baseball bat.

Horace sat rigidly in his chair, clutching the driftwood in his hand and staring vacantly. He'd been pulled into this scene with a violence that matched the fight he was witnessing. He might have figured his son to be about sixteen, judging from the hairstyle and clothes. But he didn't need to guess. He knew what he was watching.

"You owe me," Vergil hissed. "And if I can't have the money, I'll take it out this way." He jabbed at the boy, and his opponent danced and circled, avoiding the blows. Then the two-by-four made contact, and the boy grunted and fell.

Horace breathed in and out rapidly. He didn't want to see this. For decades it had been his central wish never, ever to stumble across this particular scene. The death of Vergil's friend had been a big story in their little town. His son had denied the whole thing, and in the end the police couldn't tie him to it. The bludgeoning death of the high school boy went unsolved, attributed to a drug deal gone bad, and Horace planned a quick move to the city.

"No, no ..." Horace said to himself, and worked to blur his vision as his son hovered over the boy, took the bat, and went to work.

In the living room of the little cabin, a glass of bourbon tipped off the arm of the chair and broke on the floor, spattering the amber liquor in a pattern not unlike what Horace was seeing in red. Then he stopped breathing, the scene faded to white and then black, and he slumped in the chair, unconscious.

Summer hail on the windows woke him. He sat up, realizing he had thrown up on himself. On the floor on one side was the broken glass and the sticky remains of dried-up liquor, and on the other side was the piece of driftwood.

"Ho," he breathed out. "Is this the connection? That young man Neassan. Is that to be his fate, to be killed by the man who once was his friend?"

He rose and stumbled into the kitchen, and returned with a waste basket and a spatula. He picked up the driftwood without touching it, and then carefully collected the broken glass, sweeping the shards into a dustpan. Then he tied the bag and brought it outside and put it in the back of his truck. Today would be trash day, and the souvenir of his son's murderous past would mix and decompose with the detritus of other people's lives.

...

When she pulled up to the house, Miles shot up from the back steps and rushed over.

"Hey!" he cried out in his little-boy voice.

"Pretty nice," Camilla said with an innocent smile, as if her excursion with the boy's dirt bike had been a friendly affair. She looked down to shove the kickstand into place. "You should go try it out in the woods."

Then a hand grabbed hold of her backpack, and in an instant of horror she realized she had once again made the mistake of not paying appropriate attention. This time, with her focus on her victory over red-eyed Miles, she had missed her true adversaries, Kevin and Miles's father standing in the shadows by the car.

Kevin hauled her off the bike.

"Let me go!" Camilla kicked at him.

He slammed a fist into her stomach, taking her breath away. "Shut up," he demanded.

Then the man whose birthday gift to his son she'd purloined stormed over, wound up, and backhanded her across the face. Camilla cried out and tumbled to the dirt as Kevin shoved her to add momentum. She scrambled to her feet, but Miles's protector was already on her. Kevin hauled her up a second time and grinned at the red mark already forming on her face.

"We're not done with you," he said. He held her up for another.

This time the man grabbed her by the shirt collar and lifted her completely off the ground. He shook her, staring into her eyes with a look of murder, and tossed her to the ground as if throwing away a piece of trash. The man caught Kevin's arm. "Let the little shit lie there. Miles, you've learned a lesson today, haven't you? Put the bike in the shed and then come over here and show me you can stand up for yourself. Show that little orphan bitch ..."

Camilla felt herself pulled into a different scene as the words of a new tormentor faded: *Show that little orphan bitch what happens when she tries to mess with me. ...*

"You're Tallach! Stand tall," Undine ordered, standing in the center of their small cell. "And stop wincing when I throw a punch. Tallach fighters don't wince, Tyra. And I won't hit you anyway, all right? Just learn to block."

Tyra weakly blocked the next two strikes, backing up.

"Those sentries will be coming for us," Undine demanded. "Concentrate!"

"Undine, I don't want to do this. I'm not a fighter." Tyra raised her palms and retreated. She stepped to the wall and sat.

With an angry sigh, her friend dropped her arms, her hands clenching into fists. "What's the plan, then? Sit in the dirt and let them take you? You heard the quartermaster. Damn it, Tyra, they'll kill us. Now get up! You have to fight. Fight and run."

A hand slid into the back of her shirt collar and hauled Camilla up, and she found herself standing in Miles's back lawn again. A shoe pressed against her backside and shoved her hard, and she sprawled to the ground again.

"Goin' for a ride? Get up, little shit," Kevin demanded, a smiling cat playing with his mouse. "I wanna pop you again before Miles gets his turn."

His nasal, kid-with-a-broken-nose tone almost made her laugh. But this time she was losing. Camilla groaned and pushed herself to her hands and knees. *Fight and run.* Una said, *fight and run.* And no wincing. *Your power comes from your mind*, Sensei Taniemon would have said. *Stand tall and make your strike.*

The sentiment was right, but Camilla had learned a different set of rules for a street fight. Instead of standing tall and showing her resolve, she made a show of her distress, exaggerating the pain in her shoulder and feigning an injured leg. Kevin loomed over her, gloating. Behind him she could see Miles sheepishly pushing the bike around to the shed. He was probably more frightened than she was of "getting his turn."

"Don't hit me again," Camilla begged. She raised a defensive, imploring hand. "Please, Kevin, don't."

Then as Kevin's eyes tracked her hand, she kicked the big boy in the crotch as hard as she could. The boy doubled over, and Camilla turned and ran.

Let the sensei try to tell her *that* wasn't a karate move, she thought, grinning as she tore across the yard. It was a damned fine kick.

Hiding behind the bushes in a neighbor's yard, Camilla clutched her shoulder and fought to hold back tears. The adrenaline rush was gone, and there was no one to save face with now, no one to not wince for. But she wouldn't cry, damn it! Her shoulder hurt like hell, and her stomach ached, and her face stung. Her tee shirt was ruined, the collar stretched out of shape and the fabric distorted where the man had clutched and twisted. She had grass stains and dirt on her backpack, and her knees were scraped and bleeding.

From her backpack she pulled a half-empty bottle of water. She poured some in her hand and tried to clean the dirt out of the scrapes on her knees. It wasn't working. All she was doing was wiping dirt into the scrapes. She stuffed the bottle back in the bag and rose, whimpering in pain.

It took longer than usual to get back to the trailer. She didn't want to be seen, so she crept through back yards, watching for weekenders and barky dogs. The only thing in her favor was that Marie was gone for the weekend, and she assumed Mack would be too drunk to give her a hard time, if he was home at all.

The door was unlocked and the porch light was on. She stepped inside.

"Humph," she grunted, as she saw the usual devastation in the living room, beer bottles, empty chip bags, overflowing ashtrays, and flies buzzing around the remains of dip in plastic tubs. She peered into the bedroom to make sure. Perfect. With Marie gone, they had wrecked the place and moved on to trash another venue. She could clean herself up, find some aspirin, and pack her things.

7. The Hawk Bill Inn

Soldiers came for Undine before dawn. She was given a riding cloak and bundled into a covered wagon.

"Keep this closed, if you would," the driver said, pulling the canvas cover shut. "Rap when you need to stop. I'm ordered to ride hard and lose no time. I'm told I'm to call you Una."

"Una? All right," she said with a smirk. At first she silently scolded the gunners for it. Why use her real name as a cover name? But then, why not? No one knew her as Una except for the gunners, and she wouldn't have to work to get used to it.

Her seat was upholstered and comfortable, and on the seat opposite was a basket containing a fresh loaf of bread, a wheel of cheese, and a flagon of wine. All right, then. She couldn't complain about the accommodations. The driver snapped the reins, and the horses pulled them onto the road.

Undine sat back and looked through a slit at the early light flickering through branches. The wagon bumped along, slowing on the uphill parts and picking up speed as they descended. She smiled. This was certainly better than being locked up in the dungeons of the Twelfth Station.

But as they rode on and on, the excitement faded, and she found herself mulling over her predicament. She and her friend had been seized by northern troops and manhandled into jail cells in a soldiers' station. It was an affront. Why not jump from the carriage, run back, and break Tyra out? But that was nonsense. She couldn't break into a border station, and Tyra had probably already been moved, anyway. She could be anywhere.

Then she moved to thoughts of how she might turn the tides against the northern gunners. Maybe two could play at this game. She'd snatch someone of value to the gunners and propose a trade. But that wouldn't work, either. The only northerners she knew, other than the gunners themselves, were the Gatto master Aideen and the girls who had been novices when she had been there eight years ago. She was no match for Aideen, even with four turns of the spiral on her face. And kidnapping a Gatto fighter who had been training for as long as she had herself was about as bad an idea as trying to break into a border station.

Hours wore on, until she felt that she was a prisoner just as much as Tyra was. The driver stopped to change horses, and passed the reins to a fresh driver. Late in the evening she fell asleep to thoughts of revenge.

She was awakened as the wagon slowed and stopped.

"This is it for tonight," the driver said, pounding a palm on the side of the carriage.

Undine pushed the door open and climbed out. "But where is this place?"

"Just a place to spend the night, miss. We'll start up again at dawn. Come. I'll show you to your room."

Her first night as the gunner's agent was spent in the tack room of a horse barn. She started to grumble, until she realized the cot in the corner was the driver's own bed. He could have left her to sleep in the wagon, or on the ground. She thanked him for the generosity, and as the driver headed off to sleep with the animals, she dropped down and fell asleep.

The second day on the road was the same as the first, except that the wagon had been replaced by a carriage with the curtains drawn shut. Early in the day, there was a moment of excitement, a disturbance up ahead. The driver pulled to a stop, and Undine thought he might order her to get out and seek cover. But horses rushed past them and thundered off.

"Just a bit of a squabble, miss," he called back. "No need for concern."

The vague encouragement didn't help. Undine wished she had a blade.

They rode on, and her musings ventured into darker territory. She could run to Deadrise Bay, tell Captain Armand that his daughter had been seized by northern soldiers, and they could return with a Tallach army. Why not take on the gunners? She was a Fourth-Level Talla, after all.

But none of these scenarios made sense. For all the options she could think of, the likely outcomes were worse—much worse—than simply doing what the gunner wanted her to do. She couldn't see all that much danger in their plan. First, go overseas. Tyra had done it many times. Undine herself had daydreamed about taking a trip to the mainland. In another context, she might beg to go. Then find a person. She didn't have the details yet, but how hard could it be? The purpose of this ride to the ninth sector was to meet with a team who would prepare her to identify the target. She wouldn't be going in blind. Surely she could find a man. Possibly it would require subterfuge. She might have to talk her way past roadblocks along the way. But that kind of thing was her special talent. Then she had to get the man onto a ship and get to sea, and that was that. She would make the voyage back and deliver him to the gunners.

Thoughts of subverting the gunners' plans dwindled further when late in the evening the carriage pulled up to the magnificent Hawk Bill Inn in the ninth sector, and the driver slapped the side of the carriage again and announced that this was her destination. When she looked out and saw where they were, her mood improved considerably.

In the times of the Alliance, before the dictator had been killed, the Hawk Bill Inn had been commandeered by the Alliance guard. It had ironically come to be known as safe lodging for travelers by virtue of the fact that it was crawling with Red Guard. No one would try to rob the place or accost its patrons. In a back room, the northern soldiers had even set up a clandestine meeting place, right under the nose of the enemy. Then after the overthrow of the dictator, the inn continued to flourish. As commerce returned to a more normal state, the upper crust sought fine dining and fine lodging, and the Hawk Bill had both.

"Your veil if you please, miss," the driver said, stepping in front of the carriage window. "Unless you prefer to apply the face paint. There's no hurry. The inn will wait."

Undine understood, and closed the curtain. A Tallach woman with the spiral design of a Talla fighter on her face would be a spectacle. She pulled her veil down. As she hopped to the brick drive, a graying woman in a matron's dress moved onto the porch and down the stairs. They traded pleasantries, and the hostess led her inside, the driver following with her bags. Her room was on the second floor. It was elegant. The canopy bed was large and tightly made, the dressing table was topped with marble and featured a spectacular oval mirror, and the balcony looked over a rolling lawn, a large patio on one side set with tables and chairs for the evening meal.

"I'm told your contact will meet you at the dinner hour," the driver said softly. He bowed and left.

Undine locked her door and went about the task of covering her tattoo.

Tyra reflected that seafarers were not built for climbing. She mopped a hand across her brow and took another step, and then another, each one a chore. She had sailed overseas, and had traveled on schooners, barges, and row boats. Never had she attempted to climb up so high on the land. She had read about the northlands cliffs and passes, and had heard of the triumvirate's hidden underground halls. There were stories of war meetings in the old times, and peace meetings in the new. But no one she knew had ever been there. Now the gunner was leading her up a mountain path. She glanced backward and swooned. Bad idea.

"Just walk," Ailmili said. "You're not going to topple over and fall into the abyss. It's just a walking trail."

Tyra nodded and took the next step. One step, then another, and then another after that. Keep it up, and sooner or later she would be at the top, wouldn't she? It must be so, although it also seemed as if they were just going to keep climbing forever.

When finally they entered a crevasse that led into the side of the mountain, she was apprehensive, but the walking was immediately easier, and she felt less ill at ease. She understood small spaces. Berths in a merchant schooner were confining. The crevasse felt more like home.

"The passageways are soothing, aren't they?" Ailmili said. "Like stepping into an oasis in the wastes. Come."

They headed down the dark crevasse until finally the gunner realized that her captive was lagging behind, unable to see.

"Take my hand. I should have brought a lamp. I don't usually have someone with me." She towed the young woman through a series of turns and drops, and finally they stepped into a small room. The gunner struck a match and lit an oil lamp. "There. Is that better?"

"Oh!" Tyra said, startled. "This is quite nice."

On one side was a sturdy bed with a thatched mat, and on the other a table on which a goblet was sitting, right-side-up. The gunner turned it over, fished into an opening in the stone wall, and clicked a latch, and a stone door slid open.

"Come in. I'll show you to your room."

Tyra's eyes widened as they stepped into a warm corridor, the floor lined with furs. The little room with the table and the goblet was merely a foyer. Inside, oil lamps lit a long passage. Ailmili pushed the stone door closed and led her down the hall.

"This room is yours," the gunner said, motioning to a doorway on their left. "A girl will come by tomorrow. Tell her if you need anything—different bedding, a reading chair, a table—whatever you want. You'll sleep here. Set it up as you like."

The room was opulent compared to a berth on a schooner. There was a thick thatched-mat bed covered in furs, a table with a lantern on it, a straight chair, and a trunk. The walls were covered in tapestries.

"I arranged for some clothes for you," the gunner said, nodding at the trunk, "but if you don't care for what you find, tell the girl tomorrow. You'll be expected to maintain your health, and to assist with duties here in the hold. Have the girl bring what you need. When you're called on, you'll be expected to cooperate."

Tyra nodded. "Yes, gunner," she said.

"You may go wherever you like within the shelter, but you're not to venture out into the passages. It's not that it's forbidden, but there are dangers, not the least of which is the likelihood of getting lost in the maze. Do you understand?"

"Yes, gunner."

"You'll have plenty of opportunities to go outside if you want. You don't need to feel that you're trapped down here."

The girl nodded.

"Tomorrow your regular routine will start. I'll come for you first thing. For today, why don't you spend the remaining hours below. This way." She led her along the corridor to a set of stairs winding down to a lower level. "I'm expected up on the plateau. You go ahead. Take the lamp. I think you'll be content. There will be a meal for you later."

Tyra held the lamp in front of herself as if to ward off whatever might be lurking down the stairs. She descended slowly, and came to an iron door. At first she considered running back up the stairs. What was forcing her to go into this dungeon? But she breathed in, and imagined what her friend would say, were she there.

"You're not going to look?" she said to herself, mimicking Undine's voice. "What if there's a feast of fine food in there, or a dozen man servants with orders to see to your every need? Or for you, maybe a stack of books. Live a little, Tyra. Don't be afraid of your shadow."

She laughed softly. Then her face soured, thinking of her friend off on a mission for the gunner, probably something dangerous. Maybe deadly. Would she see Undine again? She pushed the door open, and a warm, flickering light met her. She took one step into the room and stopped dead, her eyes wide and her mouth open.

"Ho," she gasped. "Oh, dear me." Not a stack of books, but an entire roomful of them. Floor-to-ceiling shelves covered the walls, filled with volumes. She almost dropped the lantern, she was in such haste to hang it on the stand to free her hands. "Undine," she muttered, "fare well. But don't finish your task too soon!"

Two redheads sat side-by-side, one quietly complaining as the needle pierced her skin again and again. The other stared forward, frightened to the point of panic, although no one was doing anything to her. The soldier's orders had been clear: The Gunner Ailmili had said, *Treat her as you would treat me, should you have happened upon me in earlier years.* They would never have dared touch the gunner at all, but the soldier standing behind Tyra interpreted the command practically, and patted the girl's shoulder, encouraging her to sit still and relax.

"Miss Tyra," another soldier said, "are you thirsty? We could fetch a drink. And is your chair to your liking? There are cushions."

Tyra glanced over. "I'm fine. Thank you."

"Well, I'm not," said the redheaded woman sitting next to her, as the inked needle moved on her forehead. "Damn it, this hurts."

"Only a little more, Miss Tansie," said the man working the tool. "And you, miss, head up."

Tyra snapped her chin up.

"So tell me, Miss Tansie," the man said, pausing, "where'd the gunner find you? She collect all the redheads in town an' pick out the one that resembles her most?" He waved the tool at Tyra.

Tansie grinned. "She fetched me up from the southlands. The gunner saw me when I was a child."

The man dropped his voice. "In the days of Shular? In the time of the dictator, before they …"

Tansie nodded. "Right in the thick of it. Ever heard of the millhouse out near the reaches?"

"Smugglers. Fine grade of whiskey. Get mine from a trader who gets it from one of them outfits."

"I run them."

The man set down the tool. "You? Well, shit. You're *that* Tansie? I've heard of you, honey. You an' that old feller, you run all the distilleries down there. That's a hell of an enterprise. And the gunner found you as a kid? There's gotta be a story there."

"They were on their way to the far reaches and stopped in. Needed horses," Tansie explained. "I'd hooked up with Butch and Quick not too long before. It was just the one millhouse back then. We didn't have the other places yet. So the gunners and Lord Torin stopped by, and they stayed the night. Taught us kids some sparring just to pass the time. And I've worked ever since then to try to get anywhere close to as good as what I saw Gunner Ailmili do."

"That'd be a tall order. But it seems she noticed you, eh? 'Cause here you are."

Tansie flashed another grin, and tipped her head up. "Okay, go ahead. I'm ready."

The man got to work again, and soon finished the small flower. "Good, good," he said, sitting back to review his work. "And tell me, lassie," he looked at Tyra, "is the little flower on your forehead all there is? I'm to replicate your'n upon this 'un. Is there any other on you?"

"Just the flax flower," Tyra said, staring.

"You're sure? 'Twon't do to hold out. If there's a tat on your buttocks or such, girl, best just to own up an' show. The silver-eyed sylph can't be tricked. Gunner Ailmili will find you out."

"Nothing. Just this. My buttocks are untouched." Tyra smirked.

"Oh, untouched?" The man stopped and gave her a mock-mournful look. "How sad. Untouched."

"Quiet, you," Tansie scolded. "That's my butt you're talking about."

"Apologies, Miss Tansie. I didn't mean ..."

"I am *not* Miss Tansie. I don't even know what you mean. Do I remind you of someone else?" Tansie pulled back. "My name is Tyra. I'm the daughter of a Tallach ship captain. My backside is not to be discussed."

"I'm sorry."

"My father is a ship captain, from ... from ..." Tansie looked over at the captive seated next to her. "Damn it."

"Pedlar Inlet. On the southern coast of mainland Ben Attallach," Tyra said.

"Right. Damn it all." Tansie rapped her fist to her knee. "Pedlar Inlet. Why can't I remember that?" Then she clenched her eyes shut. "Ow," she complained, dabbing a finger on her forehead.

Everyone stiffened as the gunners entered the room, except for Tansie.

"This hurts," she whined. "Please tell me, Tyra, that this is really the only one, and you don't have another one of these on your ribs."

"You're complaining?" the blonde gunner said.

Tansie's eyes flew open. "Complaining? Oh, buzzards, no, gunner! You know I want this. Fire and daggers, a trip to Ben Attallach? I've been dreaming about this kind of assignment forever. But the needle hurts."

"And I chose you for this task because of what I saw in you then, and because of what you've accomplished since then—not just because you bear a resemblance to the ship captain's daughter. You have three weeks to learn to be Tyra. You and Undine are to make the next run of the *Margay*, six weeks from today."

"Gunner!" The woman bowed her head, stifling a grin. "I'll be ready." She was giddy at her good luck. A trip to Ben Attallach! An actual trip overseas, to the mainland of the Tallachs.

A man in his middle-forties, graying at the temples, sat on a bar stool at a high café table overlooking the rear gardens of the Hawk Bill Inn. Every seat along the bar was filled with guests waiting for their table, and more people were leaning in behind them, with even more in the foyer. But while the café table would easily seat four or five, the man had it to himself. He drew looks of envy and resentment, but no one had the nerve to step up and have a seat. The pin on his collar, a silver bar with three ruby cabochons, warned them off. That was the mark of an officer of the Tynan triumvirate of the north. Best not to get involved.

The man rose as the matron of the house stepped past the waiting guests with a young woman on her arm. The woman wore a pressed white shirt and a black satin vest and pants. Black silk stocking covered her legs, which were exposed from mid-shin, and she had black sandals on.

Una's eyes widened. She had been told that her contact was an officer of the north, but was taken aback by the bar on his collar. This assignment must be more important than she'd thought.

"Stiles," the man said, rising, "Officer and attaché of the gunners." He removed his hat from the stool next to his and motioned for her to sit. "And I take it you're Una."

Una offered her hand. "Pleased to meet you, Commander Stiles."

"Wine, if you please," Stiles said to the matron, and she nodded and departed.

"We're to meet here?" Una looked around the crowded room, all eyes on her.

"Just for a little chitchat." He leaned in. "And to give the guests a chance to see us. We'll have a glass of wine, and then take a stroll on the bridge. That should do it."

They sipped their wine, and Stiles asked how her trip had been, and what she thought of the inn. Una nervously mentioned the lovely terrace and how she admired the little bridge. Then Stiles rose and offered his arm, and they took their glasses and walked outside. Patrons snatched up the café table.

The wooden walking bridge was far enough from the inn that they wouldn't be overheard, but cozy enough that guests spotting a man with a young woman on his arm would leave them to their courtship, even if there weren't a commander's bar on his collar.

"This place is magnificent," Una said, looking back at the inn.

"Isn't it? It has a long history. A firm connection with the north. I thought it would be a good place for our meeting. And the gunners have told me I'm to see to it that you're comfortable. You'll have a few weeks here. You're satisfied with your room?"

"It's excellent, thank you."

"Be sure to tell me if anything is lacking. The matron will arrange anything you need." He sidled up to her.

"No, it's fine. And it's, uh, very nice out here." Una trilled a quiet laugh, and looked away.

"Be at ease. You're not being forced into a courtship." Commander Stiles smiled. "In fact, the purpose of our little stroll is to see to it that you're not accosted. I want every randy young man at the inn to see you talking to me. They'll look for easier targets, and you'll be left alone."

"Oh. Oh, all right," she said, relaxing. "Thank you."

"And it should save you the trouble of having to paint your face each day for fear of an adventuresome lad daring to lift your veil for a look at you. Ailmili told me what's under that makeup, Una. Quite impressive. But come. They've seen us. Let's get to the meeting."

She took his arm again, and he led her across the lawn and inside through a side entrance to the kitchen. The staff were expecting them, and nodded silently as they passed through to a rear storage room. Stiles swept aside a curtain of dried peppers and garlic, and pushed through a hidden door to a private meeting room.

A short, bald man rose from the table and bowed. "Commander Stiles," he said. "And you must be Una. Come in, come in. My name is David." He pulled a chair out for her, and they sat.

"David is a general of the northlands," Stiles said, causing her to raise her eyebrows again.

"And Commander Stiles is an officer of the Gunner Ailmili," David said, "and so I suppose it's unclear which of us outranks the other, eh, commander?"

"I would propose that when the gunner tells me what she wants to do, I outrank you. And when you're telling her that she shouldn't do it, you outrank me, as I wouldn't dare tell her."

David laughed. "True enough. All right then. We don't have a lot of time. Una, you'll take your meals and your walks outdoors with, and only with, Commander Stiles."

Stiles nodded. "Call on me any time, day or night. Ring for a servant to fetch me, or just bang on my door."

"You're not to go out on your own," David insisted. "The guests won't interfere with a young woman seen on the arm of the commander, but once you step outside of his reach, you become a target."

Una nodded dumbly. A commander and a general of the northlands!

"I'm going to tell you a story, such as we know it. You'll need to discover which details are true. Do you follow?"

"Yes," Una said, looking confused.

"Good. Then let's begin. Years ago, during the time of the Alliance, a girl was taken into slavery by the Tallachs."

"A girl!" Una exclaimed, her heartbeat rising.

David held up a hand. "I'm not telling you your own story, Una. No, this was years earlier, and the slave trader took a girl on purpose."

"But we … uh, they only took boys as slaves."

David smiled thinly at her slip. "No, you go right on maintaining your role as Undine of the Tallachs. Your initial inclination was correct. *We only took boys as slaves.*"

"Yes, sir."

"You'll travel as a Tallach woman and use the name Una. But we expect it to be a thin disguise, and that people will see through it. Everything you do and say is to be consistent with a fourth-level Talla in disguise as the daughter of a southern trader."

"You want them to know?"

"We don't want you to proclaim it out loud. But consider what it means to travel overseas without an escort, just you and the other girl. Ordinary girls might face considerable obstacles. And Undine of Deadrise Bay would draw too much attention. But a rising young fighter traveling incognito, now that's an intriguing story. Who would want to spoil it? Watch for allies, Una, and let them be proud of their cleverness in spotting you. They'll be anxious to play along and help a fourth-level Talla along your trail."

"Yes, sir."

"All right. As I was saying, a six-year-old girl was taken as a slave. It's true that the Tallachs traded almost entirely in boys. But the men who took this little girl worked for a man with a particular taste in women."

"I don't understand," Una frowned. "An interest in little girls?"

"Let's pour the wine."

When their glasses were filled, David continued. "As I'm sure you know, Una, before the overthrow of the southern dictator, the slave trade was the Tallach cartel's bread and butter. Young boys were poached from the southlands and even sometimes from the northlands, and were shipped overseas to Ben Attallach, where they were sold. Most became plantation laborers. On this particular run, a young man, still really just a boy, had tagged along with a team of seasoned slave traders. His father had recently died, leaving his older brother to rise to the position of governor of one of the largest districts in Ben Attallach, the district now called Green Hills. ..."

No longer were they Conn and his big brother Crinan, privileged children of the governor running around the manor doing what they pleased. Now it was Crinan, governor of Green Hills, and an irksome little brother.

"You see how busy I am," Crinan complained as the boy pestered him for attention. Finally Crinan arranged to get his little brother out of the way. "I need you to go overseas to the east. If I'm to be an effective governor, I need eyes on those lands," he told Conn. "Can you do it? Your cover will be as a man in the slave trade." As an aside to his soldier, he added, "Keep him alive, but see to it that it's a long trip."

The boy boarded the ship, pleased to have landed such an important position. But the journey was less exciting and less leisurely than he had expected. He was made to work as a deck hand, as were the soldiers sent to accompany him.

"There's no room for privilege on a slave ship, master Conn," one soldier said, when the boy started to show signs of resentment. "We all work."

The soldiers worked without complaining, and so Conn did, too. But when they landed on the Western Shores and the real work started—the raids and the killing, the chaining up of young boys and forcing them onto the ship—he realized what was going on. He wasn't a spy for the powerful new governor of the Green Hills. His brother had sent him overseas to get him out of the way.

"Crinan is governor, boy," a solder snapped, at his renewed complaining. "And you're a step away from being governor yourself, you see? A step over his dead body. So he puts some distance between you and him to teach you your place. I'd be looking for ways to show him what a fine brother and loyal subject you are. Else he might settle the matter another way."

Young Conn clamped his mouth shut. He knew about sibling rivalries at other plantations. The soldier was right. His brother held the scepter, and the younger brother would be wise to find his place—or at least to make it appear that he had.

But what could he do that would put him into the good graces of his brother? He realized they had little in common. Crinan was interested in alehouses, women with doe eyes and jet black hair, and dominance. Even fresh after his marriage, he spent his nights drinking and whoring, and each time a new dark-eyed girl grew tired of his overly rough style and put an end to their nighttime trysts, he became a raging boar, stomping around and bellowing.

Conn was interested in girls too, but not in wrestling them to the ground. To him, Crinan's wife Gavina seemed like a catch. She was attractive, smart, and in fact better connected than he and Crinan, if one were to set aside the matter of the governorship. Gavina's family controlled a manufacturing business that spanned Ben Attallach and sent ships overseas. Yet Crinan treated her like just another of his whores.

Then on a slave run Conn spotted a little girl with big eyes and dark hair, cowering in the corner. "Well, well. Don't you look familiar," he said. He put out a hand and caught the arm of the soldier who was about to gut her. "Hold. Bring this one along. She resembles a girl my brother used to fancy. In some years she'll be a match, I think. That might be a gift he'd appreciate."

"This little runt?" the soldier scowled.

"She'll take time to mature, but then he'll have a girl he fancies, who can't run from him."

David paused in his story to top off the wine glasses, and Una tipped her head. "All right, then," she said, "so this man Crinan is governor, and Conn is trying to get into his good graces, so he finds a girl to be made a present. It sounds a bit foolish. But what's my role in all of this?"

David sat back. "You're to recover the girl."

Una snapped her eyes to his. "The girl?" She halted, surprised. "Oh. I wasn't expecting the target to be a girl. But all right, the girl, then. What can you tell me about her?"

"Not a little girl anymore. She was around six then, so let's say she's twenty-two now. Dark hair, dark eyes—and to see her brother, I'd expect her to be quite lovely."

"Her brother ..."

"Her brother wasn't taken by the Tallachs," Stiles explained. "Fortunately for him, he was away when the raid took place. Not so fortunately, he returned home to find his mother dead and his sister gone."

"He's here, then? Am I to meet him? He could fill me in about ..."

David put up a hand. "Commander Riley knows nothing of this plan, nor is he to learn of it."

"Commander!" Una gasped, looking to Stiles and then to David. "The slave girl's brother is a Tynan commander?"

"And to be plain, he unarguably outranks us both when it comes to the gunners," Stiles said. "Commander Riley is the gunner Rachanna's innermost guard. He was her soldier when she cut Shular in his pavilion."

"Ho!" Una expelled a breath.

She knew the story of the young gunner sneaking into Shular's compound, getting caught, and then slashing the dictator's leg and escaping. It was a favorite among the Tallach fighting instructors, an inspirational story for the female trainees, and a lesson for the young men not to underestimate their opponent.

"Why keep it a secret from her brother?" Una asked. "Commander Riley could tell me more about her."

"Because," David explained, "the danger to the young woman is significant and growing. The gunner wishes to recover the young woman. But if it can't be done, she would like to spare telling her man that his sister lived, but oh, I'm sorry, now she's dead."

Una nodded mutely.

"You're not to breathe a word about who she is. You understand? Not until you return with the girl and deliver her to the gunners. Your official task is to fetch a slave from Ben Attallach. That's all you're to say about it." David stared at her. "The gunners want you to recover Commander Riley's sister, *secretly.*"

There was a rap on the door, and dinner was brought in, a fancy rolled pork roast with boiled potatoes and braised greens. Dishes were set, glasses filled, and then the serving crew nodded and departed, closing the door behind them.

David stood and started pacing. "Go on you both. Eat. I'll finish the story. Now, this next part is less confirmed, and so the facts could change. But I suspect most of what I'm about to tell you is accurate. First there's the matter of Madam Ben Yett—which is to say, Gavina, the wife of Governor Crinan. ..."

Green Hills was the largest and most prosperous district in Ben Attallach. The family trade was in stonecutting, but the district got its name from its vast fields of flax and wheat. And while his father had taught him the family trade, Crinan didn't inherit his father's genius at running a large district. On the old man's death, the new, green governor of Green Hills faced immediate challenges. Traders dickered for lower prices. Slave traders demanded higher prices. An endless stream of underlings harassed him with requests for promotions and perks. Everyone wanted in on the game.

Familial tensions rose, as well. The younger brother Conn returned from the east silently fuming. There was no lavish welcome-home feast or celebration, and his gift fell flat.

"Doesn't she look like that other one?" Conn crowed, putting on a smile in spite of his anger. "She's still a child, but look at her face, and what it will become. Give her six years, or seven."

Crinan shook his head and sighed. "Send the girl to the kitchens," he ordered his clerk. "Conn, I've something for you to do."

The younger brother was assigned to another year away, this time with a team of pay scouts sent to make collections. Conn was a year older and a year wiser, and wasn't fooled this time, but there was nothing he could do about it. He packed and left for another year of exile. And at the end of the stint he returned home only to be sent off on yet another long assignment away.

For five years the pattern repeated. The little girl reached age eleven, and Conn hadn't been wrong about her. She promised to grow into a beautiful woman. Crinan still showed no interest, but Madame Ben Yett, who might have quietly disposed of the young slave, instead took young Adelaide under her wing. Instructors were brought in to see to her education, and Gavina taught the girl to ride horses.

To the rank and file, Adelaide seemed to have become Gavina's surrogate daughter. She had children by Crinan, but Gavina spent more time grooming Adelaide than seeing to her own brood. On his brief visits home, a much wiser Conn recognized the basis of their relationship. He saw it in their faces: Two pairs of dark, indignant eyes drilled into Crinan as he strode past without bothering to acknowledge them. Solidarity. They were comrades in their fate, the jilted wife and the girl being raised to sleep in her husband's bed.

Then one year Conn saw his opportunity. Instead of a long trip to the far north or overseas, he was once again assigned to a round of tax collecting. This time the receipts didn't make it back to the Green Hills. Conn took the money and sailed for the islands.

"Let him come for me, if he wants his money," he laughed, as he absconded with a satchel of his brother's gold.

More years passed, and as expected, the slave girl in the kitchens transformed into a stunning young woman. This created a new problem, for in fact she was a dead ringer for an early conquest of Crinan's. When one day he stepped into the kitchens to berate the servants for something not to his liking, the girl looked up at him, and it was as if he had stepped back to his early twenties. There she was, preserved at the peak of loveliness.

"Leave her alone, you old wolf," Gavina scolded, following her husband into the kitchens and stepping between them as Crinan looked the girl over. "Adelaide is my ward. You leave her be!"

"Oh, but I believe Adelaide is my slave," Crinan crooned. "Aren't you the girl Conn brought to me as present? Come, let's get acquainted."

Crinan took his slave girl, and expected his wife to accept it. Instead Madame Ben Yett took their children on a trip to the east, with no intention of returning.

"She abandoned the girl?" Una's eyes went wide. "After bringing her up, she just left her there?"

"It's complicated," David explained. "The woman loved Adelaide, and Adelaide loved her surrogate mother. But neither could stop Crinan's advances. Adelaide was his slave, and Madame Ben Yett was, well, not the governor. In the end, Crinan could do as he pleased."

"Hmph!" Una grunted. "Why didn't she take this Adelaide with her?"

"She may have considered it. But there would be two problems. First, Crinan is smart enough that he'd anticipate that, and so he'd have the girl guarded. Second, to abscond with his prize would be a direct challenge. He'd send men after her. She would be running for her life rather than just leaving."

"And so this woman ran away and allowed him to bed the girl she'd brought up?"

"Allowed? Oh, I don't think she had much choice. Neither did the girl. In fact Gavina left in part, I suspect, to protect Adelaide. Her young ward could be used as a tool, after all. With Gavina gone, there would be less chance that the governor would punish his wife by venting his anger on the girl. Better for them both, all things considered."

"It doesn't seem like such a wonderful plan to me." Una folded her arms and glared.

"You'll hear no debate on that point from me. And in fact it seems her plan didn't work. For you see, things have changed. ..."

Stories spread, and unrest swept across the Green Hills: Crinan's wife had abandoned him, his brother had absconded with a small fortune, and the governor was whoring with a slave. Disputes among traders broke out. Trades were lost, and partnerships broken. Rumors of challenges to his governorship grew. Then amidst all of this turmoil, Conn was found and brought back in chains to bow to his brother, who ordered him to make humiliating reparations.

Then new rumors circulated, that Madame Ben Yett might not be so far out of the picture as Crinan might wish. The Ben Yett family had wealth and power. Maybe his estranged wife would seek to have her husband taken out of the picture, and take over herself. Her pedigree was finer than Crinan's, after all.

Whispered stories ran through the district, of Lord Crinan cursing at the help and shouting at his advisors. Once he struck the slave girl Adelaide so hard he almost broke her arm. And this story, when it made its way overseas, forced the rumor of Madame Ben Yett's return to become real. Her plan to protect herself and Adelaide by staying away was no longer working. It was time to return and make her move.

"And the prospect of Madame Ben Yett's return is not the only danger to Governor Crinan," David said. "There are reports of other factions, powerful people focusing on the Green Hills. Military leaders are ready to move in. It's quite unstable, Una. We don't know to a certainty that Crinan's wife means to make a play at the governorship herself, but we know others are prepared to do so. And whatever her reasons, Madame Ben Yett is on her way. In fact, she'll be on the *Margay* when you sail."

8. Dressed in Black

The part of his son's past that Horace least wanted to remember was his own role in the death of the local boy. Horace hadn't been the one to beat the high school boy to death, but accepting his son's implausible story had been a gratuitous act of cowardice. He would never forget that day.

"Yeah, so we got into a fight," Vergil told him, scrubbing at his shirt. "Big deal."

Horace watched his son lean over the sink trying to remove a blood stain. "You got into a fight," he echoed.

"Neil owes me money. He said he'd pay me back, and then he took that girl out and blew the whole pile. Big, fancy dinner and all. With *my money*. So yeah, we got in a fight."

"I don't understand your animus toward that young lady, Vergil. I know you and she played together when you were small children. But children grow up and change. Childhood friendships rarely persist."

"This isn't about her!" Vergil spat, turning to flash his father a glare.

"Isn't it? It seems whenever you and your friend have an issue, that young lady is around the edges of it."

"I don't care who he goes out with. But he can't use my money for it. Is that so hard to understand?"

"Neil didn't come home last night, Vergil. His parents are worried."

"So what? I'm not his mother. I don't know where he went." Vergil scrubbed more vigorously at the shirt.

"Is that your blood or his? If something happened to him, Vergil, you could be in trouble." Horace winced. "Even if it happened afterward."

The boy turned and glared again. "You want to take a sample? He was fighting too. Not just me."

"And what if it turns out something happened to that boy, and they find his blood and yours?"

"So we got in a fight. Nobody was there to say who threw the first punch. It's his word against mine."

Horace let out a sigh. Vergil seemed angry rather than frightened. Was he merely putting on a good show, or could it be true that the fight was unrelated to the other boy's disappearance?

"Listen to me. Get a garbage bag," Horace ordered. "Put your clothes in the bag. That shirt, too. Then you take the longest shower you've ever taken."

His son turned and stared. "Dad, I got in a fight. It's not some kind of crime that's got to be covered up."

"I think I know a bit more about this kind of thing than you, son. Do you think you'll get a fair shake if something happened to that boy and they find your blood mixed with his?"

"Fuck," his son said, looking at the floor.

"Do as I say. While you're in the shower, review your day. I want to know every place you went, and every single thing you touched."

Horace retraced his son's steps and removed all incriminating traces. When he came to the kill site it took great power of will to see it merely as the scene of a couple of teenagers fighting over money. There was no body, but only fatherly love could blind him to the story the scene told.

When weeks later the body was discovered in the quarry pond, nature had already taken care of removing any remaining evidence. Vergil was brought in for questioning, but the police had nothing. They filed the case and moved on.

"You killed him," Horace muttered, staring out the window of his cabin. "I suppose I always knew. My son was not only an assassin but also a common murderer."

Horace felt hollow. Dumping the old piece of driftwood with the other trash had been a ritual with no cathartic value. It was a relief to have it gone, out of reach. But getting rid of it seemed somehow akin to his cover-up so many years ago. Instead of settling things, it brought his guilt once again into raw focus.

He considered disposing of the rest of the items. Maybe with time, and with all of these things gone, the memories would fade again. But as he sat thinking, he recognized that in the wider picture, he'd batted a .50 with Vergil's keepsakes. The driftwood had brought back a little piece of hell. But the granite chunk had led him to Una, a little girl who for some reason reminded him of his granddaughter. Maybe the only connection was that Una was a young girl, as was Camilla. But he'd spent some pleasant hours thinking about it. And then the driftwood had led him to murder and death.

"Camilla," he said out loud, "I hope these are joined only in my own mind. Don't let my son's life consume yours, child." He sat back, closed his eyes, and fell asleep.

...

In the movies, hot water flows over the hero's head and a dramatic swirl of blood goes down the drain. It was a lie. Or maybe, Camilla considered, the difference was that she was a sorry, beaten reject, and not a hero. There was no photogenic rivulet of red for her. Instead she bent over in the shower and retched on an empty stomach. She groaned, wiped stringy bile from her mouth and waited for the waves of nausea to settle down.

Kevin had hit her hard, and when Miles's father had thrown her down, she'd landed shoulder-first. It hurt. She picked up a flexible ice pack from the side of the tub and pressed it onto her shoulder, and stood half under the shower, with cold on her shoulder and hot on her back.

As the pain temporarily subsided, she found herself distracted by a flood of useless worries: Mack would be angry that she had taken his ice pack into the shower. Marie would be pissed that she'd left the shower curtain open and had gotten water all over the bathroom floor. And if either one came home and caught her padding through the house soaking wet because she'd forgotten to get a towel, there would be a full-scale freak-out. She dropped the ice pack in the tub and cranked off the water. She needed to concentrate on making a plan, not waste time fretting about the foster parents she was about to abandon.

She left a trail of water down the narrow hall and found a bin of unfolded laundry that Marie had carried in from the laundromat and left inside the front door. Marie would probably find a way to blame that on her, too. *You didn't fold the laundry? What do you think I am, your servant?*

Camilla pulled out a towel and padded back to her room. She dried herself, tossed the wet towel on the floor, and returned to root through the laundry bin to get clothes for the road. Marie would be double-pissed to find clean clothes strewn on the floor. Camilla deliberately upended the bin.

Her black backpack was old, but it held more than her regular one. Camilla packed a few outfits and some other things she needed for the road, and went to the kitchen. Mack and Marie were not good shoppers. The cupboards were mostly empty, and the few things there were items nobody wanted, or that they'd bought too much of. Camilla found a jar of peanut butter, the unsalted kind that Marie had bought by mistake and Mack refused to eat. There was a canned ham that didn't even look palatable in the picture. She left them and a jar of mayonnaise, but took a box of crackers that was still half full, and from the refrigerator she took a pack of American cheese slices, a loaf of white bread, and bottle of salad dressing.

She was just zipping the pack shut when she realized she'd forgotten something important. "Closet," she said. That's where it would be. She pulled open a closet door and fished around, and found what she was looking for. When Camilla had first moved in with Mack and Marie, Marie had made a list. She told the agent about all their plans for happy family bonding. Camping was on the list, a trip that would never happen. But she had picked up a flimsy pup tent and some other cheap camping gear to put on a good show. They needed the money.

"Ha!" Camilla said, pulling out the tent in its small nylon bag, the paper label still on it. Marie had forgotten to return it to the store.

Now for money. She had discovered Mack's stash a long time ago, when she'd been sitting in the dark living room and he'd reached up to the high shelf to fetch a ten-spot without noticing she was there. Camilla had investigated the moment Mack was on his way to the corner store. Close to fifty dollars, most of it in singles. She slipped out a few for herself. Probably he never counted it, she reasoned, and if he did and it came up a little short, he would assume he'd spent more than he remembered. She pilfered a little pocket money each week from then on, and Mack never caught her.

This time, luckily for her, he'd just been paid, and she found a jackpot of almost a hundred dollars. She stuffed it in the backpack and slipped outside. She'd hide out in the clearing in the woods and wait for dark, and then slip out of town at night.

It took much longer to get up the trail to the boulder on foot. "If I'd kept the dirt bike I wouldn't have got beaten up," she grumbled as she climbed. "And I could ride it out of town and never come back."

Her shoulder still hurt, making the walk especially unpleasant. The aspirin bottle in the bathroom scored her one lonely pill, and it wasn't enough. Even carrying the backpack over her good shoulder, the bad one hurt.

"Assholes," she said, trudging along.

She turned her attention to making plans for getting back at Kevin for the hit to the stomach and Miles's father for backhanding her. Mack would have called the police, or maybe stormed over and gotten into it with the man. She knew how this would go: *You hit her in the face? She's twelve!* Camilla felt a twinge of guilt at stealing his money. But Mack's occasional after-the-fact support for her didn't amount to actual protection. It didn't help to go punch the asshole after he'd beaten her up. And she didn't want Mack to fight her battles, anyway.

She reached the top of the hill and stared down at the trash piles. Streetlights had started to come on, showing lines of lights in a grid all around the dark dump. She looked to one side. Kevin's house would be over there. And over there, opposite, was Miles's house.

"And me right in the middle," she huffed. Then she looked again. She hadn't really thought about it, but the dump, Kevin's house, and Miles's house formed a triangle with Mack's trailer smack in the center. "Wait," she said, slowly rising. "Kevin's house, Miles's house, and the dump. And me right in the middle. Ha. It's perfect!"

Pleased to have thought to dress in black, Camilla stepped into the trailer one last time, and stopped to listen. Mack wasn't home yet. Good. Maybe things were going her way for once. She slipped through to the back and stopped in the kitchen to get the key to the shed. Mack was always swearing about neighborhood thieves stealing his gas. Camilla knew it was Marie emptying the can into the car to save using her own money at the station, but Mack never put two and two together. He finally bought a padlock for the shed. It didn't prevent the real thief from getting in, but it worked anyway. Marie couldn't very well claim that twelve-year-old Camilla had filched the gas. The kid couldn't even drive. Not that they knew of, anyway.

The can wasn't full, but it still held almost three gallons. Once again Camilla cursed her enemies as she hefted the heavy can. She cried out at the shooting pain in her shoulder, and switched hands.

She was sweat-soaked and irritable when she got to the dump—which she reflected was just goddamned fine for the present circumstances. It boosted her resolve. She ducked through a break in the chain link fence and cut out across the open space, heading for a particularly enormous pile of trash.

In the movies, she reflected, someone with a gas can shakes it all over the place, and then dramatically drops a match or a lit cigarette to start the blaze. That had always bothered Camilla. It was idiotic. She'd seen a neighbor try to do that when prepping a brush pile for burning. Maybe he'd seen it in the movies, too. The man splashed gasoline all over the place, including on his pants and shoes. He cursed and stormed inside to change, and the brush pile had to wait.

But there was no need to shake gas all over the place, anyway. Camilla knew this from simple observation. Gas is very, very flammable, and a little bit usually does the trick. She carefully poured some on one side of the pile, then backed up making a long trail to a point well away from the pile. She did this partly to be farther away when the fire started, but also to use most of the gas. The can was heavy.

She struck a match, waited a few seconds to confirm that there was no break, and when fire leapt up in the trash pile, she was gone.

One more to go, she thought, sneaking through back yards. By the time she'd made it to Kevin's house, she realized she didn't need to be especially careful to avoid being seen. The sky behind her was already lit up in gigantic, towering flames, sirens were coming on all over town, and people were streaming down the street toward the trash fire to watch. Nobody was looking for culprits yet.

The wooden back porch of Kevin's house was perfect. Camilla emptied the gas can, tossed it onto the porch, and threw a lit match, and once again she was gone, and safe from prying eyes. When she reached the third point of the triangle, all attention that wasn't on the conflagration at the town dump would be on the house fire down the road from it.

As she approached Miles's house, she heard the screen door slam, and she ducked behind a tree.

"What the hell," said a voice she recognized as the father. "Holy shit, look at that!"

"Can we go see?" begged Miles's squeaky little-boy voice. But his father was already hurrying down the street to gawk with the rest of the neighborhood.

Camilla stepped up and rapped on the screen door. There might be someone else home. She'd never met Miles's mother, but that didn't mean there wasn't one. No one answered. She pulled the screen door and shoved the back door open with her foot.

"Anyone here?" she called out. No answer. "I'm looking for Miles," she lied. "Miles, you home?" She stepped inside and sized up the kitchen. It was a familiar looking space, a dingy room with piles of dishes in the sink and on a cheap round table with some chairs around it. On the table she spotted what she was looking for, a keychain with a big red "S." She grabbed it and hurried outside—then stepped back in and snatched a black helmet from a hook by the door.

The motorcycle was enormous for her, and it was heavy, a full-sized Suzuki with all the trim, from the sculpted nose and windshield to the curvy storage bins behind the seat. At first she was worried she wouldn't be able to lift it off the kickstand. But it just required a bit of courage and persistence. If she tipped it over she would be in trouble. But it wasn't all that hard just to get it off the stand. She started the engine and slipped the second strap of her backpack on, cursing at the pain in her shoulder. But she ignored the pain, kicked the big bike into gear, and let out the clutch as she gave it some gas. It pulled into motion, and she practically laughed out loud at how easy it seemed. Once she was moving, it was a piece of cake. All she had to do was steer.

With everyone's attention on the fires, nobody noticed the figure in black riding the other way on a motorcycle. Camilla drove out of town, got on the highway, and got up to speed. She was finally free.

9. The *Margay*

Una sat in a tavern on the Western Shores. Although the spot was far to the south, outside the reach of Saor Tieg, she wore a hat with a veil. The ships that sailed to the southern ports might be in different fleets than those that frequented Deadrise Bay, but sailors moved around. She didn't want to be recognized. Not yet.

She understood the social politics of the thing, as did the gunners. Achieving the fourth level of Tallach fighting brought both status and opportunity. People admired fourth-level fighters, and would make special efforts to ingratiate themselves to them. For the fighter, the transition meant taking on a new set of responsibilities. There would be a new position, and new duties and work. And so it was expected that after the ceremony a new fourth-level fighter had a right to spend some time reveling in the achievement.

But there was also an undertone of raw excitement. People who came across a freshly minted fourth-tier enjoying a good wander were eager to join the party. To add the element of traveling incognito—without trying hard actually to remain unrecognized—was a genius idea, Una mused. People would see her and her companion on their travels, and those who realized who she was would revel in the conspiracy. They would be anxious to get in on the secret and help her on her way.

"It would be perfect," she muttered to herself, "if Tyra were with me." Then her eyes widened, and she rose from her chair as a redhead pushed through the door and strode up to the bar. "Tyra?" she muttered, amazed.

The girl turned and smiled. "Ah there you are!" She strode over and wrapped her arms around Una. "Pleased to meet you," she whispered in Una's ear.

Una pulled back and stared. It was not Tyra's face, but the gait was perfect. And, she noted, the flax blossom on her forehead was a flawless copy. "Raptors," she muttered. "I see they've trained you."

Tansie laughed, and pulled on a fancy hat to cover the tattoo. "I know her better than she knows herself. But come, let's go up to the room. We've a lot to talk about."

The gunners had chosen the flagship of a transportation line that sailed the more southerly route. That the wife of the governor of the Green Hills district would be aboard had clinched the decision. They would travel under the names Una and Tansie, the daughter of a Tallach trader and her companion. Tansie wore a stylish headband that covered the little blue flower tattooed on her forehead, and Una applied face paint the color of her skin and added a fancy hat with a mesh veil, trendy and acceptable for a rich young woman.

The *Margay* was not for peasants. To be on the ship at all was a mark of status. Those who wished to travel in style would pay a high price for a tiny room in the lower levels. And in the upper level the ship boasted the most luxurious staterooms on any ship, at prices only the richest travelers could afford. Una and Tansie giggled with excitement as they were led on board and up the stairs.

Their neighbors were a regional Tallach governor on one side and Madame Ben Yett on the other. Across the hall were an older man who appeared to be a baron, next to him a Tallach general, and in the last and smallest of the staterooms, four young men who seemed to have pooled their money in order to travel with the upper class.

"It's the finest passenger ship on the sea," Una gushed. "I've always wanted to get on board the *Margay*."

Their stateroom was opulent. The canopy bed was enormous, more than adequate for the two of them. And the room itself was lacquered mahogany and polished brass, rich and elegant. Porters had left clean water and bowls of bread and fruit. They learned that the residents of the staterooms took their meals in an extension of the pilot house, a clean, tidy room with a large table and cushioned chairs, and windows looking at the sea.

But neither a stateroom with a canopy bed nor an extended deck house could stop the ship from rolling. Una had been on short runs, but never on a long trip at sea. She had no need to hide her discomfort. Being a fourth-level Talla did not exempt her from seasickness. Tansie, however, playing the part of Tyra, daughter of a ship captain, was afforded no such latitude. The gunner had told her to *be Tyra*, in every detail. And no one would believe that the daughter of a merchant ship captain could be seasick, especially on a luxury ship like the *Margay*. For two nights she feigned a need to catch up on her sleep, and skipped the evening meal. Then by the third day the nausea started to wane, and it became less of a struggle. She plastered on a smile, wore extra makeup, and concentrated on a poised walk with an even step—and resisted the urge to vomit.

At meals they both started to notice the looks. The Tallach general seemed almost to wink at Una, and she wondered if he thought she might be a conquest. The man was well into his sixties. But Tallach generals didn't achieve their rank easily. No doubt this old man was still a proficient fighter, and perhaps fancied himself a proficient lover. She would need to be on her guard.

Her opinion of the man rose, however, at an evening meal. The aristocrat Gavina and her cubs sat at one end of the table. The children ranged from seven or eight to perhaps twelve, four of them picking at the fine meal as if it didn't altogether meet their standards. Madame Ben Yett was distracted. She made repeated, low-toned threats. *Don't come complaining later on that you're hungry, Osmond. And Myreth, I'll not replace that lace if you foul it by wiping it with your hands.* The children ignored her. Osmond pushed a piece of carrot around his plate, and Myreth, the youngest, glanced away as she deliberately wiped her hands on her dress.

But while the woman seemed to want nothing more than to avoid an embarrassing altercation, the young men at the other end of the table were impatient for some entertainment. One kept staring at Una. He was twenty or so, Una's age more or less, and dressed in an ill-fitted suit of dark linen, sturdily made, but without the cut or the fine needlework of an authentic upper-class Tallach suit. The young man's hair was oiled and slicked back in the fashion of the time, and Una found him rather attractive. She would have forgiven him the clumsy effort to emulate a high social position. But she couldn't forgive his lack of manners. He talked too loudly and too much. A few pointed looks from the general and the aristocrat didn't quiet him. Instead it seemed to embolden him.

"Fresh from the Shores, are you?" he said, looking over at Una.

She turned and raised her veiled eyes at him, and looked back to her plate, disinterested in the overture. She focused on the meal. Tyra had harangued her endlessly with her critiques of ship food. But the food on the *Margay* was excellent. The boiled meat was tender and salted, the cabbage was firm, not over-steamed, and the carrots were sweet. What was there to want? There was even a nice, light wine. She caught herself flashing a glare at the spoiled, picky children, and forced herself to adopt a more neutral expression. It wouldn't serve her purpose to join the young man in forgetting her manners.

"Where are you bound, then? You and your friend travelling on your own? Maybe you'd like some company."

Una scowled and didn't answer.

"Mind yourself, boy," the old general growled. "You'll show these young women proper respect."

"Humph," the young man grunted, and stared at Una. "I could offer company to that one."

Una turned her head slowly to the boy. She flared her fingers beneath her chin and scowled, a gesture of annoyed challenge.

"Oh, ho!" the boy said, his companions breaking into grins and chuckles. "Aren't you fresh."

Una raised her chin and didn't look at him. She didn't need to play-act at this. It was exactly how she would have responded had she been travelling as the daughter of Saor Tieg. Although, she reflected, had she been in the company of the merchant of the Western Shores, this boy would have been evicted upon his first remark.

The old general, taking the place of her protector, set his fork down, slowly pushed his chair back, and rose. "Why don't you hold your tongue, boy? Or do you require a lesson?"

The room fell quiet, the young man staring at his plate.

The general slowly sat, and smiled at Una. He leaned in. "I beg your pardon, miss, for interfering, but I take issue with the boy's tone. I hope you don't mind."

"Not at all," Una said quietly. "There must be better conversation to be had than *that*," she nodded disdainfully.

"You call on me any time, should you need something."

Later, on their way back to their quarters, Tansie leaned in and whispered to Una. "Watch that boy. He's planning to try something. I know that look."

Una shrugged. "Try what? Let him try something." She pushed her hand under her veil and scratched at her face. "Damn it, Tansie, the face paint itches."

In their stateroom they discovered a wrapped basket containing a fancy bottle of after-dinner liqueur, a pair of tiny crystal glasses, and a neatly wrapped parcel containing sweets. A note tucked into the basket read, *Compliments of General Ryndin, with hopes that you enjoy your journey.*

Tansie pursed her lips. "I'm not going to sleep with him. Let's get that straight right now."

Una laughed and popped open the bottle of liqueur. "Neither am I. But I could use a splash of this. And the chocolates smell wonderful."

Una pulled off her veiled hat and tossed it on the bed, and they each had two glasses of cherry brandy, and wolfed down the chocolates.

"It's important to eat something when you're drinking," Tansie said with a smile.

"But we just had dinner," Una said.

"That was to offset the wine. These are to offset the brandy." Tansie raised the little glass, laughed and downed it, and then took another chocolate.

Una scrubbed the makeup off her face, scrubbed again, and then rubbed oil onto her skin. The light through the porthole window waned and then went away altogether, and they sat in the lamplight and finished the chocolates.

"Let's walk outside before we go to sleep," Tansie urged. "It's windy, but it's warm tonight. I need to see the sky."

They changed from their fancy dinner outfits into more casual attire, calf-length pants, pleated shirts, and embroidered vests. Tansie wrapped a black shawl around her shoulders. She stood impatiently by the door. "Come on!"

"I'm coming, I'm coming." Una pulled on a black hat with a silk veil. "Let's go."

The moon at the bow was low on the horizon, and lit up the choppy surface of the ocean as if they were sailing along a rippled path of light.

"Lovely," Una said, as they stepped out onto the forward deck.

But Tansie had no chance to reply. Four figures appeared in front of them and fanned out.

"Here you are," the boy said, "with no irritating old generals on hand to interfere."

"Already?" Tansie hissed. "Should we go back?"

Una rolled her eyes beneath the veil. "Might as well get this over with," she whispered.

The three other young men held back to watch as the first circled in. "I thought you seemed almost unfriendly at dinner. But that can't be right. I must have misunderstood."

"Leave us be," Tansie said, putting a hand on Una's arm.

"Oh, but that wouldn't be right. Leave you all alone?"

Then he stepped one pace too close, and without saying a word, Una dropped to a smooth, clean fighting stance. "You heard her. Leave."

Tansie backed up, resisting the urge to match the stance herself. She clenched her hands into fists and wished that she were playing a stronger character. Tansie the mill house brawler would have pushed up her sleeves and stood at Una's side. Instead she clutched her arms across her front and made an effort to look frightened.

"Oh, come. That's awfully aggressive. Let's have a little fun, you and me." The boy laughed and stepped even closer, arms out as if to scoop Una up in a big hug. She struck out with a double-arm inside block, throwing his arms wide, and then shifted back and pegged him in the stomach with a kick. The boy let out a hiss of air as he crashed backward to the deck.

"I might have a bit of fun tonight," Una said coolly, her eyes now on the other three closing in, "but not with you."

The boy grimaced and struggled to his knees, doing his best to appear unhurt. "Oh, yes you will." He nodded to his companions. "Bring them both."

Una didn't give them a chance to come at her. She swept in, the first boy's howl only partly masking the cracking sound of her foot smashing into his shin. As he stumbled forward, she swung her knee up and caught him hard in the stomach. On his way down, she struck a two-fisted blow to the back of his head. One down. In her peripheral vision she caught the second boy coming at her, and she ducked and spun under his swing, pegging him in the kidney with a punch as she moved around behind him. Her foot struck the back of his knee and his leg crumpled. As he tried to turn to engage, she rushed him, using his momentum to put him entirely off balance. He spun to the deck and she kicked him in the chin and heard his teeth crack together.

The last boy, thinking better of taking on Una, went for Tansie, instead— only to receive a neatly placed, very hard knee to the groin. Tansie would later complain that it was unfulfilling to be denied the chance at even a single good punch. But she had gotten the job done, and hadn't blown her cover as the bookworm of the traveling pair.

Now the first boy rose and ran at Una again. Una jumped back to avoid his kick as he attempted to even up the score, and she stumbled over the sprawled legs of a groaning boy. She flew into a backward roll and rose, but the first boy was already coming at her, and there was very little room on deck. She dodged and ducked, and caught him a blow with her foot— but not quickly enough. His swing strafed the side of her head. The fancy black hat with the veil flew up and was caught in the wind and swept out to sea, and Una reeled, her head ringing from a blow to her ear.

Then it came to her again, the suggestions in her head that formed themselves into words. "You're going to take that?"

"Horace?" she hissed, rising and looking around.

"Take his teeth out. Throw him off the boat. Whoa, watch it, girl! Down!"

Her ear still ringing, she dropped straight down as the boy came at her again. He lunged for her, and as he swung hard and missed, she rose and pegged him with a vicious kick to the back. He slammed into a mast and fell to the deck.

"Perfect. Now dump him over the rail. Quickly. Men are coming."

Tansie rushed in to find Una breathing hard and holding a hand to her face—not because of the blow to her ear, but because her hat was gone, and she hadn't covered her spiral with makeup. Deck hands had heard the commotion, and were heading over.

"Raptors, Una," Tansie hissed, feigning amazement, should anyone be within earshot. "You're bleeding! Come, let's get you to the room."

"Good plan," the Horace voice said. "Who's your smart young friend?"

Tyra pulled off her shawl and wrapped it loosely over Una's head as if to help with the injury, and hustled her back to their stateroom.

Above them, standing silently on the flying bridge, two figures stepped out of the shadows holding crystal wine glasses. They looked down at the groaning young men.

"Dear me," said Madame Ben Yett, almost inaudibly, "that young lady knows how to manage herself, doesn't she? Look at what's strewn over the deck."

The general sidled up to her and wrapped an arm around her waist, leaning in close to her ear. "Yes, but while you were watching the boys receive a lesson in manners, perhaps you weren't watching the young lady. Very interesting face, that one. Very interesting, indeed."

As the cabin door closed behind them, Tansie broke into a nervous grin. "They weren't expecting that, were they?"

"But they'll be up and around and making nuisances of themselves soon enough," Una grumbled.

"All too soon," the voice in her head grumbled. "Why didn't you throw him over? Were you worried about the man and the woman watching from above?"

"I want a turn," Tansie insisted. "Can we lure them into a dark corridor next time so I can have a chance?"

"Watching?" Una wetted a cloth and held it to her face.

"What? No, I don't want to watch," Tansie scowled. "I want to fight. I hate sitting on the sidelines."

"No, I wasn't talking to you, Tansie."

Tansie stepped up and tipped her head. "Maybe you need to lie down. He hit you pretty hard."

Una pushed her away. "I'm all right. You're saying you want to fight?" she said, trying to work through the scene in spite of her throbbing head and the impression of the old man suddenly coming back. She adopted a strained smile. "But wouldn't you rather read a book? My friend Tyra would be more likely to hide beneath the stairs." It was a good try, but bringing up Tyra soured her mood, and a gut-wrenching feeling of guilt washed over her. It dulled the adrenaline rush.

Tansie saw it in her face. "She'll be fine, Una. I know the gunners are holding her, but I don't think they'll harm her."

Una sighed and closed her eyes. "Can I tell you something, and you'll promise to keep it to yourself?"

"Absolutely. I promise," came Horace's words.

Tansie nodded. "Yes, of course. I promise."

Una tried to shake the voice away. "What the gunners are doing—Tyra would say it's *elegant*. She'd quote something from a book about a great benefactor saving a lost soul. You know, if the Gunner Ailmili had just asked me straight out to do this, I would have bent over backward to say yes. Damn, sailing to Ben Attallach? On the *Margay*, no less?"

"Ben Attallach," the voice in her head mused. "Are you talking about a real place, or is that a fictional place, like Shangri-La? Sail to Ben Attallach. Maybe it's from a book."

Una shook her head and a clutched a hand to her ear.

"I'm pretty sure it took me a full second to say yes," Tansie said. "I had to recover enough to speak."

"But that's just it. They *asked* you. They didn't ask me. They came to Deadrise Bay to ask for my father's help. They didn't even know I was there until they saw me at the ceremony. And even then they didn't ask me. Then my friend and I ..." Una sighed out loud. "My friend and I decided to try to rob a pay run from the north, and we got caught."

Tansie nodded. "Yes, they told me about it."

"And the Gunner Ailmili intervened, and offered me a way out."

"I was told that she ordered you to do this, or she'd lock up your friend for life. Isn't that more or less the deal?"

"That's what she said. And of course I mean to keep Tyra from harm. But I'll bet she's happy as a clam, wherever the gunners have her. That's not it. The thing you have to promise not to tell anyone is that I have to do this for a different reason. You see, I think this assignment by the gunners is my real fourth level trial."

"Your ... what?"

"The Tallach masters gave me my ring and the dragon-serpent, true enough. But I cheated. And everyone who hears the story knows it." She pointed to her face. "This mission is a chance for me to prove that I'm worthy of the markings of a fourth-level Talla."

Horace pushed into her head again. "I'm not following this story." He halted. "But listen to your friend and get into that bed. Do it now."

Una jumped into the bed and pressed her cheek to the pillow to hide the spiral. She remembered from her childhood that to listen to that voice tended to be a good idea.

At a light rap on the door they hushed. Tansie stepped over to a dressing table and pretended to brush her hair, as if feigning innocence of a conspiracy. "Yes?" she said.

"May I enter? It's your neighbor, Gavina."

"You have to let her in," Una whispered.

"Madam Ben Yett," Tansie said, pulling the door open. "Please come in."

The woman looked around as if afraid someone might be watching, and stepped inside. She pushed the door firmly closed.

"Please, won't you sit?" Tansie offered a polite bow. "I'm sorry, Una is ..."

"That's why I came." Madame Ben Yett took a chair and pulled it close to the bed. "Dear me. You're hurt." She put a hand on Una's shoulder. "Those nasty ruffians."

Una froze. "You were watching?" She silently willed Horace to shut up and let her think.

Tansie hurried over and sat on the edge of the bed.

At Una's wide eyes, the woman held up a hand. "Now, now, be at ease, child. I didn't come to confront you. Much the opposite." She looked around again as if someone might be listening, and leaned in. "I came to tell you that your secret is safe with me. And is mine safe with you?"

"Madame Ben Yett, your secret?"

"Please, call me Gavina. I don't need to be Madam Ben Yett when I'm at sea, do I?" she winked and smiled.

"All right. Gavina, then."

"And listen, I may only have a moment or two. If you hear something breaking in the next room—well, the little monsters are quiet for the moment, ripping through a box of sweets, but they'll tire of it and turn to something else soon enough."

The girls glanced warily at each other.

"I apologize for their behavior. I'm afraid I failed to contract with a servant to care for them on this trip, and I'm awful at it. But anyway, let me get to the point, and then I'll let you be." She turned her gaze to Una. "I've been to Deadrise Bay. I've met the master there."

Tansie's jaw dropped, but Una said nothing.

"Only as a visitor, mind you. It's not my place to arrange trades. Not yet." She offered a crafty smile. "That said, I can tell you with great confidence that my family would be agreeable to speak one day of trade in the northerly ports of the Western Shores." She held up a hand as Una started to rise. "No, no, please. Rest, dear, and don't feel that you need to speak. I'm not here to talk of trade. Not tonight. And I need not mention names, Talla. I'll tell my friends of a lovely voyage with a most delightful young woman who cleanly put some rude young men on the deck for presuming to accost her."

"So you *were* watching."

"The general and I were having a nightcap on the flying bridge. I realize you're being polite and pretending you didn't see us. It's very nice up there at night, and usually no one is about after dark. Join us one evening if you like."

"For a nightcap." Una looked confused.

"And I must say, when those boys came for you, you did quite a proficient job, didn't you? I like that. Spare the chitchat and get down to it." The woman gave a soft laugh. "It's exactly what I mean to do—but that's another story."

"It can't be known that we're here."

"Well, that's my point, dear. It's a long voyage. You have your secrets, and I have mine." She winked. "I'll count on you not to mention my evening drinks with General Ryndin, and no one will hear a whisper from me that Saor Tieg's daughter and her friend were berthed next to me."

Something banged in the next room, and the woman rose and held up a hand to stop Una from getting up. "Lie still, child. I'm a stone cutter's wife, not a queen. Let's enjoy the voyage, and should you find yourselves in the western valleys, I'd be delighted to show you around." She pressed a glass vial into Una's hand, and departed.

The vial of laudanum dulled the pain and silenced the old voice, and Una drifted off to sleep in a state of confusion. Horace hadn't come to her in eight years. She had dismissed him as a childhood delusion. And now he was back?

She stayed in the state room the next day, partly to nurse her wounds and partly because she wanted time alone to consider Horace. The first time she had been twelve, and had just been brutally beaten. Then there was brief encounter in the dungeons of the Twelfth Station, and now she'd been hit in the head, and the voice had come back yet again. Was this how she responded to trauma, by imagining an old man talking to her?

She feigned a tremendous headache, and insisted that she needed a few hours of silence. Tansie finally left.

"All right. So, are you there?" Una said to the empty room. There was no answer. "Well?" Still no answer. Nothing. She rose, washed her face, and poked at the redness on her cheek and ear. It felt warm. "Just a hit on the head. There's no old man in there."

Tansie returned in the afternoon, and informed her that the four young men were not present at breakfast or lunch. The doctor had visited them. They would recover, but the general had declared that they were not to be seen on the upper decks anymore. The stateroom was emptied and cleaned, and a new resident moved in.

"The new resident is someone the general knows," Tansie said. "You're coming to dinner, aren't you? Gavina says the general will be disappointed if you don't. He wants you to meet this new member of our party." She described him as a man in his early thirties with close-cropped hair, a tidy, conservative outfit, and a remarkably calm demeanor.

"I'll come." Una pulled out the makeup and covered the spiral. It mostly hid the injury as well. She glanced in the mirror and thought she looked almost normal.

At dinner, the new stateroom resident rose and bowed as she entered the room. "Czabor, of Fort Ania," the man said. "Pleased to meet you, Miss Una. My friend the general speaks highly of you."

Una nodded and smiled, and sat down to a very fine, calm dinner. The new man kept quiet and listened, and there were no young men leering at her from the other end of the table.

Life on the *Margay* settled into an easy routine. They passed leisurely hours playing cards and walking the upper decks. Tansie sat and read, working to maintain her persona. At first it was a chore. All she could find to read was a book of the history of Tallach military campaigns that some-one had left in the pilot house. She found herself staring blankly at the page while her mind wandered.

Then the general caught her at it, and with a click of his tongue, gently pulled the book from her lap. He glanced around to make sure no one was looking, and with a wink, he tossed the book overboard. "It won't do to have you bludgeoning that lovely head of yours with Tallach military tomes," he said, with a conspiratorial smile. "I'll bring you some books. There's a shelf full of them in my cabin."

He returned with an armload of leather-bound volumes. To the typical wealthy traveler, they would be decorations. But to a southern stray playing at being a bookworm, it was a gold mine. She thanked him profusely, and playing at being Tyra-the-reader became much more entertaining.

Una's time on the *Margay* took an interesting turn, as well. A few days after the altercation, a porter carried a message to her written in the old, formal style, calligraphic letters drawn with a very fine brush and ink.

House Kamine offers a mat under the sword of House Kamine, should the general give his permission.

"Well," Una said, "It seems word has spread."

"What does it mean?" Tansie leaned in.

"House Kamine," Una said, nodding her head approvingly. "It's Tallach. Only the top young fighters get in."

"It's a fighting school?"

"The best on the mainland. I don't know who wrote this, but he's inviting me to train with him, or with others from the house who might be on board. This part, *under the sword of House Kamine*, that means he guarantees my safety. But I'll only be allowed to go if the general approves. I suppose the general must have told someone about the night the boys came at us."

"Will you go?"

Una grinned. "Oh, yes. Absolutely. Why not?"

Not only did the general approve of the invitation, he elected to accom-pany her. "To see to your safety," he added with his little wink.

The general brought her to a part of the *Margay* that she wouldn't otherwise have seen. There were no fighting pavilions on board. But after the evening meal, the dining room of the servant class could be converted to a makeshift sparring room by stacking all the tables and chairs along the narrow walkway outside.

Two young men in gray gis flanked the door. They bowed and waved Una and the general in. There were ten young men in the room, two sparring and the others at attention, watching. They all wore the same plain gray gis as the two guarding the door, except that one of the men sparring wore a lighter gi and a dark gray belt. This was Czabor, their new neighbor.

Una flashed him a smile. A Tallach trainer, then. She felt overdressed in her fancy blue-black gi, the belt edged in shimmering gold thread. All she had with her was her formal outfit, and here she was among Tallach trainees in their everyday gis.

The sparring pair stopped and bowed, and Czabor hurried over and bowed to her. "Talla," he said, in a conspiratorial whisper. And then added in a loud, confident voice, "We're honored to have a fighter trained in the east visit with us. And General Ryndin, my thanks to you for the courtesy of attending. I hadn't expected the honor of having you come yourself." He bowed again.

"I want to see what the young lady can do as much as you do, I suppose," he laughed.

Una tugged at her fancy belt. "I apologize, master. I hadn't expected to spar during the voyage. It's rude of me."

"Ah, not at all," Czabor waved a hand. "You do us an honor to attend our makeshift pavilion." Then he slid in close again. "And although it's covered, I'd venture the mark on your face stands out more than the finest gi could."

Una smiled again and put a hand to her cheek. It seemed the makeup covering her spiral wasn't fooling anyone.

"My house—House Kamine," Czabor explained, "is sister to a Tallach house in your eastern city of Steerageway. We trade students."

Una had to think for a moment. She had always thought of Steerageway as a western city, but of course from the Tallach perspective, her entire country was eastern.

"My students and I are returning from a year abroad," Czabor continued, "and on its next trip, the *Margay* will bring home a number of easterners who have been guests in my pavilion this past year. Come, let me introduce you." He nodded at his students, who stepped forward and bowed as he recited their names. "And now shall we do a kata?"

On her second visit to the below-decks pavilion, Una wore a veil over a clean face. When she set it aside, the fighters of House Kamine stood and gave her a cheer, and then bowed.

"And a serpent. I'd been told of that." Czabor added, noting her uncovered leg. "Mark that," he told his students. "The dragon-serpent. You won't see that very often."

Una learned that the fighting houses of Ben Attallach were every bit as serious and disciplined as those she had trained in on the Western Shores.

As she sparred with them, she felt that she was acquiring quite a few admirers, and not just for her fighting skills. She was thankful that the voyage was almost over, or she might find herself having to ward off suitors.

But the ship approached Ben Attallach, and everyone on board shifted to preparing for departure.

"Come visit our pavilion, should your travels bring you to the Fan, Talla." Czabor bowed.

"The Fan?"

"Our village in the delta. The roads follow the rivers, and fan out. It's Fort Ania on the map. But to those of us who live there, it's the Fan."

Una smiled. Now she had two invitations, the first from Madame Ben Yett and the second from this Tallach trainer. And she hadn't even gotten to port yet.

10. The Girl in the Forest

Horace stared out the window. The stone from his son's things sat on the windowsill. He had come to consider it an inert keepsake, only to reconnect with Una unexpectedly.

He hadn't been thinking of her. He had left early for the long drive to pick up bulk supplies. Then on the return trip, he stopped at a small store with a gas pump to stretch his legs and see if the coffee was acceptable, and his eye caught a notice on the bulletin board. It was a police notice, an advisory that camps in the area had been broken into, and cash and jewelry stolen. Police were looking for four men, possibly in a red pickup truck with a noisy muffler. Residents and campers were advised to stay in groups and not to engage, should they spot these men.

"Here?" Horace had growled. "They're breaking into camps here? Aren't there better pickings down south?"

He was back in his cabin and still mulling it over, wondering if he needed to consider better security than a chain across the drive, when he absentmindedly picked up the stone, and was drawn in. First he caught a brief glimpse of Una in a dungeon sitting with another young woman. She was older, and called herself Undine, but it was Una. Then later he saw her again, in a scene that was so outlandish that it took him a minute to realize it was also Una. Two young women and several young men were fighting on the deck of a gigantic sailing ship, like a scene out of an old swashbuckler movie.

It didn't last long. Una had learned to fight, and was holding her own. He warned her to watch out when her opponent was making a move for her, and then in moments it was over. She and her companion went below decks, Una took a sedative, and the scene faded.

"Much older," he said to himself, excitedly running through the visit in his head. "She's a fine young woman, now. A fighter. And a tattoo on her face." He took a sip of his drink. "Well, well, Una. It's very nice to visit with you again."

This new connection raised a lot of questions, but answered others. He had suspected that the connection to Una might involve a matter of when, and not just where. That was settled. First he sees a young girl, and a month or two later she's grown. Clearly the timeline was not his own. "But not just a matter of where and when, is it?" he muttered. "Perhaps there's also the question of who's visiting whom."

He had always assumed that he was the visitor, the protagonist in these little dramas with others. He had found the chunk of stone in his son's things, and had jumped to a girl. He had found her in a surreal environment, a virgin forest that to the best of his knowledge didn't exist in the present. But he'd been the one to pick up the stone. He'd been the one to question what connections it might offer, and to give it a try.

When he connected with little Una, he had been curious, and felt compelled to offer a paternal, helping hand. He realized this was partly an effort at vicarious familial experience. The girl was his granddaughter's age, and he had been thinking about Camilla. This girl in the forest was running from danger and trying to find her way. She seemed strong and capable, and was doing a fine job adapting. Was Camilla like that? Was she strong? Had she found a way to adapt? Surely Camilla would hardly remember her grandfather.

And now he had seen Una as a young woman. Were these scenes coming to him out of a concern for what his granddaughter would be like when she grew up? Was he subconsciously worrying that his granddaughter would follow the path of her father, and bring misery to people all around her—and that he would once again be guilty of having done nothing about it?

But now something new occurred to him. Maybe this girl Una was initiating the contact. Maybe she was contacting him, and not the other way around. It would explain why most of his efforts had failed, and the gap in the time frame. Maybe Una was driving.

Horace sighed. This was a dodgy game. He could talk himself in circles when it came to sticky questions of time and causality.

He stepped over to the window and picked up the stone again, and turned it over in his hand. "So, Camilla," he said, "where are you these days, I wonder? Are you doing all right? Is your mother caring for you, and keeping you safe? Wouldn't your old grandfather love to see you. Poor child, to lose your father—although, honestly, you might be better off in that regard. But you know, I do think of you. I'm sorry, Camilla. I'm sorry that I'm not there for you." He tossed the stone in his hand, but all he felt was a growing sense of something missing.

...

If pressed to recall a good memory of her mother, Camilla might have picked the time she and her mother went on a bus ride to Richmond. Susan, her mother's cousin, lived alone in an apartment on the south side of the city. Camilla had never ridden in one of the big coaches, so she was excited. They sat in large, soft seats with lots of room, and watched a movie on a little screen. Her mother even brought snacks for the trip. They sat side-by-side, and Camilla talked and laughed with her mother. It was a rare happy event.

The visit didn't go as well. There were cordial greetings, and Susan took them out for a fried chicken dinner. Normally dinner was leftover pizza from the shop where her mother worked, or sometimes nothing at all, if her mother didn't come home. But this time Camilla got to eat all she wanted. The conversation was friendly, and Camilla started to think she might have a real familial connection besides her mother.

They returned to the apartment and Susan opened a bottle of cabernet. "There's a TV in the bedroom, honey," she told Camilla. "Go on. Your mother and I have some catching up to do."

Camilla retreated to the bedroom, delighted to find a cable TV box, another luxury. So many channels! She found a cartoon station and sat and stared, stomach full, content. It was a fine hour of quiet happiness and entertainment.

Then the voices rose.

"Carla, are you serious? What did you do with the money I gave you last time? You said it was for a car. You needed it to get that job. You did get the job, right? With the car?"

"Look, I've got a job. Part time, anyway, but ..."

"So you just spent it. Is that it? It was *five grand*, Carla. Did you even get a car, or did you just spend it all on weed or something? Jesus. You promised you'd pay me back."

"And I will, okay? But what am I supposed to do? They were gonna evict. I've got the kid. Listen, I promise, all I need is a little help. ..."

Camilla turned up the volume to drown out the voices. She sat and prayed she could at least see the rest of the cartoon before they were invited to get out.

That night she slept stretched across a row of plastic seats in the bus station, her mother pretending they were waiting for a bus. Then early the next morning they hitchhiked back home.

Aunt Susan didn't come to mind until Camilla had ridden fifty miles on the big bike. At first she was absorbed by the sheer thrill of the ride. It was empowering. The summer wind whipped past, and several times she glanced down to realize she was going twenty miles over the limit. She found a pack of cars doing just a bit over the limit and fell in behind them, letting them set the pace.

As the adrenaline subsided and her speed moderated, Camilla started to consider where she was headed, and Aunt Susan popped into her head. She could go to Richmond. Her aunt would let her sleep on the sofa, or at least take her out for fast food before sending her away.

But in the short term she needed a bathroom and gas. And that was a problem. On the highway she was a small figure on a big bike. People might think she was Asian, or just an especially small white girl. No one would look at her and think, *My god. A twelve-year-old is driving a motorcycle!*

But once the helmet came off, she would be a little kid.

A solution came to her as a car filled with children slowed and took an exit. Camilla followed them, correctly guessing that they needed a pit stop, too. She pulled around behind the service station, parking the big bike next to the dumpsters, and headed around on foot. Five kids tumbled out of the wagon, and Camilla blended in, one more kid heading inside to get some snacks and use the bathroom.

She picked out the cheapest large bottle of soda she could find, added a bag of chips, and at the counter picked up a mini-flashlight from a display of impulse items. A flashlight would be useful.

"Oh, and dad says to give you ten bucks for gas at pump seven," she said, and handed over the money.

The clerk punched it in without noticing that the station wagon was at pump eight. She rode the bike around to the gas pump, and keeping her helmet on, put every penny of the ten dollars in. As she was putting the gas cap back on, a woman in a silver compact car pulled up to a pump behind her and got out. Camilla had her helmet on, but the woman gave her an odd look anyway, and then glanced around. It was easy enough to read her thoughts: A kid is pumping the gas. Her mother or father must be in the store. When Camilla got on the bike and rocketed out of the station, she glanced in the side-view mirror and caught the look of surprise.

"Aunt Susan." Camilla smiled. It wasn't her mother's cousin, but Aunt Susan had the same car, and that was exactly the look they'd gotten last time, when they showed up on her doorstep. "Well, here I come again," she said, heading for the highway.

It was too late to drive straight there. To show up uninvited and by herself in the middle of the night would ruin any chances she might have of soft-pedaling her situation. But she needed to get as far away as possible. Sooner or later, people would be looking for her. She wondered why no one had called her phone yet, and then realized maybe they had. She checked at her next stop, and discovered she hadn't charged it, and the battery had gone dead.

"Shit," she cursed, and stuffed it back into the pack.

At least they wouldn't be able to try to track her phone and find her—that is, if they were even looking for her. Mack might not have noticed she was gone. He might stumble home drunk, curse about the mess in the house, and vow to take it up with her in the morning. Maybe he'd crawl off to bed and wouldn't even hear about the night's excitement until tomorrow.

And the police might never fit all the pieces together. Miles's father would find out soon enough that his motorcycle was gone, but he wouldn't mention having backhanded the girl who was now missing, and Kevin wouldn't fess up to punching her in the stomach.

That whole story would be altered: "First she steals my kid's bike and goes out on a joy ride," Camilla imagined him saying. "We woulda reported it stolen, but then I found it by the shed when I went out to dump the trash. No idea where she went. Left the bike and boogied. But when you find her, you tell her there's gonna be a little talking-to about this. She rode it all through the mud and made a big mess. You know how long I spent cleaning that bike up?" Something like that. Plenty of righteous indignation, and not a hint of culpability.

But the story of the small girl breaking the big boy's nose had spread. And everything happening the same night—the fires, the theft of the motorcycle, and the disappearance of the girl—would raise a lot of questions. It would be hard for the police not to figure out eventually that they were connected.

Her campsite was a hidden spot at the far end of a subdivision where the builders had extended the road and were clearing a lot. It was the weekend, so she figured nobody would come by. And if they did, they wouldn't notice the tire tracks leading behind the pile of downed trees. In the worst-case scenario, if she heard someone coming, she could abandon the tent and ride away.

Sleeping alone on hard ground in a pup tent should have been exciting, or maybe frightening. Instead Camilla felt lonely. There was no one to talk to, and nothing to do. She clicked on the tiny flashlight and sat eating chips, and then made herself a sandwich of cheese and dressing on white bread. She missed Sasha, and felt guilty about leaving without even saying goodbye. Somehow she even seemed to miss having Mack shuffle through the room in his boxers and complain about what she was doing.

Camilla woke in a panic, and would have leaped out of bed except that she was cocooned in the little pup tent. "Run!" she said out loud, and then dropped down, realizing she had been dreaming. But had she? It was already getting murky in her mind. First Una and her companion sat in a wooden room talking. Something about going north. Then there was something scary in a restaurant or a bar, and then she was running down streets and through back alleys, pursued by killers.

She sat up and let out a long breath, waiting for her heart to slow down. It wasn't real. And how many times had she had that kind of dream? "Damn it," she cursed. "I can't be a scared little mouse." She packed up, got on the motorcycle, and headed for Richmond.

At a convenience store she bought a map of the city, but it didn't show the names of the apartment complexes.

Finally she thought to ask the clerk. "My dad wants me to ask for directions." She told him the name of the complex. "I think it's pretty close to the river."

The clerk opened up the map and made a circle in pencil, and she thanked him and left.

It was still early when she pulled in. The minute she drove into the complex she remembered where Susan's unit was. But she parked around the back rather than by the main entrance. She backed the motorcycle into a spot between a van and a fenced area for the dumpsters. Someone casually driving by wouldn't see it there, but if someone did spot it, it would just be someone's motorcycle. It wouldn't stand out.

Her backpack slung over her shoulder, she walked around to the front—and stopped dead. A police cruiser was parked in the spot next to Aunt Susan's silver car. Susan stood on the sidewalk talking to an officer, arms folded. Camilla ducked back around the corner of the building and peered out. She couldn't hear all the words, but she caught enough to understand the scene.

"Okay, ma'am. If you hear from her, you'll give us a call? We just want to find her and get her to a safe place." He tipped his hat and stepped over to the cruiser.

Camilla turned and slunk back to the motorcycle. Damn it! Now what could she do? As she peered around the van watching for the cruiser to leave, she spotted people with backpacks heading out of the apartments. Two of them climbed onto a motorcycle and pulled out. Should she follow them? Pretend they were together? They looked like college students heading to summer classes. Then two more got into an older model car.

The cruiser backed out, and then started slowly driving across the lot, canvassing, and Camilla panicked. "Hey," she said, stepping up to the two students in the car. "Could I bum a ride?"

The boy at the wheel rolled down the window and tipped his head.

"I just transferred. I'm making up an English class, and I'm gonna be late if I catch the bus. You could just drop me anywhere on campus."

"Um. You're taking a college course?"

Camilla sighed. "I know. I look like I'm twelve, right? Everybody says that. I skipped a year. But never mind. I'll wait for the bus." She turned.

"Let's give her a ride, Stephen," the girl in the passenger seat said.

The boy nodded, and Camilla quickly got in the back seat. She leaned down as if struggling to work the seat belt as the cruiser rolled past the side of the building. But she missed the woman standing on the balcony above them, looking down. She felt the sense of panic rising as they drove off. What now? Where were they going?

The campus in the Fan district was only a few miles from the apartments. They drove over the James River, and at the first college-looking building Camilla saw, she leaned forward. "Right here is good. Thanks."

She got out and strode up the steps of a random university building as if it were her daily routine. The doors were locked, but by the time she was yanking on the handle, the students who had given her a ride were already down the block. She turned, looked around, and hurried back down.

"What the hell am I doing?" she muttered, looking around. Why had she bummed a ride into the city? Why not hide around the back of the apartment building? Then she saw a cruiser, and she ducked behind a bush and watched it pull up behind the car, which was stopped at a red light. As the light changed and the boy drove through the intersection, the cruiser's lights came on. The boy pulled over. Damn it! Someone had seen her!

Camilla hurried around the building and broke into a run. About now the cop would be leaning in to question the boy, and he would turn and point. *I dropped her off right there, officer. She said she had a class.*

At the next intersection Camilla ran across the street in spite of the *Don't Walk* light, and kept going. She needed to hide. Ahead she spotted a narrow alley between two elegant old brick buildings. These had once been stately downtown homes of the wealthy, but now were university property. One held the philosophy department, and the other seemed to be offices. She ducked down the alley.

Behind her she could hear the bark of the cruiser's siren as it made a U-turn, and she quickened her pace. The officer gave short blasts of the siren—moving through the traffic light, no doubt—and the sound grew louder. Had he seen her running around the side of the building? Then Camilla heard a siren from another direction.

In later moments of calm reflection she would realize that it hadn't been a dragnet. There weren't a dozen cops in cruisers closing in, weapons drawn, ready to take her down. Probably the agency had told the local police that Camilla had a relative in Richmond, and they had made a call: could you have a local officer do a drive-by? But as she ran around a corner and crossed another street, it felt like a full-on pursuit.

"I have to get away!" she said out loud in a panic. She turned, expecting to see cruisers everywhere. Then she spotted a bus approaching. She ran for the bus stop and waved her arm. *Highland/Jeff Davis*, the destination sign said. She climbed on, rummaged in her pocket for bus fare, and sank down in a seat as the bus pulled away.

Camilla had no idea where the bus was going. She was relieved when it crossed the James River. At least she was heading generally in the right direction. At the next stop, as people were getting off, she stepped up behind the driver. "I think I'm on the wrong bus," she said, and told him where she needed to go.

"You'll need to transfer," he told her, and explained where to get off and what bus to take.

When finally she reached a stop near Susan's apartment complex, Camilla looked all around before she got off, prepared to tell the driver that she'd made a mistake and this wasn't her stop. But she didn't see any danger signs. There were no police officers waiting for her. She got off the bus and took the long way around to the lot where she had parked the motorcycle. It was still there. She got on the bike and pulled away, unsure where to go next.

"What would Una do?" she asked herself. In her troubled dreams, Una had been running down back alleys as she herself had just done. *We have to go north.* That's what Una had said.

"I have to go north," Camilla echoed, and headed for the main road.

11. The Fan

Tansie wandered down the gangplank and stopped near the end, staring in awe at the vast, busy port in the height of the day's activities. As far as she could see in either direction, everything was moving. Merchant wagons were lined up, sailors were loading and unloading ships, and people were crowding around food carts or congregating in groups. The main road stretching off toward the city was busy, a dozen port roads converging onto it. On the wharf where the *Margay* was docked, fancy carriages were waiting, and smaller carts and wagons were lined up behind them, ready to receive disembarking passengers.

"Miss," a soldier said, drawing her attention back. He held out a velvet-lined wooden bowl. "The port tax."

"Oh." Tansie dug in her pocket and withdrew money for herself and Una, and dropped it in the bowl.

Then Una stepped up next to her, and the soldier held up a hand, halting them. He fished the payment out of the bowl and quickly handed it back to Tansie. "Apologies, Talla," he said quietly, offering Una a shallow bow. "The general announced you to me. Enjoy your day."

"Well," Tansie said, sidling up to her as they stepped off the gangplank, "it seems you're famous. But raptors, Una, look at this place!"

Una was less impressed. It wasn't all that different from Deadrise Bay. She took Tansie's arm and led her toward a small wagon near the back of the line, but another arm looped under hers on the other side.

"Don't even think of climbing into that filthy thing," said a stern voice.

"Oh, hello, Gavina." Una smiled at Madame Ben Yett, who steered them forward. "Thank you for helping to make our journey so much more enjoyable."

"And I'm not quite finished." Gavina waved at one of the fancy carriages, and the coachman stepped down to take their bags. "Take these young ladies wherever they wish to go, if you please. Just the two of them. Don't crowd them with others. You know who I am?"

"Yes ma'am," the man said with a slight smile. "We all know who you are."

"Good. My man will settle with you in town. That will do?"

"Yes ma'am," the coachman bowed.

Madame Ben Yett took hold of Una's hand and Tansie's, and gave them a warm grasp. "I do hope to see you again in your travels." She smiled and turned to fetch her children, who were already wandering toward the edge of the wharf.

"Sixteen Back Hill Road," Una said, and the coachman snapped the reins.

"The gunners didn't tell me what happens once we arrive at Ben Attallach," Tansie said, as they sat back in the coach. "You know what we're to do? I know the mission generally, of course, but do you know the steps we're to take?"

"We need to make our way to the Green Hills and extricate the target."

"The Green Hills," Tansie repeated. "But Madame Ben Yett, isn't she going there?"

"Possibly. As she said on the ship, she prefers to stay in the valleys. But we can't ask her to help us, anyway. She might be planning to make a play for the Green Hills. We can't get entangled in that."

"Oh."

"Don't worry about it. We'll figure it out."

"All right. Of course."

They rolled over worn gravel roads at the wharf and onto cobblestone streets. A mile down the road, the coach turned and took a narrow road into the village of Fort Ania.

"This is where the man from the stateroom lives," Tansie said. "Isn't that right?"

"This area, yes. We're staying in the place Czabor calls The Fan. But just for tonight. We have to go north. I'm told we can arrange transport to the north from this place."

The lodging they found in The Fan was a notable step down from their berth in the *Margay*. The room was tiny and Spartan. There was a single cot and a chair, and enough room on the floor for their bags. The porter hovered over them until Una slipped him a coin, and then he scowled and retreated.

"Wear your simplest Tallach outfit," Una said. "We'll have dinner. I suppose this area is safe enough, but we need to maintain a confident poise, and not draw attention."

Tansie nodded, and put on a white shirt and a neutral gray vest and pants. Una was forced to be a bit more fancy, with black silk stockings to cover the tattoo on her leg and a dark blue outfit. She covered the spiral on her cheek with makeup.

"Ready? Let's go."

A block from the rooming house they stepped into a saloon, where a man on a platform played a three-stringed instrument. He missed a note as they walked in, but kept playing. The barkeep was a swarthy man of forty who seemed to stare at first, and then looked away as if he had been expecting someone else.

"Not very friendly," Tansie whispered.

They sat at a table halfway to the back of the room. Una scanned. There were people at three other tables: Two couples, and one table with five men in charcoal gray gis.

Tansie leaned in. "Do we have a contact to help us get where we need to go?"

"Not exactly. I know where we need to go, but we need to find our own way." Una scanned back to the men in gis, and tipped her head. "Huh. What's this?" she muttered. Then she stiffened. "Oh, no. Oh, no, Tansie."

Tansie looked around, and leaned in. "A problem?"

"Our first night, and we walk into this?" Una hissed. "Damn it! Why didn't I case the place first? Stupid!" She leaned in close. "Those five. And look at the barkeep. I thought he seemed indifferent, but that's not it. He's afraid."

Tansie immediately saw what her friend saw. The barkeep kept glancing at the men in gis, then checking the door to the rear, as if confirming that a ready exit was still available.

A waitress stepped up. "Dinner tonight?"

Una put up a hand. "Give us a moment," she demanded.

The woman gave a huff and retreated.

"Do you have your blades?" Una whispered.

"My blades? Just short blades, Una. I was ordered to carry them in my vest," Tansie whispered back. "What's happening?"

"Look at how they sit," she whispered. "It's a kill team. It will happen any moment. Damn it, Tansie."

"A kill team?" Tansie whispered back, wide-eyed.

"When it starts, you go left and I'll go right. Do you follow? Two or three will step out to the sides, and the others will move forward to the target."

"The target?"

"Whoever the mark is. He's about to walk through the door. It's a kill team, Tansie. And they won't leave witnesses. They'll kill us too."

"A kill team?" Tansie repeated, numbly. She unbuttoned the vest and fingered the blades sheathed inside. "All right. I'm ready. But five? With short blades?"

"You can take one. I can probably take two. We have the element of surprise. We'll have to hope that whoever comes through that door can fight. We'll need a third on our side."

The waitress returned and brusquely set a ceramic jug of water and two glasses on the table. "Are you planning to place an order?" she snapped. "The tables are for patrons." It seemed the waitress hadn't picked up on the situation. She stepped back half a pace and folded her arms.

"Just give us a minute, all right?" Una snapped back. She looked to Tansie. "Ready?" Una's head spun, and her heart pounded. "Damn. You'd better be ready."

Then words came to her, in her head. "Not a good play, Una. Five of them? It's too many, and you don't know who the target is."

"Horace!" Una hissed. "You have a better idea?"

Tansie shook her head, confused. "Me?"

"Spoil the setup," Horace demanded. "Do it now. Damn it, girl, do it right now!"

"Shush," Una hissed again.

"I'm sorry," Tansie said, "no, I don't have a better idea."

"Not you. I need to think." Una's hands clenched into fists and she pressed her eyes shut.

"Listen to me," Horace demanded. "Sometimes there's not a clean way out, but I'll give you a messy one. Make a ruckus. Get into a fight with the barmaid. Break the water bottle. Spoil the scene. Then get the hell out. *Move*, girl!"

Una saw a figure outside approaching the door, a shadow across the window. Horace was right!

"Change of plans. Follow my lead," she whispered to Tansie. She jumped up abruptly and pushed the barmaid hard. "Didn't I say to give us a minute?" She picked up the jug of water and hurled it across the room at the entry door. The jug smashed against the door in an explosion of water and clay shards. "If I wanted water, I'd have asked for it!"

The barmaid reeled back in surprise and indignation, and everyone in the room turned to stare.

"Let's get out of this place. What possessed me to come in here?" She grabbed Tansie's arm and pulled her toward the door, and they rushed out into the night.

"Run!" Una hissed. She tore down the road, Tansie right behind.

They ducked down the first alley and kept running. Una heard pursuing footfalls, and turned a corner to hurry down another alley toward what ought to be a larger street opposite. Then she saw her mistake. The roads in The Fan weren't a tidy gridwork. The alley was a dead end! She spun and drew her blades, and Tansie halted and drew hers. They backed up as a shadow moved along the building opposite.

A solitary shape appeared, the silhouette of a man in a gi. They raised their blades, but the figure held up his palms. "Talla?" he said, almost in a whisper. "From the *Margay*. Is that you?"

"Czabor?" Una kept her blades up and ready.

"Yes. Come! Follow me. Quickly."

Una nodded, and they emerged from the alley and followed.

He took them on a long run, winding through streets and alleys, until finally he slowed and motioned for them to duck under the footings of a wharf. He put a hand to his lips, demanding silence. Above them, shadowy shapes stretched across the planks and moved off.

Czabor stepped quietly into the water and waved them on. They sheathed their blades and waded in and swam beneath the wharf. A fishing boat was tied on one side, and they moved quietly along the hull. The crew had arrived late, it seemed, and was working into the night to offload their catch.

This way, Czabor motioned. They swam silently to the bow. He caught hold of a mooring line, and they climbed hand-over-hand and silently boarded. Czabor peered around, and when there was a moment's distraction on the wharf, they slipped into the pilot house. He rapped a signal on a floor and the hatch swung open. A sailor popped up, looked at them, and then half pulled them down.

"A problem? Come, quickly," the sailor urged.

An oil lantern lit the chamber. It was a small room equipped with a hammock, a bench, and wooden lockers.

When the hatch was closed, the sailor turned to them. "Czabor. What's going on? I was told our meeting tonight was called off. Something is wrong?"

"Blankets," Czabor ordered.

The man quickly pulled blankets from the hammock and offered them to Czabor.

"Not for me. For the Talla and her friend. I'm sorry, Talla," he nodded at Una, "to guide you into the water. But those men who emerged from the saloon, those are very dangerous men. What happened? How did you get entangled with them?"

"That was you? You were the one about to enter?" Una said.

Czabor nodded, and glanced at the sailor. "To visit my friend here, both of us recently back in port." Czabor tipped his head. "But ..." He put his hands to his temples and let out an exasperated sigh. "But I'm a fool. They were coming for me, not you. I didn't send word to call off my meeting. Someone else did. Those men were there to ambush me. Here I thought I was saving you, Talla, and it was you who saved my life."

"As an accident of saving our own," Una said, shivering. "I've been told about the kill teams, that they don't leave bystanders alive to report."

"No, indeed. And so you created a distraction and ran." Czabor nodded his head in approval. "That was a good plan. A brilliant plan, Talla. I counted five gray-gis in pursuit. Far too many to take on. I wonder how many of my young trainees would have had the presence of mind not to engage, but instead to find another way. Here's a learning tale to tell."

Una felt her face grow warm at the undeserved compliment. She'd been all set to jump in and fight until Horace had stepped in. It was just as it had been when she was little and running from The Hidden. Repeatedly when she'd been ready to rush into danger, the old man in her head had cautioned her to consider something more clever and less rash. Then tonight, as she had sat staring at an impossibly difficult obstacle—five assassins!—the question had popped into her head: What would Horace say? And there it was, the sensation of him, her mind forming an answer into words: *Spoil the setup ... Do it right now!*

House Kamine was a compound of four buildings with high stone walls from one to the next, forming a large, closed courtyard with the buildings in the corners. Along the top of the walls between the buildings were narrow walkways, just wide enough for one man. As three figures dressed in the daily garb of fishermen approached, a man on the wall spotted them and made a sharp, chipping bird call. Czabor returned the call, and an iron door in the wall swung inward. They stepped inside, and the door thumped shut and a bolt was dropped.

"Master," a young man said in the darkness, "we have guests?"

"Double the wall guards. Then set two extra places for the meal." He turned to Una and Tansie. "Come. We'll find you some water to wash and something dry to put on that doesn't smell of fish." As they stepped inside, Czabor waved at the young recruit to come along. "See to their needs."

"Yes, master." The young man looked inquiringly at his master's odd getup, a fisherman's jacket over a wet gi, and then at the two women in similar jackets, much too big for them. Then his eyes widened at the smeared makeup on Una's face and the tattoo showing through.

"Exactly what you think it is." Czabor answered his unasked question. "Fetch wash water and dry clothes. Quickly, now, or we might have to put you on the mat with her." He winked, and the recruit gave a bow and a smile.

"The guest quarters are upstairs," he said. "This way, Talla."

The House Kamine meal was not at all what Una had expected. In the Tallach fighting houses along the Western Shores, meals were formal affairs, long benches filled with quiet recruits. Talking was considered discourteous, except when the master should choose to offer instruction. But at House Kamine, wine was passed, everyone talked, and there was laughter mixed in with the conversation.

"Forgive the lack of decorum," Czabor said, seeing Una's look of surprise. "We've three things to celebrate tonight. It warrants a bit of merriment."

"Three things?"

"First is our safe return, myself and the students who accompanied me. Second, the fact that I wasn't taken down by that kill squad. And the third reason, my personal favorite, is that we have a fourth-level Talla and her companion at the meal with us."

Everyone at the table gave a cheer.

"But tell me," he said, "what can House Kamine do for you? Aside from a meal, I mean. How can we return the favor?"

Una smiled. "The meal is fine. Maybe afterward I can ask for one thing."

She would have loved to linger at the House Kamine compound and train with the recruits, but that wasn't her mission. After dinner Tansie went upstairs, and Una followed Czabor into a quiet, private room.

"We need passage north to the Green Hills, and information," she told him. "As you might have guessed, my travel here isn't for pleasure."

"Although running from a kill team provides a bit of adventure, doesn't it? There's some pleasure to be had in that." Czabor smiled.

"We'll have stories to tell," Una smiled. "But can you tell us how we might find passage?"

"I can arrange passage. It won't be in grand style, I'm afraid. It would be a ride with a merchant caravan."

Una nodded. "That will do nicely. Thank you."

"And there's one among the slaves at the manor who might be of help, should the need arise. He's young. Your age, I suppose, or perhaps a bit older. He's a friend of House Kamine."

"A friend of House Kamine? At the Green Hills?" Una asked. "Then you have an association with them?"

"No, no. That's above our station," he chuckled. "No, Abel is often with the team that carries goods to the merchant ships. His master is a friend of this house, and enjoys training at House Kamine when he's here—and he brings the boy with him. I think it's a paternal thing. My friend has no son of his own. But Abel is a fine young trainee. He comes to it naturally." Czabor leaned in and spoke quietly. "You see, he's the son of an eastern fighter, a woman lost in the slaughter in the southlands there, years back."

Una involuntarily pulled back. "An eastern fighter?"

"Lost in the slaughter at Nonney Field."

"Nonney Field? So, who was this woman fighter, then?"

"A woman called Aideen."

Una froze.

"The boy was taken as a slave in the aftermath, just a child, and he's lived at the Green Hills all his life since then," Czabor continued, not seeming to notice Una's blanched face. "You can rely on him. His master has taught him discretion, for the boy's sake and his own. And ours too, for that matter. Not that it's expressly forbidden, but for House Kamine to train a slave in Tallach fighting methods would be—well, let's say, frowned upon. Best all around to keep it quiet."

Una recovered her poise and gave a strained smile. "Well, then, I thank you for the meal, and we'll take you up on the offer. We'll be grateful for a ride in the caravan."

The sleeping quarters at House Kamine were an upstairs dormitory. Cots were lined up in rows along two long walls, so that twenty people could sleep comfortably. But for the night, Una and Tansie had the room to themselves.

Una slid the bolt on the door and spun. "Aideen's son!" she blurted out. She pulled her cot closer to Tansie's, and dropped down and stared at the ceiling.

"Aideen's son? Who's Aideen? Have you met someone important?" Tansie asked.

"I … let me think. What do we do?"

Tansie perched on the edge of the bed. This was the first time she had seen Una struggle with resolve. "I'm not sure I follow. What do we do about what?"

Una let out a breath. "It's a complication," she improvised. "Have you heard of Master Aideen?"

"The Gatto master? A little bit. I heard the gunner mention her. What of her?"

Una drew in a breath. She needed to tread carefully. The gunner had promised to keep it secret that Una wasn't really the daughter of Saor Tieg. Una had to make sure she didn't give it away herself. "I sound like a wreck, don't I?" she forced a smile. "Czabor just told me there's a slave named Abel at the governor's mansion, and he's the son of a fighter lost at Nonney Field."

"But Master Aideen wasn't killed at Nonney Field," Tansie objected. "She runs a Gatto house up in the north."

"Listen to me. There's a close tie between Master Aideen and the triumvirate of the north," Una continued, as she settled on a plan. Maybe the truth—or a piece of it, at least—was the best option. She couldn't tell Tansie everything, but there was no need to pretend she didn't know Master Aideen. "That place in the north where her pavilion now stands? The boy king Torin and his gunners fought Shular there,"

Tansie drew in a breath through her teeth. "And this Abel, he's Master Aideen's son? But wouldn't that seem to be an ideal contact, then?"

"You said the gunner mentioned Master Aideen. Did she mention that she has as son who's a slave in Ben Attallach? Did she ask us to fetch this Abel and bring him back?"

"Well, no …"

"And that's the problem. You see, either the gunners know the master's son is here and didn't tell us, or they don't know."

"Yes," Tansie said, and then halted. "Oh, I see. Either the gunners don't know that the master's son is a slave at the Green Hills …"

"In which case, what do we do?" Una said.

"… Or they do know, and for some reason chose not to tell us."

"In which case, what do we do?" Una repeated. "Do we bring him back with us? Or is he a spy, or a threat? We need to be careful. I don't understand all the pieces in play."

Czabor sent trainees to fetch the bags from the room Una and Tansie had rented. They returned to report that the room had been ransacked, the lock broken and the bags overturned.

Una patted her hip. The money was safely strapped around her waist. "It's just clothes and things." She poked through the bags of items, and scowled. The jar of makeup was missing.

"Broken," the trainee explained when she looked up. "Smashed on the floor."

"Damn. Tansie, let's choose what we need, and travel light. We'll be safer once we're in the merchant caravan."

12. Two Turns of the Nautilus

Horace slung his rifle over his shoulder, checked his water bottle, and headed to the path. He would hike to the small river today. There was something about it, the stretches of calm water broken by rapids. Were it not for the occasional hikers, it might be the most perfect spot in the county.

August in Maine was hot and humid in the open areas, but cool under the cover of woods. His insect jacket protected his arms and head, and light gloves protected his hands. He would have no quarrel with the natural world.

Then as he was ready to strike out, he heard an engine. Normally he would guess it might be a lost delivery van, or hikers looking for a trail. But this was purposeful, a truck with delusions of being an assault vehicle, harsh and overly loud. This was a driver who considered the horsepower and racket of his truck to be a manifestation of virility. Then came a sound that was not merely purposeful but threatening, metal on metal. Someone was breaking through the chain at the end of the drive.

Horace came around the side of the cabin moments before the truck. It was big and bright red, jacked up on enormous tires. "Like a gigantic substitute penis," he growled, as he took a position behind a tree stump. He swung the rifle down and racked the slide.

Four young men tumbled out, whooping and hollering. Beer cans cascaded to the ground.

"Look at this!" The driver said, stretching an arm out. "Gotta be some good shit in this one, right? Come on. Let's go. Get the crow bar." And then a .22 round made a neat hole in his shoulder, and he went down.

The other three looked over, confused by the unexpected sound of gunfire and their companion screaming in pain. The rifle fired again, and a second man went down.

"Shit!" called the third. He darted for cover behind a tree as the fourth man dove into the truck, narrowly escaping Horace's third shot.

Now, Horace knew, the real work would start. Putting two out of commission right off had been an excellent opening: reduce the threat by half, an offensive defense. But the element of surprise was gone. Horace shattered a headlight of the truck with another shot to give himself an extra second, and ran for the shed.

Then the return fire started. Shots rang out, six rapid barks. Horace guessed a 9mm semiautomatic handgun.

"Go around!" One man shouted to the other. "Get him!"

"Yes, come on around," Horace said quietly. He popped open a plastic tub and drew out a shotgun. Ducking down, he darted to the rear of the cabin and pressed himself to the wall, aiming the rifle at the corner. When a cautious arm reached out, he fired, splintering the clapboards at the corner of the hut. A howl of pain told him his aim had been good. Unless the man could fire left-handed, it was three down.

Next came a piece of guesswork. The fourth man could certainly hear the howls of the third. He knew as well as Horace that he was the last man standing. A smart adversary would get in the truck and get the hell out. Three of his boys were down in the first minute.

But Horace guessed the fourth man was as untrained and reckless as the others. He guessed the man would try to get clever, try to get the jump on his opponent by unexpectedly coming around the same way. Horace continued around the cabin and ducked behind the stairs to the side entrance. He listened for movement behind, and watched in front.

The fourth man was stupider than he had expected. He ran right around the side of the cabin, his arm extended and his finger on the trigger, as if certain the shooter was still in back. Horace fired one more time, and it was done. He switched to the shotgun and raised it to his hip.

"The rifle hurts, fellas," he said, stepping out. "You don't want to experience the shotgun. Understood? Splatter you all over the place. Don't try and pick up those guns." He collected their guns, popped the magazines and racked the slides to empty the chambers, and tossed them on the ground. "Get in the truck. Time to go," he said, and waited while the groaning men rose to their feet.

They stumbled to the truck and climbed in, cursing and threatening to come back and finish the job.

"Any time, fellas," Horace said. "But next time I'll be aiming tighter in."

The driver put the truck in gear and spun the tires backing up. He scraped one of the stone posts at the entrance, but managed to get the truck into the fire lane, and roared away.

"Well, now, Camilla," Horace said out loud, unzipping the hood of his insect jacket and pulling it off his head, "I suppose I'm glad you weren't here to see that. Ironically, I was wondering how well your mother was caring for you, and if you might not be better off up here." He laughed quietly. "Do the news stories reach you, honey? I suppose not. It's the big buzz around here, ten burglaries in the space of two weeks, all within a few miles. Well, eleven now, but no one will read about this one. And I don't suppose you see news from the County, anyway, wherever you are."

Horace considered that he could have killed the men and eliminated the risk. Dead men don't come back to gun for you, and no DA would try an old man for shooting four dangerous criminals in his own yard. On the contrary, Horace would be a celebrity: *Old Man Stops Rural Crime Spree*. And that story would make it into papers all down the coast—and of course he couldn't have that.

But he wasn't a killer, anyway, he reassured himself. And dead bodies don't get back in the truck and drive themselves off the property. Besides, with his insect hood on and a cap on his head underneath, they couldn't see his face clearly. Even if they were foolish enough to report it, the men wouldn't be able to give a good description. In the short term, they would be interested in getting medical attention. It would give him time to decide what to do.

"I do like this spot, Camilla," he said out loud. "But it may be time to move along, soon. Maybe a nice little cottage over the border."

Horace hosed down the bloody spots on the lawn and carried his toolbox to the driveway to pound the chain loop back into shape. This left one more task. He grumbled about the lost day of hiking to the river, and cursed the invaders as he collected their guns and put them in a bag.

With his rifle and his day-hike pack he climbed into his truck. A few miles down he turned onto a gravel road that stretched into the woods. The road gradually became rougher, until he found himself on a new, raw stretch of logging road. He bumped along the rutted, branch-strewn path, and came to a rise above a pond. For a moment he stood by the truck, looking out at the water. Everything was peaceful. Then he poked a few holes in the bag and hurled it out over the water, and watched the guns disappear.

"It's not the morning I had in mind, Camilla," he said, talking out loud as he turned the truck around and headed back along the new cut. "I'd hoped to dip my feet in, and listen to water rush through the rocks. Instead it seems I'm doing target practice on the local thugs. And now I'm having a closer look at the other hot topic up here. Very industrious, this clear-cut, don't you think? The whole side of the pond. I hear hikers complaining about it when I'm in town. They don't like seeing the trees come down."

He chattered away in a one-sided conversation with his absent granddaughter as he drove home. "I'll miss this place, when it's time to go. This old house," he pointed to a white colonial, "is on the historic register. And the Harrison family lives down that lane. Thirteen kids. And you thought your little room in the basement was small, back in Massachusetts, eh? Imagine having a pack of brothers and sisters crowded in there with you. ..."

The next morning he stepped into the back yard again and stretched. He felt better than usual. Was it the altercation with the men in the red truck? Had it distracted him from his persistent reverie? Somehow, even facing the prospect of having to move on, things seemed calmer and less worrying. Vergil wasn't plaguing him, and his mind was oddly free of worries about his little granddaughter.

"So, Camilla, I wonder where you are now," he said out loud to the woods.

"I think I'm at the front door," a young voice answered.

Horace spun, and his face blanked. "Camilla?" He pulled the rifle off his shoulder.

"Grandpa Rand? This is your house, right?"

Horace stepped into the front yard and lowered the rifle. A small, skinny girl stood peering in through the window, looking into his cabin. She had dark hair, and wore a black mini-skirt over black lycra pants, a matching tank top, and heavy black hiking boots. She looked like a stick figure in boots. A black backpack sat on the stoop next to her.

"Camilla?" he repeated.

The girl turned and froze.

The first thing that struck him was the abundance of mascara, and all the black clothing. Goth. He'd read about it. It had been a fashion trend shortly after punk rock, as he recalled. Evidently it wasn't dead yet. The second was her face. She had stretched out from the pudgy-cheeked little girl he remembered into a stringy adolescent. But his focus was on the tattoo on her cheek, two turns of a nautilus shell in black.

They stared at each other, and then Horace turned and made a visual sweep. "How did you get here?"

Camilla shrugged and nodded at a motorcycle pulled up just outside the chain at the end of the drive.

Horace stepped closer, incredulous. "Camilla, you're *here*?"

She folded her arms and put her weight on one foot. "I'll go if it's a big problem. I just thought …"

"No, it's not a problem." Horace looked around again. "You're here alone?"

"This was a bad idea. I should go." She turned and snatched up the backpack.

"Please stay." Horace stepped forward and caught her arm, and then let go immediately when the girl stiffened and pulled away. She ran backward three steps and dropped to a fighting stance. "I'm sorry." Horace held up his palm. "But please, you're here. Won't you come inside? Are you hungry? Camilla, look at you." There was no mistaking her face. This was his granddaughter! He smiled, and almost laughed. "I've been thinking about you a lot lately."

"I know," Camilla growled. "You've been in my head for two months."

Horace led her in, and fussed in the kitchen for a long time, first putting together a glass of ice water for his granddaughter, and then mixing a very strong martini for himself. Camilla perched on the edge of the recliner, so

Horace pulled in a chair from the kitchen and sat. He chased an olive around his martini glass with a toothpick.

"Camilla, I've been in your head for two months? What does that mean? Do you mean you could hear me?"

"I'm Una. I changed my name."

His eyebrows went up. "You changed your name to *Una*?"

"Yeah."

There was a long silence, and then Horace nodded. "All right," he said under his breath. "That could get confusing." He plastered on a smile. "So, Una, you could hear me?"

The girl stared at him, taking stock. Her eyes narrowed, and she folded her arms. "No. I was just saying that." She looked away. "How could I hear you? That would be crazy. I was in Virginia."

"In your head. Thoughts that form themselves into words. Not like a voice."

She stared at him, unblinking.

"It's not a new thing to me, child. I've had that in my head since I was younger than you are now."

"Thoughts that form into words," the girl echoed, staring. "You ... get it, too?" Then her eyes clouded. "Wait. Next you're gonna say it's a psychological thing, or a chemical imbalance, right? You're gonna say you know this guy who can help me, and why don't we make a phone call to the agency."

Horace smiled sadly at her. "I've very much wanted to meet you, Camilla. And I've no agenda with you, dear. It's the plain truth. All my life I've connected with people in the way you describe. And I have little use for psychologists."

The girl's jaw dropped. "You're serious. You don't think I'm crazy? You really were talking to me? Oh, god, you were! It wasn't just in my head." She gave a trilling laugh of relief, and her shoulders relaxed. "You hear the voices too? And you see them? I knew it!"

"You could hear me," Horace echoed, more to himself than to Camilla. "And you changed your name to Una." Maybe it was because he was out of practice in talking to people, but he felt slow and inept. "You see Una too, then?" Horace looked stupidly at her. "Hence the name. Not a very common name, Una."

"She gave me the idea for this." Camilla pointed at her face. "Me and Sasha got our black belts."

"Black belts?" he repeated, feeling stupid, trying to catch up.

The girl seemed to drop her guard. "I mean, it's not like we're gonna beat up Jackie Chan, or something. And Una—I mean, the *real* Una—she could totally kick my ass. Did you see her in that dojo on the ship, with

153

the guy Sabor, or Zhabor, or whatever the hell his name is? God, she's good. No, it's, you know, a kid black belt. And relax. The tattoo's henna. I stopped at a fair on the way here. You can't get a real tattoo on your face when you're twelve. At least not anywhere I could find, anyway. I'll get the real thing when I'm a real black belt. Like Una."

Horace tipped his head. "Wait a minute. Slow down. Fighting in a dojo? But you mean on the deck of the ship, don't you? You saw her beat those young men?"

"Those four guys? They were just a bunch of assholes. No, I mean, the what-do-you-call-it—House Kamine, right? The House Kamine guy." Camilla gave another shrill, little girl laugh. "That's a great name. When I have a dojo, I'm gonna call it House Kamine."

"Camilla, I didn't see Una fighting in a dojo on the ship."

"I'm Una."

Horace exhaled. "Una, I didn't see Una fighting in a dojo on the ship."

"You didn't? It was great. God, she's got the moves. I mean, the House Kamine guys do, too, but she's better than they are, and she's a girl. It was excellent. And her spiral. That's so cool. I sorta thought the nautilus was cooler than the spiral of diamonds, and they had it in the book, so that's why I picked it. But it works the same. You can add another ring and it spirals out."

Horace's sense of his world was getting blurry. First his granddaughter shows up out of the blue. Then it turns out the girl knows more about Una than he does. "Honey, tell me. When did you first see Una?"

"The first time? You mean, like, grown up? In that jail. You know, the twelfth station, or whatever. Where the hell is that, anyway? She got hit in the head, and then she's in a cell and Tyra's crying."

"Tyra?"

"Not the one playing Tyra now. That's Tansie. I mean the real Tyra."

Horace shook his head, confused. "And what do you mean, I've been in your head for two months?"

"How do you think I got here? You're always talking about the place. *Look, that house has thirteen kids living in it. And this big white house, it's historic. And there's been all these robberies right near here. And people are trying to stop the logging around this pond.* I just had to look up some stuff. It wasn't that hard to find you."

Horace suddenly rose from his chair, realizing that his sentimentality at seeing his granddaughter was clouding his judgment. "Camilla," he said, standing up, "we need to leave. We'll talk once we're safely away, all right? Come over here. Do you know how to put bullets in a magazine?"

"Like, for a gun?" Camilla's face fell. "Nobody followed me. I swear."

"The motorcycle. Where'd you get it?"

She grimaced. "I kind of borrowed it. God, I'm in so much trouble." She put her face in her hands.

"It's stolen? It might have an anti-theft tracking device. Or someone might have seen it. Or seen you. They were probably watching you. Probably have been the whole time."

"No, honest."

"I'm not blaming you. We have to leave. You ride the bike. We'll leave it somewhere to create a bit of misdirection. But first we have to pack some things."

"What are you talking about?" The girl folded her arms and flashed him a pout.

"Camilla, I'm not living up here for the fresh air. You think you're in trouble? So am I. We have to get out of here, or we might both have more than we want. Now, listen. Here's what you can do to help. …"

Camilla reflected that she ought to be frightened, but instead she found her grandfather's exit plan to be a comforting diversion. Something other than her own problem was the focus of attention. Her grandfather hadn't even asked her to fess up to what she had done. Instead he was pulling guns from drawers and showing her how to snap bullets in—a task that she thought was about the coolest thing ever—and constantly looking out the windows. She didn't know what he was afraid of, but he wasn't yelling at her for her massive fuck-up.

They packed the guns into plastic cases, and packed the cases and several others into the back of the truck. Then they covered them with buckets of tools and scrap lumber. Nothing to see; just a carpenter in his work truck. Soon Camilla was on the stolen motorcycle following her grandfather.

Horace watched in his rearview, struck by the sheer improbability: A stick-thin little girl in black was riding an enormous motorcycle behind him as they raced up a rural road in Maine. After some fast driving, he led them down a dirt road to a pull-off by a boat ramp to a little pond. There was a pickup truck with a boat trailer parked on one side, and an old Subaru wagon.

Horace hopped out of the truck and came over with a rag. "Get your stuff. We'll leave the bike here." Camilla climbed off, and he wiped down the motorcycle. "Don't leave anything. Hop in the truck."

He roared back to the road. "Next we find a phone, and then we're gone. All right?" He glanced at the girl, belted in and leaning against the door. "I don't suppose you have a passport."

"No. Why? Where are we going?"

"Canada."

13. Moonlight

The merchant caravan moved slowly, but it was better than walking. Una and Tansie sat in a cart and leaned against their luggage, pared down to one bag each. At mealtimes the master of the caravan invited them to join the crew, and overall, the journey was fine. Una's only complaint was her hat. Her other hats had been lost or ruined, leaving only a black one with a heavy, dark veil.

"I can't see with this thing on," she insisted, tugging at it. "And I look as if I'm going to a funeral."

"Czabor said we can find what we need in the village shops," Tansie said. "We can find face paint there."

"That's where we need to go, anyway. We're staying there, in the village."

"Oh. In the village?"

"The gunner assures me the lodging will be comfortable," Una said. "It's arranged. But if someone comes at us in the short term, I'm a blind old cow. You'll have to fight for us both."

"I'm fine with fighting," Tansie grinned. "But it seems safe enough."

"It seems quite safe, indeed," said a voice in Una's head.

Una sighed. "We were fortunate to get out of that saloon," she said, rolling her eyes and offering her Horace voice a bone.

"I don't know how you knew what to do," Tansie said. "I didn't even realize we were in trouble."

"And you were ready to fight them, Una," Horace's words scolded her. "Not that to fight isn't sometimes the only choice. But don't neglect your options. You have a great mind for trickery and subterfuge. Use it. Winning without fighting is always better."

"Sometimes it's best to avoid a fight." Una scowled. "All right?"

"Oh, no argument from me," Tansie agreed. "Especially with five of them. As Master Shiskin wrote, *best to defeat the enemy without a fight.*"

"You sound like Tyra."

Tansie shrugged. "Sorry. It's part of her character. I'm supposed to drop little quotes here and there. I keep forgetting."

"She's always doing that, yes."

"I got that one from a book in the lounge, before General Ryndin threw it overboard," Tansie said. "He said something about not filling my head with the military tomes of old men."

"That one is a borrowed quote, of course," Horace piped in. "It's Sun Tzu, from *The Art of War*."

"I concur, Tansie," Una smirked. "Old advice from old men. It can be annoying."

"Much older than you or I, that one," Horace said. "Sun Tzu wrote that around twenty-five centuries ago. For me, anyway. Perhaps it's much more ancient for you. And yet that annoying advice persists. You might pay it some mind, Una."

Una shook her head, trying to rid it of Horace.

As they neared the borderline of the Green Hills manor, the caravan leader stopped and called for Una and Tansie to come forward.

"We'll be inspected at the approach to the manor. You could ride up front and play at being servants, or disembark here and make your way on foot."

"On foot, of course," Horace urged. "Maintain control."

Una exhaled loudly. "Thank you for taking us this far, sir. We'll make our way on foot. Is the village nearby? That's where we're bound."

"I'll drop you at the crossroads. It's a mile down from there." He nodded and called an order, and the caravan pulled forward.

"And thank you, Horace. I don't always need you to tell me what to do."

There was a sensation that translated as mirth. "You called out to me, dear, didn't you? I'm just a passenger on this ship."

"Una," Tansie said, "who are you talking to?"

Spinning to look at her companion, Una screwed her face into a scowl and then halted. "I'm ... It's ..."

"It's a method," Horace urged.

"It's a method," Una echoed. "It's a method, Tansie."

"A method?"

"Oh, dear. Is that a term you don't have?" Horace said. "It's a technique. Tell her it's a technique of—what's your fighting method called?"

"It's a Tallach technique," Una said.

"Right, right. Tallach, that's it," Horace said. "I'll have to research that. Never heard of it. Tell her it's to help make sense of options. To help choose the best one. Horace is your spirit voice, or whatever you would say. I don't know if spirit voice makes sense to you."

Tansie nodded slowly. "A Tallach method?" she repeated, intrigued.

"Something I was taught in my Tallach training," Una said, "my instructor told me to listen for my inner voice, and to call on it." Una waved a hand. "I know, I know. It sounds foolish. But it's the idea of it. You picture your inner voice and concentrate on what it has to say. It's a means of reflecting on your options."

Tansie nodded again, and Una smiled back. She was buying it!

"Nicely done," Horace said. "See? You're good at this."

"I guess I do the same thing sometimes," Tansie said. "Maybe I should be a Talla, huh?" she laughed. "But you call your inner voice *Horace*?"

"Tell her that ..."

"Shut up," Una hissed. She turned to Tansie. "Not you. Sorry. Sometimes Horace speaks up when I don't ask him to. Sometimes he's a nattering old man."

"Your muse is an old man?"

"The Tallach way mixes the generations," Una improvised. "An old man, a little girl, a king, a stray—the vessel isn't important."

"Oh, very nice!" Horace glowed. "Quite eastern. I like it."

"It's not something you choose," Una continued. "So although you might in fact find old men to be incredibly annoying at times," she rolled her eyes, "your inner voice might take that form."

"The wisdom of age can be irritating, can't it?" Horace teased. "It stops you from executing brilliant plans like trying to take on five assassins with just two of you."

"Please, please shut up."

"I'm annoying you. I'm sorry," Tansie said. "I was just curious. I don't know the Tallach ways."

"No, no. Not you. I meant Horace. Here I am, yammering away with my muse. It's rude of me. I'll stop."

"Run! Damn it, girl, run!"

Una's head swung around. "Run!" she commanded, not seeing anything.

Then they heard footfalls behind them, and they ran. They rushed down the road and rounded a turn, Una whipping a hand out to catch her hat and veil. Then they stopped short as a pair of road scouts crashed out from the woods and dropped into the road, cutting them off. Una and Tansie froze, and the road scouts also froze. They stared at each other. Then a hundred yards down, a young man crashed out of the woods. He halted, saw the road scouts, and ran.

"There he is! Begging your pardon, Talla." The scouts nodded and tore down the road after the man.

"Not after us," Tansie said, in a relieved laugh, bending over and resting her hands on her knees to catch her breath. "Raptors, Una, they're not after us. They're chasing someone else."

"No, not after us. It seems sometimes my muse gives false alarms." Una scowled and stalked down the road. "And now we've been seen by the road scouts." Nonetheless, she pulled the hat back on, and tugged at the veil to cover her face.

To call it a village seemed almost silly. Una figured it was supposed to sound quaint. The village of Green Hills, in the valley below Green Hills Manor, was astonishing in its wealth. It made Deadrise Bay look simple. Neat, smooth roads of tightly fitted cobblestones were flanked by city mansions with fancy flower gardens and servants stationed at the entrances. In the middle of town was an enormous, ornate park with wrought-iron benches, statues and reflecting pools, and winding brick walks for afternoon strolls. The shops were big, sunny, and filled with the most expensive goods that could be had.

"Can we afford to shop here?" Tansie whispered in Una's ear.

"It's arranged."

"But, do we have enough? I know you have your money belt, but ..."

Una smiled. "My father is wealthy, Tansie, but I think in setting up this ruse the gunner might have overestimated his wealth. The purse is extremely generous. And the gunner gave me a token. Arrangements were made some time back with a shop called The Moonlight. It's a clothier, but I'm told they do business across the board—privately, if you take my meaning. We're to go there, and they'll get us whatever we need."

"A token?"

"The gunner's token. I'm to present it to the mistress of the shop."

The Moonlight was easy to spot, the center of attention in its block. It was a square three-story building painted a rich, deep gray, with a copper-clad mansard roof and trim painted gold. The front was mostly glass, offering passers-by a view of the wealthy patrons inspecting the wares inside. And in the center, above the entry door, was a gleaming white, round window, illuminated from the inside by lantern light. Even in the late afternoon daylight, it was a giant, shining moon.

The attendants flanking the entryway wore suits of black silk. They hesitated when two plainly dressed young women stepped up. This was not a shop for commoners.

One of them looked at Tansie, as he couldn't read Una's face beneath her veil. "May we be of assistance to you young ladies?"

Una lifted her chin and strode past them, up the steps. She knew this world. Deadrise Bay might be a port city, but she understood wealth and power. Tansie smiled sheepishly at the attendants and hurried after Una.

Inside, a woman stepped up to block their way. "Might I help you find a suitable shop, ladies?" she said, in a slightly cloying, upper-crust tone.

"Why, is there something wrong with this one?" Una glanced around as if looking to see if it measured up.

"You might find some bargains down at the depot. Shall I point the way?" The woman flashed a smile and took half a step toward them, suggesting that they turn around.

"Oh, I don't know. Perhaps we won't be disappointed with what this shop has to offer. Might as well look around."

"Well, now, miss, I think you'd find the shops at the depot much more to your taste and station."

Another woman stepped up, older and primmer, and dressed in a black silk vest with a watch chain, the outfit of a store owner. "And what have we here, Marianne?"

By this time, several of the wealthy patrons had stopped fingering the merchandise and had turned to watch, adopting smug expressions of superiority. A pair of country girls had wandered into town. It would be amusing to see the mistress turn them out.

"Just a couple of young ladies on their way to the shops at the depot, Miss Kendall." The woman looked at them and pointed toward the street. "If you turn down the next lane, and then …"

"Are you the proprietress, then?" Una said, cutting the woman off. "We do need a few things, if it's not too much trouble. Here, I have it some-where." Una reached into her pocket and pulled her closed hand out. "Ah. Here it is." She turned, putting her back to the woman who had stopped them, and quickly opened her hand to show the proprietress what she held, a short ebony token decorated with three ruby cabochons set in silver. She slipped her hand back into her pocket and smiled. "Would the shop be available, oh, perhaps right now?"

The woman froze, then put on a big smile. "Right now would be splen-did. Marianne, I'll see to our guests. Could you please close the shop? Offer our apologies to the patrons, and assure them that we'll open later today or perhaps tomorrow."

Marianne stared. "Close the shop?"

"Immediately, if you please. You and the other attendants will meet in the salon right away. Inform the doormen that we're closed until further notice. Draw the shades." She smiled at Una and swept an open palm to usher them in. "Right this way, ladies. I apologize for the misunderstanding and the delay."

A few short minutes later, the patrons had lost their smug expressions and were muttering to one another as they strode down the walk to find other places to shop. The doors were locked and the doormen stood in front of them; and a dozen attendants lined up inside, waiting for orders.

"Well, now, the shop is yours, miss. What can we get for you today?" Miss Kendall said to Una.

Marianne sidled up to her. "I'm not sure I understand."

"It's not hyperbole, Marianne," she said in a low tone. "The shop is *hers*. I told you it was purchased."

"You said by a concern overseas."

"And here she is. Now, hush." She flashed a smile. "So, ladies, freshly arrived at Ben Attallach, are we?"

"Yes, on the *Margay*," Una said, raising some eyebrows. "It was a lovely trip. Fine conversation. Does Madame Ben Yett come here, I wonder? She's a darling." Una flashed a wink at Tansie.

The name drop worked. The staff immediately stiffened, and the whispering stopped.

"Now, here's the thing," Una continued. "We can't very well go around town in dusty traveling outfits." She motioned at her road-stressed clothes, covered with a fine coating of dirt. "But we don't wish to stand out. Understated, I think, is the word. Wouldn't understated be best, Tansie?"

"Yes, I think so," Tansie nodded, and lifted her chin a bit. She could play this game. "We aren't queens, after all. Just the daughters of traders," she added, riffing on Gavina's words as she had left their room on the *Margay*.

The staff offered a strained, light laugh.

"And—Miss Kendall, is it?—I suppose I can count on your discretion, and that of your associates?" Una glanced at the row of attendants standing stiffly like soldiers.

"Of course." They all nodded solemnly.

"Good. Because I can't see with this on." Una pulled the hat off and tossed it to one of the attendants, who almost dropped it when she saw the spiral on her face. "So, please, this is my friend Tansie, and my name is Una. Never mind if you hear any other names. We need proper Tallach outfits, top to bottom, and I'm hoping one of you might find a suitable shade of makeup for me." She motioned at her face. "I wish to be Una, the daughter of a trader on the Western Shores. Now, let's see what my new shop has to offer, shall we, Tansie?"

The staff scattered through the store, and some went on errands. Outfits were picked out, some sent for tailoring and some delivered to the hotel down the street.

Soon Una and Tansie were being ushered up a grand stairway at the hotel to an upper-level suite with a balcony overlooking the park. Servant girls lugged in wash water and basins, and the dusty travelers were transformed into stylish young Tallach women.

The dining room at the hotel was already filling up when they descended the stair, but the attendants at the store had handled this detail as well. The matron greeted them and led them to a reserved table for two on the far side of the room. It was a fine spot for observing, Una noted, and there was a lot to see. At the front were two enormous bay windows looking out at the manicured gardens that flanked the entry to the hotel. A large, round table had been set in each bay window, and adorned with candles and flowers for centerpieces. But no one had been seated there yet. The rest of the room was filled with smaller tables for groups of two or four, and only a few were empty. People were lining up in the foyer, ready to fill them.

A waiter stepped up and poured water and wine, and Una and Tansie sat and studied the patrons. Then the guests for the front tables arrived, all in a group. In the lead was a beefy redhead in his middle forties, dressed in a dark suit with gold epaulettes. Surely this was the governor of the

Green Hills, the man called Crinan. On his arm was not Madame Ben Yett, but a much younger woman with big, dark eyes and black hair tied up primly on top of her head. She wore a starched white dress, and smiled continuously as she moved through the room—as if it were an act, Una thought. The governor seated her, then sat next to her. Then the rest of the seats were filled with the entourage of finely dressed men and women.

The soldiers who had accompanied the group took up positions against the wall nearby, facing out.

"It seems we have all the royalty here," Tansie said, leaning in. "Good. We can check them out."

"Not all of them," Una said. "I don't see Gavina. But I'm going to guess that's Adelaide on his arm."

"Our target. We've found her already?"

Una nodded. "An accident of us having been spotted by those men on the road. They're here to check us out." She clenched her teeth, silently admitting that Horace's demand that they run had turned out well in the end.

"That's a stroke of luck," Tansie said, unwittingly turning the blade.

The waiter interrupted their quiet conversation to take their order.

As he turned to leave, Una touched his arm. "Say, can you tell me, who's that at the governor's side? Striking, isn't she?"

The waiter leaned in. "That would be Miss Adelaide."

"Would it be possible to send her my greetings? Perhaps we might meet. My friend and I are new to town. It would be nice to visit with some-one our age." Una smiled pleasantly.

"Oh. I'm afraid she uh … I mean, the governor doesn't … Well, what I mean to say is that we're not offered the opportunity to speak with Miss Adelaide."

She saw him eye the soldiers, and his meaning was clear enough. "All right. Thank you. Oh, and another question, if you don't mind. Does Madame Ben Yett come here? I've heard she might be coming to town."

The waiter stiffened, and his smile grew strained. "I couldn't say." He hurried away.

The food came quickly, and for the next hour a little play was acted, the new arrivals studying the wealthy locals while they in turn studied the new arrivals. Many of the guests invented reasons to walk past their table and stop to introduce themselves, but no one from the governor's table came over. Una and Tansie finished their meal and returned upstairs.

In their room, they stared at each other for a minute, unsure where to start in recounting all they had learned. It seemed that everyone wanted to figure out who this new young woman was, and to get in early, should it be worth-while to be associated with her. Everyone, that is, except for the governor and his party.

"Maybe they're too important for us," Tansie proposed.

"Or unsure what to make of us," Una offered. "But Adelaide was well guarded. We know that much." Una had watched the woman carefully. Occasionally the young mistress neglected the plastered-on smile, and another sentiment had come through. She was frightened.

"Are your meals at the Shores like this?" Tansie said, pulling the curtain back to peer outside. "It's exhausting."

Una smiled. "Sometimes. Although I prefer to eat down on the docks when I can get away with it. Less fuss and more food. But what a show, Tansie. We show up at The Moonlight with the gunner's token, and half the town shows up at the hotel the same night."

"And Adelaide. He brings her? Isn't that a bit brash, to bring his slave to dinner? Especially with Gavina back on the mainland."

"That's the real story, isn't it? I'll bet he brought his slave on purpose. He's telling the village that Gavina has no power. But where is Gavina, and what's her play?"

"And how do we get to Adelaide?" Tansie added.

"Yes, and how do we stay out of the crossfire?"

At the morning meal the room was abuzz with the latest gossip: The street scouts had captured a slave trying to escape from Green Hills Manor. They said the dark-eyed slave girl had helped him escape, although the story was that Adelaide had vehemently denied it.

Una waved the matron of the house over. "What's this I hear about an escaped slave? It seems a lot is happening around here in the short time since I arrived."

The matron fussed with the table settings. "Don't pay it any mind, miss. A street scout met the governor on his way to his carriage last evening, and said he'd caught one of his slaves. It seems to have upset the young lady. The slave got a beating, and the word is, he's to be sold."

"And who is this slave? Is he known in the village?"

"Nice enough lad. I haven't known him to get into trouble. Been at the manor since he was a young thing. His name is Abel."

Una clenched her teeth, but held her poise. "And he's to be sold? Through a vendor?" Her heart raced. This was Aideen's son!

"There's buying and selling of all sorts of things at the manor. I suppose they'll sell him direct. Probably he'll be gone today, off to the valleys or who knows where."

"Thank you." Una's mind raced. "Speaking of the manor," she improvised, "we were hoping to visit. With all the people here last night, I didn't have a chance to greet the governor. Do you know if there's a carriage we could employ?"

"I'd be happy to arrange it for you, miss."

When they returned from the morning meal, one of the attendants from The Moonlight was waiting outside their suite with freshly tailored outfits.

"Just in time," Una said, as she closed the door. "Put on the best one, Tansie. This is where we start to earn our pay."

The matron of the hotel not only arranged a carriage for them, but sent a runner ahead. When they stepped down at the entrance of the enormous stone manor, staff were there to greet them. They were whisked inside and shown directly to an opulent sitting room. Una gave a quick shake of the head, signaling to Tansie that they would not sit.

She leaned in. "Sitting means waiting. And waiting means you're less important than the person you're waiting for."

The host arrived promptly. Crinan smiled widely and kissed Una's hand. "Miss Una," he said. He kissed Tansie's as well, then led them down the main hallway to a much cozier, darker sitting room that smelled of pipe tobacco.

"Well, then," he said, motioning for them to sit, "I'm told you're the new owner of The Moonlight. A fine shop. I've parted with quite a few coins there, picking up this and that."

"I heard about the place from a friend, and it seemed interesting," Una said, offhandedly. "I suppose I'll keep it for a while." She smiled sweetly, almost condescendingly. Tansie kept quiet.

"And so I suppose I'll have to stop in again soon." He matched her cloying smile. "Will you be managing the establishment yourself?"

"Me? Oh, no," Una waved a hand dismissively. "Marianne will handle it."

"Oh, too bad," he said, with mock disappointment, "then it will so much less interesting to shop there. But tell me, if you're not to be on the floor at The Moonlight, how will you spend your days here in the Green Hills?"

"I'm sure we'll find things to keep our interest," Una smiled.

"Well, then." Crinan sat back, "tell me what the governor of this drafty old place can do for you lovely young women."

Una had to stifle a scowl. This was laying it on rather thick. "I'm told that your family produces a fine grade of stone for finish work. I might decide to build here, or to renovate one of those adorable old homes in the village."

This was laying it on thick in return, and the governor bit his lip. "Of course. But you didn't come all the way out here to inquire about stone for a renovation."

"No, no," Una laughed. "Of course not. And we don't mean to hold you up. I'm sure you're busy. We just wanted to offer our greetings. We saw you at dinner last night, and weren't able to make it to your table. Next time you're in the village, would you honor us by being my guest?" Una rose and offered her hand again.

This time the governor took her hand in both of his and held it firmly. "That sounds fine. Let me see if I can arrange it. And now shall I call a servant show you to your carriage?"

"Oh, one other thing," Una said. "I heard that you might have a slave for sale."

"Possibly."

"Does he know his way around the village? It would be handy to have a slave who's familiar with the area. If he's not already spoken for, I might be interested."

The door swung open, and a younger version of Crinan burst into the room, gnawing at a chunk of bread. "So what did Abel do?" he said with a sneer. "You're selling him? What, you're afraid he'll take your governorship, brother? Or is that particular unfounded fear reserved for me alone?"

Crinan barely moved. He turned his head and gave Una a slow nod of the head. *Sorry*, it said, *but do you see the things I have to deal with?* "Conn, have you met the new proprietress of The Moonlight?"

"The Moonlight!" Conn said, with an exaggerated expression of awe. "You're the new owner? Oh, then surely you must be a nabob from the east. Are you a princess?"

Una's eyebrows lifted, but she kept quiet.

"A princess from overseas," Conn continued, holding the floor, "deigning to buy a little piece of my brother's district. Isn't that something, big brother?"

"Well, *little brother*," Crinan said, teeth clenched, "I would wager she's closer to a throne than you are—or ever shall be. Is there a reason that you've barged into my sitting room? Perhaps you saw the notice for volunteers for the deep northern expedition this winter, and you're game to sign up?"

"I'm certain you have something much less amusing in store for me."

"Is the treasury paid back, dear little brother? At the last check, I believe you weren't quite halfway there. Perhaps you should take a kindlier tone. In my magnanimous grace, I've offered you a way out. Maybe you'd prefer the stockade."

Conn exhaled an exasperated breath. "Crinan, in fact I came to tell you that I've made the payment, all right? It's been recorded."

"Delightful. At this rate I should say you'll be solid in five years, give or take. Am I right?" Crinan mocked. "And I've business to attend to. This eastern nabob is interested in purchasing a slave. So why don't you get out of my sitting room, Conn, before I decide to reconsider our arrangement."

"All right. I'm leaving." Conn raised his palms. "But I'd advise against selling the slave. Especially to an easterner." He grimaced at the visitors, and Una and Tansie pulled back. "One day it's The Moonlight, and the next she'll be taking over as governor—before I have a chance to." Conn laughed and stormed out of the room.

Crinan sighed, and led Una and Tansie to the door. "So, you're interested in a slave. I think we might arrange something."

Looking down from a high window, Crinan watched the carriage pull away. Behind him stood a man in a black gi.

"Follow," Crinan told the man. "Remain unseen. There's something here I don't quite understand."

"You suspect the boy?"

"Conn?" Crinan smiled. "My brother is angry because he was caught, and his little jaunt to the islands with my money is over. No, never mind Conn. It's this girl from The Moonlight. Who is she? My little brother is an ass, but his guess might not be so far off, Dorren. A nabob from the east. Or maybe a spy from the east."

"And what of Conn? He takes liberties."

"You had a fine idea, Dorren, to keep my little brother alive and set him to the task of repayment. It keeps him occupied, and the focus of his attention is on getting money to repay me. But he does grow tiresome, doesn't he? Let's raise the interest. Have the quartermaster inform him that his debt doubles on the fortnight, and the stockade awaits, should he fail to make a payment. See if that slows his tongue and quickens his pace."

It wasn't until the carriage reached the hotel and Una saw the young man wince as he stepped down that she realized he was in pain. The story of the beating had been true.

"Bring him in," Una said to the driver. "And would you mind checking with the matron? I'm sure she can arrange a space for him, perhaps across the hall. Or maybe there's a storage room that would suffice. Tansie and I will take a turn around the park before the noon meal." She looped her arm under Tansie's, and pulled her along.

When out of earshot, Tansie shifted up close. "Raptors, Una. You bought a slave."

"Did you have another idea? He's Master Aideen's son."

"No better idea. But what now?"

"Now we go to The Moonlight. We need some things."

Una kept to a casual pace through the park, in spite of her urge to hurry. This time when they stepped up the walk to the store entrance, the door-men rushed forward to escort them inside. Miss Kendall was there in a flash, and while all the patrons in the store were staring, this time it wasn't with disdain.

"Do you need the store again?" Miss Kendall said.

"Just a few things. Could we speak in private?"

She listed what she wanted, and attendants were sent out. In the back room, two boys changed into servants' attire.

"And you're to treat him with respect," Una admonished, as the boys emerged prissed and preened, ready to enter the hotel.

"Just between you and me," Miss Kendall quietly confided, "if that slave ran from the manor, he had a reason. Strange goings-on up there, since the old governor passed."

Una said nothing, but nodded slowly. Another leisurely stroll brought them back to the hotel, and the matron smiled and stepped up to greet them.

"We've set things up as you've requested, miss," she said. "Is there anything else we can do for you?"

"Would it be too much trouble to have our noon meal upstairs? And perhaps an extra plate. I'm sure my new slave must be hungry. Bring us a healthy portion, and we'll leave something for him."

"It will be our pleasure."

The moment they had closed the door to their room, there was a rap on the door. Tansie cracked the door open and let one of the boys in.

"He got a good lashing, miss," the boy said to Una. "But he'll pull through all right. Ain't nothing broken. Just raw. We got him wrapped up and dressed presentable. You want us to stay?"

"No, thank you," Una said. "Tell him to report to me immediately, and then you may go."

At the next light rap on the door, Tansie let Abel in. He was dressed in a simple Tallach outfit. He bowed and stood just inside the door as Tansie closed it behind him. At another rap on the door, Tansie was about to reach for the knob once again, but Una shook her head. Tansie retreated, and Abel stepped forward and opened the door.

"The quarters of Misses Una and Tansie," he said to the hotel staff waiting in the hall.

"Is that our meal? Let them in, Abel," Una said, and Abel stepped to the side.

A cart was wheeled in, and in moments the table by the window was wiped down, a tablecloth draped over it, and two places set. Dishes were placed in the middle, a half dozen covered tureens. Silverware was set, a bottle of wine decanted into a crystal carafe, and then at Una's nod they rolled the cart out, leaving an extra plate on a small table by the door.

Abel closed the door behind them. "Shall I wait in the hall, master?" he said, tentatively. "Or would you like me to serve?"

"In the hall? Of course not," Una said. "Put the bolt on the door, and come sit with us. And don't call me master."

"But, you mean …"

"Lock the door. I don't want someone wandering in. Then get your plate. There's plenty of food."

Abel locked the door and picked up the plate. He stood by the door, confused.

"Don't make me order you to come sit."

Guardedly, he brought the plate over and stood by the table. "Master …"

Tansie slid a chair over with her foot. "I'm Tansie. This is Una. Let's eat. I'm starving."

Abel stood frozen. "Shall I serve?"

Una exhaled, and held up a hand. "I'm being unkind. This all seems very clever from where I'm sitting, but I should know better. I've been in your position, Abel, at the mercy of those I stood before, and unsure what to do. Please sit, and I'll explain."

He sat, and winced as his back touched the chair. He scooted forward, clutching the plate.

Una took the linen napkin from her lap, dipped it in her water glass, and wiped it across her cheek. Then she did it again, and a third time. The young man's eyes widened. "It's a rumor spoken of in whispers, but it's true. My name is Undine. I'm the daughter of Saor Tieg of Deadrise Bay on the Western Shores."

Abel nodded. "Talla," he said.

"Have you heard those names? Mine or my father's?"

He nodded again. "I've heard both, master. On the trade routes. Some of the ships sail to Deadrise Bay."

"Don't call me master," she repeated, brusquely, and then held up a hand. "Please. I don't like it."

Again Abel nodded. "Your father is the freedman merchant of the Western Shores?" He bowed his head in respect. "A very powerful man. And you a fourth-tier Talla."

"We met a friend of yours on our journey here. Czabor. He seems to be a man of honor, and he's a damned fine fighter."

Abel smiled, and relaxed a bit. "Czabor! You know Czabor, master— uh, miss …"

"Just call me Una. He told me about you, Abel. He mentioned that you spar at the House Kamine pavilion. And he said you're the son of a woman fighter named Aideen, who was lost at Nonney Field."

"Yes, Talla."

"And so you see, I know who you are, as well." She looked him in the eye. "I know your mother. She wasn't lost at Nonney Field, Abel. She's a Gatto master in the northlands."

14. Street Café

Camilla huddled against the door, keeping her distance. Her grandfather spoke to her occasionally, asking if she needed food or a pit stop. But he understood her reluctance to warm up to him. He was a stranger. She had little grounds for trust.

When they stopped for gas, Camilla considered striking out on her own. But she didn't have anywhere to go, and her mother had never blamed her grandfather for what had happened. That had been because of her father, and he was long dead now, and her mother long gone. And maybe all her grandfather had going for him was that he was the last man standing, but at least he was taking her with him. He didn't seem to be trying to fob her off on someone else.

"I don't have a passport," Camilla said, as they passed a sign announcing the border crossing ahead.

"I know. You told me. It'll be fine."

"They won't let us through."

"I'll take care of it." Horace pulled to the side of the road a mile before the crossing. He got out of the truck, and stretched his arms out in a big yawn. He walked around to the passenger side and pulled Camilla's door open.

Her eyes widened. "You're gonna dump me here?" she hissed, pulling back.

"What? Good lord, child, of course not. I'm going to hide you. Hop up, and watch your head." He pulled up on the seat cushion, and it came loose. "Get in. And don't worry. It's not ideal, but you'll have air, and it's only for a short time. I'll let you out the minute we're past the border station."

Camilla peered in. There was a cavity under the seat with some kind of burlap material at the bottom.

"A customization," Horace winked. "Used to store things in there. So we'll store you for a little while, all right?"

Her mouth fell open, but Camilla crawled in, and Horace gently put the seat back down. He closed the truck door and gave one more big yawn for the benefit of a passing car. Just a man stretching his legs.

"Everything all right in there?" he said as he pulled the door shut and turned the key.

"It stinks," came Camilla's muffled voice.

"That's *old truck*," Horace explained with a smile. "Decaying foam and vinyl. Sorry about that. Just keep still at the border station, honey, and don't worry. I'll get us through."

Camilla clenched her hands into fists and closed her eyes, and willed the border guards not to pick them for an inspection. Never mind the girl hiding in the seat. There were cases of cash and guns in the back of the truck.

But Horace was calm. He pulled up to the booth and turned on the charm, adopting a French accent. He told the border guards that he was on his way to visit his daughter in Montmagny. Some repairs always needed doing, didn't they? And his daughter was always so busy. The front door needed work, and last time he visited he noticed some windows that were hard to open. He sprinkled in little details about her home and his favorite place for lunch.

Even Camilla, for a brief moment, wondered if her mother actually was in Montmagny. Damn he was good, she thought, silently kicking herself for almost buying it.

They drove on, and Camilla kept silent. Horace pulled over and let her out, and she resumed huddling against the door. But this time she showed a little grin.

After a long time on a smooth highway, the sounds and motion of the road lulled her to sleep. She slept for hours, and was so quiet that Horace kept looking over to make sure she was all right. At a rough stretch of road she finally woke up. She rubbed her eyes and stared out the window. Horace kept quiet as well. He understood. She was twelve, he was a strange old man, and they were hightailing it out of the country. It was lot for a little girl to handle.

They stopped a couple of times for bathroom breaks and for fast food, and kept driving without talking. It wasn't until they had made it to Québec City and were leaving the front desk of a hotel with a key card that she finally broke her silence.

"They speak English," she said, as they walked back to the truck to drive it around to an entrance near their room.

"It's Québec City," Horace said casually, as if they had been chatting all day. "They speak English when they have to. They can't turn down English-speaking patrons."

"I thought you spoke French. Mom said you did."

"French, Spanish, and a bit of Latin, for what it's worth."

"You could have talked to them in French."

"I could have. And they would remember me as the old gentleman from the States who spoke excellent Parisian French."

"That's bad?" Camilla climbed in and slammed the truck door, and Horace climbed in behind the wheel.

"If I talk to them in English, I'm one of endless hundreds of Americans that they have to put up with. Much less interesting, and much less notable. Come. We'll freshen up."

They pushed into the room, and Camilla tossed her backpack onto one of the beds and sat on it while Horace splashed water on his face. Camilla found the TV remote and flipped channels. Then she remembered her phone, and pulled it out and plugged in the charger.

"Need the bathroom?" Horace said, wiping his face with a towel. "Take a shower if you want."

"Nah."

"Okay, come with me, then. We have to switch vehicles. We need to get to the airport."

"The airport?"

"The truck is too conspicuous. We'll drop it off and switch to a rental. And we need to change some dollars."

It took a long time to make the switch, first parking the truck in a long-term space, then making their way to the rental, then driving back to the truck to transfer the cases. It was late in the evening when they finally parked in the old city and walked in for dinner.

Camilla was wide-eyed at the unfamiliar environment, steep, narrow streets flanked with shops. This was nothing like Virginia. Horace drew in the night air and almost laughed. He loved the place. It was among his favorite spots on Earth, and it was a beautiful night.

"Come," he said, taking Camilla's hand. "We have some time."

She stiffened, but didn't pull her hand away, and didn't ask, *time until what?*

He led her to a restaurant with tables on the sidewalk, and this time he spoke in French. The waiter smiled and led them to a café table under an umbrella. Horace and the waiter traded some comments and a laugh. Camilla didn't know any French, but she picked up some of the words. She heard *Montmagny*, and he said something about Michigan. The waiter bent down and said something she didn't understand, except for *mon petit chou*, which she knew meant something like, *my little darling*. She forced a scowling smile at the condescension. This little darling might like to punch him in the face, she mused.

"I told him I live in Montmagny," Horace told her, "and that your mother recently moved from Ontario to a suburb of Detroit, and sent you to stay with your grandfather for the summer while she got the new place set up."

"Detroit? I gotta live in Detroit?"

"Detroit's a fine city," Horace said. "Maybe I'll take you there some day. But listen, I assume the waiter knows enough English to get by, so we'll be judicious in what we say, all right?"

Camilla shrugged.

"You said you're in trouble. Do you want to talk about that, or shall we talk about Una?"

"I'm Una," Camilla said, frowning.

"Camilla, I can't call you Una. It will just be too damned confusing. If you and your friend want to be Una and Tyra, that's fine. But for the sake of clarity, can we just stick with Camilla for now?"

"Fine." Camilla looked away.

The waiter came back with a cocktail for Horace and a soda for Camilla, and Horace ordered in French.

"So am I gonna be eating snails, or something?"

"Pasta and sauce. I thought that was safe. And a salad for me. That okay?"

She nodded, and even almost smiled. "Yeah."

"So. Trouble. Let's hear it."

Camilla sighed out loud and looked away again. "It wasn't my fault. There's this kid who's always making fun of me. You know, 'cause I'm skinny, and I'm small. Like, the shortest girl in my class. Or maybe just because he's an asshole." She peered over at him, expecting a rebuke for the language, but her grandfather just tipped his head and rolled his hand, motioning for her to move along. "He's thirteen, and way bigger than me. He's always calling me stick girl, and saying rude things. You look like a boy, that kind of thing—except a lot more rude than that."

"Mm." Horace said. "All right. I've experienced teenaged boys. They can be trying."

"He's always trying to grab my chest, and stuff."

Horace's eyes narrowed. "Wait. That's not acceptable. Teasing is one thing ..."

"So I kept telling him to cut it out, but he wouldn't. So me and Tyra— I mean, my friend Sasha—we're going to the lake to go swimming, and Kevin comes along with his friend. Miles is okay, I guess, but when Kev is there, they're like this team. They have to show off for each other."

"Yes—teenaged boys. It's in the genetic code. Their brains are mal-formed at that age, you know. I believe there are studies."

"And Kevin comes over and grabs my top, and pulls me over."

Horace scowled and folded his arms. "That's assault, Camilla. Did you report it?"

"Nah. I smashed my forehead into his face and broke his nose."

Horace's eyebrows went up, and he stifled a smile. "Okay, then. Not the solution that jumped to mind. But all right. I'm with you."

"Yeah? Nobody else said that. Everyone freaked. I had to do all these sessions."

"Sessions?"

"Counselors and all. You know."

"But he assaulted you."

"Yeah, tell them that. God, I just wanted them to leave me alone. And then he comes at me *again*. Only this time it's Miles's father, too. They start hitting me."

"Whoa. Who is this *Miles's father*? An adult was hitting you?"

Camilla exhaled. "Miles got a dirt bike for his birthday. And to get him back for what happened at the beach, I took it out for a ride."

"A dirt bike."

"Yeah, you know, a motorcycle that you ride on trails."

"I know what a dirt bike is. I'd say you're young for that, but I saw what you rode in on. So you took his new bike for a ride. And this was a problem?"

"I kinda did it without his permission, okay? And it's not like I wrecked it or something. I brought it back. Eventually."

"And his father took exception."

"He hit me in the face. And Kevin started punching me."

Horace crossed his arms again, angry. "Did you report it this time? That kind of thing is absolutely not okay, Camilla. Especially for an adult. He could go to prison for that."

"What, like tattle on them?" She clicked her tongue. "How's that gonna help?"

"You could tell your counselor. Or your mother, for instance. They could file charges."

"Mom took off years ago," Camilla scowled and looked away.

"She ... oh." Horace stared, momentarily speechless.

"Foster family," Camilla spat. "And they're not gonna do anything except send me back."

"Oh, dear. Your mother took off? I'm sorry. I didn't know that."

"That's what she does. She runs away."

Horace nodded slowly. "And so, this boy and the other boy's father. I gather you addressed the situation in another way, then."

Camilla crunched her face into a scowl. "I kinda set Kevin's house on fire. And I stole the motorcycle from Miles's dad."

Horace's eyebrows went up again. "Well. Once again, a different level than I was thinking of."

"I'm so screwed." Camilla put her face in her hands. "They're gonna put me in juvie. I'll be in there forever. And Kev wasn't even there. Nobody was home. They were probably all watching the big fire like everybody else."

"The boy wasn't in the house." Horace breathed a sigh of relief. "All right. Wait, the *big fire*?"

"The sensei is gonna tell me I didn't get set. I didn't size up my opponent. God damn it. All I did was light some fires and run. It was useless." She looked over to find her grandfather staring at her. "Look, I needed a distraction. So I set the town dump on fire. What was I supposed to do?"

Horace locked eyes with the girl, and then glanced away and held up a hand. "All right." He softened his voice. "But Camilla, let's hold on a minute. We can't solve all the world's problems en masse, but maybe we can tease out a few strands to work on."

"What do you mean, tease out a few strands? They're gonna *arrest* me."

"In Québec City? I think we can keep the Virginia police at bay up here."

"It's not funny," the girl sneered. "I came to you 'cause there's no other place I can go."

"And that's fine," Horace said. "My voice was in your head because I've been thinking about you. I didn't realize I was actually talking to you—and I'm sorry to hear of the troubles you've been facing—but in spite of that, I'm very glad you came. But, do you know why we packed up and left my cabin?"

"You said someone might've followed me. Cops, or something, I guess. But I don't think anybody followed me. Not since Richmond."

Horace took a sip of his drink and leaned forward. "We left because I have a problem, too."

Camilla looked up.

"My problem is that I stole a whole lot of money from some very powerful, very bad people."

"Yeah?" Camilla said with a growing smile of solidarity.

"My first inclination, frankly, had been similar to yours. Kill the bastards. Burn their houses down with them inside, and put an end to the threat. Instead I went for the long game, and stole millions of dollars from them."

"Wow. Millions?"

"I gave some of it to the victims—the few I could find. The family members of my son's victims, I mean." Horace sighed.

"People my dad killed." Camilla hung her head again. "Mom told me he was a psycho. They're gonna put me in prison once I'm too old for juvie. I'm a psycho with a psycho for a father." She looked up, then suddenly hushed.

Horace noted that Camilla naturally went quiet as the waiter came over with the food. She sat up and even made an effort to smile, playing her role: a kid visiting her grandfather in Canada. Good instincts. The waiter smiled back and set a plate of pasta and sauce in front of her, and a large, fancy salad with different kinds of olives for Horace.

After asking Horace in French if they needed anything else, the waiter nodded and left. In spite of the sour mood, the girl wolfed down her food. She sat and ate without talking, and when her plate was empty, he caught her looking longingly at the remains of his salad.

"Take it," he said, pushing it over to her. "And Camilla, if you're anything like your namesake …"

She looked up from stuffing olives into her mouth. "What name's sake? Someone else in the family is named Camilla?" She spat the name with disdain.

"What's wrong with Camilla?" Horace smiled. "It's a fine name. A classy name. But no, I mean your new namesake. I mean Una. If you're anything like her, you aren't eager for an old man to give you advice. But let me just offer one little tidbit. Don't lump everything together. You have several problems, not one gigantic problem. So do I. For my part, I have a number of different, powerful people after me, and they'll kill me if they can."

The girl stopped eating and stared.

"And probably they were watching you in order to get to me. You see? And if they were following, then they will have found my little home by now—which means that just like you, I don't have a home to go back to. And it seems you're in trouble with the law, and your mother has run off. Quite a list we have, you and I. But we don't each have a single, huge problem. You have to split them up."

"They're gonna put me in jail. It's a huge problem." Camilla stared at him.

"Let's try this. Let's set aside the boy and the burned house, and the stolen motorcycle. And let's set aside the extremely powerful men who want me dead, and the cabin we can't go back to. And a few other things that I hope I didn't mention when I was *in your head*, as you say." He winked. "We can talk about those things later. For now, set them all aside. Let's try talking about something else, and see where it goes."

Camilla shrugged. "Like what?" She fell silent again as the waiter stepped up.

"Dessert?" Horace said, and they ordered. "For starters," he continued, the moment the waiter had stepped away, "there's this elephant in the room. Two of them, actually. First you said that I've been in your head for two months. And then you told me that you saw Una. Let's start with that one. You told me the first time you saw Una, she was in a jail cell, and then you mentioned the ship, and House Kamine. I know about the fight on the deck of the ship, but I don't know about this House Kamine."

"Yeah, mostly you're not there. It's better when you are, though. It lasts longer."

"It—what? Wait. Just exactly how often do you visit with Una? If you can call it visiting. You know what I mean."

"God, all the time."

"You just pop in whenever you want?"

"Sure. I mean, only for a little while. It's hard to hold onto it for long. Except if you're there, it's longer. Here, I'll show you." Camilla closed her eyes and stiffened.

Horace set down his drink and felt himself pulled in. Una and another young woman—the one from the ship—stood in a richly decorated room that looked like a parlor in a Victorian mansion. A hotel room, Horace guessed. An older woman stepped up and embraced Una. Horace recognized her from the ship as well. This was the woman who had clandestinely watched Una fight the boys on the ship, and who had later visited Una in her stateroom.

" … and I'll visit one day," the woman said.

"You'll be welcome. More than welcome! We'll do a fire dance for you," Una smiled. "And we'll keep your secrets, Gavina, and you'll keep ours. Isn't that also right? …"

The scene pulled away from him, and he found himself staring into young, dark eyes.

"That's Tansie with her," Camilla said. "And the other one is Gavina."

With a few rapid blinks, Horace worked to center himself. "Yes. All right. Of course."

"They're gonna poison the governor. I mean, not Una and Tansie. Adelaide's gonna do it. Una gave her a vial of something called conium macu-something."

"Conium maculatum?" Horace's eyebrows rose. "Una has prepared a tincture of poison hemlock?" He stared.

"Yeah, I guess. They're gonna poison the governor guy, and then Gavina will take over. It's really cool. God is Una smart. Maybe I should have used poison."

Horace shook his head. "Whoa. Slow down."

15. The Governor

"It can't be so," Abel insisted, standing by the table. "Begging your pardon. There are pavilions in the northlands, and perhaps a woman called Aideen. But it can't be my mother. She was killed in the slaughter. She's been dead these eighteen years."

"She escaped Nonney field," Una said. "Lord Neassan gave her and the others refuge, and when the old king was killed, his son Torin allowed them to stay. They call themselves The Hidden."

"She would have come for me."

"She thought you were dead. She flew to the north thinking her son was lost."

The young man's face adopted the safe, bland expression that all slaves at the Green Hills learned to adopt. "If you say so. It's not my place to disagree," he said.

Una sighed. "Tansie, could I ask a favor? Could you see if they have any brandy? Something nice. Not the house brandy. Ask at The Moonlight. I'd kill for a good brandy."

"I'd love one, too," Tansie said, and rose and left the room. She understood. Una wanted to try one-on-one.

When the door closed, Una dropped her voice to a conspiratorial low. "Abel, you're not to speak of what I'm about to tell you. Understand? Not to anyone."

Abel nodded with the neutral expression of a slave accepting an order.

"I know who this woman is because I trained under her as a child."

"But you're a Talla. You said she runs a Gatto house," he said. Then he retreated a step and winced. It wasn't a slave's place to question his master. "My apologies," he gasped. "I overstep."

Una blew out another long breath. "There are only a few people who know about my time before I came to my father's house."

"Before …"

"You'll find out eventually, so I might as well tell you. One is your mother. Also the gunners of Lord Torin."

"The triumvirate of the north. You've met the gunners?" His eyes narrowed skeptically.

"I met them when I was nine years old. I was a slave at an inn at Stockton Line called the Rose and Star."

"But, the daughter of Saor Tieg?"

"Please, I'll explain." Una held up a palm. "I came from overseas," she said, neatly blending fiction with fact, "and was taken to the inn and made a slave. This inn was part of the northland's underground transportation route. I'm speaking of the times before the overthrow of the dictator, mind you, when Lord Shular ruled the south. The gunners came to the inn and they found me there. And Gunner Ailmili, in her grace, released me from servitude and sent me to learn the art of the Gatto fighting style. I was sent to learn from Master Aideen, your mother, a refugee who escaped Nonney Field."

Abel pursed his lips, and then his face again turned to a mask. "As you say, Miss Una."

She caught him looking at the mark on her face. "You may have heard the story of my journey overseas to find my father. The part that's not widely told is that I didn't reach him directly." Una drew the token from her pocket and set it on the table, and Abel stared. "Do you know what this is?"

He nodded, and stared at it. "I know the Tynan mark." Abel looked at her. "It says you're their agent."

"And it says that I'm telling you the truth. They don't hand these out like candy. Do you remember a girl named Caterione? She must have been about your age."

"Caterione?" Abel stiffened. "There was a girl in our village by that name when I was little. She was my friend."

"Dark skin. Quite pretty. Annoyingly capable. Doesn't speak much, and doesn't smile a lot."

Abel shrugged. "My childhood friend was like that. As are many others, I'm sure."

"Her father and your mother were in the same regiment, and so their children—you and Caterione—played together."

"Yes, Miss Una. How do you know that?" The neutral expression started to break.

"I can fill in some things you wouldn't know. Such as, when Caterione's father was killed by the guards, Lord Torin sent the orphaned girl to the northlands, to be brought up and trained by a woman her father knew and respected, the Gatto fighter Aideen."

Abel glanced around, unsure what to fix on. "Caterione. And my mother?" He put a hand out to take hold of his chair. "You're not making stories?"

"Master Aideen runs the pavilion of The Hidden. And Caterione is there as well."

"But, I don't understand. You're a Talla. And you said Czabor told you about me. Did you know I was here? Did you purchase me from Lord Crinan at my mother's order?" Abel's face was pale.

"Sit. Please, sit. I'm a Talla. I don't take orders from The Hidden. I left there and found my father. Czabor told me about you, Abel. And it terrified me, because I hadn't been informed by the gunners. Frankly, Abel, I bought you because if it should be discovered that I found you and didn't do anything about it, the thrashing I would get from Master

Aideen would make the thrashing I once got from Caterione seem like a minor argument."

"I don't understand." Abel sat, confused and tense.

"And I don't have time to explain everything just now. But I need to get the main points across. It seems the northern triumvirate doesn't know you're here. Nor does your mother. I'm quite convinced of that. And as a simple matter of self-preservation—my preservation, if not yours—I have to take you with me. But finding you is not my mission, Abel. Do you know the woman Adelaide?"

Abel twitched, and looked into her eyes. His guard went up again. "Since we were small children. We rode the same slave ship here. We're bound to one another."

"Bound to one another? But she's the governor's mistress."

Abel turned his head and growled.

"You can speak freely, Abel. I'm no friend of the governor."

"The animal," he muttered. "I'd kill him if I could get close enough. I will one day. Just give me the means. What of Adelaide?"

"I'm here for her."

"For Adelaide?" Abel snapped out of his angry reverie. "You're here for Adelaide?" It seemed not to register. "Why?"

"She has a connection to the northlands, as well."

"A connection?"

"Again, I need to cut the story short. I need to get you both back to the Tynan north. All that's left is to figure how to fit the pieces together to make it work."

The young man stared. "Promise me, Talla. Promise me this isn't a trap," he hissed.

"Abel, I'm here to bring Adelaide home."

"Talla," he said, dropping his eyes.

Una sighed, and broke her stare. "I mean to prove that I am," she said, half to herself. "Talla, that is. But you're not to call me that."

Abel nodded. "I know someone who might help," he said. "Another who would like to see Adelaide out of harm's way. Do you know of the governor's wife? I mean his wife by marriage, Madame Ben Yett. Do you know of her?"

"Tansie and I had a very nice voyage on the *Margay* with Gavina. But I suppose she's hiding somewhere. I've inquired after her, and no one seems to know where she is."

"She's hiding, yes. Just across the hall."

"Here? Gavina is here in the hotel?" Una rose. "Bring me to her!"

Abel led her down the hall to the last room. A notice hung on the door that the resident was not to be disturbed. A tray of dishes had been left for a servant to carry away. He rapped a pattern on the door. A peephole cover was drawn back, then the deadbolt slid, and the door was pulled open.

"In, in," said a familiar voice. "Dear me, Abel, I've been so worried! I'd wondered if …" She halted as Una stepped in after him. She flashed a look of surprise; then instantly hid it with a well-rehearsed smile. "Una. You've come to visit the Green Hills? What a fine surprise."

"Abel, could you wait outside," Una said. "Bring Tansie when she returns."

When Abel led Tansie into the room a while later, Una and Gavina were seated on a divan, intently reviewing details.

"On the road, Tansie," Una said, looking up, "when you and I were approaching the town, Abel wasn't trying to escape, although I suppose his crime was worse than trying to escape. He was running messages from Gavina to military leaders in the region. Would they accept Gavina as the new governor, should Crinan be ousted?"

Tansie looked at Abel, and he smiled a thin confession.

"And the answer so far," Una continued, "has been favorable, except that none will agree to participate in executing the coups. Isn't that right, Gavina?"

"Just so. Their answer is that should some other means be found to oust my husband, they'll support me. Until then they'll bide their time. And Tansie dear," Gavina added, "I'd been working on some plans, but our clever friend Una has a much better idea than mine."

Una stifled a smile. "Horace will be disappointed. He keeps telling me to practice my long game."

"Horace?" Gavina asked.

"Oh, a mentor, of sorts." She shot Tansie a wink. "Horace is always encouraging me to slow down and learn the long con: Set everything up and then trick your opponent into a crushing loss. And he's probably right. If done properly, you can avoid the killing and blood, and defeat your opponent anyway." She looked up at the ceiling. "I'll practice it someday, I promise, Horace. But we don't have time, so it's going to be the short game."

"The short game," Tansie echoed, leaning forward with rapt attention.

"A tidy little short game, if it works." Gavina glowed with delight.

Una rose. "Abel, I need you to carry a note to Adelaide. They think you're my slave now, so they'll allow you to deliver it to the gate, at least. The message is that the new owner of The Moonlight wishes to make a gift to the governor in the form of a particularly stunning dress for the beautiful girl she saw him dining with. But it's to be a surprise for the governor. Understand? And so, could it be arranged for the girl to come to the village on some pretense, and to drop in at The Moonlight for a fitting?"

"Crinan will be informed," Abel said. "No message will reach Adelaide without being passed by him first."

Una shrugged. "And so he'll have two choices. Allow her to go, and see his prize decked out in the finest The Moonlight has to offer ..."

"Wouldn't that be a delightful slap in the face for his errant wife?" Gavina winked.

"... Or he can refuse, and she won't get the dress," Una said.

Abel nodded, and offered a conspiratorial smile. "Crinan will see your gift as an effort to win favor with him. I'd wager he'll allow it."

"And Tansie," Una continued, "you'll go back to The Moonlight. I'm sorry to make you run out twice. Thank them for the fine brandy, and tell them we need a carriage and horses, a driver, and gunmen for the road."

Tansie rose and headed for the door. "And do I meet you back in the room?"

"Before dinner. I have a task, as well. When we were walking along the road to the village and the road scouts leaped out of the woods at us, I spotted something. A plant my mentor calls conium maculatum. You might know it as hemlock."

"I've not heard that name for it," Gavina said, "but I know about hemlock. We've had enemies use it on arrow tips. Don't you have an interesting mentor."

"*Interesting* doesn't begin to cover it," Una grinned.

"And of course I have a job to do also, don't I?" Gavina added. "I need to practice at being the bereaved wife of the dead governor, pained by his early death, but silently judgmental. My eyes will take his corpse to task for having allowed his weaknesses to overcome him. And now it's for the badly used wife to stand up and assume the burden of his failed governorship and turn things right." She drew an arm to her forehead, and then tipped her head back and laughed.

"That's it exactly," Una said.

"Just one more thing, Una. I have something for you. And Tansie, before you leave, would you pour a round of that brandy for your friend and me?" Gavina rose and stepped over to a desk. "I thought of this on our trip, and had the papers drawn up so that I'd be prepared, should I wish to move forward." She pulled out a case and rifled through some papers. "Ah. Here it is. Something for you to bring back to the Western Shores, assuming we pull this off and tomorrow sees you on your way there." She handed Una a leather pouch with a document inside.

Una unfolded the paper and stood reading. Then open-mouthed, she looked over. "Gavina. Do you mean it?"

"By this time tomorrow I'll either be governor, dead, or exiled. The deal is off if it's the second or third. But if it's the first, then I mean every word. I've been planning this since we met on the *Margay*, although I didn't expect things to happen quite this quickly." She raised her glass.

Una picked up her glass and clinked it to Gavina's. "To a long friendship," she said, and they downed the brandy. Una rose and gave Gavina a smile and a parting hug, and she and Tansie left the room.

"What is it?" Tansie couldn't help asking, as they stepped back into their own room.

"A contract," Una grinned. "A contract to move the trade from the Green Hills up from the southerly ports of the Western Shores, and land all of it at Deadrise Bay."

"And that's good?"

Una laughed out loud. "If you were the person you're pretending to be—my friend Tyra—you'd have fainted dead away. Her father's fleet will have ten times the business. The port at Deadrise Bay will be cheek to jowl with ships."

"That's good, then." Tansie grinned.

"Oh, yes. And it means there's one more reason to make this work. Now we have Governor Crinan, Master Aideen, the Tynan gunners, Tyra, and my own father—and they'll all be gunning for *me*, if I fail."

Adelaide stepped up to The Moonlight flanked by the governor's soldiers, who displaced the doormen and stood guard outside. She was to have her fitting, but his men would see to it that she returned directly after.

Miss Kendall adopted a wide smile and took Adelaide's arm. "Come in, come in," she said.

A small crowd of attendants gathered, and Una watched them walk Adelaide around the shop, talking up the dresses. When several had been brought to the fancy fitting room, Una shooed everyone away, insisting on a one-on-one with the young consort of the governor. The staff complied without question, and she and Adelaide were finally alone.

"You're most generous, Miss Una," Adelaide said, as a matter of expected courtesy. "Do you wish me to try a particular dress?"

Una made a dismissive gesture. "Pick one." She dropped her voice to a whisper. "And take your time putting it on. We have a lot of ground to cover."

"Miss Una?"

"This one is lovely," Una added loudly, facing the door. She grabbed the first one on the rack. "Let's see this one first. Oh yes, this is a gem. I must see it on you." She leaned in. "Don't worry if doesn't fit, and I don't care what it looks like. But when I raise my hand like this," she waved, "I want you to say something about it, loud enough for them to hear. Do you follow?"

Adelaide froze, then looked around. She nodded, opting to go along with this new intrigue for the time being, whatever it was.

"Let's practice." Una waved her hand.

"Yes, I had my eye on this one," Adelaide said in a loud voice. "It might almost be overpowering though, don't you think?"

"You go behind the screen and put it on." Una waved at her to go put it on, but instead of waiting, she followed her behind the screen and sat. "This must seem terribly rude," she said. "I apologize. But we need to make every minute count. I need to tell you something that will startle you. Please don't cry out."

"Miss Una?"

"Call me Una. I'm not a baroness. You were taken from a home near the Western Shores. Your mother was killed. Your brother was not there."

Adelaide halted and stared. Her mouth dropped open.

"I'm sorry to be abrupt. I have to cover many years in a few minutes. Do you recognize this?" She pulled out the token with the three ruby cabochons.

Adelaide's mouth dropped even farther. But she quickly composed herself. "What is this? Why did you bring me here? The governor will punish me."

"Put the dress on. Say you're having trouble with the laces." Una waved her hand.

"Miss Una, I wonder if you might help with the ties," Adelaide nervously called out to the closed door, quickly shedding her dress and working to pull the new one on.

"I have a story to tell you. Please just listen. Get that dress on, and we'll take a turn around the shop for their benefit, and return to continue our conversation. All right? So let me get right to it. You know that the northern part of the lands overseas are under the rule of the Tynans."

Adelaide nodded. "I've read a history of the east, and have been told a little bit about the recent years."

"Then I assume you know that ten years ago the new triumvirate— the boy-king of the north and his gunners—killed the dictator of the southlands."

"Everyone knows that."

"The gunners sent me. The gunners of Tynan."

"The gunners!"

"Quiet, please. The walls are thin. Yes, the gunners. And Gunner Ailmili was not asking if I might kindly choose to come here. I was directed to do so. Although the mission is actually Gunner Rachanna's."

"The one who marked him," Adelaide hissed pulling the ties tight. "The one who cut the tyrant Shular."

"Good. You know that part of the story, too. Yes, Rachanna made her way into the dictator's pavilion and cut him before rushing out into the night and getting away. In that same story there's another important figure. One of her team on that mission would later become the gunner's personal guard. He doesn't carry a token in his pocket. He wears it on his collar."

"A commander."

"Exactly. I met another man who wears the mark of Tynan on his collar. And let me assure you, that little bit of metal and stone is both sword and shield. No one dares accost a commander of the northern triumvirate." Una glanced at the door. "Come. We'll show this one, and I'll say that I'd like to see another."

Adelaide plastered on a strained smile and stepped out for the benefit of Miss Kendall and the attendants. They gushed and glowed, and Una gave them a minute, and then proposed trying another.

Safely behind closed doors again, Adelaide grabbed a random dress and started to change. She understood the game now.

"This other man who wears the mark of Tynan, along with one of the generals of the northlands, gave me my orders for this trip," Una continued. "I was to sail to Ben Attallach to retrieve a person sold into slavery years ago, and only recently discovered. This person is of great interest to Gunner Rachanna. For, you see, the brother of this person I'm to retrieve is the gunner's man. I'm speaking of the gunner Rachanna's private sentry, the very man who went on that mission to Shular's pavilion with her."

"You're here to retrieve a slave whose brother is the private sentry of the lord's gunner?" Adelaide asked, with a note of wonder. "Is he a slave in the Green Hills, then? Am I to help you get to him? I'll do what I can. ..."

"He's not a slave in the Green Hills. *She* is. The gunner's inner guard is Commander Riley. Your brother."

Adelaide spun around and stumbled, and Una caught her arm. Adelaide fixed a stare and stopped talking.

"Another walk outside. I'm sorry. Can you manage it?"

A nod of her head was all she could manage, but Adelaide forced the familiar smile, and they showed the second dress to more cooing and praise.

Safely back in the dressing room, Adelaide practically ripped the dress off, and snatched up another. She turned to Una, tears in her eyes. "My brother? Do you mean it? Riley is alive?"

"He's not merely alive, Adelaide. Do you follow what I'm saying? He's a high commander to the Tynan triumvirate. The gunner wants her man's sister returned. Gunner Rachanna wants this mission to end with you stepping through the door to greet her commander, your brother."

It took three more dresses to get through the whole story, and to repeat parts of it, and to move Adelaide from astonishment to muddle-headed emotional breakdown, and finally to a state of mind suitable for planning. But they kept up the ruse, and neither Miss Kendall nor the attendants seemed to sense anything out of the ordinary. Adelaide was practiced at pretending. A few remarked that the young slave woman seemed a bit emotional, but others pointed out that it wasn't every young slave who got fitted at The Moonlight.

Una finally picked the dress she thought Miss Kendall seemed to prefer. "You'll box it up for her then, once the alterations are made?" Una said, polishing off the ruse. "I can't wait to see her wear it. If you hear tell that the governor will be visiting the hotel again, please let me know."

Miss Kendall nodded and smiled.

Una saw Adelaide to the door of The Moonlight, and the soldiers moved in. A woman servant stepped forward and frisked Adelaide thoroughly.

"What might she be hiding?" Una snapped with a scowl. "Is this entirely necessary?"

But Adelaide stood and allowed the search without responding. The soldiers moved to the side and motioned for her to accompany them.

"Well, then, Adelaide," Una said, stepping forward and offering her hands before the soldiers could whisk the girl away, "it's been a lovely afternoon. I hope to see you again in The Moonlight soon." She took Adelaide's hands in her own, and palmed her a small glass vial.

"Thank you. I'd like that," Adelaide said with a smile.

The soldiers led her to the carriage, and Una offered a final, friendly wave, and stepped back into the shop.

Now it was back to the hotel to meet Tansie, a nip of brandy before dinner, and a quiet meal.

16. The Ace

"Let me see if I understand this," Horace said. He had ordered coffee and brandy for himself and another soda for Camilla, and they were sipping them slowly. They were lingering, dessert long over, and the waiter had started to look impatient. "You can visit with Una any time."

"Not *any* time, but usually," Camilla said, with a shrug of her shoulders. "When I hear you in my head I can hold on for longer."

"And you pick up on me talking to you and to Una."

She shrugged again. "It's not like hearing somebody talking. It's like you said before. The ideas come into my head, and I can tell it's you. Or her."

"Right, right," Horace nodded. "Do you speak to Una?"

"Nah." Camilla looked away. "I can't say anything. I dunno how to do that. I'm just watching."

"And how many times have you sensed me there?"

"That fight on the ship, and then in the cabin on the ship. Then when those two scouts or whatever they're called ran at them on the road. And that place with the assassins. The other times it was just me."

Horace scratched his chin. "Fascinating. I had thought Una might have been calling to me, that she was driving, so to speak. You follow? But maybe that's not quite right. I wonder if for me to connect with her now requires the token—and you."

"What do you mean, *the token*?"

"I suppose you don't know about that." Horace sighed and looked away. "It's a painful subject, Camilla. This part involves your father."

"I don't want to talk about him," Camilla scowled.

"We don't have to." Horace put up a palm. "All you need to know is that he could connect with people, too. Differently than you and I, I suppose. But I think he formed the connection to Una. He started it all. The token is an object that directs you to connect to something, Camilla. At least, that's the kind I mean. The token in this case is a stone. Just an old rock. It's an object from my son that represents his connection to Una. I suppose you could think of it as a souvenir—except that he's gone now, and the connection is still there through me. And more through you, it seems."

"Everyone thinks it's crap," Camilla growled. "Sasha is the only one who believes me. And I'm not sure she even really does. I tried to tell my foster mom about it, and she got all nervous, and then I heard her whispering with my foster dad. Probably planning to send me back."

Horace pushed back his chair. "I want to show you something. You up for a walk?"

Camilla shrugged, took a final drink of her soda, and followed. They walked a long way, out onto an enormous wooden terrace and up the stairs of the Governor's Promenade. The stairs and walkways led up and up, until finally they reached the stone fortifications looking over the old city and the water.

"You see that?" Horace swept his arm out at the breathtaking view. "This place is hundreds of years old. Now imagine it's 1690, and the New Englanders are fighting the French. The French are up here looking down, and the ships of the Massachusetts Bay colony are down there, the soldiers looking up."

"This is really cool," Camilla said. Then she shivered as the wind picked up.

"It is, isn't it? Quite impressive to be looking down from the same place. Now imagine all the people between then and now who have stood here looking down, or who have stood down there looking up."

"Lots of 'em."

Horace smiled. "Lots, yes. Countless thousands of people, Camilla. And that few hundred years is just a little snippet. Now imagine endless hundreds of intervals of a few hundred years, stretching back from 1690 and forward from now. Pick a random sample."

"What do you mean?" Camilla clutched her arms across her front.

"Come, you're cold. Let's go back. I know a place for a nightcap."

She clicked her tongue. "A nightcap? I'm twelve."

"Yes," Horace laughed, "you are, aren't you. At the moment. We'll get you an ice cream soda then, all right?" He led her back to the walkway, and they descended, taking their time. "What I mean is, think of a random block of time. Earlier, later … picture that time in your mind. What do you suppose is here?"

"The fort would last a long time. It's all stone."

"Was it here another three hundred years ago? Let's say, in 1390?"

"How would I know?" Camilla said, and then stopped. "Wait. No, it couldn't have been. We read about Samuel de Champlain in history class. That wasn't until sixteen-something. So the fort wouldn't be here in the 1300s."

"Very good, very good. So consider your random time segment. Suppose you're looking at a segment a thousand years from now. Is the fort here?"

"I dunno. Maybe not. I mean, a bunch of guys had to build it. A bunch of guys could take it down."

"Exactly. Or there could be earthquakes, or floods. Maybe famine. Disease. Maybe nobody is here."

"That's depressing," Camilla said. "Maybe there's super cool people here. Maybe Una's here."

Horace stopped and raised a palm, and Camilla instinctively high-fived him. "Exactly!" he said. "I have no idea if she's been here. She could be anywhere. But she could also be any-when. That's my point."

"Any-when?"

"Any time," Horace said. "Before us or after us. You and I, we're here right now. And we're connected, we two, not just by being in the same place at the same time, and not just by the token. Una's not here just now. But we're connected, we three."

"What, like she's my great grandmother, or something?" Camilla stopped and leaned on the rail, looking out over the water. Horace put an arm around her shoulder, and she let him. She smiled, even. She did feel connected for once. She liked it.

"It might be many, many greats. Great times a power of ten. Who knows? But I don't think we're looking back. It's just my sense of it. I don't know for sure. But I think we're looking forward. She's not your great-something-grandmother, Camilla. You're hers."

Camilla looked up at him, and her jaw dropped. "Yeah? You think so? Wow. That's so incredibly cool."

"These connections, Camilla, for me they come and go. Maybe because I'm old. Maybe you see more of our Una because you're young. Or maybe it's a fleeting connection for both of us. Who knows? But whatever the case, each time you see her—and each time you see her make a decision about what to do—think about your place on the timeline. If I'm right, then you come before. Look at her, and think about what you want to do."

She leaned her head against him, and suddenly he felt her sobbing. "God, I've screwed everything up. I'm gonna let Una down."

Horace waited, leaving her to think about it and cry. He smiled to himself, and patted her on the shoulder. He had intended to describe a sense of wonder and excitement at the grand sweep of time—not to make a little girl cry—but her tears in this context raised his spirits considerably. This wasn't a psychopath sobbing on his shoulder. There was a chance for his granddaughter. A good chance.

When she stopped sniffling and wiped her eyes, he leaned in close. "Well," he said, "come. Let's head back. It's been quite a day. Why don't you tell me about what you've seen of our Una while we walk back?"

Camilla nodded, still sniffling. "Okay," she said, working to put a brave face on. "So you know about the governor. Una's plan, I mean. With Gavina and Abel. ..."

They ambled back down, Horace's eyebrows rising repeatedly as his little granddaughter trotted out the story of Una's plan to assassinate the man called Crinan and abscond with the slaves. He listened and didn't ask questions, although he had plenty. It was a good story, and it was making her feel better to tell it. He kept quiet and let her talk.

Finally they reached the bottom of the promenade and headed back onto the old city roads. As they approached groups of people, Camilla instinctively stopped talking. Horace patted her shoulder and they walked along quietly. They both had a lot to think about, and neither wanted to share their stories with strangers.

Twice he turned his head, thinking he'd seen something across the street, a figure who seemed to be trailing along behind them. But there were plenty of people walking around. Then he saw it a third time, and started to watch for it. He took a few turns down streets, and the figure turned as well, following.

"Camilla," he said in a low tone, "what do you have with you?"

"You mean like money?"

"Anything. In your pockets. A phone, or keys, or anything. What do you have on you?"

She peered up at him as he picked up the pace. They headed toward a group of people gathered by a tour bus, and stepped among the group, pretending they were part of the tour. Horace scanned across the street, trying to pick out their pursuer.

"I left my phone at the hotel. I had to charge it. I've got half a pack of gum. You want a piece?"

"Your phone? Damn it. What else?" He pulled her through the group and around the end of the bus, and hurried her across the street toward a row of shops that were still open for the late evening tourists.

"Um, a little money. Forty bucks. And some mints." She tensed, realizing that something was wrong.

"No electronics? No pads or pods, or what have you?"

"I can't afford that stuff," Camilla said. "All I ever got was the phone, and it's Mack's old one."

"Did you buy the gum or the mints before you left home or after?"

"After. Why? Is there some kind of problem? It's just gum and mints."

Horace ducked into a shop. It was cramped, narrow passages between racks filled with key chains, stuffed animals, snow globes, shot glasses and other trinkets. Scanning the wares, Horace found a rack of tee shirts and grabbed one, a white cotton tee with the Canadian flag embroidered in red on the back. From a rack below he snatched a pair of white shorts with a draw string and a giant red maple leaf on the backside.

"Just these," he said to the clerk, handing over some bills. Horace took Camilla's hand and pulled her back outside.

"Where are we going? What's going on?"

"Someone's following us."

"What?" Camilla hissed. "And you're shopping? Jesus!"

"Improvising. I can only spot one, but there are probably more. "In there." He nodded at an alley between the shops. There was a metal gate, but the lock had been broken. It sat slightly ajar. The alley was used as a shortcut to the apartments in back, Horace figured. "Come on." They pushed through and he shut the gate behind them and hurried her along. "Fast!"

They ran, Horace scanning as he went. "Wait. Stop a minute." Tucked behind a drain pipe were some remnants of an old repair, ends of 2x4s and scraps of plywood. Horace pulled out a two-foot length of 2x4 and rose. "Okay, go!"

They hurried to the end, Horace peering back repeatedly.

"Hide in the stairwell." He pointed to an old wooden staircase on the back of the building. Below it, brick steps led down to a lower level.

Camilla hurried over and ducked down, peering out wide-eyed from the darkened stairwell. Not even a minute passed before a shadow darkened the narrow slot of light from the alley. Camilla froze, and Horace flattened himself to the corner of the building, holding the scrap of lumber like a bat.

They both watched the shadow moving, and then heard the figure approach. It paused at the end of the alley and stepped out. Horace's arm was ready, and he swung. Camilla clamped a hand over her mouth as the man crumpled to the ground. She turned to bolt.

"Camilla!" Horace commanded, and the girl froze. "Come here."

He knelt down, ready for another swing if needed, and rifled through the man's pockets, pulling out a wallet, a phone, and a handheld tracking device. He crushed the phone and the hand-held under his foot. Camilla crept up and stared as he stuffed the wallet into his pocket.

"Let's go. Quickly, now." Horace grabbed her hand.

They rushed along the back of the buildings and circled to the main street. He led her away from the heart of the old city. When he reached the street where he had parked the car, he pulled her into a dark entryway. Camilla shivered, and clutched her arms across her front.

"You're cold?" he said, absentmindedly.

"I'm fine. Fine," she stuttered. "I'm okay."

"Try to relax. We'll get out of this. Things never go exactly as planned. And so the surprise is on us this time." Horace pulled the Sig out of his jacket pocket, flipped off the safety, and racked the slide. "So we adapt. Calm down, and stay right behind me. Let's go."

They walked at an over-fast clip down the sidewalk, and as they approached the car, Horace pushed her head down, and they ducked and ran the last stretch in a crouch.

"Get in back," he quietly ordered, opening the doors on the curb. "And keep down."

She jumped in, and he slid behind the wheel. He checked the headlight control and turned it to the off position, and then started the car and pulled away from the curb. He turned down the first side street and accelerated, lights off. It wasn't until he had gone around the block and was merging onto a main road out of the city that he clicked the lights on.

"Camilla," he said, turning to look at the figure peering between the seats, "get your clothes off."

"My clothes? What are you talking about?"

"They've got a tag on you. Probably in your shoes, but we don't have time to search for it. Just get changed. Put these on." He tossed the shirt and shorts over his shoulder.

"But … oh, Jesus! My clothes? They're tracking me?"

He heard the panic in her voice. "Stay with me, Camilla. I need you to focus. There's probably a car on the perimeter, and maybe two. We're not out of the woods yet. So get moving. Get changed. It'll be fine."

"Oh, god," Camilla choked, tugging her boots off.

He sped forward, and sure enough, a black convertible with the top down pulled away from the curb and accelerated. High beams blared through the rear windshield.

"Keep down!" Horace barked. "And hurry!"

"Jesus, are they gonna shoot us?" Camilla whined.

"Just get changed, fast." He hit the gas and they rocketed forward. "And don't panic. I've got this. I do cars, Camilla. Neassan uses blades, and Una goes for hand-to-hand, right? And you with that Kevin boy. For me it's guns and cars. My stock-in-trade."

In the back seat, Camilla was hurled back, and then ducked down behind the seat. "God, I'm so stupid! They tagged my stuff? This is all my fault!"

"No it's not, Camilla." Horace took a turn, fast, and Camilla slammed against the door. "It's entirely my fault. They're not after you. But we're in the middle of it now. We have to play this out."

Horace knew the streets of Québec City, and he knew a few tricks for losing a tail. He slowed at a traffic light, and just as it turned red, he floored it and turned the wrong way down a one-way street. A horn blared and a driver swerved, and a moment later Horace spun the wheel and careened down another side street, this time going the proper direction. He turned again, then rolled back onto the main road and floored it. They shot forward, the girl tumbling around behind him.

"Jesus Christ!" Camilla cursed.

"Needed to give us a little room. You ready?"

"I'm bouncing around like a goddamned playground ball. It's a little hard to change."

"They'll be back on us in ten seconds." He raced down the road. "Now? You ready now?"

"Shit," the girl cursed. "Goddammit."

Horace accelerated hard as the car chasing them pulled back into the road behind them and raced forward. "This next light, Camilla. I need you up here and buckled in."

"I'm not ready."

"Quickly! Just get up here. I don't care if you're ready. There's no airbag back there." He pushed a button, and the driver's window went down. Warm wind whipped in. "Now!"

"Oh, Jesus." She snatched up the souvenir tee shirt and struggled to pull it on, and clambered over the console and into the passenger seat, tugging at the hem of the shirt and squealing as the collar slid down her arm. "Don't look!"

"Attention's not on you at the moment. Get your seat belt on and cross your arms across your front." He looked in the rearview. "Relax your muscles. Be like jelly."

The convertible chasing them was gaining fast, and someone was rising on the passenger side pointing a gun.

Just before the intersection, Horace stomped on the brakes, screeching and shuddering to a stop. The car chasing them slammed into them from behind. Glass shattered, metal grated, and something big hit the rear windshield and went over the top of the car. A figure tumbled down and rolled off the hood, his gun clattering across the pavement.

Inside the airbags deployed, and in the moment of blind confusion that followed, Horace found himself thinking about the opacity of the air bag material, and how it provided a benefit at times like this, preventing a little girl from seeing the body of a man roll into the road in front of them.

He shoved the deflating bag down, got the car in gear and struggled to turn the wheel. As the car bucked and pulled to separate from the one crumpled into its rear, Horace leaned out and fired a full magazine into the front and side of the stopped car behind him. He sped down the side road as cars in all directions slowed and stopped.

"You okay?" Next to him, Camilla was frozen, pressed back against the seat with the air bag half obscuring her. He leaned over and put an arm on the girl's shoulder. "Camilla. Are you all right?"

Camilla uttered a keening laugh. "I have no fucking idea."

"That'll do." Horace already had his pocket knife out, and was slicing off the airbag. "Now get in back again. Get your clothes together. Next step is to toss them into another vehicle. You understand?"

She nodded, shoving at the airbag and struggling to get her seatbelt off. "So they'll follow someone else," she said, her voice cracking.

"Exactly. A pickup truck will do, or a parked car with the window open. We can't be choosy. Get back there and wait for my word."

Shaking, she climbed back over the console.

He pulled through a set of lights, thankful that the car was still running after the impact, and especially thankful that the rear windows went down when he pushed the buttons. That would make the next step a lot easier. At the next intersection they had some luck. An old, noisy pickup truck was already waiting at the light. Horace pulled into the turning lane next to it.

"When the light changes, I'll hit the horn and wave like I'm a friend. You toss the clothes into the back of the truck."

Camilla nodded, shaking.

"Get everything."

The light turned, he honked and waved, and the man in the truck turned and waved back—and didn't notice the girl in the back seat of the car tossing things into the bed of his truck. Horace took the turn and they parted ways, and he reached back and patted Camilla's arm.

"Nice work. Now we need to make a little more time."

He sped up and raced down the street, feeling the car pulling hard to one side and hoping it wouldn't die before he found a replacement. His knowledge of the local streets helped once more. He went through several turns, and came to an access road that led to a parking area down by the docks. He identified a model of sedan that would do, and pulled up next to it.

"Wait in the car. There's broken glass, and you don't have shoes," Horace said.

"No shit. I have a goddamned extra-large tee shirt, and gigantic shorts," Camilla said. "Do I look extra large to you?"

Horace smiled. Humor was good at times like this. "I was in a hurry. Didn't think to check the size."

She climbed into the passenger seat again and watched mutely. The terror of the crash was pushed away as she looked in wonder at another talent of her grandfather's. In seconds he had gotten into the parked car, and was in the front seat popping the trunk.

Their pursuer's windshield had splattered over the back of their car, and glass pellets scattered to the pavement as he wrenched the trunk open.

Horace quickly transferred everything, lugging the cases and packing them into the new car. He closed the trunk and came around. Without asking, he swept Camilla up and carried the barefoot girl over, and deposited her on the passenger seat. Then he ran around and climbed in behind the wheel. "Ready?"

She offered a surreal grin. "Where'd you learn to do that?" she said, as he started to work on hot-wiring the car.

"To carry you? I'm a grandfather. I've carried kids before."

"What? No, stupid. Where'd you learn to hot-wire cars?"

"Oh," he grinned. "I told you. Cars and guns. My strong suit." In moments they were pulling away in their new ride. "Now, Camilla, you're okay? Nothing hurts?"

"I feel like an idiot in this dumb shirt, but aside from that, I'm fine." She smirked, holding the collar together at her neck and tugging at the hem, which reached almost to her knees.

"I'm sorry. I just grabbed the first thing I found." He looked at her, and tipped his head. "Oh dear."

"You might've grabbed something like, say, a dress. This is like wearing a tent," Camilla giggled nervously.

"Sorry," Horace repeated.

"Forget it. I just look like a complete idiot, is all."

Horace pulled onto the main road and headed back to the old city.

"Hold on," Camilla said, her voice tightening again. "We're going back? But we gotta get out of here!" She peered up and down the street staring at the people, certain each one was another pursuer.

"Yes we do. But we'll cool our heels and get out of here a little later, when there are fewer eyes out for us."

He parked and looked over. Camilla was shaking, terrified. He got out and came around to her door. "No shoes. Come on."

"Yeah, no shoes," she said blandly, with a strained smile.

"And we need to look like we're not the people they're looking for. Hop up and pretend you're asleep."

She nodded and raised her arms; and he picked her up and wrapped an arm under her backside and strolled up the street carrying her on his hip as if she were a small child.

"It'll work," Horace said. To people passing by she would look like a kid in a nightgown, too tired to walk on her own.

Camilla leaned on him and wrapped her arms around his neck, playing the sleeping child. And then she pulled tight and hugged him, and shuddered. "So that's not all of them?"

"No."

"You can get the rest of them? Like you did with Juliette?"

Horace's eyebrows went up. "You saw that? Camilla, aren't you full of surprises." Horace felt her rapid heartbeat, and felt a pang of emotion. He was holding his granddaughter, and she was clinging to him, pressed to his shoulder, seeking comfort and safety. He wrapped his free hand onto the back of her head and gently caressed her. "I don't need to get them, honey. I just need to get them off our trail."

"You can get them off our trail?"

"You just watch me," he said, and The Ace headed for the rendezvous.

17. Cloaked in Gray

"So I'm to sit and wait?" Gavina raised her eyebrows. "Not a strength of mine, to be sure." She rose and started pacing. "Will it work? Will this finally be the end of my husband's horrible governorship?"

"We'll know soon." Una rose as well. "And if it does work, I won't see you again. Will you send word to me on the Western Shores?"

"It's a promise." Gavina gave her a hug. "And I'll visit one day."

"You'll be welcome. More than welcome! We'll do a fire dance for you. And we'll keep your secrets, Gavina, and you'll keep ours. Isn't that also right?"

"That's exactly right," Gavina winked.

Una and Tansie took another stroll to The Moonlight, and met in private with Miss Kendall. "Something calls my attention overseas," Una told her.

"So soon?" The woman's eyebrows went up. "But you arrived such a short time ago."

"I'm sure I can count on you to manage things. You will, won't you? It's the gunner's wish."

"Of course." Miss Kendall smiled, delighted. It seemed her position was secure.

"I prefer to leave without fanfare. But I don't want to be rude. Would you help me draft a few letters? I'd like to send my thanks to Governor Crinan and a note to Adelaide. And maybe a note for Gavina, for whenever she might arrive." Una offered a friendly smile, and silently nodded to Horace in her head. *Here's your long game*, she projected. The letters would help dampen any speculation that the exodus of the new owner of The Moonlight might be connected to the events about to take place. That could be important in coming years, as new arrangements were forged between the Green Hills and the Western Shores.

A man in a black gi slid around to a lower entrance and glided up the stairs. The soldier guarding the door moved aside and allowed him to step into the foyer. This was a man trained in the east, back in the days of the powerful tyrant Shular. He was one of the notorious black-gis, the elite fighters of that old regime. Now he served in the court of Lord Crinan.

He rapped lightly on the door of Crinan's inner quarters and stepped in. "Lord," he said.

Crinan lounged on a divan, sipping a cocktail. He looked up. "Dorren. Back so soon?"

"Things moved quickly, lord. The Talla hides in the woods at the rear entrance."

"Does she? Outside the manor? Shall we invite her in?" Crinan swung his legs around and sat up. "And did she meet with my slave?"

"She did, master. At the shop called The Moonlight, as you had described. They met inside, and then Adelaide emerged and they parted."

"And what do you say of this meeting?" Crinan scowled.

"The Talla, lord, I can't say for certain, but I believe she palmed something to your slave."

"Don't they work swiftly, indeed. One day the young Talla shows up and purchases a slave, and the next she's conspiring with another. So you say she slipped something to my Adelaide."

"Too small to be an edged weapon, unless it be a tiny blade. And there would be no need to pass her a message, unless there's another party involved that we've not identified. They had ample time to talk. No, it's something else."

"Something else," Crinan repeated. He rose, and strode over to a window. "And what's your guess? What has our young Talla slipped to my slave? An aphrodisiac might be useful." He chuckled malevolently. "My Adelaide might benefit from that. An icy thing she is, lately. Has me wondering why I keep her."

Dorren offered a neutral nod. "There are weapons as powerful as a blade that come in small sizes."

"Yes there are indeed. Well then, Dorren, we'll see what little gift my Adelaide brings to me. Send for her. You may go."

Adelaide's heart was pounding as she ascended the staircase. Why was she so nervous? She had climbed these stairs countless times. A guard stood at Governor Crinan's door as usual. He stiffened into something resembling attention, but his expression was a leer, not the impassive look a guard ought to have.

"Int'resting night," he said. "Do you know what's happening in there? Tell me. It's got to be good."

She halted. "What's happening in there?" she repeated. "I beg your pardon?"

"The gov ain't his usual sullen self. What's it about, girl? Ain't like the governor to be all grinning."

"What are you talking about?"

"The scowl's like home. You see that, and you know all's well. Quiet night standing my post, and off I go for a sleep. Dark clouds on his face means shouting and maybe a cleanup. Sometimes takes fetching a few extra hands to get things in order. But shit-eatin' grins? Cat's got a mouse?"

Adelaide realized she was standing in her robe, mouth agape, and she folded her arms across her front. "What are you on about?" she said, hoping the tremor in her voice wasn't noticeable. "Am I to go in or not?"

The soldier gave her a wide grin, rapped twice on the door, and stepped aside with a dramatic wave of his arm. "By all means. You go on in. Can't wait to see what comes next."

Her heart pounded, but it was too late to change plans. She had to make it work. Lifting her chin, she stepped into the room. The governor was standing by the window looking out, and didn't turn as she entered. She sighed, stepped over to the divan, and untied her robe. She pulled it off and draped it over the back the way he liked it. Tonight she wore the blue silk. It was his favorite. She hoped it would lend her an edge, an added distraction. Eying a decanter half filled with grain alcohol on a table in the corner, she slipped her hand into a delicate silk pocket and fingered the glass vial. All she needed to do was to pour him a drink and get the liquid into it. Or get it into the decanter.

"Well, pretty darling," Crinan said, turning, "that old thing again?" He waved a dismissive hand at her choice of lingerie.

Adelaide blanched. "Lord? But I thought ..."

"You thought what? That what's pleasing once is pleasing in infinite number of times? Nature doesn't bear it out. With gold, perhaps," he laughed. "And sunshine, and certain carnal passions." He stepped closer, putting himself between her and the liquor table. "And wine, grain spirits, laudanum ... these things never lose their luster. But fashion, my dear. Fashion is a fleeting thing."

"Lord?" she said. The guard had been right. Something was off. This was not the Crinan she knew, all too eager to leap into bed, do the deed fast and rough, and then lounge for hours talking about himself. Was she discovered? Had the plan been detected?

"Were I to adopt the garb of my father and take a stroll in the courtyard, the people would think me a relic," Crinan continued. "*Past his time, that Crinan. Look at him, tedious and old-fashioned.* And then their eyes would turn to see if they might discover someone fresh."

"Lord, shall I pick another?" Adelaide glanced at the door.

Crinan laughed. "It so happens that I have something fresh. You had your visit to The Moonlight, and so did I."

Adelaide stiffened.

"Oh, come now. I know all about the gift from the proprietress. A fine gesture, don't you think, to fit my Adelaide out in the best The Moonlight has to offer? I'm sure it's stunning. But a dress, that's for the world to see. I thought, what about Crinan? Why not a gift just for Crinan? And so my man made a visit to The Moonlight as well, to pick up a little something else."

"You picked up something ..." Adelaide lost focus. This was wrong, unfamiliar. She absentmindedly put her hand over the pocket that held the vial.

"Take that thing off. Throw it in the bin." Crinan nodded at a wicker basket by the door. "Put this on instead." He drew a box from the window-sill and tossed it to her.

Adelaide's eyes flashed from the waste bin to the liquor table, and then to the box in her hands. Panicking, she moved to the liquor table and set the box on it, and began to open the tie. She didn't look back. Surely he was staring at her, and if she were to turn and look, she would lose the last shred of composure. She opened the box and drew out a black silk shift. It was exquisite, and must have cost a lot. Adelaide was struck by the irony: It would be a handsome gift, were it offered to a willing partner. But to her it was a slap in the face, a rebuke.

She lifted the shift as if appraising it—and then hands clamped onto her from behind. She cried out as one arm wrapped around her throat, pulling her head back, and another patted her down. Crinan's hand latched onto the small, hard item in her pocket. He stuffed his hand in and wrenched it out, ripping the pocket half off.

"Is this for me?" he said, pushing her away and holding the vial up to the light. "What is it?"

"It's ... Lord ... but ..." she stuttered.

Crinan set the vial on the table by the decanter, and then whirled around and struck her hard across the face. Adelaide reeled back and tumbled to the floor. Crinan stepped over her, hauled her up by her collar, and punched her in the face. She slammed against the wall and slid to floor, unconscious.

"The servants' entrance," Una pointed. "She'll come out of that door?"

Abel nodded, peering over the stone wall they hid behind. "Yes, Miss Una. That's the plan."

"Una. Just Una."

"Apologies. It's a habit."

"We'll work to break you of that. You're not a slave any longer, Abel. You're ..." She halted as his rapid tap on her shoulder signaled danger. Una turned. "Where?" she whispered.

Abel had dropped to a low fighting stance, and Una followed suit. She saw them too, five looming shadows in the dusk.

"Black-gis?" Una hissed. "Here?"

"Some fled here when the eastern lord was slain. Dorren is their master."

"Damn it." She looked around. "Spoil the scene. How do I do that now, Horace?" she growled.

There wasn't time to wait for an answer. The shadows closed in, and all at once the quiet was broken by fighting cries.

"Together, then separate!" Una ordered, praying that Czabor hadn't exaggerated Abel's level of training. This was one of the simpler tactics practiced in Tallach pavilions, to attack as a team in hopes of taking out one or two opponents quickly, then to separate and draw the remaining attackers apart and fight them one-on-one. But Una could see that it would be more than one-on-one in this case, even if the initial moves were successful.

They rushed forward, Abel copying each move Una made, so that to an observer it might seem that he was her shadow. Una cut in, faked a thrust, and as her adversary blocked, she whipped an arm to the side. Abel obeyed and copied, causing the next attacker to pull back, and in the space it created, Una closed and rabbit-punched the first man, catching just the right spot at the base of his skull. The black-gi collapsed.

Una yielded the lead to Abel. The second man was his. Abel darted forward, blocking blows and causing the man to take another step backward—and to take his attention away from Una for just the slightest moment. It was all she needed. She leveled a vicious kick to the attacker's kidneys, and the man cried out and bent forward. Abel finished him with a two-fisted blow to the head.

But three more were on them, and there were no clever moves to shake them. Abel split off from Una, but the next man was much more skilled. The black-gi thrust and blocked, and quickly moved in and punched Abel in the throat, taking his wind away. Abel dropped to the ground, grabbing his neck. Black-gis came at Una from both sides. And while she landed some punishing hits—one of the men would nurse a broken jaw—they overtook her quickly. She was thrown to the ground and pinned.

"And the slave?" A black-gi asked, as Una was flipped over and her wrists bound.

"Never mind the slave. The Talla is our mark. Bind her. Make her silent."

She was tied and gagged, and then something struck her in the head, and she went out.

Pain. Pain everywhere. Adelaide lay on her back on a cold, hard floor. Her head throbbed, and she tasted blood. Breathing in and out, she waited for her head to clear enough that she could tell up from down. She rolled over and rose to her hands and knees, and then sat. She felt blood on the back of her head. What had happened?

As the whirling gradually receded, she looked around. A dim light from a barred opening lit another shape on the floor. She took deeper breaths, trying to clear her vision, and crawled over to the crumpled heap. Then she recognized the expensive Tallach outfit.

"Una? Oh, no," she muttered, and slumped to the floor.

It seemed to be many hours later, but neither was clearheaded enough to count the time. They sat leaning against the stone wall of the cell, arms folded around their knees.

Adelaide sighed in anguish. "Una," she said, "we're in the dungeons."

Una closed her eyes. "Not my first time, Adelaide," she growled. "What happened?"

"He knew. Oh, I'm so sorry. I failed! The governor knew. He was giddy as a summer lark. I should have turned and run."

"Run? Adelaide, you couldn't have run. But you say he knew. How? Damn it, we made a mistake."

Then they both fell silent as a light flickered down the stairs outside their cell. A face appeared in the barred opening of the door.

"I'm most, most disappointed," said a sarcastic voice. "Adelaide, you were supposed to kill the bastard. Wasn't that your plan?"

"Conn? Conn, please help!" Adelaide rose, and stared at the face.

Una didn't move. She wasn't listening to Adelaide or Conn. Someone else was in her head. "Set up the long game." The words came to her. "Work it."

"Horace? Damn it. Not now."

"Now's the time. The woman Gavina, and Conn … This is no time to sit down. Get moving."

"And do what?" Una muttered. "How exactly do you propose I get out of Crinan's dungeon?"

"That's the twelve-year-old in a wet gi talking. You're Undine, Talla of Deadrise Bay. You're smarter than this."

Una clutched her head. Her plan had been destroyed, and now Horace was needling her about it.

"Conn, you know it would have been for the better," Adelaide implored.

"Indeed." Conn chuckled sardonically. "I'd have told you, atta girl. Raptors, I might have freed you and given you a post. Knock my brother off the seat, and elevate me? That would be a fine gift. But you didn't kill him. All you did was to make him angry. So I'll be sent to another godforsaken, nasty corner of the world. Probably something even worse than he'd initially planned. He'll blame it on me. The slave I gave to him tried to kill him."

"Please, will you help us?" Adelaide begged.

"Us? Who's *us*?" Then he saw the second figure, and held the lamp up to the window. "Well, now, Talla, you're here too? I heard about you. Spiral on your face under all that makeup. Isn't that right? What an interesting night."

Una shrugged, and let out a long sigh.

"Rub it in. Make him angry," came Horace's urging voice. "Make this

his failure, rather than yours. He has skin in the game, too. Make him see it."

"Oh, shut up," she hissed—and then halted and pressed her eyes shut. Horace was right, again. Una gritted her teeth. Damn him, he was always right. She rose and put her hands on her hips. "Is this funny?" she said.

"It's not unamusing," Conn smirked.

"I take it you're Conn, the younger brother. Are you happy with the result? It's amusing to you?" Una tossed her head and leaned casually against the wall. "So my plan seems to have failed. But you don't even have a plan, do you? Would you like me to help you form one? Or do you look forward to your next godforsaken, nasty corner? Is that how it fares for you, impotent younger brother of Crinan?"

Conn grinned sourly. "Ho, now. Aren't you fresh, Talla. Maybe I'll ask my brother to give you to me. But no, I suppose he'll want to pillory you, or hang you, or some such thing. Skin you alive, or have you drawn and quartered. Are you looking forward to *that*, sharp-mouthed Talla?"

Una gave a thin smile, and silently waved Horace away. "I see your point," she said to Horace, out loud, "All right? But time is short."

"I still have time," Conn said, pleased by the apparent success of his thrust. "But you're right to worry about it. You only have a little bit left."

"You suppose I fear death?" Una boasted, looking directly at Conn. "Bring the poison to me. I'll drain the cup in one breath."

"Delightful!" Horace interjected, in her head. "You remembered! I trotted out that old chestnut when first we met. I'm touched."

Una grinned. "I'll die quickly. And you, Conn. You'll spend another year in the snow-covered northern mountains, or the desolate islands to the south. Who will suffer more, impotent younger brother of the governor, you or I?"

There was a moment's hush. "You're a smart one, aren't you? And that's so excellently sexy. Brains. Fire and daggers, so damned rare around here."

"It seems so," Una said. "In you, for example. Rare, I mean. If you had any brains, wouldn't you use them? Or do you like being the impotent younger brother, destined eventually to be where we are now?"

"I'm not the one in the dungeons, girl," Conn snapped, turning sour at the taunt.

Una sighed again. "As I thought. Never mind, dullard."

Conn pulled back, scowling. "You're a sour little Talla."

"And you're a stupid little brother."

"Fine. Enjoy your dungeon." The light moved away as Conn huffed back up the stairs and slammed the door.

Adelaide shivered and turned to Una. "Is that wise, Talla, to vex him so?"

"Long game," Una growled, then she looked up. "Yes Horace. I'm playing your long game, damn it. Longer than usual for me, anyway. Anger the young lord, instead of begging. That's what I'm supposed to do, right? So, next steps? You're usually so full of suggestions. *Jump, Una. Stop, Una. Hide, Una.* I don't hear anything."

"Oh, I think you've worked it out already," came Horace's words. "All that's left is to play out the hand. You can do it."

"Una, are you all right?" Adelaide leaned in and put a hand on Una's arm. "Did they hit your head? What did they do to you?"

"There were too many, Adelaide," Una snapped. "What do you think happened? The black-gis swarmed us. And as my dear, dear friend Horace would say, five is too damned many for two to take on."

"Horace? Who's this Horace? And, two?"

Una laughed. "Who's Horace? He's that voice in my head that won't let me give up."

"Oh. But you said two. Was Abel to wait with you?" She blanched. "Oh, no, Una. Don't tell me ..."

"They left him there, I think. I suppose that means there's one small part of the plan they don't know about."

Adelaide breathed a sigh of relief. "Alive, then?"

"But it doesn't mean he's safe. And obviously neither are we. So, listen. We're not finished yet, Adelaide. Here's the game. The *new* game. You'll have to play your part."

"So, brother, I suppose you'll blame this on me." Conn stepped up to the table. "I gave her to you, so this must be my fault. Isn't that right? I must have put the wench up to it. And so you'll decide that I'm needed in the glacial passes, or in the festering swamps of the southwest. An important mission."

"Conn, she had a vial of poison. For once, I don't suspect you. This is too daring for my little brother to have planned. No, I've no doubt where it came from. That Talla." He spat the word. "That damned Talla from the east. I'll let her blood, brother. I'll bleed her, and hang her from the walls. I'll leave her for the crows, and leave her bleached bones to turn to dust in the sun. Her and your damnable slave girl."

Conn poured liquor into a pair of glasses, and clinked them together, picking them up with one hand. "That's excellently dramatic, brother. The crows will peck out their eyes, and all that." He laughed, and handed his brother a drink.

"You're not the governor, boy," Crinan spat, and slugged back half the glass. "The weight of it isn't on your shoulders."

"Most assuredly not." Conn grinned, putting his glass to his lips and then pulling it away, as if a thought had just occurred to him. "Although, I do feel a weight. It's the debt I owe the treasury. A debt that will never be repaid, no matter the sum I forfeit. Isn't that right, big brother? Wasn't that your message? That I'm to be your slave as much as Adelaide is. Do you plan to bed me as well? Bend me over and ..."

"You robbed the treasury, Conn. Would you prefer the stockade? It could be arranged." Crinan downed the rest of his drink.

"I'd prefer the governorship. Being second doesn't suit me. And maybe I'm a sour-tempered younger brother at times, Crinan, but even at my worst, people like me better than they like you. Who will object? Why would they?"

Crinan raised an arm and wagged a finger at his brother. "It could be ... It could be ..." Crinan smacked his lips, and his eyes lost focus.

"What? It could be what? Better for everyone, were you to be poisoned by your slave and die in these chambers? Oh yes. Not only could it, it *will* be better." Conn set his glass down. "What a lucky thing that I didn't take a drink as well. Too much drink, Crinan, it's no good. It's a weakness."

"But you're ..." Crinan's pupils expanded. "But you ..." The wagging finger steadied, and then dropped, pointing from Conn to the floor—and Crinan slowly leaned over and fell to the spot he was pointing at. "You ..."

"Yes? What is it, Crinan?"

"You ..."

"Come, Crinan, you said that already. But let me help finish the thought for you. The wench—the treasonous wench, may she rot in the dungeons for a hundred generations—the wench had already poisoned the carafe before you discovered the vial. The druggist will confirm it. The same poison. Oh, the treachery!"

Crinan's eyes peered up at him and turned vacant.

"It's something nasty, that's for sure." Conn set his glass on the table and knelt down by his brother. "We'll wait a bit. Let the poison set." He knelt quietly, watching intently.

Crinan's breathing stopped, and Conn waited another full minute.

"All right," he said, "Are we both ready? You just need to lie there, but I have to start howling. Oh, my brother! Treason! That kind of thing, only very loudly. Sorry, brother, if it pains you. I can't tell if you're dead yet."

In the dungeons, Conn found the two women sitting in the same spot, arms around their knees, staring. Even from the dungeons, they heard the commotion above. Everyone was running around.

"Well, murderess," he crooned, "and your accomplice. You'll have a rough go when they figure it out."

"As will you," Una said dully, "if you get this next part wrong."

"I? Oh, I don't think so. The governor, my dear brother, was murdered. Murdered, I say! And by an errant slave in a conspiracy with an easterner. The punishment will be gruesome. Blood and pain."

Adelaide stiffened, but Una put a hand on her arm, silencing her. "And for you," Una said, "a war you can't win, followed by death or exile. But I suppose you're used to exile. You'll have a different master, but the same result. That's if you're lucky, and you aren't killed."

"What's this nonsense?" Conn folded his arms.

"Smart women," Una said, "and stupid men. That's what you meant earlier, right? You fancy smart women because you're not so bright yourself. You think that with Crinan gone you'll ascend. Go on. Admit it. That's what you were thinking."

Conn puffed up his cheeks. "Of course I will."

"Oh feh! Madame Ben Yett will crush you."

"Gavina? She's hiding overseas, afraid of her own shadow."

"No she's not," Adelaide said. "She's here, Conn. She returned on the same ship that brought the Talla."

"You lie," Conn spat. But then he looked at Adelaide's face, and he blanched. "Wait. Do you know this for a fact? Gavina has returned?"

"I've seen her."

"And she has the ear of the generals, I'm told," Una added. "Go on and gloat, Conn. But not too much. You'll be next to us as we hang for the crows."

"But, Gavina? No, it can't be. She's …"

"She's what? Much more resourceful than you? Ten steps ahead of you? And unfortunately, the only person you know who could mediate an arrangement on your behalf is sitting in this cell. Enjoy your last days, brother of Crinan. And tell your friends to prepare to bow to the Ben Yett family."

Conn stood open-mouthed. He hadn't considered Gavina. In spite of having been absent, she was still the governor's wife, and could claim the right to ascend to the governorship. He could contest it, but would he win? The Ben Yett family was extremely powerful. This Talla was making terrifying sense. "Mediate for me?" he muttered.

"Raptors, Adelaide," Una said, "did you save any of that poison? I'd like to get this done with. This young lord, so clearly bound for his death, stands here gaping. It's hard to take."

"Gavina," Conn repeated, stupidly.

"Yes, Gavina," Una huffed. "I sailed with her. She offered her services to me, should we meet in the Green Hills. So you see, Conn, there's a way out of this mess, if you're ready to listen."

A horse came around the corner at a run, and slowed. Two figures dismounted and ran to a stopped carriage, its lanterns dark. Just as quickly, two other figures mounted and rode on, turning at the next crossroad to divert the pursuers. Una closed the carriage door, grinned at seeing both Abel and Tansie, and pounded on the roof. The carriage driver snapped the reins.

Adelaide dropped to the seat and threw her arms around the figure next to her.

"Ow! Ow! Gentle, Adelaide," Abel scolded. "I've been beaten enough for one day."

On the other seat, Tansie raised her arm, and they bumped fists. The carriage pulled away, picking up speed.

The driver kept the lanterns unlit, relying on moonlight and his knowledge of the road until they had rounded a turn. Then he lit the lanterns and snapped the reins, and they flew.

"It worked!" Una said, grinning. "Damn it, it worked!"

Adelaide and Abel nodded, and then they all burst into relieved laughter. Adelaide grasped Una's hand and bowed. "Thank you, Talla! You've winged us away."

Una smiled. "You played your part, Adelaide. And Horace," she looked up, "Horace, here's to you!" Una bowed. "Next time I tell you to stop nattering at me about the long game, I give you my permission to wag your finger and tell me to recall the Green Hills! Tell Una to shut up and listen!"

"Your muse," Tansie said. "It helped you again?"

Una sat back and slapped her on the shoulder. "Tansie, we were all done. The whole damned thing had failed. And then Horace—that inner voice I consult …" Una nodded her head reverently, laughing inside, "Horace told me to play it out. Build the story and set up the long game. You can't fight your way out of a dungeon. But maybe you can engineer your way out."

"And will she go along with it?" Adelaide said, long-faced. "Madame Ben Yett, I mean."

"What did you do, Una?" Tansie said, leaning forward. "Come on. Give. What long game?"

"Yes, tell us," Abel urged, his hand slipping into Adelaide's and squeezing. Adelaide leaned against him.

Una gave a trilling laugh. "The oldest game in the book, Tansie. Raptors, Horace, I hope you approve."

"Damn it, Una, tell!" Tansie demanded.

"You have to play the opponent in front of you. Figure him out, and write a story he'll believe. That's what Horace always tells me. Don't try to do something fast and tricky."

"And? And?" Tansie smacked Una's shoulder.

"And the person in front of me was Conn. Adelaide and I were caught. Crinan had discovered our plan and put us in the dungeon."

"No!" Tansie said, eyes wide.

"But when Conn found out—when he discovered that Adelaide had tried to poison Crinan—he saw a way out of his own problems. Finish it. Poison Crinan, and let it fall on Adelaide and me."

"Oh, dear," Abel said. "Conn poisoned his brother?"

"All it took was a bit of coaxing. Well, needling. Foster his sense of injury, and call up his feelings of inadequacy. Make him angry enough to build the conviction to finish the job himself. Of course he hadn't thought it through. It's a long game," Una grinned, "Conn was only thinking to finish what Adelaide started. He wasn't thinking about what might happen next, who else might want to assume the governorship with Crinan gone."

"Madame Ben Yett," Abel said. "Conn didn't know she'd returned!"

"Exactly. Conn hadn't considered Gavina. Wasn't that a surprise. Even Conn came to realize the odds were against him. So I offered to fix it. Fix the whole mess. Conn lets us go, and I solve his problem with Gavina."

"You found a solution," Abel said, leaning in.

"Yes. Marry her."

Tansie, Adelaide, and Abel hesitated, then broke into laugher.

"Of course!" Tansie said. "The widow marries the brother. That's an old story, indeed! But how did you get Gavina to go along with it?"

"First I had to make Conn believe it would take some masterful convincing," Una grinned. "I needed him to let us out. Truth is, if he'd thought of marrying her, he could have left us to die and arranged it on his own. It probably would have worked anyway. But his confidence was low. Someone had been belittling him," Una grinned.

"You kept at him," Adelaide said, "Calling him the impotent younger brother. So that was why."

"Then I dropped the problem of Gavina on him, crushing his adrenaline high. And then came the deal. He takes me to Gavina, and if I can arrange a solution that they both agree on, Adelaide and I are free to go. If not, we go back to the dungeon, and he's no worse off than he was."

"But Una," Tansie complained, "you have to tell us how you got Gavina to agree. Marry Conn? Why would she?"

"Tansie, you should know this part. Don't you remember our conversations on the *Margay*? Gavina doesn't want to live in the mansion. She wants to spend her days in the valley. She might be heir to the governorship, but she doesn't want to run things. And Conn is itching to take over. For Conn to marry Gavina solves everything. Conn gains the power of the governorship with the blessings of the Ben Yett family. And while Conn is seeing to the day-to-day work of governing, Gavina can do as she pleases down in the valley."

They all sat silent, working it through.

"Una," Tansie hissed, "that fourth turn of the spiral, and the dragon-serpent—I think we all see why you have them!"

They arrived on the wharf in the same style as they had left. People moved out of the way as the elegant carriage halted. The driver hopped down and opened the door for two rich young women, and they strolled along the wharf in no particular hurry.

There were more soldiers than usual moving about, inspecting the flow of people, and the overall mood was tense. Everyone was talking about the assassination of the governor of the Green Hills district. No one paid attention to the trainees preparing to embark. It might have seemed odd that they wore their hooded cloaks for cool weather, given that it was still summer. But the soldiers had important things to do, and didn't waste their time with the eastern trainees returning home from the House Kamine compound in the Fan district. They were looking for an assassin, not a student.

A pair of soldiers moved toward Una and Tansie, and were about to intercept them when the ship captain rushed over and offered a gushing welcome.

"Oh, so nice to see you again, misses! I was so very pleased when they informed me that you would be gracing us with your presence again on our voyage. May I see you to your stateroom?" He talked nonstop as he offered Una his arm and led them onto the ship. The soldiers moved off.

A cart arrived carrying more trainees and a lot of gear. There were cases, sacks of goods, poles, canvases, and all manner of items. Ten gray-clad students lugged items toward the wharf and showed their entry papers to board the ship.

"We'll return for the rest of the gear," the oldest of the group said, waving off a porter. "No need to bother about us. The students will carry their own things."

It took several trips, small clusters of gray-gis moving down the gang-plank, loading up with items, and lugging them onto the ship, and the man checking papers lost interest and waved them through. No one noticed that on two of the trips back onto the ship there was an extra gray-gi lugging packages. With hoods pulled low and their heads down, Adelaide and Abel boarded the ship and were safely hidden with the homebound fighters.

When the *Margay* sailed into the southern port, their return journey over, Una and her companion disembarked without fanfare, and moved with the crowd to a line of carriages waiting on the wharf. This time Una selected an unremarkable carriage, waved two more from the crowd to get on board, and told the driver where she wanted to go.

And this time when they pulled up to the Hawk Bill Inn, there was no matron waiting at the door to rush outside and usher them in. They unloaded their bags themselves and went inside.

"Will we have a problem?" Tansie whispered. "No one greets us."

"We're not announced. And it's a different matron," Una whispered back, as a woman stepped up behind the desk.

"Do you have reservations?" the woman said.

"We're just in from overseas," Una said. "You weren't here before."

"I'm afraid I've just handed out the last key, miss," the woman said, looking at the road-weary group. "Might I recommend you to an establishment in town? I think they might have rooms."

Una scowled and was turning to leave, but stopped. "Wait, I think I have a key. She fished in her pocket and pulled out the token. She clicked it onto the counter. "Would this open a door or two for me and my companions?"

The woman halted, staring. "That ... Are you ... Yes, yes," she gave a nervous laugh and plastered a smile on. "Let me call a porter immediately. Have you had dinner? I could arrange a table in the dining hall, or we'll bring it up to you if you prefer. I apologize. I didn't know."

"It's no matter," Una said. "I think we'd like to clean up, and then a table in the dining room would be grand. Last I was here I met with a gentleman." She picked up the token and held it at her collar.

"The commander," the matron whispered. "Shall I send word?"

"If you would."

Commander Stiles arrived the next day. A porter brought a note to Una's room: A visitor waited for her at the bar. She put on her nicest Tallach outfit, chose a hat with a veil, and strode into the room. Commander Stiles sat in the same place as the first time she had met him.

"You're back quickly," he said, rising with a note of concern. "A problem?" he added quietly.

"No." Una grinned and sat, and accepted a glass of wine that the waiter immediately poured for her. "It was a good trip. She's here."

His face lit up. "You've brought her!" he hissed. "You have the girl? She's well?"

"She is. And I've brought one other."

"Another?"

"The gunners will be interested in him as well. Would it be possible to arrange to meet them and Commander Riley at Master Aideen's fighting pavilion?"

18. The Long Game

Horace ducked into a tourist shop and reluctantly set Camilla down. This time she didn't leave it to him to pick things out. She found long black socks with a Canadian flag logo, a pair of black flip-flops, and a black scarf. Horace found a baseball cap and a tote bag, and picked out another tee shirt. They left the shop and slipped around behind a shrub border, and emerged a minute later, a couple of tourists enjoying the warm night.

"This is better, don't you think?" Camilla grinned. She had wrapped the scarf twice around her waist and tied it in back, and the socks went up past her knees.

Horace winked. "Very stylish."

"Right," she rolled her eyes. "I look idiotic. But at least it looks like I meant to do this."

"All right," he smiled.

"So where are we going?" The tension returned to her voice.

"Dessert."

"We had dessert."

"Second dessert. Come on. We're late."

"Late for what?" Camilla took his hand, looking all around for threats.

They received a few sidelong glances from patrons and the bartender when they stepped in, a skinny girl wearing a huge tourist tee shirt like a dress and an old man in a matching shirt and a Québec Capitales baseball cap. Camilla seemed to have pegged it. The looks were of distasteful amusement at the silly American tourists.

But Horace spoke in French and charmed the waitress, and soon they were tucked away at a café table in the corner. Camilla scooped whipped cream from a tall ice cream float, and Horace rifled through the wallet. There was no ID and nothing with a name on it. He pocketed the bills and quietly dropped the wallet on the floor and shoved it under the table with his foot.

The atmosphere of friendly bar chatter and laughter was soothing, and Camilla started to calm down. The shocked expression faded and changed to a grin. "That was excellent," she whispered.

"The float? Do you want another one?"

"Jesus. No, dummy, not the float. I mean, how you got that guy in the alley, and then the car crash, and then stealing the car. God, that was cool. But do you really think we're safe? I thought you were gonna say we had to get the hell out."

Horace raised an arm as a waitress passed by. "Another float for Calista," he said in French. "And a cognac." He slid his empty glass over.

Camilla got the gist from the first time he had ordered. "You mean we're staying? Are we meeting somebody?'"

"Very perceptive, Calista. Yes. We missed them earlier, but they'll be back around. So another float for you."

"What, so I'm *Calista* now?"

"You can't be Una. It's too unusual. And you absolutely can't be Camilla. So yes, dear, you're Calista. And it's not clear how we know each other, I should add. It might be random, as with Juliette, for instance. Someone happened to cross my path, and here you are. Don't worry. They won't interrogate you."

"Who won't interrogate me? What are you talking about?"

"Robbie and Grace. Two of the finest agents I've ever met. Careful and efficient, and invisible when they need to be. And those aren't their real names either, Calista. But they'll follow my lead. You understand?"

"Not even a little." Camilla frowned.

Horace leaned in again. "I made a call before we left the States. Do you remember? I left a message, and I'm sure it was received. We're going to meet some people who will help us. And unless you care to propose some other names, we'll call them Robbie and Grace, and you'll be Calista."

"Okay."

"And they'll roll with it, easy as pie. And you will, too. We need to be careful and efficient, Camilla. Rule number one is to say what you need to say, and don't say what you don't need to say. Understood?"

"So you've got people coming to help us." Camilla offered a weak smile.

"We were supposed to meet with them earlier, but we missed the window, so now we wait. They'll return. When they get here, follow my lead. Tell me you understand."

"I'm Calista, and I don't say much." She crunched her face up in disdain.

"And I'm here to protect you. You're my client. Understand?"

"Yeah? But wait. … Oh, I get it. You don't want them to know why I'm really here."

"Keep it simple. You're my client, and they're meeting us here to help with the mission."

"So who are you gonna be?"

Horace smiled. "We'll find out when they get here. Now let's get back to our conversation. We've other things to address. I've been mulling it over. Here's my list of things you need."

"Things I need? I need some clothes," Camilla smirked.

"Tell me if I've missed anything." Horace waved her off. "You need a mother, a father, a home, a school, and a friend or two. Would that settle things?"

"What are you talking about?" She looked at him and dropped her voice to a whisper. "We just escaped from a bunch of guys trying to kill us. And you wanna talk about my parents and stuff? Now?"

"Just to be clear, hon, they were trying to kill me, not us." He almost added, *and they're not finished.* "But yes, life moves along quickly. It's prudent to use your free time to plan your next steps. So do I have it right? Is that what you need?"

Camilla stared at him. "I don't have any of those things. I had a friend, I guess, but I can't go back to Virginia. So I don't even have Sasha anymore."

Horace held up his hand. "Long game. Never mind what you have right now. I'm asking about what you need in the long term. We're going to determine what you need, and then we can engineer those things for you. And something for me as well. That is, if you're up for it."

"Up for it? Well, duh. And yeah, that's a good list, I guess. Unless you can make me eighteen, and then we can skip the parents."

"You'll be eighteen soon enough," Horace said. But let's consider a slightly less long game than that, eh? Do you think you could work with me on this?"

She shrugged. "Like how?"

"Carefully. You don't want bad parents, bad friends, and a bad school, right?"

"I've had those already," she huffed.

"So let's do some planning and find you some nice ones."

"I don't see how. It took them more than a month to get the last foster family."

"But they weren't playing the long game, were they? Think about it this way. Let's consider parents and a home. Who would benefit from adding a twelve-year-old girl to the family?"

"Nobody." Camilla looked down. "Don't be stupid."

"Not true." Horace put up a hand. "People want all kinds of things. And among the things people want are companionship, attention, love, family ..."

"Nobody wants a juvenile delinquent psycho who hears people talking in her head." Camilla folded her arms and crunched her face into a deep frown.

Horace clicked a fingernail against the side of his glass. "You just told me about how Una set up the operation with the governor to get the young woman and the young man away. What do you think of that?"

"It's super cool."

"And it's good, too, isn't it? She found a way to oust the governor and also to help others—not just the young woman and the young man, but really the whole district, don't you think? Surely many people benefit from the removal of a bad governor. Good all around."

"Yeah."

"And the young man Neassan," Horace paused, thinking. "That's something of a connection, isn't it? His actions were much to the same purpose. It wasn't bloodless either, but he found a way to hold his enemy at bay and protect his people."

"Who's Neassan?"

"Oh. You didn't see that part? Someone else from Una's time, I think. A young lord of a place called the northlands, and his adversary, a man called Shular."

Camilla's eyes widened. "Shular! That's the governor. The slave owner. Una was in a slave wagon, and one of the men said the slaves were for Shular. I remember it. It's a strange name."

"Is that so?" Horace looked at her. "The slave mongers she escaped from as a child were Shular's men? Well, well."

"I did see that part. I think maybe I might have even helped a little, but I'm not sure."

"Did you? Well, dear, it seems our friend Una is right in the middle of things, isn't she?" He looked around the room. "As are you and I. But Camilla, look at the big picture. Look at how a properly planned effort can lead you to your goal and also help others. Wouldn't you like to be able to do things like that?"

"Una's this smart fighter girl, with all kinds of connections. I'm just Camilla, the crazy daughter of a murderer."

"Mm," Horace said. "Una was a slave, Camilla."

"I know. But she's not now."

"No indeed. She escaped from all that. And then she was adopted by a very powerful man, and she became the fighter that we've both seen. My point is that it took several long steps for her to become Talla Undine."

Camilla shrugged. "But that's *Una*, not me. I'm a nobody orphan, and I'm gonna get put in jail when they catch me."

"Do you know what I see when I look at you?" Horace said. "Maybe I have to squint a little." He tipped his head sideways and crunched his eyes. "No, it's not a juvenile delinquent psycho. That's not it. I think I see an imaginative and bright girl with a strong streak of independence. I see a fascinating, clever creature who's going to be quite something, one day."

"Right," Camilla rolled her eyes again. "So you're telling me you're gonna be Saor Tieg and adopt me, and make me a Tallach fighter?"

"Let's just see what I can put together, shall we? Ah. Here they are." Horace rose as a couple stepped in from the street. "Grace! Robbie! Is that you? Well, I'll be. Come, come!" he waved them over. "Calista, dear, slide over and make room. Look who's here!"

A dark-haired woman of thirty stepped over, pulling along with her a blond man the same age. The woman had dark eyes, almost black, and smooth skin. Camilla stared. She was gorgeous. And the man wasn't so bad looking, either. They were dressed nicely in casual street clothes, the woman in snug blue jeans and a white blouse, and the man in khakis and an Oxford shirt.

"Why, look who it is, Robbie. I didn't know you'd retired up here, Howard," the woman said. She gave Horace a hug. "And who's this with you, then?"

"This is my granddaughter Calista," Horace said.

Robbie reached across the table to shake Camilla's hand, and then turned to Horace, paused, and gave him a hug instead of a handshake. "The department is lost without you, Howard. Are you sure you're happy in retirement? Accounting would take you back in a heartbeat."

"Come. Sit, sit. Tell me what you've been up to."

The bar was a popular spot. People stopped in for a late drink and wandered back out, and no one took notice when an old man in a tourist shirt walked out with his son. A few men at the bar turned as the beautiful black-haired woman left with her young daughter, but only to watch the woman's backside as she stepped out.

Horace and Robbie chatted as they strolled down the street, and Grace held Camilla's hand and led her the other way.

"So, Calista, you spent all your money in the gift shop?" Grace said, for the benefit of the people on the sidewalk. She offered Camilla a clandestine wink.

"It's my money," Camilla played along. "And I like it," she lied, stopping to pose.

"You're not wearing that to school. Don't even try it."

They turned the corner, and Camilla watched the woman. Horace was right. She was good. The woman was casing the block, but no one would think she was.

"Come along now, hon," she said. She stepped up to a scooter backed into a narrow alley and hooked a finger into the ring of a keychain hidden under the back seat. "Hop on back and hold on, okay?" She turned the key, pulled onto the sidewalk, and when traffic cleared, pulled onto the street.

They rode for a while, Camilla enjoying the cool night air and wondering where this was leading. She hadn't liked the idea of splitting up. Why did she have to go with the woman? But Horace had given her the hairy eyeball, silencing her protest.

Grace pulled the scooter into a tiny parking area behind a building. She led Camilla up an exterior stairway to an apartment, unlocked the door, and led her inside. The place was tiny, but nicely furnished. There was a miniature living room with a dormer window facing the water, and the smallest kitchenette she had ever seen, neatly tucked next to a tiny bathroom.

"Shower," the woman said, clicking on a lamp and drawing the curtain over the window. "Go on. I'm guessing you're dying for a shower. And lord, girl, you don't really dress like that, do you?"

Camilla smirked. "You don't like it?"

"It's got Horace stamped all over it." She held up a hand as Camilla opened her mouth to explain. "No need to trot out the details, hon. I've worked with the man before. Always one step ahead, and if you start questioning him, you're just wasting time. I'm sure there's a fine reason you're dressed like a tourist shop mannequin experiment."

Camilla grinned, peering at her reflection in a mirror on the bathroom door and striking a pose.

"Go on. Shower. I'll get you something to wear."

"You're going out?" Camilla flashed a look of concern.

"Out? Oh, hell no, child. You're my assignment. Nothing gets to you unless it goes through me first."

"I'm your *assignment*?"

"Maybe I've known the man longer than you, Calista. When Horace says, *you take Calista and we'll meet you tomorrow*, it means I keep you safe. But listen, nobody will find us. Robbie and I cased everything in a four-block radius before we entered the bar. It's all clear. Horace just wants me to see to it that you're okay for the night."

"And how come you're calling him *Horace*? Isn't it supposed to be *Howard*?"

"Aren't you a smart one," Grace grinned. "He gave us a safe word. Anything family means you already know who he is."

"A safe word?" Camilla tipped her head.

"If he'd said you were his friend, or his neighbor's kid, or something like that, I'd still be calling him Howard. But he said you're his granddaughter."

"I am his granddaughter," Camilla blurted, and then snapped her mouth shut, wondering if she'd made a mistake.

"Of course you are." Grace winked. "Now go on and get cleaned up, and I'll get you something to put on. We'll find a store tomorrow."

"In the hotel room." Horace handed the room key to Robbie. "They'll be casing it for certain. She told me she left her cell phone there. That was careless of me. It never occurred to me to ask if she had a cell phone."

"That's how they found you?" Robbie raised his eyebrows.

"No, they had a tag on her. But I'm sure they're tracking the phone as well. Damn it, this one was messy."

"Usually is with kids."

"I should have expected it. But listen, we'll use it to our advantage. They took a shot at us in the old city. And they'll have someone on the hotel room. Rent the room next to it, or figure another way. Get her back-pack. Put everything in it, and get to the back of the building. I'll find us a car and wait for you."

"Why do they want her?" Robbie halted and put up a palm at Horace's raised eyebrows. "Never mind. Forget I asked. I just mean to say that the kid's got to be a high value target, Horace, if they're throwing all of this at her."

Horace turned and put a hand on Robbie's arm. "She's my highest value target ever. I want these people off her."

"Understood." Robbie nodded. "I'll lead the bastards on a wild goose chase like they've never seen before. They'll be looking for that girl on the other side of the globe."

And me with her, Horace thought, smiling.

19. Gatto Girl

Back in her role as Undine, daughter of Saor Tieg, Una paced impatiently. The driver was late. Finally she saw a coach approaching, and she stepped into the road.

"Tyra!" She wrenched the door open and wrapped her arms around her friend.

"Undine! You're all right?"

"Me? Oh, better than all right. But what about you? Tell me!" Undine grabbed Tyra's arm and led her inside, where she had already reserved a table. "Tell me everything, Tyra." She dropped her voice. "The gunners. What did they do to you?"

Tyra laughed. "The gunners? Who cares about that? I want to hear your story."

"I have to know. Did they mistreat you? You have to tell me, Tyra."

"Mistreat me? Undine, it's the most amazing place I've ever seen. They took me to the White Cliffs. It's like an underground palace. There's a library with so many books I could never read them all, even if they kept me there for ten years. They fed me, and gave me a fine room to sleep in, and taught me to fight." Tyra leaned in. "The Tynan lord himself! He sparred with me. Do you believe it?"

Undine blinked. "Lord Torin sparred with you? Damn, Tyra. You're trying to steal my thunder."

"And I learned a lot. My father will be so surprised. Gunner Ailmili said I'll make a fine fighter if I keep it up. And Gunner Rachanna said I had good style."

"I see." Undine folded her arms in mock condemnation. "I suppose they'll be going to *your* parties instead of mine from now on."

"What? Come on, Undine. You went overseas. Tell me what happened. I'm told that you returned with someone important."

"But I didn't spar with the dragon king. Honestly, Tyra, weren't you supposed to be locked in a dungeon? And instead you come out of this as a fantastic fighter girl who spars with the northern lord and chats with his gunners?"

Tyra waved an arm. "Wine," she called to the waiter. "Undine, there wasn't any dungeon. The only difficulty was worrying about you. And now you're back, so everything is fine. But damn it, you have to tell me! I want to hear the whole thing. Right from the first day. I won't leave this table until you finish."

"Two bottles!" Undine called after the waiter.

"Wait. I almost forgot," Tyra said, dropping her voice. "There's something the gunner says I have to tell you." She leaned in. "We have to keep up the story, Undine. Tell me everything that happened, but only partly because I insist. The other part is that when we go back to the Western Shores ..." She giggled at the prospect of their return "... When we go back, everyone has to think I went with you. Even my father, and yours. The gunners don't want anyone ever to know."

"Very sneaky. And appropriate," Undine said with a shrug. "If you're going to upstage me by learning to be a Gatto fighter, you'd better also learn to be sneaky."

"I mean it, Undine. I promised. It was a condition of my release."

"Frankly, Tyra, I don't think it will be a problem. Not with what we brought back with us. They'll be too distracted. Nobody will question our account."

"What we brought back? You mean the woman Adelaide? The gunners told me that's who you were to retrieve. But she'll be going north, won't she?"

"Not Adelaide, and not Abel, either. He's the other one I brought back. No, I mean this." Undine pulled out the leather document pouch Gavina had given her, and dropped it on the table. "You're not the only one who's been rubbing shoulders with important people, Tyra."

Tyra pulled out the paper and scanned down the page, and froze. She looked up and stared. "It's real?" she hissed. "All of it? This is real? And Madame Ben Yett, she can do this?"

"It's real. And yes she can. She's governor now. Or will be soon, if she's not already."

"Undine!" Tyra hissed. "Raptors, do you know what this means? All the commerce from the Green Hills, coming to Deadrise Bay? Ha! My father will be able to buy the *Margay*, if he wants!" She let go, and dropped back in her chair, grinning giddily.

"And he won't be questioning your decision to run off with me for a trip overseas, will he?"

"Tell me the story." Tyra leaned in, perched on the edge of her chair.

"I'll tell you the whole thing as soon as the wine gets here. But Tyra, the story isn't quite done yet. Tomorrow we're going to Master Aideen's pavilion."

Undine and Tyra stood with Adelaide and Abel on the brick terrace overlooking the forest of The Hidden. In the eight years since Undine had last been there, the terrace had been extended and a large canvas pavilion erected on one side. No longer would the tea ritual be rained out, or performed hastily in a cold sleet, or under cover of a shady tree in an effort to get some relief from the sun. Master Aideen's students, a dozen of them, sparred under a canopy. They were proud novices of the pavilion of The Hidden.

From inside they heard young boys calling out and engaging.

"Should we go in?" Tyra asked.

"They'll come to us," Undine said, and nodded to Adelaide and Abel, standing nervously behind. "Let me do the talking. They know me."

"They know you?" You've been here before?" Tyra's eyes widened.

Undine had prepared for this. Her strategy had come to her when she'd met Abel and needed to convince him to listen to her. On the return trip she had spent sleepless nights mulling over this very moment, and in the end had opted to take the same approach. Keep it simple, and stick to the story she and Saor Tieg had invented eight years ago—but with a small, harmless addition.

"I told you that I came overseas to find my father," Una said.

"When you were twelve. Yes, you've told me that story a million times."

"But I didn't come over at twelve. It was earlier. Years earlier. It took me until I was twelve to find my way to the Western Shores. Part of that time I was here."

"Raptors," Tyra said. "You never told me that."

Tyra's flood of questions was cut short as the canvas parted and a tall, dark-skinned woman in a white gi with a black sash around her waist stepped out. She halted, noting the visitors on the terrace, and then strode over. Her eyes narrowed. She stared at Undine, working to reconcile what she was seeing.

"Una?" She said, in an almost hostile tone. "You've come back." She stepped up close.

Una had prepared for this moment as well. She leaned in to Tyra "I called myself Una back then, instead of using my real name," she whispered. Then she grinned and moved into a high fighting stance, a silent challenge to the Gatto girl who had once beaten her almost unconscious on this very terrace. She had waited eight years for this. The stance said, *want to try me now?*

Caterione grinned back, retreated a step, and flowed down into a full fighting stance. *Yes I do*, she silently said.

Tyra had learned enough during her time at the White Cliffs to understand this. The gunners had told her that she would be expected to maintain her health. What they meant was that she would learn to fight, and she would practice daily. Oddly, she now knew more about Gatto fighting than she did about Tallach fighting. But the sign of a challenge was common to both. Tyra put her arms out and backed up, moving Adelaide and Abel with her.

Una called out a ready cry. Caterione attacked first, moving in quickly with a series of strikes meant to overtake her opponent without a fight. But

Una deftly blocked and moved, and Caterione flashed past her entirely. Then they circled, and Una was next to engage. She faked a direct attack, at the last moment pivoting to the side and leaping up. She caught Caterione on the back of her shoulder with a reverse kick before tumbling into a roll.

They both leaped up again and faced off. Young fighters crept out from the pavilion and spread out in a line to watch their trainer sparring with this stranger on the terrace.

Caterione got the upper hand in the next volley. She darted in, ducking low, and forced Una to jump backward to avoid having her legs taken out. Una had to lean forward and turn to keep her balance, and Caterione took advantage and landed a fast blow to her shoulder, throwing her to the ground. But Una rolled out of it, avoiding a series of kicks as Caterione closed in. She spun around, and in a move that Caterione had never seen before, leveled a sideways kick to Caterione's shin. This time Caterione was forced to jump backward, and Una got to her feet.

Una ran in and faked a high, two-arm strike, pulling Caterione's focus upward for a mere moment, and in the same motion snapped a kick to her middle, catching her by surprise. Caterione was forced back.

They volleyed, circling, fighting and separating to circle again. Una executed moves twice more that were unfamiliar to Caterione, forcing her to retreat. Caterione maintained a stoic expression, but Una thought she detected a slight hesitation in her opponent, a shred of doubt.

Neither the fighters nor their audience noticed when two more watchers stepped out of the forest. Two figures in black robes with silver-stitched sashes silently appeared behind Adelaide and Abel.

Una came in fast with another feint and a double inside block, throwing Caterione's arms outward and putting her off balance. She was about to throw a victory strike, a swift blow held back from making contact, the sparring version of a kill shot. Caterione was hers! But then she caught a glimpse of the new visitors, and her eyes went wide. She leaped backward and thrust her arms out with a ready cry, calling a halt to the sparring match, and then ran up and dropped to her knees before the gunners, pressing her forehead to the ground. Caterione's jaw dropped, and she hurried over next to her old foe and did the same.

"Gunners!" they said, in unison.

The young students, seeing their trainer bowing to these unknown visitors, followed her lead and dropped to the ground. "Gunners!" they called out.

"Rise, Master Caterione, and your students," Ailmili said, stepping forward. "And you, Una."

They all rose and bowed. The students formed a line and stood at attention.

"Caterione?" Abel said, softly. But his reunion with his childhood friend would have to wait. Tyra held a stiff arm across his chest, warning him to stay put.

"Una, that was very interesting," Ailmili said, stepping forward. "I've wanted to see the Tallach fighting way. I should have thought earlier to ask you to show me." She pulled off her robe and stepped out in her fighting leathers, ebony-handled blades at her shoulder showing a glimmer of red from the sun reflecting off the ruby cabochons. "Show me."

"Show you? Um, show you what, gunner?" Una said, flustered.

Ailmili laughed. "That's what I said, the first time I stepped onto this terrace. Caterione was here. Do you remember? Torin had you perform the twenty-one strikes."

The students lost their poise for a moment, smiling and elbowing one another, until Caterione flared her fingers at them and they halted and fixed their positions.

"I hadn't seen it before," Ailmili continued. "The exercise, I mean. The twenty-one strikes. So Caterione performed it, and Torin said, *now you show me*. And I said, *show you what?*"

"You want me to perform the twenty-one strikes?" Una asked.

"No. I want you to show me those moves you just did with Caterione. The Tallach moves." Ailmili dropped into a fighting stance. "Come. I want to try them. Give them to me twice."

"Ho!" Una gasped. But she faced the gunner, and dropped into a stance.

Caterione stepped back and stood in front of her students as Una and the gunner sparred. They watched in wonder as Una executed the Tallach moves she had used to gain an advantage on her opponent. On the first move, Ailmili performed Caterione's response, exactly as Caterione had done it, except that she pulled her strikes, as did Una. The second time through, Ailmili proposed a different response that overcame the move.

At the end, Una stood and bowed, staring, and Ailmili smiled and gave a trilling laugh. "It's cheating, of course. The moves weren't a surprise to me, since I'd just watched you execute them. Caterione didn't have the same advantage. Isn't that right, Caterione?"

On the sidelines, Caterione smirked and struggled to regain her neutral expression. She bowed, and then turned and bowed to Una. "The Talla bested me this time."

"Those moves are splendid, Una. Can we do more later? But look, someone is coming. Let's gather inside," Ailmili said. "We have some introductions to make." She pulled her robe back on.

They didn't see anyone approaching, but followed her and Rachanna into the pavilion without question.

"Aideen will be here in a minute," Ailmili said, "but while we wait, tell me, Caterione. Don't you know one of our guests?"

Abel had his eyes locked on the dark-skinned fighter. "Caterione," he said, softly. "Do you remember me?" He wiped his eyes, and stepped up.

Caterione tipped her head and looked at him. "Abel?" she said, losing her poise and gaping. "Abel?"

And then Una saw something she never thought she would see. The severe, tight-lipped Caterione burst into tears and hugged her old friend.

Then another figure appeared, a silver-haired woman in a white gi like Caterione's.

"Master!" the students all chanted, snapping to attention.

"Master Aideen, look!" Caterione said, unable to regain her poise. "Look, it's Abel!"

Aideen stopped cold and stared in astonishment. There was a moment of utter silence as the young man's eyes met his mother's—and then his mother stepped forward and wrapped her arms around her son. All semblance of decorum was lost. The students cheered, and Caterione waited a moment and then joined them in a hug.

Master Aideen looked to Ailmili and Rachanna. "Gunners," she gasped, choked up, tears in her eyes. "You found my son!"

"My agent found your son," Ailmili said.

Master Aideen turned to look at the young woman dressed in Tallach garb. She tipped her head and then straightened. "Una?" she said. "Una, is that you?" Then her eyes widened at the spiral on her cheek. "Talla! Fire and daggers!" She bowed low to Una. "Welcome to the pavilion of The Hidden, Talla Una. Or, welcome back, rather."

Una bowed back. "My Tallach name is Undine," she said. "My father is Saor Tieg of the Western Shores. I was reunited with him soon after I left the north."

Aideen stared again, and then both broke the formal stance and stepped forward to grasped wrists. "Well," the master Gatto fighter said, dabbing a hand to her eye as her son put a hand on her shoulder, "Talla Undine, today the Pavilion of The Hidden is yours. You've brought me my son." She offered a short laugh of delight. "I think we're done with training for today."

The students cheered. Their exercises were over. The pavilion would be transformed into a banquet hall.

But there was one more reunion. The gunners stepped outside and Rachanna waved a hand, and her commander emerged from the woods with a dozen soldiers.

"Gunner," Riley said with a bow. "Apologies. We didn't mean to crowd. We'll retreat."

"You always crowd," Rachanna said, with a bit of a grin.

Una and Tyra stepped outside as well, and Tyra moved in close. "My god, Undine, who's *that*?" she whispered. "Look at him."

"Look at him, indeed," Undine whispered back, a low lilt in her voice. "Commander Stiles wasn't joking when he compared the sister to the brother. Here's one to get to know." She nudged a conspiratorial elbow into Tyra's side, and at the gunner's nod, snapped her sleeves and stepped forward.

"Undine," Emma said, "meet Commander Riley."

Riley bowed. "A fourth-tier," he said. In the fashion of one fighter meeting another, they met eyes as they bowed. But Riley's eyes locked onto Una's for an extra moment, until Rachel tapped his shoulder with the back of her hand.

"Talk to the Talla later," she said. "Someone to see you."

"A pleasure to meet you, Talla." Commander Riley bowed again, and reluctantly turned. "So, gunner, someone to see me, you say?"

"Home from overseas. Come." She pulled the canvas back and gestured for him to enter. Commander Riley stepped inside, and Adelaide emitted a shriek of joy and flew at him.

Food and drink were brought in, and the celebration stretched through the day. At first Tyra clung to her friend, but after a glass of fine northern wine, she let go of Una's arm and took up a conversation with one of the students. "The master teaches you Gatto," she said. "Tell me about your lessons." The boy grinned and launched into the story of his latest achievement on the mats.

Una spoke quietly with Caterione for a while, then drifted off and found the gunner's young commander, one arm around his sister and the other resting on the hilt of a blade at his hip.

"Ah. Here you are," Riley said, patting his sister on the shoulder and releasing her. "Undine. I've met your father, you know."

"My father?" Undine said. "You've met my father?"

"Come, shall we take a turn about the terrace? The gunner commanded that I talk to you didn't she? *Talk to the Talla later*, I believe she said. So you see, it's my duty to walk with you." He smiled.

Una took his arm. "I'll walk. But I want your promise that your duty doesn't involve reassuring me that you mean only to see to my safety. Commander Stiles has told me that story already."

"The northlands are dangerous, Undine," Stiles said with a little smile. "You never know what could happen."

Master Aideen's students had gathered around the redheaded woman from the south and were all talking over one another, eager to brag of their fighting exploits. Tyra looked up and flashed a smile, and Una gave her a wink as she and the commander stepped past.

Outside they found Caterione standing at the edge of the terrace. Caterione stood stiffly, unsure how to respond to all the merriment. But as her old adversary walked past on the arm of the commander, she gave Una a bow. "Talla Undine," she said, and stepped away to give them their privacy.

Una felt a shiver run up her back. She looked down at the sweep of the river and raised a hand to touch the tattoo on her face: Talla Undine.

As the sun set, Una found her friend and led her out of the pavilion. The gunners were outside already, standing at the edge of the terrace watching the canopy turn orange. Nearby a contingent of northern soldiers waited. In the presence of the gunners, Commander Riley stood at attention, but nodded at Undine and her friend, and risked a wink.

Ailmili turned. "Are you ready?" she said. "Commander Riley has volunteered to accompany you back to the Western Shores."

Una smiled. "We're ready."

"All right then," Ailmili said. "It's been an interesting road. I'll look forward to our next meeting. Live on, Talla Undine, and join in the hunt tomorrow."

20. Pater Familias

She still wore too much mascara, Horace mused, but Camilla looked decidedly less severe in her school uniform than in her typical all-black. She looked rather adorable, he thought.

"It's itchy," she complained, tugging at a plaid skirt. "And god, I have to wear tights?" A woman standing next to her pulled at the collar of her white shirt, fussing over her. "Mom, will you cut it out?"

"Oh, for heaven's sake, Calista, could you stand still for just a second? Do you want to go to your first day of eighth grade all rumpled?" The dark haired, dark eyed woman took a step back to check her work.

Camilla exhaled loudly. "Fine. Just stop pawing at me. And Dad, no pictures." She held up a palm.

A blond man in a business suit stood by the door snapping shots on his phone. "Sure," he said, smiling. "No pictures, Callie." He snapped a few more, and then looked at his watch. "Gotta go." He leaned down and kissed Camilla on the forehead. "Love you. Have a great first day, honey. I'll pick you and Nicola up at the dojo at six, okay?"

"Awright." Camilla caught her grandfather looking at her, and rolled her eyes. "What? I'm wearing the stupid uniform, okay? There's no rule that I can't wear makeup."

"The makeup is fine." Horace laughed and gave her a hug, which she reflexively pulled away from.

"Stop it. You're gonna mess up my perfectly fixed collar," she complained, turning to flash a glare at her mother.

"Do you have your karate gi?" Horace asked.

"In my pack. I'm all set, okay? God."

"Make sure Nicola has hers too," he added.

From outside came a toot of a car horn.

"Go on," the woman said. "Andy just pulled in. Don't keep him waiting. You and Nicola have a good day." The woman kissed Camilla on the cheek and shooed her out the door, waving as she climbed into the car. "Bye, Calista!" she called out. "Love you!"

"Bye, mom."

She watched the car pull away.

"So, Grace, things are all right?" Horace said as she stepped back inside and closed the door.

The woman gave a wide smile. "She's got a long way to go with—you know, the dark streak. It's not all roses and smiles. But Robbie is making progress with her. He's good at that, you know."

Horace nodded. "And so are you. She needs a mother, too. Don't give up on her. And don't take your eye off her."

"We weren't expecting to be a model family. She's got her ghosts just like Robbie and I do. Me especially. I keep waking up thinking, is it really true? No more running? No more always keeping my back to the wall?"

"They'll never find you here, Grace. Nobody will think you two have picked up a thirteen-year-old daughter and an elderly father, and we're all living in Chestnut Hill." He winked.

"Best dad I could pick," the woman smiled and gave him a peck on the cheek. "Come on. I'll make coffee."

"And you make a fine daughter." Horace followed her to the kitchen. "And this is for me as well, Grace. I'm safe here, too."

"They figure you went overseas to France, or something. I'm sure you arranged it, right?"

"Hidden in plain sight. They're looking for a widower on the run, and I'm right in their back yard."

"I've been meaning to ask you, Horace." Grace lowered her voice. "I see how it fits together. It always does when you engineer something. You took that girl from something bad. I don't know what, but it's clear there was something seriously wrong. And now Robbie and I have a new home, and something to live for. We'll do all we can for Callie. A hundred percent. Maybe it sounds sappy, but I feel as if her salvation is ours as well."

"She's your daughter now. She's counting on you."

"And she's your granddaughter."

Horace smiled. "That she is. A hundred percent."

"And I think it's working. Not just for Robbie and me, but for Callie, I mean. I see the guard coming down. She's finally starting to think she's part of a family. Not always, but sometimes, as least."

"It's good to see that." Horace said.

"And I know you can't tell me everything. She never talks about it, you know. Not a word. I understand that. She needs to be safe from it, whatever *it* is. But Horace, it's been six months, and I still don't even know her real name."

"She's especially important to me, Grace," Horace said. "And isn't she spectacular? You just give her some time and watch what she becomes. She'll tell you, one day. She calls herself Una. And she's a fighter."

Acknowledgments

Thanks to my editors, Sarah Dole and Lisa Wesel, for making my writing better, and thanks to Braden Todd Curtis for the fine cover art.

Also by Todd Woofenden:

The Gunners Trilogy

Gunners of the White Cliffs
Trail of the Gunners
Gunner's Blade

Sign up for email notifications of publishing dates and author news:
https://www.gunners-book.com/subscribe

The Gunners Trilogy:
https://gunners-book.com

About the Author:
https://www.gunners-book.com/about

Signal Light Books:
https://www.signallightbooks.com

www.ingramcontent.com/pod-product-compliance
Lightning Source LLC
Chambersburg PA
CBHW070444260626
47161CB00004B/1198